Ogulia Kvell

MORRIGAN
Killala, Co Mayo, Ireland

morrigan@online.ie

© 2002 Conan Kennedy

ISBN 0907677 59 2

10 9 8 7 6 5 4 3 2 1

Typeset by Carole Lynch
Printed by Techman Ireland.

Morrigan Books neither applies for
nor receives any financial assistance
from the Arts Council.

All rights reserved. No part of this publication may be reproduced,
stored in a retrieval system, or transmitted, in any form or by any means,
electronic, mechanical, photocopying, recording or otherwise,
without the prior permission of the publishers.

Ogulla Well

Conan Kennedy

Morrigan

1

A YOUNG MAN STOOD IN THE DOORWAY. The scar on his face was the shape of a bird. A birthmark, raised, and bubbly blue, he fingered it, nervously.

It was a habit of his to finger the scar when he was nervous. And now he was very nervous. Nervous about entering, nervous about not entering. Caught between these two fears, he stood, without moving.

He watched the woman's leg.

It was bare, the bare back of a woman's leg. The sole of her foot was the palest of yellow. And all the rest of her was the palest of white. It was the time of the dawn, and there was no colour in the light. Just different shades of white. And among all those shades, her skin shone out the brightest, the very whitest.

He watched. The pretty ankle. Two bangles there. The pretty curve of her calf. The back of her knee. Two more bangles just above the knee.

He watched.

The bangles glinted, tight, and the flesh curved to their tightness.

His eye moved on.

There was a blue tattoo on her heavy thigh.

He knew what that meant.

But nonetheless he would have looked further if the covers on the bed hadn't put a stop to his eye.

The Storyteller lay in the bed, watching, this young man at his door. He recognised him, knew him. A messenger. One of those lads who hung about the place, relaying messages, running errands. All sorts of things. Important messages, some were, while some were not. Some were just. . . messages! But while the messages were very different, these lads, the messengers, they themselves were somehow similar. Yes of course not all had scars on their faces in the shape of a bird, but they were all of a certain look, and a certain age, and bright, and clever. But not too bright, not too clever. A message is information, and information is power. And the wise man picks his messengers among those who cannot make that connection.

The Storyteller nodded, vaguely satisfied. If nothing else, he thought, there was at least that much wisdom left in the place. Wisdom enough to pick the right messengers.

'Boy, what is it?' he called out suddenly, 'come in, or go out, talk, or don't talk. . . but please. . . do. . . something.'

First words of another day!

One day there'll be the last words, of the last day!

The Storyteller nodded, listening, hearing the words he had just spoken, hearing them again in his head. And what he heard was the voice of an irritable man, himself, his voice, and the shock of it in the silence was like one of those reflections suddenly seen. . . and the thought that follows. . . oh by the gods is that me. . . and do I look like that?

The young man took a careful step inside.

And as he moved away from the doorway the light came rushing in behind him, like he was dragging it, or like it was a breeze about him.

Morning.

The Storyteller shook his head.

Not particularly enthusiastic about another morning.

Where do the nights go?

Where do the days go, for that matter?

And, wherever they go, do they go to the same place?

He smiled at this notion, and chuckled, and the young man said 'why are you laughing?'

'Why not, Boy? Aren't I better to start with a smile? Won't the day make me cry in its own good time?'

'I don't understand. . . your words. . . '

'You're better off. Knowing enough *not* to think. . . sure that is half the knowing.'

'I don't understand that either'

'Well don't worry about it. Just tell me. *Why* are you here?' The Storyteller followed the young man's eyes, and they led him to the bare leg of the woman stuck from out the covers on the bed. The back of the woman's leg. And it bare from the toe to the thigh. And two broad silver bangles around the ankle, glinting. And two thin silver bangles above the knee, glinting.

'I have a message.'

'And?' prompted the Storyteller, thinking it strange the ways of things, how a young man may not understand too many words, or complicated sentences, but he will always completely understand a woman's leg.

'The King will see you now.'

'That's good of him. . . very good of him. . . very *very* good of him. . .' The Storyteller stretched. . . and yawned. . . 'Only thing is. . . I didn't ask to see him.'

'Now. He will see you *now*,' said the messenger, still looking at the woman's leg. The Storyteller's stretching had moved the covers, slightly, and there was one bare buttock to be seen now. And that there was the blue tattoo of a married woman, glowing.

'Aahh. . . I hear his order in your words. . .'

The Storyteller squeezed the flesh of the buttock, squeezed it tight, and loose, and tight again. The woman stirred, and muttered something, but did not wake. . . 'So. . . the King sends for me, but why? What happened over there. . . in his house? What is he doing, up and about, at this time in the morning?'

'Men came.'

'Men came?'

The Storyteller stroked the buttock.

'What men?'

'From the west,' said the messenger, watching the stroking of the buttock.

'Men? Men *of* the west. . . or are they our people, travelling *from* the west?' asked the Storyteller, thinking of his hand on the smooth skin of the woman, and how it was not his hand anymore, but the hand of the young man too. A hand without a particular person attached.

'Men *of* the west,' was the reply, 'wild people.'

'Well just kill them!' That voice of an irritable man again. 'Where are our warriors? Will you not be stirring me in my bed!'

'These are not fighting men. . . they are magicians. . . hairy people. . . and they have a woman witch. . . there's mud in their hair. . . and they come with a story.'

'What story? Oh for the gods! What story? What story gets the King out of his bed? Do we now listen to muddy savages from the dark places? More important, what story gets the king to send for his Storyteller, to get *him* out of his bed?'

'I don't know.'

'Well. . .' The Storyteller rose, and swung his legs to the floor. That knee was still an ache. And the ache was the old man he would be in the future, reminding him that the body is a book. And the pages of the end are already written.

'Well. . .' He scratched himself. . . 'This news. . . is it good, or is it bad?'

'It is not good.'

'Not good?'

'The King has sent messengers to the east. . . and to the north. . . and to the south.'

'What message has he sent. . . to those parts?'

'I don't know.'

'You do know.'

'I cannot tell.'

The Storyteller looked at the boy, and smiled, and said 'alright, alright my boy, I will tell you. He has sent them to raise men, fighting men, to gather his people here, his sons and those who follow his sons, to bring an army here.'

'How do you know?'

'Because. . . oh. . .' The Storyteller paused, and sighed, and looked to his roof. And he counted the row of six hams hanging there. One two, three four, five six. Close together in twos, they looked rather like the backsides of three women. He sighed again. He thought of his three wives. Life would be simpler if they too hung from the ceiling like hams, waiting. He sighed yet again, and as he did he realised he had sighed three times, once for each of the wives.

He shook his head.

He looked over to another part of the roof, at the rows of herring hanging. Far too many of them to count. . . but he knew there was enough anyway. Yes, indeed. He was well set up. With ham and herring he was well set for any winter. But, he knew, and sighed again, he knew that no matter how well set up, a man was going to be disturbed anyway! By things of life, and thoughts of death. . . and messengers! 'How do I know' he said, putting tiredness into his voice like a man salting a meal, 'you ask me how I know, how do I know he plans to bring an army here?'

He rose to his feet and sighed for the fifth time and stretched his arms and looked at the young man. 'I know because I know. And I know because that's precisely what a king does when he gets bad news. He raises an army. I know that and, unlike you my son, I *can* tell. Because I am the Storyteller. So. . .' He slung a cloak about him. . . 'tell the King I'm on my way.'

The messenger moved to leave the room.

The Storyteller paused him with a gesture.

'Do you know, boy, do you know what the penalty for seeing the naked backside of the Chief Wife of the king's Storyteller is?'

'I saw no nakedness.'

'Hah. . . he shall have his eyes plucked out.'

'I didn't look.'

'Hah. . . that's worse. . . *not* looking at the naked backside of the Chief Wife of the king's Storyteller is an insult. . . to both the wife. . . and the Storyteller. . .'

'You're tangling me in words.'

'It's what I do,' murmured the Storyteller, 'it's what I do. Now off with you.'

The messenger left, and the Storyteller after him soon. And the woman left behind in the bed, she stirred, as if she were dreaming. As if she would remember the coming of a messenger, and the voices, and the movements, as if they were parts of a dream.

⌒•

THE CATTLE'S LEGS were hidden, and for all the eyes could see the animals were legless things, carcasses, floating in the mist that filled the hollows. Legless, all of them, and some of them headless too, the grazing ones, their munching heads hidden in the mist. But others held their heads up high, watching the Storyteller as he passed. That is the way of cattle. Some guard, while others graze.

The Storyteller's feet squeezed the silver dew out of the grass, and he left behind him dark footprints, and he thought yes, this is a beautiful morning. And then he thought another yes, yes he should get up earlier, and see more of these beautiful early mornings. But. . . he realised. . . to get up earlier he'd have to leave the woman in the bed. . . earlier. . . and he'd have to leave the drinking of the beer the night before. . . earlier. . . he'd have to abandon the conversation, and the laughter, and that particular revealing wisdom of men halfway between drunk and sober.

And was the loss of all that really worth it?

Not at all, not at all.

And the solution?

Well. Instead of giving up his simple pleasures. . . he *could* lie abed. And there he could quite easily *imagine* the beautiful morning, just bring a picture to his mind, a picture of the grass and it silver touched with dew, and the mist in hollows so the cattle turn into those strange legless creatures, he could picture all that. And the woman's backside would still be in his hands!

He walked on.

It was all a matter of choice. . .

The alternative was that he *could* give up his simple pleasures, and picture *them* in his mind while he walked in the early beauty of the morning.

Indeed.

A man chooses.

He chooses which way to live in the flesh, and which way to live in the mind. And the sum of the ways of the flesh, and the sum of the ways of the mind, they all add up to the same number. And that is life. And when that number is added to death, then the sum of life and death is existence. A man's existence.

He nodded wisely to himself.

Pretty much pleased with this line of thinking!

Yes, a man's life adds up to numbers.

And in actual fact the number that it adds up to doesn't much matter.

Any old number will do.

It's just a number he scrawls in sand, like an idle man on a shore will draw in the sand with his foot. A drawing for an idle wave to wash away.

And the wave, what of that, the idle waves?

They are the gods.

And that is the way of things.

And without the knowing of that, a storyteller has no story.

He walked on, grinning to himself at his early morning philosophy.

If. . . he realised. . . if. . . if the messenger had not come, I would now be fumbling for the woman in the bed. . . and my hands would be full of her hams. . . and I'd be thinking of the pigs' hams hanging from the ceiling, and the similarity. . . and I'd be grinning to myself. . . happy!

If the messenger had not come!

But the messenger *did* come, and so he walked on. And as he walked he looked at his empty hands, at the palms of his empty hands. And he saw there how long he would live. And how he would die. And how many wives would warm him, and the children of his sons, chuckling. He saw all that, written in his hands. And he realised. . . by the gods this early morning air is certainly good for the mind!

He decided yes, yes it was definitely best to be out and about. Because, if he *were* back abed, and if his hands were full of woman's meat, well then it would not be possible for him to see anything at all, either written in his hands or written anywhere else. . .

Is that the plan of women?

To stop a man thinking?

Perhaps.

Who knows the plan of women.

Who *wants* to know the plan of women!

The Storyteller walked on.

He walked to the mound where the ancestor waited.

They said he came from across the sea, that ancestor.

They said his name was Eremon. And they said his wife was Tea, and it was her name on this place. And it was from her they called it Tara.

They said!

But who are they, and who are they to say!

Eremon and Tea were silent now, dead for a thousand years, and there was no asking the truth of them.

Well, the Storyteller thought. . . there certainly *was* the asking of them.

But as for the answering?

He smiled, and then his thoughts of the ancestor wandered off as a girl came passing him, carrying water. Looking at her, she added to his morning, to the advantages of being up and about. Yes, he made his final decision on the whole matter. . . get up early in the mornings, see the beauty, see the girls carrying water and the first smoke of fires and the stirring of the place, get up and see all that. And bring along in the mind the picture of that fine woman's backside in the bed. . . that's having the best of both worlds. . . the world of the eye, and the smell and the touch. . . and the world of the vision too. . .

The girl carrying water smiled, as if she were smiling at his thoughts.

And he smiled back.

He recognised her.

He never forgot a pretty face.

And this one belonged to one of Irial's cumhals.

And Irial was a drunken man who slaughtered pigs and beat his women.

Though both seemed happy, pigs and women alike.

Fate. . . destiny. . . sure isn't a pig's throat born for the knife, and a woman's back for a whip? And isn't it only the fighting against fate, the argument with destiny, isn't it only that that brings the unhappiness?

'Good morning girl, the gods have given you today.'

'And a good day it is, Storyteller.'

'You will have many of them. I can tell it in your smile.'

'I smile for today, not for tomorrow.'

'Aren't you the wise girl!'

'It has been said.'

She stroked her hair from her eyes, and looked at him silently.

'And will be said again,' murmured the Storyteller, looking her up and down, 'among many other things!'

Her feet were bare.

There is something about a girl's feet, no matter how filthy.

Would Irial sell her to him?

Yes of course he would.

But for how much?

Three pigs?

Maybe.

Was she worth three pigs?

The Storyteller thought of his house, and the six hams hanging for the winter. And he thought of those hooks empty. And he thought alright, she *was* a pretty girl, and lively, and not afraid to jest.

But was she *worth* three pigs?

Two?

Two might be the sensible number.

Calculations. . .

If he bought the girl he'd have to feed her.

But then, of course, if he bought her for three pigs he'd no longer have to feed those three pigs. But, there again, to be positive, pigs breed pigs which can be sold. . . and, to be negative, women breed children which must themselves be fed!

By the gods!

Was the worry worth it!

The Storyteller nodded his goodbye to the girl, and she walked away, not looking back, but swaying a hip as if to say I know your mind. . . your calculating mind. . . and be it known I'm worth *six* pigs. . . you mean bastard!

He smiled.

Yes, he got the girl's thoughts, picked them up. From the morning air and the sway of her hips.

Yes maybe I am a mean bastard.

But times are hard and death. . . he shrugged. . . pretty certain!

He walked on.

Laoghaire lived on the south side of Tara, the Storyteller on the east, and thus the simplest journey between the two raths would be a route running in a south-west direction. But the Storyteller never took this simplest route! It was his habit to walk due west from his house to the mound which was the grave of the ancestor and then, from there, to turn due south. He never broke this habit, even when summoned urgently. In fact, *particularly* when summoned. A man may not choose his destination. But surely he has to be free to choose his own journey!

It was his habit also, when he got to the mound, the grave of the ancestor, the ancestor who now would never tell us whether he came from across the sea. . . or merely from over the mountains. . . it was his habit to walk around it.

Three times!

And so he did, now, around that grassy mound, his morning ritual, three times. And when he'd done with walking, he stood there, and faced the north. He raised his left hand in a curse, and cursed the men of Ulster. That made him feel better. And then, his morning cursing done, he stooped down, picked up a bone that came to his hand like it was chosen. A leg bone, it seemed, come tumbled from the heap of sacrificial bones that lay on top of the mound.

Children!

I have told them!

Countless times!

I have told them not to play up there. . . but I might as well be talking to myself. . . it's the parents. . . I blame the parents. . . I've told their parents too. . . have they no control? What is the world coming to? Children running wild, parents taking no interest. . . they'd sooner be drinking. . . and gambling. . . and arguing about cattle. . . racing horses. . . when they should be bringing up their children properly. . .

It can't go on.

I'll talk to the king.

He will issue an order.

But will they even listen to him?

Children!

They've had it too easy.

And they have no respect.

The little bastards!

The thought of careless children spoiled his mood and angered him but, as luck would have it, precisely at that moment a silly hen pecked its way across his path. He danced a step to get it right, and then he kicked the hen which sailed a fluffy squawk away and landed, bouncing in a ball.

Felt better after that!

2

THE KING WAS in no mood for bones or talk of bones. The Storyteller realised that as soon as he saw him. Blood, the more like!

The king was in the mood for blood.

He paced his hall, going up, and down, and up and down again. And those that walked with him walked with him in an anxious little gather, and those that stood around opened a whispering path for him as he passed. And then they closed in behind him, watching for his return, and then opened up again like he was a saw through a tree, and his footsteps were the teeth of the saw and the people were the dust of the wood, scattering.

The Storyteller watched, and saw all this, and waited for his moment. Not for the moment of his choosing, but for the moment that would be chosen for him. There is a difference in those two different waitings.

The king passed, one more time, and not a flicker of his eye noted the Storyteller's arrival. The moment has not been chosen yet, the Storyteller told himself, watching the king and his people walk by. The usual people, the ones who stay close to a king, advisors, lawyers, chiefs and warriors. The leaders of warriors. Dressed in the old way, traditional old men, they carried brown skulls hanging from brown belts.

The leaders of warriors have white hair, thought the Storyteller, while the white skulls of their enemies have taken on the colour of young men's hair. And that is a strange thing to see, stranger to realise. As if the colour lives on, and does not care where it lives. As if the colour were like flesh, which rots in a grave, but lives on in the leaves that grow above.

The Storyteller waited, watching, thinking.

Thoughts. . . of life. . . and death. . . but mostly death.

And then at the end of the hall the king turned, and walked back in his direction. And the people with him, they too turned, and started walking back alongside. Suddenly the king paused, held out his hands, and walked on. And his warriors and advisors and the old people about the place stopped. And the king walked up to the Storyteller alone.

'Did I take you from a woman's bed, Storyteller?'

'Laoghaire,' said the Storyteller, bowing his head, 'for my king.' His bow implied that nothing was too much trouble. Although in truth he didn't actually bow his head *very* much. Not because he lacked respect. No, perhaps more because he had found that those who bow their heads too low to kings tend to have them chopped off eventually. A king does not trust the bowers and the scrapers. A king likes to look in a man's eyes, not at the top of his head where he can't see what he's thinking.

'The news is bad from the west' said Laoghaire, King of Meath.

'What news is that?'

'The girls are dead.'

'The girls?'

'The daughters of this house,' said Laoghaire, father of children.

'Eithne. And Fidelma?'

'Eithne and Fidelma.'

'Eithne the Fair?.'

'And Fidelma the Dark. They are dead.'

'How?'

'That is for you to find out, Storyteller, the how and the why of this. There is a witch from the west, among the men who came. You must talk to her.'

'Why?'

'She has a story. I do not believe her. I'll put her to the fire. But first you must talk to her.'

'Why. . . why talk to her. . . if you do not believe her?'

'Isn't a lie a step to the truth?' murmured Laoghaire, thoughtfully. 'Listen to enough lies, and the truth comes out. And anyway, something in her story. . .'

'So you *do* believe her?'

'Don't trick words with me, Storyteller,' snapped Laoghaire. 'Remember that the fire is big enough for her and you.'

The Storyteller smiled. But not too much. the girls were dead, not the time for humour. He spread his hands. 'I eat well. I drink beer. I have my wives about me. And a good roof. Horses. Cattle. My apple orchard. And fourteen pigs.'

'And?'

'All these things I have from my king. What I am saying is this, Laoghaire. . . I am paid well. . . I am paid well by you. . . to trick with words.'

'Hah! All storytellers trick with words. And not for their payment either. It is the way of them. And witches too. Storytellers and witches, you're seeds from the same field. So, that witch from the west. . . talk to her. . . I am a warrior. . . I am a king because my father Niall was a king. . . I have no understanding of witchery and magic things.'

Laoghaire walked away and, when they saw him go, his followers and retainers and advisors and servants who had waited still, they moved after him in a crowd. And the storyteller watched, Laoghaire alone in the crowd, a great king, the greatest of kings.

The Storyteller watched, and he saw the great king lonely.

⌒·

THE WITCH FROM THE WEST WAS OLD.

Thirty five if she was a day.

She was ready for the fire. They had stripped her bare, and tied her to a post. And small boys were dragging branches to add to a heap.

But, although she was naked and tied, the witch had the air of someone who was dressed in the finest, someone quite free of the cares of people. She watched the children and the branches, with something of a smile. And although she was old, the Storyteller noted, because he noted women generally, an interest of his, he noted that she had the body of a woman who has had no children herself. Everything about her was young, and strong, and firm. And it was a pity to burn her. But then it's a pity too when the storm takes off your roof, and the waves wash away your fish trap, and the winds flatten the oats in a field. It's a pity. But pity and sadness and regret are things of the world of men. The gods have no pity. And the storm will blow and the witch will burn.

The Storyteller looked her up and down, silently. And he reached out with the leg bone in his hand and lifted her dark hair from her white shoulders, and let it fall again. It fell silently. And he thought that strange. He didn't quite know what sound he expected from hair falling on shoulders. . . but nonetheless the silence of its falling was strange, unexpected.

'Laoghaire is the greatest of kings,' he said, 'what madness was it to kill his daughters?'

She shrugged, silent.

'Why did you come, witch?'

'Daithi sent me,' she replied.

'Oh right enough and maybe so. But let me tell you. . . it's not a witch that Laoghaire will be sending back! There's messengers gone to the north. And the south. And the east. Laoghaire will gather an army here. And move into the heart of Connacht. There will be slaughter. And the burning of houses. And the driving away of cattle. And the selling of children into slavery.'

'If it happens,' said the witch, 'it happens.'

'Well that's a very calm way of looking at things,' said the Storyteller, 'particularly for someone who's about to be burnt.' He looked her up and down. And he reached out with the leg bone in his hand and poked at her. A fleshy woman, she squirmed to the poking but otherwise took no heed. The look on her face was amused, mocking. He lifted one of her breasts, and toyed at it with the knobbley end of the bone. And pressed it into her, watching the meat wrap itself around the bone, and feeling the love of the meat for the bone, and the love of the bone for the meat.

'Flesh clings to the bone,' he said, thoughtfully.

'It surely does,' agreed the witch.

He lifted the breast with the bone, and felt its heaviness, and it travelling along the bone into his hand, and at the same time he felt his own body sending strength to his wrist, so that her heaviness and his strength balanced each other out, so that neither heaviness nor strength existed for a moment.

He felt that.

And he didn't know what it meant. And then he took away the bone, and the flesh fell into its shape again. It fell into shape silently. And he thought that strange. He didn't quite know what sound he expected from a breast falling into its natural shape. . . but nonetheless the silence of its falling was strange, unexpected.

'Flesh falls from the bone,' he said.
'It surely does,' said the witch.
Both said nothing for awhile.
A vee of ducks quacked towards the dark skies in the south, flapping.
Boys called to boys about the gathering of the fire, squabbling over branches.
A young woman sitting nearby on a tuft was combing her hair, silently, watching. Her hair was long and coarse and the colour of straw.
The quacking, the flapping, the squabbling, the watching, the combing of the hair, the sound of the silent moment.
'Now. .' said the Storyteller, 'to the matter. . . what is the story?'
'It is long.'
'And you will make it longer? To avoid the flames.'
'Whose bone do you carry?' asked the witch, ignoring the jibe.
'I found it. Beside the mound where our ancestor lies. The old people would sacrifice to him, captives, and whoever. And the bones of the sacrificed are piled on the top.'
'Why did you carry it away?'
'It had rolled to the bottom of the mound. Children play up there. . . these days. . . they have no respect. . .'
'The old ways are changing.'
'Is it like that in your country too, in Daithi's kingdom?'
'The Roman moves about.'
'He has passed through here. I told Laoghaire to kill him. And his followers. But he didn't. I think he was afraid.'
'Why did you tell him to kill him?'
'Perhaps because I myself was afraid!'
'I know, Storyteller.'
'You seem to know a lot about me, Witch. . . perhaps too much. . . it's I who would learn about you. . . so tell me. . . what is this story, what is the story you and your muddy magicians bring from the west?'
'The Roman and his followers were in our country.'
'Come to think of it, where *are* your muddy magicians?'
The witch nodded, in a certain direction. And the Storyteller followed the nod and over there he saw a row of heads, new heads,

on new stakes, in a silent row, looking the one to the other like they were surprised to be dead. Their mouths were open, as if they were talking, but the only voices in the air were those of women, chattering women, bending about the stakes, with pots, containers.

The young woman sitting nearby on a tuft still combed her hair, silently, watching. The Storyteller noticed that she turned her head to follow his eyes when he looked at the magicians. And then, when he looked back to the witch at the stake, she too looked back. And all the while she combed her hair. He noticed how the comb in one hand followed the flat of the other. A rhythm, of smoothing and combing and patting. Are women born with that in them, that rhythm?

Perhaps.

But no matter. He put his attention to the witch. 'The crones collect the blood for spells,' he explained, 'do they do that in your country too?'

'Not so much. Not now. The old ways are changing.'

'Yes, everywhere, 'said the Storyteller, moodily. 'The shrines are neglected. And there's weeds in the wells. And I heard the great tree of Munster has fallen. Did you hear that the great tree of Munster has fallen?'

'It fell in a storm'

'I heard that too.'

'The storm came from nowhere. On a summer's day.'

'That is a god. . . wearing the cloak of a storm.'

'An angry god,' said the witch, and her tone was that of someone ending a conversation, like its purpose was over.

'But still, but still,' said the Storyteller, a mite irritated by her disinterest, 'but still, all is not lost. . . round here I keep them on their toes. . . reminding them. . . the old ways, the old magic. . . little things. . . it's in the little things. . . like when you burn,' the Storyteller poked the witch's belly with his bone, 'when you burn they will collect your fat. . . for special candles.'

'I will light their darkness,' she murmured, and that was a mockery in her voice, the Storyteller realised. Well, he thought, when she dances with the flames she'll be in need of all that mockery. A burning witch is not a pretty sight. Nor her screams a pleasant sound.

'You seem remarkably happy about your present situation!'

She shrugged, as if it was of no matter. 'I will light their darkness. . . but with my darkness.'

'Oh don't riddle me, woman,' the Storyteller snapped angrily, hitting her across the thigh with the bone.

She said nothing.

'Now,' he said sternly, 'now to the matter and no more nonsense. Tell me the story. Tell me about Eithne the Fair and Fidelma the Dark, the Auburn Haired. But first. . .' He hit her again with the bone. 'First, tell me your name.'

She said nothing. And he was about to hit her again when she nodded, directing his eyes back to the row of heads beyond. And over them now the Storyteller saw a bird, flying, flying low, along the row of heads, back and forth as if about to choose a perch. A black bird, a large black bird with ragged wings, and the feathers like a bunch of jagged knives.

He did not like the look of that bird.

'Tell me your name,' the Storyteller repeated, in a mutter, not expecting an answer, vaguely watching the bird. And how it choose a head, and landed, and fluttered its feathers that were like a bunch of jagged knives, and settled, watching. He did not like the look of that bird.

Whether it was watching the chattering women about the stakes, or watching the Storyteller and the witch, it was not possible to say. But that was not the point. The Storyteller just did not like that bird, and did not like it looking at him. Or even *not* looking at him. That was a bad bird, in his opinion. And a bad omen. And he was thinking how bad an omen it was when he noticed her again, the young woman combing her straw coloured hair. And how she was watching him, and the witch, and the bird, one to the other, turning her head. And all the while combing, and smoothing, and patting her hair.

'Boy,' he called out to one of the boys dragging branches to the witch's fire.

'Storyteller?' asked the boy, nervously.

'Do you see that bird. . .' he pointed. . . 'go kill that bird.'

'I cannot kill a bird.'

'Go. Kill. That. Damn.Bird.'

'I cannot kill a bird,' the boy insisted.

'What is your name, boy?' asked the Storyteller, sighing, hoping the question might bring a better answer than it had from the witch.

'Conor.'

'Ah. Alright. With a name like that you surely cannot kill a bird, you are well taught. But tell me, what can you kill?'

'I can kill a rabbit. Or a dog. Or a pig. Or a cow. But I cannot kill a bird.'

'By the gods ! What boy here can kill a bird?'

'Felim can kill birds. But he cannot kill a pig.'

'Oh good. That's good to know. And if that were a flying pig, over there on the head, then we wouldn't trouble Felim. But seeing as it's not. . . just you go tell Felim to kill that bird.'

'Would not telling Felim to kill the bird be the same as me killing the bird myself?' said the boy, carefully.

'No. Not a bit of it. Entirely different thing. I know about these geiseanna. Trust me. Go tell Felim. Now.'

'Oh,' the boy was still doubtful, 'oh, alright.' He wandered away, not in any hurry, like his footsteps were worries.

'You lied to that boy,' said the witch. 'He who orders another does the deed.'

'Of course I lied. . . nothing would be done without lies.'

'Or truth. . . nothing would be done without truth.'

'Yes, but lies are more certain than truth. A lie is always a lie. But the truth is sometimes. . .' He spread his arms.

'That is the way of it, Storyteller.'

'Lies are the rocks in the stream, and the truth is the water, washing them.'

'Some would say the other way, the other way around.'

'Some would say. . .' the Storyteller paced about, exasperated, 'some would say. . . sure they'd say anything. . . to get a hearing.'

'The Roman says there is just one god.'

'For sure. And I bet he says it's his!'

'Indeed. He came to us in Magh Ai. . . we must put away our gods, the Roman said, and listen to this one god. . .'

'What did your king Daithi say?'

'He would have no heed of him.'

'Should've killed him. All foreigners should be killed. They're here to take, not give. In the days of the old kings there'd be no

Roman bands, wandering the country, talking nonsense to the people, disturbing things. One god! Hah.' The Storyteller spat on the ground. 'How can there be one god?'

'That's what Cathad asked...'

'How *is* old Cathad?'

'Well. But old. When the Roman came and talked to Daithi he sent for Cathad. And said there is a mad man here from over the sea... he is a Roman...'

'What did Cathad say?'

'Does he trade wine, he asked.'

'Ah,' the Storyteller laughed, 'the same old Cathad... he likes his wine.'

'Do you like wine?'

'Surely. But I prefer women.'

'Have you many wives?'

'Enough,' said the Storyteller. 'Or nearly enough,' he added, seeing an image of the slavegirl with the water jug, and the image walking past his mind like she was there, dirty feet and all.

'The Roman says you must have one wife, only one wife.'

'Hah,' the Storyteller laughed, 'to go with the one god I suppose! And then we'll all have one cow? One pig? It's ridiculous. Why do people listen to this Roman?' He spat on the ground again.

'Cathad the Druid listened to him. And then told Daithi not to kill him.'

'That man is getting old... befuddled with drink! So, Witch... is this the story? Is this the story you bring from the west?'

'Not yet,' she replied, vaguely, her mind elsewhere.

The Storyteller followed her eyes. And over beyond where the heads of the muddy magicians were staked he saw some boys, with spears, chasing the bird with raggedy wings, trying to spear it. And with very little success. It hopped from head to head as soon as a spear was thrust in its direction, and it fluttered, and slid sideways through the air. But not, the Storyteller noted, not in any agitated fashion. Calmly, easily, just doing enough to avoid getting speared, like an old person indulging some children's game. Expending enough energy to be part of the game... but not totally involved.

'What bird is that?' he asked, aloud, but not a question of the witch, although she heard, and answered.

'Mark that bird well, Storyteller,' she said.

'What bird is that, Witch?' he asked her, directly.

She looked at him, and laughed. But there was no sound of laughter, although her face had the movements of someone laughing. Instead of sound of human the Storyteller heard the scraw and the screech of the bird.

He jumped back. And with the end of the bone in his hand he drew a quick circle about himself in the ground. And he said words to himself that were secret.

'Too late, Storyteller' she said. 'Remember. . . and remember this on your journey.'

'Remember? Journey? What journey?'

'Flesh clings to the bone.'

⌒•

'HE WALKS IN HIS GARDEN,' said the wife to the wife.

'He picks apples from his tree,' said the wife to the wife.

'But he only takes one bite, and throws them away, and walks on. . .'

'He looks at his bees.'

'He talks to the stableboys.'

'He walks in his garden.'

'He picks apples from his tree, but doesn't eat them.'

'That witch has unsettled him.'

'What did she say?'

'I don't know. . . they burn her tonight.'

'Good riddance I would say.'

'And I would agree. . . do you remember Eithne?'

'And Fidelma. Yes I do.'

'They were pretty girls.'

'Which was older?'

'Eithne. . . but not by much.'

'They were always together.'

'Different mothers, hadn't they?'

'Yes, half sisters. One is fair, the other dark.'

'Nice to see half sisters getting on.'

'Sometimes they don't.'

'Who're you telling!'

3

'THE STONE IS silent, Storyteller, the stone is silent now.' 'That stone has spoken, long ago, Laoghaire. You *are* the king.'

'But king of what? Look over there, the sun. The sun is going down, Storyteller, and if I say slow or hurry it will make no difference. The sun will still go down.'

'Surely.' The Storyteller looked up at the king, anxious at his mood.

They were alone, at the centre of Tara, on the mound where the kings are crowned. Laoghaire stood on the stone, the Stone of Destiny, and the Storyteller stood beside him on the grass. He noticed how the grass was long, too long, neglected looking. And the ground was burrowed with rabbits. And something had eaten something, and there was fur and scraps of skin. And there was rabbit droppings, and cattle shit, and it was good to be wearing good sandals. And the Storyteller looked at all this and knew it was the turn of times.

He clacked his bone against the stone.

He'd carried it throughout the day, and the habit of it was in his hand. And the truth was, he didn't quite know what to do with it. *Something* had rolled it his way... and until he had more information on that something, well, perhaps it would be better to hang on to it.

That was his thinking anyway.

He looked to the far west, and the red disc of the sun setting, and he saw a cloud the shape of a hand, a hand that was streaked and dripped with blood. And he saw a leaning tree on a hill and it looked like a spear that was stuck in the ground, some battle over.

'What king,' asked Laoghaire, 'what king tells the sun to fall, and the sun to rise?'

'The old people believed that the sun *was* the king' replied the Storyteller.

'The old people are dead,' said the king.

'But do their beliefs die with them?'

'Why question me? Ask me what I know!'

The Storyteller held his silence, watching. The last of the sun going into the black land, like the tip of a red tongue into a black mouth. Watching, watching. How many sunsets does a man watch, and what does he learn from each? Is a sunset like a woman, where a man learns a bit from each and adds it to his understanding of the next? No, it's not like that at all. A man could watch a thousand sunsets. And still fumble foolishly with the next.

The Storyteller held his silence, listening. The bang of drums now, and the clang of metal bells, over there, behind the Storyteller and the king. They turned around, and over there among the buildings they saw the people gathering, ones and twos becoming groups. They carried lights, and the lights bounced to their footsteps. A stream of lights, thought the Storyteller, like sparkles on a black stream in sunlight. Yes, just like that! How like the day is night, he realised, one the other through a mirror glass. Is life, and death, like that, he asked himself, one through the other like mirror glass?

No answer.

'Why are you burning the witch?' he asked Laoghaire.

'Revenge,' said the king, a one word man when asked the hard question.

'Daithi will not be pleased, you burning his witch, beheading his magicians.'

'He'll be pleased less when my armies come and burn Rathcroghan!' said Laoghaire coldly.

'What did the witch tell you?'

'What did she tell *you*, Storyteller? I sent you to ask her, to understand her story.'

'I got no sense from her.'

'You only stayed the hour. . . or even less.'

'Who tells you this, who spies on me?'

'And you went walking in your garden, and in the fields alone. With a black dog and a white dog.'

'Who tells you this? Can a man not walk his dogs?'

'The black dog you call Night, and the white dog you call Day.'

'Are we to talk of the names of dogs? Who tells you what I do, and where I go?'

'I asked you for the witch's story. But you left her. To walk your dogs.' The king shook his head. The shake implied that he was astonished, but not surprised. Such bad behaviour was all he could expect. The disloyalty of men!

'I took the witch's story to the fields, to think on it. Who spies on me?'

'You talked to children. And you talked to the old man who guards my bulls. And you talked to a man visiting from Eamhain. And you ate two meals. One with the wife they call the daughter of the moon. Why do they call her that?'

'She was born at night.'

'Many children are born at night. Are we to call them *all* the daughters or the sons of the moon?'

'Her father called her that, ask him!'

'Her father? Old Anluan of Connacht. . . he's dead these couple of years, as well you know, Storyteller.'

'Well then, my king, well then we'll never know. Unless. . .'

'Unless?'

'Unless that spy who spies on me. . . unless you send him to the Otherworld. . . to enquire. . . to report. . .'

'You have a quick mind, Storyteller, and a quick tongue. There's many a quick tongue dug a grave. . . slowly.'

'I am my father, and he was his, and he was his, and he was his.'

'Indeed. I haven't a notion what that means. And you probably don't either. So tell me more. . . '

'About?'

'Your day. It interests me. That pleasant quality of leisure about it. And the ease. Particularly the ease with which you ignored my request to question the witch.'

'There is no talking to that witch. Her answers to questions are riddles and spells.'

'Aren't riddles and spells your business? But. . .' Laoghaire raised a finger. 'Knowing what goes on is mine. . . so I will tell you. . . more of your day. . . and a pleasant day it was. . . later then you had your evening meal. . . in the house of your chief wife. . . and you played chess with your son. . .'

'It is good for his mind. Too many parents these days spend too little time with their children.'

'And too many storytellers ignore the orders of their king?'

'Laoghaire. . . this I know about the witch. . . her story is not to be told in my words. Nor understood in words either. What did she tell you, when she came first?'

'She told me the daughters of this house had died.'

'Died, not killed?'

'Died. They met the god of the Roman. . . and died, and their shadows went with him.'

'I wouldn't be believing that in a hurry!'

'Me neither. . . that's why you will go there.'

'I will go where?'

'To Rathcroghan. . . to find out what really happened.'

'But. . .' The Storyteller didn't think this was a good idea at all. 'But you are leading an army into Connacht. To destroy the kingdom.'

'That will take days. For my sons to gather the warriors. There's more to war than marching, you know. Oh a lot more! There's the gathering of men. And weapons. And horses. And men must eat. All takes time. In the meantime, you will move fast.'

'Fast?'

'So that you will find out. . . what really happened to my daughters.'

'Why?'

'If this Roman really has a powerful god. . . and if my daughters have gone to that god. . . well I'm thinking it may not be a good idea to destroy Connacht. . . so. . . by sending you, I will know before the army arrives. . .'

'And?'

'And then I may change my mind.'

'But. . .'

'Yes?'

'But you mean I am to go to Daithi. . . and I am to tell him his witch is burnt. . . and the heads of his magicians are on stakes. . .'

'Sure he'll know anyway. Such news travels fast. Traders and travellers. What do they do but gossip!'

'Daithi may not take kindly. . . to this news. . . he may decide that Laoghaire's Storyteller should meet the same fate as Daithi's witch.'

'That's a risk we have to take.'

'We? We? What do you mean *we*, King?'

'Well, *you* take the risk of the fire, *I* take the risk of losing a good Storyteller. Now, no more. Let us listen for the witch's screams.'

The Storyteller looked gloomily across the field.

It did not take any great imagination to see himself shortly in a similar situation as Daith's witch. This was a tricky situation, a very tricky situation indeed. And the solution was not entirely clear. The Storyteller brooded, and looked across the broody night into the darkness, and the dark happenings beyond.

Over there, to the west of the Slope of The Chariots, at the traditional place for burning witches, over there he could just about see her, a finger of white on the black mound of sticks. It was that time of night when the earth is darker than the sky, even though the sky itself is very dark. The black mound over there was very black indeed, much blacker than the sky. Breast shaped, it looked to him, rising up. But then, he realised,. a lot of things look breast shaped to him, a man particularly interested in women. However. . . whatever about that, the thing was definitely breast shaped, and the little white figure of the witch made the nipple.

How quiet things are.

Yes, everything seemed quiet, still. And then, in the way of these things, everything suddenly burst into action. Little black figures of people darted in and out with flickers of fire. And then the fire took hold. And soon the black mound was ringed with a bracelet of light, like a black slavegirl might be decorated for dancing. But not really like a black slavegirl might be decorated for dancing, because the black itself did not move, it was the light that moved, danced, and grew as the fire took grip. And the little white figure that was the witch wriggled and writhed.

Not like a nipple now, thought the Storyteller, what is it like?

He knew what it was like before he admitted to himself what it was like.

It was like a finger beckoning.

And it was a beckoning ever more urgent.

Come here, come hurry, come here Storyteller, beckoned the finger, the finger that was the witch burning. But not there, not over to the fire, that was not where it beckoned to. . . it drew him to somewhere else. Yes, the burning witch was beckoning him. He felt a chill inside of him, and a silence, and he was glad when the silence was broken by the king's words.

'I don't hear her screaming,' he said.
'Me neither.'
'That's very disappointing.'
'It is indeed.'
'What do you hear, Storyteller.'
'Drums. . . banging. . . distant voices.'
'No no,' said Laoghaire, pointing a finger into the sky the way a man does when he wants another to listen. 'No, hear that.'
'What?'
'It's like a moaning.'
'Yes it *is* like a moaning.'
'But it's in the sky.'
'Yes it is in the sky.'

Both men looked up into the darkness, their heads acock so each had an ear pointing upwards.

'What would that be?' asked Laoghaire.
'I have no idea,' said the Storyteller, 'but. . .' With the legbone he'd carried since morning he drew a circle on the ground around himself and King Laoghaire. . . and muttered certain secret words.

'Are we safe now?' asked Laoghaire.
'Safer than we were,' said the Storyteller, without much conviction.
'But not safe?'
'From what? From what are we not safe?'
'You're the Storyteller. . . do you see anything?'
'No. . . yes. . . no. . . yes yes yes. . .'
'What what?'
'No. . . it was nothing. . . a shadow. . .'
'The moaning is going. . .'
'Yes it is going now. . .'
'And we saw nothing. . .'
'We saw nothing.'

The Storyteller looked back towards where they were burning the witch. And there was nothing now there but fire. There was no black breast, no nipple, no finger beckoning. Just fire, fire, fire, burning and twisting, and the flames were like devils having sex with each other.

'Well I'm for bed,' said Laoghaire, 'we might talk in the very early morning, before you go.'

'Go?'

'To Rathcroghan.'

'Oh yes, of course, my king,' said the Storyteller, gloomily. And gloomily he watched Laoghaire slapping a leather cloak about himself, and shifting a sword at his belt. A bronze sword, he noticed, some old thing handed down through fathers, not a fighting sword, not for now. Now the young men fought with iron. Their swords would slice through bronze like knife through butter.

Everything was changing. But Laoghaire as the king did not need a new iron sword. All the king needs is a symbol. To show he is the king. His sons are armed with iron.

'I'll have a woman this night,' said Laoghaire.

'Enjoy her,' said the Storyteller.

'Burning a witch puts a man in the mood for a woman,' said Laoghaire. 'Particularly if she screams.'

'She didn't scream,' said the Storyteller.

'No but we did hear moaning in the sky. . . something anyway.'

'That we did,' said the Storyteller, 'that we did.'

He watched King Laoghaire leave, and he wondered why he had lied to his king, why, why had he not told him. . . that in fact not only had he heard the moaning, he had also *seen*, seen something in the sky.

⁓•

'WHO BLOCKS THE PATH OF THE KING,' said Laoghaire.

A voice with a foreign accent replied.

'It is I, Cassanus, O King.'

'Oh by all the gods,' said Laoghaire, exasperated, looking at the Roman priest. 'What do you want. . . now?' He was tired of them all, the Romans, and their silly haircuts. He was tired of them, and their asking, their forever asking.

Can we have a plot of land for a church?

Can we put a cross at the well where the women wash?

Can we light a fire on the hill to celebrate a saint?

Can we do this, can we do that, can we, give us, help us. . .

And what in return for this? The promise of eternal life!

Laoghaire wasn't at all sure about eternal life. But one thing he was sure of, a promise makes an easy bargain.

'What do you want, the king is tired. What are you doing in Tara tonight anyway? Didn't I give you land, on the plain of Eachnach, to build a church? Isn't that enough?'

'There must be no more burning of witches,' said Cassanus.

Laoghaire looked at him, thoughtfully, and then a vague and cunning smile drifted over his face and he said 'Would you prefer the burning of Roman priests?'

'Jesus Christ the Lord God would not approve of burning witches' was Cassanus' answer.

'Should I nail them to a cross, the witches?'

'They should be baptised for the Lord,' said Cassanus.

'Baptised for the Lord,' repeated Laoghaire.

'Yes.'

'Baptised for the Lord,' said Laoghaire, again. And held up his hand. A command. 'Do not speak to me, and I will speak to you.'

The priest shuffled about, silently.

'I will tell you of two daughters of this house, my daughters, Eithne and Fidelma. Eithne is the one they call The Fair, and Fidelma is the Dark. Each take the colour of their mothers.' The King raised a finger. 'And tell me not again to take one wife. . . or your head will join the wizards of the witch. The burnt witch!'

The priest shuffled about, nervously.

'It is the custom among the people here. . . you people wouldn't know this. . . being ignorant foreigners. . . but it is the custom to send our children away to be taught. . . my sons go to the houses of farmers and soldiers. . . my daughters go to other kingdoms. . . my sons grow up with the children of farmers and soldiers. . . and my daughters sometimes marry the sons of other kingdoms. . . this custom weaves us together. . . do you understand that?'

'Yes, King Laoghaire,' said Cassanus.

'All customs have a meaning. Eithne and Fidelma were sent to Rathcroghan. There is a great school there. Cathad the Druid has that school. Eithne and Fidelma would learn those things. Would you prefer our women learn nothing?'

'A woman is the mother of children,' said Cassanus.

'And if she knows nothing. . . what would a child know. . .

do you know what I think. . . I think you Romans are afraid of women. . . but that is no matter. . . I am tired. . . and one of the women who you're afraid of waits for her king in my bed. . . so about the witch. . . the witch burned because she came with wizards to my house. . . I will have no Connacht witch nor wizards in my house. . . Daithi knows this. . . and he sent them for a mockery. . . and he sent them with a story, to add insult to the mockery. . .'

'What is that story?'

'The story is that Eithne and Fidelma are dead. That they have died to go. . .' King Laoghaire paused. . . 'to go to your God. . .'

'God awaits us all.'

'Indeed. . . indeed. . . the story brought by the witch and her wizards says that Patrick, your leader, he is in that country. . .'

'He travels in the west, baptising many for the Lord.'

'The story brought says that Patrick prayed with my daughters, Eithne and Fidelma, and that they then died. . . and went to your God. . .'

'It's a miracle.'

'And a bigger one if I believe it. . .'

'So what will you do now, King Laoghaire.'

'I have sent my storyteller to the west. . . he is a man who understands. . . he will find out what really happened. . .'

'And then?'

'And then I will burn Connacht. . . Daithi's head will hang from my bridle. . . and his sons' heads from my warriors' belts. . . and his daughters will be sold to the Picts. . .'

Laoghaire smiled at the priest, reading the shock on his face.

'Or,' he said, pointing at him. . . 'or. . . depending on what my storyteller reports. . . 'or I shall turn my army against the Romans. . . and burn their churches. . . and tear down the crosses on the holy hills. . . and drown their priests in the wells they've given to their saints. . . and I'll hunt down their hermits in the mountains with my hunting dogs. . . and I'll give their nuns to my soldiers as harlots. . . that is what I will do. . . but not now. . .'

'Not now?,' said Cassanus.

'No, not now. *Now* I go to bed. But thanks to you my wife is probably asleep by now. And a king wouldn't wake a woman for sex. So be glad, your delaying has taught me chastity. . . for one night anyway.'

'The King will sleep in the arms of God.'

Laoghaire looked to the sky, and sighed, deeply. He saw no Christian heaven in that sky. He slapped his cloak about himself, and walked on.

⌢•

THE STORYTELLER SAT, with the black dog he called Night, and the white dog he called Day, and at his knees sat his youngest wife, the one they called the daughter of the moon. Her hair was blonde, a harsh and unattractive yellow blonde with a touch of red, and the fire in his hearth was grey, and the night was cold for the time of year. He looked at the ashes of the fire, and the girl's hair between him and the fire, and the yellow and the red colours of her hair reminded him of the flames that had died in the hearth.

'Do you hear the wind, girl?'

'I hear the wind, husband.'

'Will it rain?'

'Not tonight. . . tomorrow.'

'These are bad seasons. . . and tomorrow I travel to the west.'

'Oh will you take me to the west? I'd like to be in my own place. . . again. . .'

'I will take my black dog, and my white dog.'

'You will be lonely for the want of a woman.'

'The white dog is a bitch. . . I'll sleep with her.'

'She's not so pretty as me.'

'Almost! Anyway my prick is not looking for prettiness.'

'She cannot sing. Or cook. Or laugh at your jokes.'

'It's far too dangerous. . . for you to travel. . . there is talk of war.'

'There's always talk of war. . . and I'd really like to go. There's nothing to do here. And your Chief Wife doesn't like me. Orders me around when you're not here.'

'We all must follow orders. The king orders me. I order my Chief Wife. She orders you. Discipline! This is the trouble with you young people. No discipline.'

'Stop speaking like an old man.'

'Just because I am wise. . . would I call you foolish because you're young? Why call me old because I'm wise?'

'You often call me foolish.'

'You often *are* foolish.'

'Why did you marry me then?'

'I owed your father a favour.'

'Hah. . . if that's your jest. . . you'll be getting no favours from me tonight, Storyteller!'

'I'll sleep with my white dog so.'

'And I with the black.'

'But he's called Night, and you're called daughter of the moon. . . oh. . . enough of playing with words.' The Storyteller reached out, and touched her hair. 'Sing for me, girl.'

'What would I sing. . . a sad song, or a happy song?'

'There is a song you sang. Once. When I was bringing you from your people. Across the river. Do you remember?'

'That was years ago. . .'

'Do you remember the song?'

'Of course I remember. . . but I can't sing that song here.'

'Why not?'

'Because that is the song of the river. . . and there'll be no music in my voice if I sing it here.'

The Storyteller laughed. And looked into her eyes. And wished he hadn't! Because he saw again how one was cold, and one was cruel. 'You're a strange foreign person. . .' he said to her, looking away, hiding a shiver. Suddenly in his mind was the witch on the fire, and the heads of the wizards from Connacht on the stakes, and all the strangeness of those foreign people.

He touched the Wife's coarse Connacht hair with fingertips. He remembered her, combing her hair that morning, sitting there on a tuft, silently. And how she watched him and the witch and the magicians, and the black bird with feathers like jagged knives. He remembered that. And now the witch was ashes. And now the dark bird was invisible in the dark night. And now his fingers were the teeth of a young woman's comb.

'Oh sing anyway,' he said, 'sing me any old song.'

And so she sang. And as she sang he combed her coarse Connacht hair with his fingertips. Remembering her, combing her hair that morning, sitting there on a tuft, silently. And how she watched then. And now she sang and he listened, but he could not tell whether the song she sang was sad, or happy. And he realised how much strangeness there was about her, how much difference. Just like her singing, it was the same about herself, whether she was sad, or happy, it always was a mystery. And the touch of her to the hands, her body, neither warm, nor cold, but something different. Oh well, marry a foreigner, a woman from Connacht, and those are the thoughts a man brings to his bed.

⁓•

'AND DON'T COME BACK,' said the tavern keeper to the man he'd just thrown out, the man who lay in the mud at the door. 'I'm sick of your drunken fighting. . .'

'But. . .' said Irial the pig slaughterer.

'But nothing,' said the tavern keeper, 'there's honest men in here. . . relaxing after a hard day. . . a few drinks. . . a joke. . . good conversation. . . you and your fighting. . . hah!'

He slammed the door.

Irial the pig slaughterer crawled to his feet. He wasn't that drunk. He'd been a lot drunker last week. He stood up, he got his bearings, and walked, not that unsteadily, to his house.

It wasn't fair.

There was drunker men than him in that tavern.

And what did the tavern keeper expect? Did he expect a man to sit there being insulted? By some half witted bogtrotter? By the gods. No, he wouldn't go there again. His money was hard earned. He wouldn't spend it in a place where a man got no respect. He went into his house and sat in a chair.

Where was that slavegirl, to take off his boots?

What did she expect, a man to take off his own boots?

In his own house?

Oh by the gods!

She was in for a whipping, no doubt about that, no doubt about that at all. He'd get some respect in his own house if nowhere else!

'Where are you girl?' he roared.

There she was, in the doorway to the other room.

'Haven't I told you to be waiting here?'

'I was waiting there.'

'*There* is not *here*. . . when I say here I mean *here*, not *there*. Go get my whip. Oh your back will be sore tonight girl, that'll be a lesson.'

Silently, she went out again.

He sat, waiting, dozing a bit.

Shook himself awake.

It'd be a pity to fall asleep before the girl was whipped.

Looking forward to it. The welts, the blood, the helplessness.

He dozed.

He heard her near.

He woke.

'About time too,' he said, 'give me that whip and get down there you whelp.'

He reached out his hand. She reached out hers and slammed the axe into his head. It split the head into two thirds and one third. The two thirds stayed on the neck, and the one third sliced away, fell from his shoulder, and tumbled to the floor.

She smiled, and sighed, relieved.

And then, fastidiously, she opened her fingers and dropped the axe beside the mess of brain and bone and blood. She watched it, fall, straight down, and she nodded as it embedded itself in the floor, remaining there, upright, a marker on a messy grave.

She went to the door and waiting for her there like the ghost of a friend was her cloak. She put it on. And there waiting also was a bag, she picked that up. And then she went out the door, quickly, her hips swaying. And as she passed through the doorway her hips brushed against the door, and it closed, creaking. And she heard the sound of it like keening and she smiled. A cold smile on her pretty face. A pretty girl. An ever so pretty girl. She was worth far more than a couple of pigs. But there was no-one there to see her prettiness, no-one there to make an offer for the pretty slavegirl. Only the dead eyeball of Irial the pig slaughterer watched as she hurried away.

Into the darkness of sleeping Tara.

Quietly around the laziness of sentries.

Into the darkness of the countryside.

4

HE WOKE TO AN EMPTY BED. The clatter of a servant boy around him. 'Break that jug, boy,' he muttered. 'break it and I'll have your head.' He was very fond of that jug.

A trader from Armorica had brought it, long ago. Samian pottery, richly red, valuable and rare. It was one of those possessions a man hangs on to, as his life changes. He gets them early in life, and builds them around him, and builds life around them. These are my precious things, a man says. Each one of these is a slate on the roof to my soul. I will keep these things, he says. And at that stage he wants no more. If he is wise. If he is foolish he keeps gathering all his life. And nothing then is precious. He has too many things about him.

This is the way of it, he thought, watching the servant boy.

Warily.

Then relief to see the good jug of good fresh milk there, safe on the table.

Alongside the bread.

Baked by the Quiet One, his middle wife, she rarely spoke, but baked good bread.

What more could a man ask for!

The second half of his brain woke up. And the emptiness of the bed he was in became more important, more interesting, it conjured up more questions.

Why is the bed empty?

Who was in it, which wife?

Where has she gone. . . the daughter of the moon. . . oh yes it was her. . . the skinniness of her still in the memory. . . but where has she gone. . .

'Have you seen my wife?' he said to the servant boy.

'Not this morning Storyteller.'

'Well go out there and find her. . . by the gods. . . now. . . go. . . go on. . .'

The boy hurried out.

The Storyteller tore off a hunk of bread, and bit a hunk of the hunk out of it.

Honey, he thought, that'd be good, why is there no honey to dip this into?

Can a man not have any comfort in his own house?

An empty bed.

No honey for his bread.

By the gods!

And a long journey ahead, a long and dangerous journey.

No wife. . . no honey. . .

He sighed.

Yes at least he knew why there was no honey. Because that damn servant boy was afraid of bees, that's why!

By the gods!

A servant boy afraid of bees!

What was the world coming to?

Would he have to starve if the servant boy became afraid of cows and pigs?

By the gods!

He chewed the bread, morosely.

He washed it down with milk from the jug.

By the gods! No woman in the bed, no honey for the bread, I might as well be one of those damn Christian hermits in the woods. . . they live on prayer and air!

'What is it now?,' he called, seeing the door open, thinking it was the servant boy, come back to annoy him with some foolishness.

It wasn't the servant boy, it was another young man, standing there.

Dithering, nervous of entering.

The Storyteller recognised the young man. Fair, and slim, and girlish. . . yes definitely girlish. . . because it *was* a girl!

'By all the gods,' he roared, leaping out of the bed. 'Wife, what have you done?' he yelled at her.

'I have cut my hair.'

'You have lovely hair,' he heard himself shout, simultaneously hearing another part of his mind whisper no she hadn't, it wasn't lovely, it was in fact rather coarse and an ugly shade of yellow red.

'Not any longer,' she said.

'What're you doing, you're mad... you are touched... the fairies have touched you... let me call the women... get the boy to call the women... they will tend you.'

'Call nobody,' she said, her confidence returning. 'I'm well able to tend myself.' She stood there, smaller as a boy, somehow, and barely reaching to his shoulder. She wore a brown tunic, and her legs were thin under it. And the tunic was belted at the waist with a belt of browner leather. But belted loosely, showing no shape to her hips. A knife to one side, and hanging loosely from the belt was that purse she always wore. She'd brought it with her from the west, those years ago. He didn't know what it contained and he didn't ask. Some woman's magic. Some Connacht woman's magic. It was made from the skin of a sow's dug.

A man wouldn't want to know about those things.

'By the gods,' he muttered, looking at her, taking in the details, up and down.

She stared back, defiantly. 'I am not mad. I am going to the west. You said it was too dangerous for a woman. So I go as a boy.'

'You stay right here, girl,' said the Storyteller, sternly, but his voice had no conviction. And the sound of his voice told him, what he knew... what something in him knew... oh yes a man always knows when a woman is about to get her own way.

'I *must* go to the west. You know that. You know who was my father...'

'He was Anluan of Ardikillan.'

'Yes, and where is Ardikillan but in Connacht?'

'That is no reason... that is no reason... they are savages... muck savages... did you see the heads on the stakes?'

'I saw them.'

'Did you see the witch?'

'I saw her.'

'They are not like you and me, Wife.'

'Not like you... perhaps... but remember who I am, and who my father was?'

'He was Anluan of Ardikillan yes I know... but girl,' said the Storyteller. 'Wife. Wife they call the daughter of the moon. Come. Sit here. Do you know me?'

'Does a woman know her husband?'

'Does she? Laoghaire is my king. He feeds me. His house is my house. Without him, I am a head on a stake.'

'And?'

'And without me he is no longer king.'

'What of all this, Storyteller?'

'What I am saying. . . what I am trying to say. . . he and I are together. . . I am the memory, and the story, and the days that are gone, and the days that will come. . . and this protects me. . . no man will harm a king's storyteller.'

'And?'

'But you. . . what do they care of you. . .?'

'I go to Connacht.'

'There are bandits there. . . like Corotocus. . . he wanders the country. . . seizing girls. . . sells them to the Picts across the sea. . .'

'I go to Connacht.'

'The Picts are blue men. . . do you want to be in the bed of a blue man?'

'The bed of men have a certain sameness for a woman, and no matter the colour! I go to Connacht. Come, it's nearly dawn. I have told the boys to prepare two horses, they had only readied one.'

'I *know* they'd only readied one. . . I *told* them to, last night.'

'Well now everything is ready for the journey.'

'By the gods, girl. . . I bought you in Connacht. . . at a bargain price. . . and now you're ordering my stableboys around. . . oh yes, it'll be the whip for you!'

'Oh whip away. . . but my mind is not in my backside.'

'Oh yes, insolent too. . . I should have listened. . . should have listened. . .'

'To?'

'To the wise men. . .'

'What did the *wise* men say?' she asked, saying the word *wise* as if it was the name of a smell.

'Never marry a foreigner.'

'Why not?'

'Because a marriage is not between two people, two individual people. . . a marriage is two histories coming together. . . and if those histories are not the same. . .'

'What happens?'

'Trouble,' said the Storyteller, 'trouble happens!'

The Wife laughed. A merry laugh, in the way of her, but the storyteller knew that if the day was up and if he could see her properly she'd be looking at him with those rather frightening Connacht eyes of hers. . .

One eye cold. . . and the other cruel.

⌒•

'WHAT DO YOU WANT TO LEARN?' asked the Storyteller of the king.

'The truth,' said the king.

'The truth may not be a good truth.'

'Is the truth not always good?'

'If Eithne and Fidelma have really gone to the foreign god. . .'

'Yes?'

'What will you say to your people here?'

'I'll tell them the truth. The people trust me here.'

'But what will they say of our gods then?'

'I see what you mean. But what should I do?'

'You are the king.'

'Oh they're only ideas, this god or that god, what matters!'

'Ideas are power, and they wander like strange soldiers in your country.'

'What will I do?'

'Ideas are scouts, sent out by armies far away. Ideas are little waves that creep before the tide.'

'What will I do?'

'What *can* you do?'

'Nothing. . . I said to you last night, didn't I, Storyteller. . . the sun goes down for all my ordering, for all my power. . . and soon it will come up again. . . so it is with the little waves you talk of, they creep before the tide. I can stop the little waves, but not the tide.'

'What will you do?'

'Nothing, probably. . . but I must know what happened to the girls. . .'

'Why must you know?'

'A father wants to know. . . go. . . go now, Storyteller. . . travel safe. . .'

'I have my battle dogs. . . and my Connacht wife, she comes with me.'

'You are well protected so. . . go. . . I sleep. . .'

Laoghaire turned his face to his wife's shoulder. And his wife's eyes said goodbye to the Storyteller, wishing him out of the room. She would mind the man, her eyes said, as best she could. Her shoulder was soft, and a good place for a man's face. Her skin was very white. And her armpit hair was very black, like a black nest in the limbs of a white tree, thought the Storyteller. . .

Or like a black bird in a white nest?

He wondered that, leaving.

⌒•

'THE BIRDS ARE SINGING in Dun Laoghaire now,' said the soldier to the soldier at the gates of Tara.

'They start singing in the east.'

'Yes, and the singing moves from east to west, from bird to bird, like the light moves west from shadow to shadow.'

'They are singing for the Ui Cumain people now.'

'And the Ui Colcan.'

'Yes, for all the people of Bregia.'

'Would you say they are singing at the the plain of Ailbe?'

'Yes, I'd say that. . . I can feel them singing. . .'

'But not hear them. I know what you mean. . . about the feeling.'

'Some mornings the light comes first, before the sound of birds.'

'And some mornings it's the other way around. . . do you hear horses. . .?'

'I hear horses,' said the soldier, standing, picking a spear from the hedge. 'Who is that?' he called out, 'who crosses the gates of Tara?'

There was no reply.

'They come out from Tara,' said his companion, standing beside him with his own spear now.

'Why don't they answer my call?'

'Who is that?' called out the other soldier.

There was no reply. But the sound of horses grew louder, and then separated into the separate sound of horses' hooves, then snorting, and the jingle of a harness.

'I see nothing,' said the soldier.

'The rising sun,' said the other, 'in my eyes. . . can't see a damn thing. . . oh yes. . . yes I can. . . see them?'

'Yes, two horses. . .'

Suddenly upon them, two horses, the black bulk of them and their riders dark shadows against the rising sun.

'Who is this here,' he called out, 'and where do you go?'

'I am Laoghaire's Storyteller,' came the reply, 'and I go where I will.'

'Pass by, Storyteller,' said one soldier.

'And a peaceful road ahead of you,' said the other. And the Storyteller passed by. And behind him a boy on another horse passed by. . . and behind him a white dog passed by. . . and behind the white dog a black dog passed by. . .

'Where does he go,' said the soldier to the soldier, 'the Storyteller and that boy?'

'That is no boy,' came the reply. . . 'that's a girl. . . a girl dressed as a boy. . . I recognise her. . . she's his wife, the one they call the daughter of the moon. . .'

'The one from the West?'

'The very one. . .'

The soldier stared silently after the horses and the dogs.

'Why are you silent?' asked the other.

'It is a strange thing. . . but now I remember. . . it's only now I remember. . .'

'What?'

'I dreamed last night of horses passing.'

'Just as well the captain didn't come round' laughed the other, 'and you dreaming.'

'Oh alright yes. . . I admit, I *was* asleep. . . and I dreamed I was asleep. And I dreamed I woke to the sound of horses.'

'That was a dream in a dream.'

'It was. . .'

'I once had a dream in a dream *in a dream*!'

'Did you,' said the soldier, no question in his voice, not interested, his mind on his own experience. 'Well in *my* dream I woke and I stirred and I called out. . . just like we did now to the Storyteller and his wife. . . but just like that there was no answer. . . and then out of the darkness came eight horses, moving from Tara to the west. . .'

'Who were they?'

'Nobody. . . they were ghosts. . . the horses were ghosts and the people on them were ghosts. . .'

'That is a strange thing to dream.'

'It was the witch they burned last night, and her magicians. . .'

'Their ghosts were going home?'

'I suppose so. . .'

'I suppose it's the natural thing. . . will you go home to Cualann when you die?'

'Before, hopefully!'

'Before?'

'Yes I've asked to be sent to the fort there on the sea. . . Dun Laoghaire. . .'

'And that's on the edge of Cualann. . . that'd be dead handy. . . for your home place. . .'

'But from what I heard yesterday it'll be to the west we're all sent. . .'

'I don't want to go to the west. . . I'm tired of war. . .'

'The Roman says we must make peace, not war. . .'

'He has it right.'

'You're getting old.'

'A man gets tired of war. . .'

'Tired of the smell of blood.'

'Tired of the screams of women being raped.'

'Tired of the smoke from burning houses.'

'Tired.'

'Tired.'

'What will you do. . . after the soldiering?'

'I'll keep sheep in Cualann. . .'

'I never liked sheep. There's a lot of work in sheep. If it's not lambing, they're being eaten by foxes. . . and if it's not foxes they're being buried in snowdrifts. No, I never liked sheep. Pigs are a better bet.'

'Some men like sheep, some like pigs.'

'They have sacred pigs in the west. . .'

'Ah sure you wouldn't mind that. . . they're all muck savages in the west!'

'Yes but you never heard of sacred sheep, did you?'

The soldiers laughed, and gathered up their cloaks and spears, and set off back up the Slope of the Chariots to Tara. Their guarding of the night was done. But the soldier who had dreamed was uneasy. He remembered more of dreams, and the darkness of the night followed him into the day.

∽•

A SPIDER RAN along a web, too late.

The horse's hoof crumped down, and spider and web were gone. Another little bit of life, unnoticed, another little bit of death.

'Do you believe the sun is a god?' said the Wife on her horse, suddenly, her eyes screwed up at at the dawn.

'Well,' said the Storyteller, looking at her, surprised at the question. Her face reflected pink from the sun rising, and it looked as if she were blushing. 'Well,' he said, 'it's certainly a lot more important than I am.'

He knew this answer sounded weak, but it really was a bit early in the morning for the serious questions of the world. A man needs a few drinks in him to be getting round that sort of business.

'But do you *believe*,' she insisted, 'really *believe*?'

'What have I here now, instead of a wife, some musty druid, interrogating me?'

That silenced her! But then, he realised, it's easy to silence the questions and the wonderings of others. Not so easy to find peace in one's own head.

∽•

A BIRD CALLED *glasán darach* twittered in the air. Green, patched with yellow, it flew this way, that. And a bird called *corcrán coille* called out melancholy from a hedge. And watched, looking this way, that.

The white dog ran ahead.

And the black dog followed her.

And the Storyteller and the Wife, riding side by side, they followed along after. But not closely. Sometimes the white dog was out of sight, sometimes both dogs.

'They know the road,' said the Storyteller.

'How do they know the road?' asked the Wife.

'Oh a dog will know.'

'That's not a very satisfactory answer.'

'I can only speak the language of humans, not dogs. But I'll tell you this. . . I knew a man sold a dog once to another man in Munster. . . and two months later that dog was back at his door! What do you think of that?'

'Well,' said the Wife, 'if the dog at the door was speaking human language and wearing a hat I might think a little more of it. . .'

The Storyteller laughed.

And looked at her sideways.

Away from Tara she was a lively girl, a vaguely different woman. Or was it that he saw her new, away from Tara? Are the people we know just parts of our place, like a table, or a chair? Always there, and probably always will be. The bits and pieces of our lives, around us. Like at home, that apple tree in the corner of the path to the hen's place? A familiar thing to pass, and at a particular season a place to pick an apple, from the habit in the hand, and walk on.

Are those the people we know, the people we live with, the people we meet?

Apples on a tree.

Which ones to eat. . . to become part of us. . . and which ones to leave rot, untouched in the grass below?

⌒•

TREES CAST SHADOWS AT A PLACE.

Alder trees and ash. And four strangely twisted pines among them. Twisted like they'd grown in pain. And were dying the same way.

There was sun to this side, and sun to that. But the place itself was in shadow, and the shadow was stronger for the sun all around. The dogs snarled at a cart they came across on the road, up there ahead, going in their direction. The Storyteller and the Wife heard the snarling, but at first the cart and the dogs were out of sight around the shadowy bend, and they didn't know quite what was going on. They looked at each other, calculating, deciding wordlessly to be curious or nervous.

They decided to be curious, and rode on.

The cart was pulled by an old horse.

An old woman sat hunched on the old horse.

There was no joy in her day, and hadn't been, for many a day.

Her heavy skirts were the colour of the horse.

It was hard to see where the horse ended and where the woman began.

A man with a stick was berating the dogs, but they ignored him, jumping at the boards of the cart, snarling.

A closed in cart, with slatted boards. There was something in there, alive, but what? The Storyteller stared. It wasn't possible to see between the narrow gaps in the boards. Movement, yes, but nothing clear. Probably a pig.

'Geddown yadogs,' called the Storyteller.

'Are those your dogs?' said the man with the stick.

'Is that your cart?' asked the Wife.

'Of course it's my cart' replied the man, 'why would I be trying to drive away the dogs if it wasn't my cart?'

'And why would I be calling to the dogs, if they weren't my dogs?' said the Storyteller.

'Oh I've no time for this,' said the man with the stick. He walked to the head of the horse, and led it on. And the something in the cart let out a squeal, an almost human squeal. And the old woman with the skirts the colour of the old horse looked at them, malevolently.

'She has a curse to curse, that one,' said the Storyteller, riding past.

'She'll soon be earth,' said the Wife, dismissively.

And they rode on, leaving the cart behind. And a red squirrel high in the tallest of the twisted trees, watching all this, its eyes like buttons on a vest closed tight...

⌒•

THE SUN ROSE higher in the sky. And the blush of reflected pink faded from the cheekbones of the Wife. And her face was its natural pale again. There's a woman needs a feeding, thought the Storyteller, a good meal! People will think I starve her. Oh yes, oh yes they will. And say it behind the backs of their hands. That Storyteller! He starves that little wife of his! That little one, the daughter of the moon. She's pale and not a peck on her. And something should be done! Gossips. The Storyteller spat at the road, gossips and gobdaws all. He spat again, and forgot the matter.

The black dog ran ahead.

And the white dog followed him.

And the Storyteller and the Wife, riding side by side, followed after them. But not closely. Sometimes the black dog was out of sight, and sometimes neither dog was to be seen.

'We travel north,' said the Wife, suddenly realising, looking about her, calculating the sun. 'Why do we travel north, when our journey lies to the west?'

'We haven't much choice but to follow the road. . . unless you want to hack through the whin. . .'

'But why *does* the road go north?'

'Because we go to the old Slighe Asail?'

'Isn't this the Slighe Asail?'

'This is the *new* Slighe Asail. . . we join the old in a few more miles.'

'Why does the old, the old road, why does that not go to Tara?'

'Because when the old road was built there was no Tara.'

'Tara is very old.'

'The road is older. . . in the time of the old people it led from the graves on the Boyne to Cruachan Ai. . .'

'Why?'

'Because the kings didn't live at Tara, they lived at the Boyne. . . and the other kings lived at Cruachan Ai. . . and kings like roads between their places. . .'

'Why?'

'Oh by the gods. . .' The Storyteller looked at her, exasperated. '*Why*? Because I suppose kings like building roads to see how far their power will stretch. . . and the roads between two kingdoms have to meet somewhere. . . life is logical. . . well, to a man anyway. . . talking of which. . . pull down your skirt and cover your thighs, those poor men walking by are looking at your legs.'

'It's not a skirt. . . it's a boy's tunic. . . a boy rides a horse like this. . . and anyway these are a boy's legs. . .'

'Do you throw away your modesty with your woman's clothes?'

'Perhaps,' she grinned, 'perhaps.'

They rode on, in silence, awhile. And then she asked 'which comes first, modesty or clothes?' And he replied 'why do you ask?' And she said, a shrug in her voice, 'no reason, really, just thinking.'

'Oh' said the Storyteller, 'you don't want to be doing that, leave that sort of stuff to a man.'

The Wife laughed.

And looked at him sideways.

⌒·

THE TWO POOR MEN WALKED ON.

They were going to Tara.

They might find work there.

There was no work in the poor border country between Meath and Ulster now. The soldiers were gone and the wars were over. . . for now! But the houses were burnt and the cattle driven away. And there was no work. But there might be work in Tara. They had heard that there might be work in Tara. And there was no harm in trying.

'That rich man who passed. . . on his fine horse. . .'

'The one with the dangerous battle dogs. . . what about him?'

'His companion. . . that was no boy. . .'

'I was thinking that myself. . .'

'Or if it was a boy he had very pretty legs. . .'

Both men laughed, and walked on a way in silence.

'No it definitely was no boy. . . it was a girl, for sure.'

'Why would a rich man travel with a girl, and her dressed as a boy?'

'And why would he have two battle dogs?'

The poor men wondered this, and walked on a way in silence.

They got no answer to their wondering, so they let it be.

'Do you think there'll be work in Tara?'

'It's a long walk back if there isn't.'

'It'd be good if there was work in Tara.'

'It surely would.'

'Yes. It surely would.'

⁓.

'WHAT IS THIS PLACE HERE,' said the Wife, 'these strange mounds and ditches?'

'Ferta-Fer-Feic.'

'Who was Fiac?'

'He was chieftain here, and these are the graves of his men.'

'Who owns that land to the north,' asked the Wife, 'what people there?'

'Our people. Well, *my* people. The road divides the kingdom of Laoghaire into two halves.

'And then, beyond? Beyond our, I mean beyond *your* country to the north?' There was a mocking in the way she spoke. He ignored that. 'Ulster, and the Ulstermen,' he replied, and spat to the ground. And the black dog and the white dog looked to the north, and growled.

'Geddup yadogs,' said the Storyteller. And they all moved on, in silence for awhile. And then the Wife spoke again. 'You talked of meaning once,' she said, 'I don't remember when, but it's in my mind.'

'I did?'

'Yes, how a place is the earth, and the air, and the meaning too.'

'I did?' said the Storyteller, surprised at her remembering something like that. . . 'What're you thinking?'

'That that makes three, the number three. And my people have a goddess in the west. . . and she is three, she comes as three. . .'

'Oh I know, don't I know her well.'

Too well, he thought, too well.

He thought of the witch they burned at Tara, she did not scream. He thought of the bird, the bird that hopped from wizard's head to wizard's head, the boys could not spear it. Then he thought of the crone, the crone that sat on the horse that drew a cart, she had the evil eye.

They come as three, they came as three.

He knew them well.

The witch, the bird, the crone.

He knew them well.

He looked at the Wife and wondered about her.
How well did he know *her*?
Did *she* come as one, or two, or three?

'Geddup yadogs,' he called, not for any reason to do with the dogs, no, just to be shaking thoughts from his head, 'geddup!'

They trotted on in silence for awhile.

Her thighs were slender and pretty against the hugeness of the horse. He noticed that, a man does, notice such things. And how her hands were strong on the reins, strong but easy, how she rode easy. The strength of the horse was hers, and they were the one thing, living. Then he saw in his mind the crone on the old horse, back there on the road. And how the crone and the horse were the one thing, dying.

He shrugged that thought away and watched the Wife, remembering. Remembering certain things that travellers had told him. About countries to the east. Beyond Armorica. Beyone the Roman country. And there, they said, and he had no reason to disbelieve them. . . there were horses with the heads and upper parts of men. And birds with the bodies of men. And lions with the heads of men. And women with the tails of fishes. Wonderful creatures, all of them.

It'd be good to travel in distant countries.

A lion with the head of a man would be an interesting thing to see.

And a woman with the tail of a fish, she would be interesting too. If not entirely practical around the house. Or in the bed for that matter.

'That hill there now,' said the Wife, interrupting his musing, 'what is that, the one there, heavy with trees.'

'It is Slane, we go there now, we will see the Neladoir.'

'To cast our fortunes for the journey?'

'Well. . .' His voice was careful. 'Well we do travel without warriors to guard us. . . and a man without warriors would be wise to know where he's going, and what might happen.'

'Do you get afraid?'

'I am a cautious man, and I live in a dangerous country.'

'And you want to live in it a while longer?'

'Exactly.'

5

'I<small>T'S A FIERCE LONG WAY UP</small>,' said the Wife, looking up at the hill of Slane.

'It is *not* a long way up,' the Storyteller contradicted, though he didn't particularly relish the climb himself. That knee was still at him. 'If you didn't want to come,' he lectured, '. . . well you had the choice. . . no-one asked you. . . you choose to come and now you're complaining already.'

'I just said it was a long way up. . . on foot. . .'

'Well, we have to go on foot. . . the Neladoir doesn't like horses on his hill.'

'Pity about him,' said the Wife.

'Oh come on with you girl, and stop moaning.'

The Storyteller led the way. Into the trees at the foot of the hill and up through the trees that covered the slopes. Oak trees, mossed with age and twisted with years, strong, these trees had nothing left to learn about the seasons. But some had bent to time, and fallen. And up through their grey bones grew new oak trees, straight and stretching to the light. And in and among these newer trees were holly bushes, untidily grabbing space where they were let, like children at an adults' table.

The path was clear, but steep, and even if the Neladoir had allowed horses on his hill they would have been of little use. A wide enough path, but not so wide as once, it wound among the trees, up and up and up. The growth at the edges creeping in, reclaiming the width of the path, cautiously, like a man adjusting his neighbour's fence.

'Will you come on with you,' the Storyteller called, using the leg bone from Tara as a stick at a very steep place.

'I'm coming, I'm coming,' the Wife scrambled behind, nimble for all her complaints.

The Neladoir lived half way up, at a place where the hill flattened, a plateau, a place to look out over the trees at the countryside, a place to see the sky, and the clouds far towards the sea.

He was old. And, like the oak trees on his hill, he too had nothing left to learn about the seasons. 'Is it the Storyteller of Laoghaire I see?'

'The very man.'

'You bring a boy. . . or is it a girl?'

'I don't know, Neladoir, I'm still trying to work that out myself.'

'I am a girl,' said the Wife, 'but I dress as a boy.'

'Why?'

'We go on a long journey,' said the Storyteller.

'And my husband says I will be safer as a boy,' said the Wife.

'Depends' said the Neladoir, grumpily.

'What do you mean?'

'I've heard some of these Romans are very fond of boys. . . use them as girls. Another disgusting foreign habit.'

The Storyteller laughed. 'So you still don't like the Romans, Neladoir?'

'They want my hill.'

'But this is *your* hill. . . tell them they can't have it. . .'

'King Laoghaire says that Ercc, the son of Daig, that he can have it. . . when I die. Now he's only waiting for me to go!'

'Well don't die,' said the Storyteller.

'That is my plan, precisely that,' nodded the Neladoir, 'but I'm not too sure I'll be able to carry it out. . . anyway. . . where are you going, this long journey?'

'You tell us, Neladoir,' said the Wife, 'are you not the fortune teller, diviner, do you not see?'

'Ahh. . .' His smile showed one single tooth. It guarded the left side of his mouth, like a weatherbeaten marker at the edge of a man's land. 'Ahh. I know you *now*, girl. . . the cheeky one from the west. . . the one with the sight.'

'That's me,' she said, cheekily.

'The one they call the daughter of the moon.'

'The very same. . . so. . . what do you see?' asked the Wife.

'Last night I saw a far city to the east. . .'

'Dun Laoghaire?' said the Storyteller.

'No, much further than that.'

'Eadar's Mountain?'

'Further, further, across the sea. . . and across the land of the Picts too. . . and across the land of the Romans. . . as far to the east as the sun rises. . . and further. . .'

'And what did you see. . . in this far city. . .'

'I saw these animals, like big huge fat horses. . . and they had snakes for heads. . . huge long snakes that trailed the ground. . . sniffing. . .'

'And what of them?'

'Nothing.' The Neladoir shrugged. 'Just saw them.'

'Oh,' said the Storyteller. He remembered not long ago thinking of lions with the heads of men, women with the tails of fishes. A strange coincidence, his thinking that. But then, many things are strange. He listened to the silence. And noticed a trickle of water in the silence, the trickle of the small brown stream that passed the Neladoir's house. . .

House?

It wasn't really a house, it was a cave, with a building coming out of it, and an old roof on the building that once was thatch but now was part of the hill, growing. Soon, realised the Storyteller, soon that roof will fall. As will the Neladoir himself. And the Romans will get the hill of Slane, and build a cross, and light their fires. And the story here will be silent.

The Storyteller knew all that, and he looked around, sadly.

The stream flowed to the side of the cave house, but out from it there was a ditch, a drain, and this led a flow of water to a pool in rocks, and then, from the other side of the pool, another ditch or drain was dug, leading the water back into the stream. The pool itself was calm, and there was no sound or seeing of it filling, or emptying. The trickling noises of water all came from the main stream. The path of that stream had been carved by the water, but the path of the ditches to and from the pool had been dug by men. A long time ago. They were fallen in, and overgrown, and looked almost natural. Almost as if they had been carved by water, and by time, by the gods of the earth. But only almost. There is always that difference. And it is always possible to see where men have been, where men have touched the earth.

The Storyteller knew these things.

But was never quite sure how the knowing might help him.

'Well Neladoir,' he said, 'we climbed your hill for an omen, and is it good or is it bad?'

'Where do you go?' asked the Neladoir, walking slowly, ever so slowly towards the pool in front of his cave.

'To the West, to Cruachan Ai.'

'That is a journey for a young man.'

'I'm not old. . .' the Storyteller protested, 'and we do have good horses.'

'Where?' the Neladoir looked around, grumpily.

'At the bottom of the hill.'

'Good, I don't like horses on my hill. . . or dogs. . .' He looked grumpily at the black dog and the white dog lying there. 'But seeing as it's you, Storyteller, you're allowed bring your dogs. . . and your wife I suppose. . . though I don't much like women on my hill either.'

'Who *do* you like on your hill?' asked the Wife, in a sweet voice.

'Myself,' snapped the old man.

'How can you tell fortunes and omens if no-one comes?'

'No-one much comes anyway these days. The Romans are telling people not to come. The Romans say fortunes and omens are works of devils. What do they know of devils? Last week I saw the years ahead, and in those years the Romans ruled, and there were devils then, oh yes, devils aplenty! There was children cut from the bellies of mothers, and the land dying, and the story dying. . . I saw that in the clouds. What know the Romans of those things?'

'Oh stop worrying about the Romans,' said the Storyteller, 'pick your stones and tell me the omen.'

'Alright for you,' said the Neladoir, picking pebbles from a heap. And then, with a sweep of his hand, he threw them across the smooth surface of the pool. . . and it shattered like a glass, reflecting the clouds.

'There is another pool in the west,' he said, 'you go there.'

'Do we?' said the Wife.

'Shush,' said the Storyteller.

'You go there. There are armies. There is a witch. There is a hare. There is a pig. There is a cave. There is a black bird. There is a boat. There is a song. And that is all I see.'

'Throw more stones. . . is the journey good. . . or bad. . .?'
The Neladoir threw more stones.
'The journey there is safe.'
'The journey back?'
'I see no journey back. . . but that is not to say there is no journey back.'
'What else do you see?'
'I see a fair girl.'
'Is it me?' asked the Wife.
'No, not you, she is beautiful.'
'Thanks a lot,' said the Wife, and the Storyteller grinned, and the Wife made a rude gesture at him with her mouth.
'What of this fair girl?'
'The water is calm.'
'Throw more stones, throw more stones.'
The Neladoir threw more stones and said 'she is with a darker girl, and they are by this pool, this other pool you travel to. . .'
'What do they do there?'
'I cannot see. . . there are people in chains. No, they're not people, one is a bear. The other a person.'
'What do they do?'
'Nothing, they stand, they're waiting.'
'Throw more stones,' said the Storyteller.
'What do you see?' said the wife.
'I see a pig on a butcher's hook.'
'What else?'
'I see a black bird.'
'What else?'
'The black bird has a woman's breasts.'
'That is a strange bird to be seeing.'
'Many things I see are strange.'
'Throw more stones.'
'I see blood now, blood in the water.'
'The water is clear.'
'Not this water, the water of the other pool.'
'Throw more stones.'
'The stones are thrown.' The Neladoir walked away. 'Now, what do *you* bring me, Storyteller, what story?'

'Laoghaire has burned a witch. And has had the heads of seven wizards from the west.'

'Are you sure? I saw no witch in Tara. . . nor seven wizards either. . .'

'Sure how would you see them in Tara, from up here?' asked the Wife, annoyance in her voice. Why that sudden annoyance, wondered the Storyteller, what had the Neladoir seen in the water, to annoy her?

'How do I see anything,' the Neladoir said, softly. 'What do you bring me, Storyteller, what food?'

'I bring you eggs, and bread, and cakes.'

'No wine?'

'And wine,' added the Storyteller, 'of course I bring wine. I was teasing you.' He handed him the basket, and the Neladoir placed it on a stone and looked at it. 'I mind a time,' he said, 'that stone was piled with gifts. The bread and cakes grew stale, I couldn't eat them fast enough. The eggs were nearly hatching, there was that many.'

'Did the wine go sour on you?'

'No, I managed to get through that alright.'

The Neladoir grinned and then, looking around at the Wife who was wandering, whispered, 'that girl knows more than you think.'

'About?'

'Everything.'

'What do you mean?'

'I mean what I mean' muttered the Neladoir as the Wife drifted back over.

'We should go now,' she said, and drifted away again. Her drifting back and forth was as if she didn't want to be too long in the company of the Neladoir. And the Storyteller wondered why.

'Yes I suppose we should be going,' he murmured, looking at the sky, and how much daylight was left in it.

The Neladoir nodded towards the Wife. 'I see her,' he said, tapping his head, 'I see her combing her hair, long yellow hair.'

The Storyteller looked towards the Wife. He too saw her in his mind, combing her hair, watching him talk to the witch. And he wondered vaguely if the Neladoir had picked that memory from his mind, or from somewhere else. Was there a place where everyone's memories gather, he wondered, where a man with the sight can go and pick and choose?

Ah sure! Too many wonderings!

He yupped at the dogs and they stood, and looked at him. He waved an arm in the direction of the path, and they knew, and ran into the woods, the black dog first, and then the white.

'They'll wait at the horses,' he said.

'Should've waited there in the first place,' said the Neladoir.

'Oh don't be grumpy, drink your wine, be well,' said the Storyteller.

'I'll surely drink the wine. . . but I will be grumpy. . . and I won't be well. . . I'm old. . . I am that bone in your hand.'

'By the gods,' said the Wife as they left him and walked in under the tress, 'he's a miserable old man.'

'Oh. . . he's old. . . and he sees times changing. . . old men don't like that. . . and anyway he has the sight. . . those with the sight get a bit gloomy betimes. . .'

'Do they,' said she, 'do they really?' And she smiled, and danced away from him down the hill. And in her brown tunic she was like a deer to his eyes, flickering like a deer flickers, from tree to tree, and then gone, with that suddenness.

The Neladoir of Slane watched them, and the woods closing about them, watched them 'til they were gone. He opened the wine, and sipped, and looked into his pool. And a fair girl there said to him. 'what did you tell, what did you tell?'

'I told them nothing.'

And then a dark girl beside the fair girl said to him, 'what did you tell, what did you tell?'

'I told them nothing,' repeated the Neladoir of Slane.

'Good,' said the fair girl and the dark girl, together.

The Neladoir sipped his wine. The fair girl and the dark girl stood beside him for awhile. Their dresses in the breeze. Their hair in the breeze. Their silence in the silence. And then they moved away, without another word. Away into the trees, and the woods closing about them. The Neladoir watched, watched them 'til they were gone.

He sipped his wine, looked back to the pool, and remembered. When he was a young man he went to the grave of Aengus, on the Boyne. He went with the old Neladoir, the previous Neladoir of Slane.

Now he himself was the old Neladoir of Slane, but he had no boy to teach, to carry on. And when he was dead it would all be gone.

And what was it for, then?

That was the question.

He remembered asking the same question of the old Neladoir at the grave of Aengus on the Boyne. A huge mound, it guards the bend of the river, and it stands near other mounds, and stones, because the gods of the old people are buried there. And when he went with the old man who'd taught him the tricks of the neladoir trade, he had said to him, asked him, 'what was it all for, teacher?'

Because the grave of Aengus was grass and brambles then, and there was no-one about. The new kings lived in Tara then, or Eamhain, or Rathcroghan. And no-one lived at the grave of Aengus on the Boyne. Except sheep. And foxes watching the sheep. And shepherds watching the foxes. Apart from that, there was nobody there.

'What was it all for, teacher?'

All the glory, all the days of war, coming home with heads, and slaves, and cattle. What for? And the days of peace too. What for? You get up in the morning and you love a woman. What for? Now she is dust, clay. So what's it for, loving women. Feeding children. Hunting deer and passing beer from hand to hand by the winter fires.

What for?

But from the old Neladoir there had been no answer. So they'd come home, from the grave of Aengus to the Hill of Slane. And he'd helped the old man up the hill, and sat by the pool watching the evening. By this very same pool. And the old Neladoir had thrown the stones and said 'I see a storyteller.'

'Tell me,' the old man who was a young man then had said, 'tell me.'

'He comes up this hill. With a black dog, and a white dog, and a girl dressed as a boy.'

'Tell me more.'

'Look for yourself... what do you see?'

'It's very hard to see...'

'Look closely.'

The Neladoir sipped his golden coloured wine. It trickled down his throat. Soon I will be mud, he thought, and where will the wine go then?

A STREAM OF GOLDEN COLOURED urine trickled towards the roadside mud, steaming. It separated into smaller streams. And then it faded into the rainwater, became part of the puddles that were there. And then it was gone, the steam and the colour gone out of it.

The Wife squatted, and the Storyteller said 'well you can dress like a boy, but for sure no clothes will let you piss like one.'

She stood, and smoothed her tunic neat around her knees. That gesture is born in a woman, he thought, waiting for reply. But she did not speak immediately. Well, not with words anyway. Instead she looked at him, a still moment, a challenge.

'How wise did you have to be to grow that beard,' she said then, suddenly moving, then scrambling up on her horse, 'or that prick? Are you to be congratulated for those achievements now?'

The Storyteller laughed.

The black dog sniffed at the last of the urine on the ground.

The white dog sniffed at the black dog's balls.

The horses moved on.

⌣•

FIVE RAIN DRENCHED CATTLE stood in a small rain drenched field. Smoke from two cabins mingled, at first with the smoke from the other, and then with the day. A man by the road raised a right hand in a greeting, but said nothing. His eyes were careful.

'Now we pass through interesting country,' said the Storyteller.

'It looks fairly dull to me,' said the Wife.

'Ah that's because you are looking at sticks and stones, at trees and hills and woods and fields, at forts and houses. . .'

'Well what are *you* looking at?'

'I'm looking at what makes a country interesting.'

'Isn't Lag-an-Aenaigh near here?'

'Yes,' said the Storyteller, carefully, sensing a trap. And then, to change the subject, he said 'what makes the country interesting is the story in the place.'

'To a Storyteller,' she murmured. 'Tell me, does the road actually pass *right by* Lag-an-Aenaigh?'

'Fairly, fair near enough,' muttered the Storyteller. He realised that, to avoid this trap, some distraction was called for. He waved an arm, like there was a brush on the end of it, and he was painting the landscape. 'It was here,' he said, 'here that the old people were slaughtered by the new...'

'But aren't we the descendants of the new?'

'We?' he snorted. 'Hah... *some* of us are... while some *others* of us are from Connacht... descended from murkiness!'

'Blah blah blah,' said the Wife.

'Anyway,' he ignored that, 'anyway I'm not making comment on the slaughter... the rights and wrongs... merely telling you what happened.'

'What happened?' She sounded completely disinterested.

'The Sons of Brogan were slain here... well... not exactly at the battle... later... when the battle scattered across the country.'

'Who were the sons of Brogan?'

'Fuad was one... and Cuailgne another... they were slain to the north of here...' The Storyteller waved his imaginary paintbrush towards the north. And as he did he noted a fair enough day in the sky, to the north, and to the east, and to the south. But to the west, where they would be going, it didn't look good, not good at all.

Rain?

Perhaps.

'Fuad and Cuailgne were the chiefs of the new people,' he said, realising that it was better to be telling a story than worrying about the weather. Also that he'd better extend the story to help her forget about Lag-an-Aenaigh.

'If the winners were slain,' said the Wife, 'it was good not to be a loser!'

'Battles can be won,' said the Storyteller, 'but people can live or die.' He knew that she was mocking him, and his storytelling, but he was well used to it. And not only from her, that mockery. People these days were impatient with the old stories, in a hurry towards the new. They'd listen forever to a Roman preaching. But to someone telling them who they were, and where they come from?

Their ears were closed.

A storyteller might as well be talking to that tree!

'Where exactly is Lag-an-Aenaigh?' the Wife's question interrupted his irritation, doing nothing to smooth it either. He realised he'd been wasting his time trying to distract her.

'Over that way,' he gestured, very vaguely.

'Do you know what it is,' she said, 'you seem to be more exact about old battles and old chiefs than where exactly is Lag-an-Aenaigh?'

'Oh I know *exactly* where Lag-an-Aenaigh is!'

'And why wouldn't you? Didn't you take your Chief Wife there. . . and the Quiet One. . . they told me so. . .'

'And?'

'And you never took me!'

'But they are free women. . . their fathers own cattle! You know the law!'

'*My* father owned cattle?'

'Yes but he sold you. . . you are not a free woman. . . you are a bought wife. . . it's the law, the fenechas!'

'Fenechas my arse,' said the Wife. 'ah go on take me through the Lag-an-Aenaigh. . .'

'The journey is hardly started. . . and you're nagging already. . .'

'I won't nag if you take me through the Lag-an-Aenaigh. . .'

'It is not the right time of year. . . Tailtenn is empty. . . all that's there are fields. . .'

'Yes but *there* is the marrying place of Lag an Aenaigh. . . and didn't you say that fields are not what makes a country interesting. . . it's the story. . .'

The Storyteller sighed. But smiled inwardly at her quickness.

'Alright. For a quiet life,' he said, 'we *will* ride our horses *through* the Lag-an-Aenaigh. . . we will *not* get off our horses. . . we will *just* ride through the hollow. . .'

'Then I'll be married,' she said, 'you'll have taken me to the Lag-an-Aenaigh. . .'

'You *are* married.'

'Yes but I'll be married in a different way.'

'You'll still be a bought wife.'

'I don't like being a bought wife.'

'Sometimes I don't like to be a Storyteller. . .'

'One day there'll be no bought wives. . .'

'Aye, and that'll be the day there'll be no storytellers either. . .'

'That river there,' she said, ignoring his grumpiness, 'there, on our left hand, what do you call it?'

'What do *I* call it? By the gods, girl, the ignorance. *We, everyone* calls it the Boyne.'

'Oh yes.'

'Oh yes, indeed.'

'We follow it now?'

'Well not forever! It rises in the south, at Sid Nechtain. . . we follow it to Nuachongbail.'

'Nuachonbail?'

'Yes, Nuachonbail. . . and there it meets another river. . . the river they call Bright. . . and then we follow *that*!'

'Where does the Bright River rise?'

'In Sliab Guari. . .'

'Do we go there?'

'Oh no. . . that's too far north. . . we follow it only awhile. . . the road will show us the way!'

⁃•

THE ROAD TOOK THEM to the Lag-an-Aenaigh.

It was quiet, a grassy place.

The horses' hooves were quiet on the grass. Like a man's boots might be on a rug, so silent almost, there was the feeling of being on the wrong feet in the wrong place. Of bringing mud into some great lady's chamber, and of sensing her polite unspoken disapproval. That was the feeling, and the Storyteller looked around, trying to understand more. But there was no understanding more. The feeling was just of that great lady, and she was the spirit of the place, aware of him. And making sure that he was aware of her!

It was quiet, a grassy place.

The white dog chased a butterfly. It was a white butterfly and she chased it through white dog daisies. And the black dog watched the white, but didn't bother running.

'It's so pretty here,' said the Wife, adding, after a tiny pause of thought, 'I would wear those daisies in my hair.'

'If you had any hair,' said the Storyteller.

'Oh hair will grow,' she said, vaguely, her mind drifting.

'What do you see,' asked the Stoyteller, 'can you see the ghost of Taillte?' He turned his horse, and started moving.

They rode up out of the hollow.

He called the dogs to follow.

'What can I see,' she asked, 'see, with my sight?'

'Why would I ask what your eyes can see, I can see that myself! Yes of course that's what I mean, with your sight, what can you see in your mind?'

'I saw a crowd of ghosts,' she said, 'running and fighting and drinking and laughing.'

'And getting married?'

'Yes,' she grinned, and then was quiet, and looked deeper into her mind.

The horses hooves flumped quietly on the grass, the only sound, for awhile. And then she spoke again. 'I see a dark haired woman, very dark.'

'That is Taillte,' said the Storyteller, 'and who is with her?'

'A fairer man, a younger man, dressed like a warrior.'

'That is Lewy,' said the Storyteller.

'Who are they?' she asked.

'She was a woman from Spain, and she was his foster mother.'

'And who was he?'

'A king. Ancestor of the people of Laoghaire. . . it was he who founded this place.'

'Founded? Was the place not here before him? Did he drop these hills from the sky?'

'The place was always here, but he gave it its meaning. A place is more than hills or fields or streams, haven't I told you that?'

'I believe so,' she grinned, that grin that'd have a man reaching for a whip, if it was close. If it was not close it'd be too late, because by then she'd have coaxed a laugh from him. 'Yes' she said, 'I believe you did. . . you did tell me that. We talked of it earlier.'

'Well I'll tell you again. A place has three things. The earth, and the air, and the meaning. And everything is either part of the earth, or part of the air, or part of the meaning. And if you take away any one of those things, there is no place, there is an emptiness. And if there is no earth to walk on, a man will die. And if there's no air to breathe, a man will die. And if there's no meaning, a man will die.'

'One day I will understand,' said the Wife, thoughtfully, 'one day.'

'One day everyone understands,' said the Storyteller, watching her, thoughtfully. He knew quite well she understood, already. But it was the way of her to act more stupid than she was. She hid her cleverness, like it was a knife, some weapon she didn't want people to know she possessed. Whereas her real knife, that she wore openly, and it dangled at her hip. He watched her, up and down. Yes she looked good, dressed as a boy. Not like a good-looking boy, no. Just. . . attractive. Not that she was beautiful, far from it.

The Storyteller sighed.

The truth was, of all his wives, he loved her.

And now he had ridden with her through the Lag-an-Aenaigh.

Already, the journey barely started, in the first few hours of a journey that would take days, she had led him here.

Women!

Where would she lead him next?

She had the sight.

What did she see that she hadn't told him?

'Geddup yadogs' he called out to the wandering animals, and he kicked his horse into a trot ahead. And the Wife followed. And behind her the white dog ran, looking this way and that for distractions. And behind the white dog ran the black, looking straight ahead.

⁓•

CROWS PECKED AT THE INNARDS OF A FOX.

Thunder rumbled in the west, but very far away, still.

The red blood of the fox was very red, the black of the thunder-clouds very black. The Storyteller saw in his mind a memory of last night, last night when they burned the witch. The flames were very red. The night was very dark. He saw that, but said nothing.

'How did that fox die?' said the Wife, looking down, her horse picking its hooves around the corpse. And the crows waiting in the ditch for their passing.

'How do any of us die,' said the Storyteller.

'Painfully,' said the Wife, 'the most of us.'

'Would you rather die in peace?'

'No I think I'd rather die in pain,' said the Wife, 'screaming. . . my innards pulled. The gods would know I'm coming then!'

'Your innards pulled?'

'The old way of execution in the west. . . when they capture you. . . put a hook up your hole. . . pull your innards out. . .'

'Who told you that nonsense?'

'Not nonsense. . . true. . .'

'Ah get away with you girl!'

'Well. . . when there's a hook up *your* hole. . . and they're pulling *your* innards. . . don't say I didn't warn you!'

'I'll bear it all in mind,' he sighed.

'Where are we now anyway,' the Wife asked, 'and what is this place?'

'Sifoc, they call this place.'

'Another mound, another mound of fairies. . . is there no end to mounds, or fairies, or mounds of fairies?'

'Think of it this way. . . time. . . time is a long year. . . but a man lives for a short minute. . . and so there is no ending to those that have lived, those that will live.'

'I see in this place,' the Wife said, stopping her horse suddenly.

'What do you see?' the Storyteller stopped alongside her.

She didn't answer.

She held her hand up, it said pause.

The Storyteller stopped his horse, and looked around. He knew this place, a hilltop, well known along the road. They would leave the river here, it flowed down from Lough Ramor in the the north west, and their road from here went directly west, downhill, straight for miles, and then uphill again, straight for miles. The next hill would be Crossakeel, and from there they'd nearly see the lakes. The lake of Lene, and the lake of Derravaragh.

Sure that was half the journey done!

Or so he told himself, but unconvincingly.

Too old for travelling now? Perhaps. He sighed. And a stand of eight old ash trees whispered back his sigh. Very high, those ash trees. And five swallows swooped, very low, and that meant bad weather soon. He looked at the Wife but she wasn't seeing ash trees or swallows, no, she stared into her trance, silent.

Those with the sight are best left quiet.

They will speak in their own time.

He watched the swallows.

Yes, it would rain again, soon, he knew from the way they swooped.

How graceful though.

Like dancing.

Though in all truth, does a swallow have to be really that graceful to look graceful? Isn't it the way that he's so alike his companions, that his movements merge into theirs? And the reality may be that each swallow is flying awkwardly as an individual. And it's only the confusion between one and the other that makes them seem graceful!

The Storyteller smiled, at this riddle.

And he wished there was someone to tell it to!

But the Wife wouldn't appreciate such a concept.

And anyway she was in a trance beside him.

'I see,' she spoke suddenly... 'I see a fort... a great fort...'

'What is it called, this fort?'

'Dun Chuile Sibrinne.'

'I know of no fort that name.'

'It's here... Fiacha Finnalchas has built this fort.'

'I know no king or chief of that name... what is his country, who are his tuath?'

'He is king, high king. This is his ceannannus... and he lives here...'

'Kings live in Tara.'

'Tara is gone...'

'Gone? How can Tara be gone?'

'The Romans have fasted against it... their priests walked round and round, clappering bells, singing... and Tara is gone now...' She nodded her head, in a finality.

'Now?'

'Now in the time I see.'

She shook her head, like shaking a wasp from her hair. And the trance was the wasp and it flew away, harmless.

'Now in the time I *saw*,' she muttered.

'You dream, girl, you dream,' said the Storyteller.

'You told me on the road, there *was* a time before Tara... that the road used go to the Boyne, where the kings lived before Tara...'

'Yes, I did, and so?'

'Well if there was a time *before* Tara, can there not be a time *after* Tara?'

'There could be, could be. . .'

'The new kings could be anywhere. . . here. . . on that hill there. . . anywhere. . . way out on the rocky sea to the east. . .'

'Yes, funny place to have a kingdom. . . but I suppose so. . . Laoghaire already has a fort there. . . now enough of this, this chatter. . . come, we ride on.'

She looked at him, silently, and rode ahead. And the white dog followed her horse. And the black dog followed the white. And the Storyteller rode along behind them all.

He knew she did not dream.

He felt in in the story.

There are times. And the beginning of times, and the end of times. And this was the end of times. The old ways were going, but the new ones were not clear to see, not yet. There was a confusion in the world. Soon, he knew, soon the new times would be there with them, and things would be clear again. There would be no confusion. People would say 'we live this way, because this is the way.'

⌒•

'YOU TALKED OF MEANING,' said the Wife, 'back there on the road. Before we climbed the hill. Before we talked to the Neladoir. And again later.'

'I did.'

'And how a place is not only the earth, but also the air, and the meaning.'

'I did,' said the Storyteller, wondering about her thinking. 'What're you thinking?'

'That it's three, three things. A place is. And my people have a Goddess in the west. . . and she is three, she comes as three. . .'

'Yes. You mentioned this, before. It's much in your thinking, I'm thinking!'

'She comes as a girl and a bird and a crone.'

'And?'

'Oh nothing, nothing at all' said the Wife, 'I just think, to shorten the road.'

'You want to be careful,' said the Storyteller, 'sometimes it's the thinking makes it longer.'

'True, perhaps,' she agreed, and then, pointing, added 'people come.'

'Well we don't own the road,' said the Storyteller, others pass here too!'

He watched the group approach.

Two on horses, a group behind on foot. And then some other horses, laden down with baggage.

'Hello,' he said.

Two women rode the two horses, and from their dress he knew them to be women of the airlaicme, aristocratic, educated women.

'Hello,' they said, together.

'I am the Storyteller of Tara, I go to Connacht.'

'I am Scire,' said one of the women, 'and this is my sister Corcaire Caoin.'

'Ah,' said the Storyteller, none the wiser about their identity.

'I am daughter of Eugene,' said Scire, and he was son of Carannan, and he was son of Ailild, and he was son of Fergus.'

'And Fergus was son of Eochaid Moimedonius,' added Corcaire Caoin.

'Ah,' said the Storyteller, 'I know your people now. . . so. . . what do you do in this wild place?' He looked at the group of people on foot, gathered patiently behind the aristocratic sisters. A quiet bunch, of the lower class of person. Not *the* lowest class of person, no, but not aristocrats, not by any manner or means!

'We go to build a church, the chief has given us land, near here.'

'A church? A Roman church?'

'Yes,' said Scire, 'we follow the Christian god.'

'Ah,' said the Storyteller, 'and he has led you here?'

'Indeed,' said Corcaire Caoin, 'and where does *your* god lead you?'

'To Connacht,' said the Wife, breaking her silence.

'That is the devil's country,' said Scire, 'full of witchcraft and evil and devilish things.'

'Is it really?' said the Wife.

'Yes,' said Corcaire Caoin, 'but our holy leader Patrick preaches there, driving out devils, baptising many.'

'Oh so that's alright so,' said the Wife.

'Well,' said the Storyteller, feeling a little argument brewing around him, 'well we'd best be on our way. . . I don't like the look of those clouds ahead.'

'And we must away too,' said Scire. 'Do you return this way, after Connacht?'

'I hope to,' he said moodily, thinking 'unless Daithi has my head!'

'Well you might visit us at our church. . . it's not far off the road.'

'I'll bear it in mind,' said the Storyteller, thinking again 'unless Daithi has my head!'

Scire smiled, and said 'chch chchh' to her horse, and rode on. And Corcaire Caoin said 'chch chchh' to *her* horse, and followed her. And after them the group of followers on foot. And after them led on long reins came the string of horses carrying baggage.

The Storyteller watched them all, thoughtfully.

And then shrugged.

Let the story tell the story!

He looked ahead and yes, definitely a touch of darkness there.

And was that a spat of rain?

'Come on,' he said to the Wife, 'let's ride on, and faster.'

'So we get faster into the rain?' came the reply, sardonic, but still she took his heed and rode faster. He saw her flick her reins, and her heels kick against the horse's side. What pretty heels she has, he thought. . . and he remembered the sexy slavegirl at Tara, and her pretty feet, although they were dirty.

Where were they now, those pretty feet, those dirty feet?

Wherever!

There's a thing about a woman's feet!

A man likes a woman's feet.

Why does a man like a woman's feet?

Is it because they are small, and make her appear childlike? And a man looks at the small childlike feet and it makes him feel strong? Because if he looks at the woman who stands on the small childlike feet she makes him feel weak?

And a man likes to feel strong with a woman.

So he looks for her weaknesses.

To protect her?

The Storyteller pondered this.

Yes, he decided. A good man looks for the weakness in a woman, to protect her. But a bad man looks for the weakness in a woman, to rule her.

So a woman's weakness is both her strength *and* her weakness.

There's a riddle for the riddlers!

⌒•

THE SLAVEGIRL RAN THROUGH LONELY WOODS.

Her feet were sore, and cut.

She clutched her bag to her chest, and even through its thickness she could feel her heart beating.

She was frightened, and tired, but she would never go back to Tara, never.

She ran on.

A pigeon flapped away from her running.

Someone's good dinner, she thought, that plump pigeon.

Skewered on a stick, roasting.

She thought of it, and felt hungry. And she saw it, skewered, turning. And as it turned she saw herself, skewered, a captured slavegirl.

What did she do?

She killed her master.

It's a cruel death ahead for her.

She ran on, hearing the whispering, it was the trees whispering about her.

Let them whisper!

Let me die a cruel death.

Better that than live a cruel life.

6

THE BLACK DOG MOVED among the trees, and the white dog too, but not together. Separately, and the Storyteller watched them, vanishing, reappearing. And sometimes the black would go out of sight, and the white reappear, in its place. And the Storyteller thought, this could be be the same one dog, changing colour out of sight. The white called Day, the black called Night, the one.

He smiled.

That lonely smile that no-one sees.

'The trees are heavier here,' said the Wife, 'darker, older.'

'This is the forest of Carn na Ross.'

'Are there wolves?'

'Many,' said the Storyteller, 'and most of them walking on two legs.' He looked ahead, and dirty men with blackened faces watched them come.

'A rich man comes this way,' said one.

His hair was long.

'And a boy on a horse alongside,' said another.

He had no teeth.

'And two dogs,' said a third.

He had no hair.

'Big battle dogs,' said a fourth. He was neat, and had the air of someone cleaner. But he was as dirty as the rest.

'I'm afraid of dogs,' said a dirty woman with a blackened face, she stood beside the men. Her legs were bare and dirty, but slender. Her lips were full, and red. And she had the eyes of a whore, sleepy, but watching.

'Well go and tend the fire then,' said the man with no teeth.

'The fire is good, it needs no tending.'

'I am the Storyteller of Tara,' said the Storyteller, riding up to the charcoal burners, and seeing them drawn up before him like a picture. The longhaired man, and the toothless one, the bald man and the neat. And the woman with the eyes of a whore, sleepy, but watching him.

'You are welcome to our shelter,' said the neat man, 'and some bread. . .'

'We want the river by the night.'

'Sure you have a river here,' the neat man pointed at a stream.

'What river is that?' asked the Storyteller.

'It has no name.'

'Well a river with no name is little use to me, it's the Shannon is my destination.'

'Oh you'll never make that by the night,' said the charcoal burner.

'It's a two day journey, from Tara to the big river,' said the charcoal burners' woman.

'You'd be best to stay here. . . and start afresh.'

'But there's plenty of light in the day,' said the Storyteller, looking down from his horse, and seeing no comfort in this camp.

'Yes, but the light will go. . . and then you'll be in a wilderness. . . in the dark. . . the houses are burned in the country ahead.'

'The cattle are driven away.'

'There's Cianachta, wandering. . . and there are Ulster bandits. . . still about. . . a few. . .'

'They come out in the dark.'

'You'd be best stay here. . . and start afresh.'

The four men talked in turns, as if they were one man. And for all the difference in their appearances and their dirtiness and their sooty faces they might as well have been the one.

'Start afresh in the morning,' said the dirty woman, 'you'll be well rested in the morning.'

She smiled.

She had the smile of a whore. The tip of her tongue touched her lips. The Storyteller thought of that little tongue a woman keeps between her legs.

'Well rested in the morning,' mimicked the Wife, and then, in a whisper, 'not if she has a choice!'

'Shush,' the Storyteller whispered, and then, aloud to the charcoal burners, 'alright, we camp here. . . have you food for my dogs. . . and my horses. . .'

'Will your dogs eat a deer's head,' said one of the men, 'we have one handy?'

'*I* won't eat a deer's head,' said the Wife.

'They weren't asking you,' said the Storyteller. 'Yes, of course they will. . . and for my horses?'

'We have oats.'

'*I* won't eat oats,' said the Wife.

'They weren't asking you,' said the Storyteller. 'Yes, of course they will. . . and for my pageboy here?'

'Dogs? Horses? Me?' said the Wife to him, 'what sort of importance is this?'

'Well,' said the Storyteller, 'the dogs can tear the throats of bandits on my way. . . and I can ride the horses there. . . can you tear the throats of bandits?'

The Wife smiled, but said nothing.

'Can I ride you to Rathcroghan?'

'Being a good wife,' she said, 'I tend to stay in the same place when my husband rides me.'

The Storyteller laughed. 'But you are allowed to move. When your husband rides you.'

'Am I? Now you tell me!'

~·

'WHY DO YOU DRESS AS A BOY?' Asked the charcoalburners' woman.

They squatted by the fire.

The Storyteller and the charcoal burners were in conversation across the clearing.

Men talk.

And women talk.

In separate places.

'My husband wouldn't let me come. . . as a woman. . . said it wasn't safe. . . in these wild places. . . so I turned myself into a boy.'

'I live in the wild places,' said the woman. Her blackened face crinkled into grey as it grinned. 'But then,' she shrugged, 'I have four husbands to protect me.'

'Four? Are they all your husbands?'

'Yes.'

'That's a very strange arrangement.'

'Not for charcoal burners. We live in the forest. The work needs men more than women. It's always been the way. My mother had six husbands.'

The Wife looked at her, thinking.

'Well how did you know which was your father?'

'I had six fathers.'

The Wife looked at her, thinking.

'But one must have been. . . your real father.'

The woman looked at her, puzzled. 'No, they were all my fathers. . . why would one be. . . what do you mean *real*?'

'But. . . but. . . oh never mind,' said the Wife. 'Where are you going?'

'I'll see to food,' said the woman, standing. 'The men will be getting hungry.'

'Pity about them,' said the Wife.

'What do you mean? Sure when men get hungry mustn't women cook?'

'And put your arse in the air when it's not food they hunger for?'

'Sure my arse spends so much time in the air I should be growing eyes in it' she said.

And they both laughed.

But probably not at the same joke.

⁓•

THE FIRE BURNS, SMOKILY.

My eyes smart.

My thighs are sore from the horse.

My husband talks to charcoal burners.

In the morning he will know everything about charcoal burning.

And he will add that knowing to his story.

My story?

My story too?

My, my, and my. . .

I clutch myself to myself.

I have the sight. The world whirls within me, but I never see myself.

Who is the me and the my that looks at the world that whirls?
Does my husband know, does he know that?
He is the Storyteller of Tara, a learned man.
And I am a girl from Connacht.
And I know nothing.
But I see everything, because I have the sight.
They call me the daughter of the moon.
I have danced with the wizards.
And now I go home.

⌒·

'THERE'S A ROMAN HERMIT in the forest here,' said the bald charcoal burner, in answer to the Storyteller's questioning.
'What does he do in the forest?'
'He's built a little hut, and prays.'
'Is that all?'
'Seems to be. . . but says he expects other hermits to arrive any day soon. . . then they're going to build a monastery. . .'
'What is that?'
'A place where lots of hermits gather.'
'What do they do there. . . in the monastery?' asked the Storyteller.
'Pray,' said the charcoal burner.
'And what does the chief of your tuath think about all this?'
'Oh he's given them a little bit of land for the hut. . . and more for the monastery. . . it's very handy having hermits on your land.'
'Handy? What use are they? All they do is pray!' snorted the Storyteller. He looked around, the charcoal burning woman was fiddling at a pot. And the dogs were gnawing a deer's head between them. And the face was half off of the skull, like the swaddle from a baby. And over there beyond the horses were grazing a scatter of oats. And the Wife was sitting alone by the fire, watching it.

⌒·

THE FIRE BURNS, SMOKILY.
I sit alone, and look into the fire, moodily.

I am death, and I dance in the embers.
I am death.
The fire burns, smokily.
I sit here thinking, moodily.
The fire burns, smokily.
I sit alone, and look into the fire, moodily.
I am a girl, dressed as a boy.
I am skinny, and have small breasts, and my husband mocks me in the bed.
But he loves me.
Not because I'm a woman.
But because I have the sight, and he is a Storyteller, and he needs me, my sight. By his side. He needs me more than he needs a woman. And I suppose if he could take the sight from me and put it in his own head he'd leave my woman's body behind, he'd sell me to charcoal burners!
Then I'd have four husbands.
Difficult enough arrangement!
Would they take turns, shagging me?
Or do they each do different things with me. . . one shags me, one talks to me, one laughs with me, one beats me. . . is that the way of it?
No way of knowing, really.
Only certainty is I'd be cooking for four men!
If I were a charcoal burner's woman.
But I'm not. Because I'm a storyteller's woman, and he needs me, for my sight, and now I see a horseman in the east, a horseman, riding, fast.
The Wife closed her eyes, looked into her mind. The picture was somewhere above her nose, between her eyes. As real as if her eyes were open, but different. When younger she'd thought this was a wondrous thing, this seeing. But now it was ordinary, and sometimes a nuisance.
It had come upon her with her first woman's bleeds. And she hadn't said anything to anyone about it. Because those were mysterious times, and there were various ceremonies, certain mysteries. The truth was she'd thought all the other girls had got the sight too with their bleeds, she thought it was part of the thing,

like swollen breasts and hair between the legs. She was very surprised when she found out that no, the other girls were not seeing things, they had not got the sight.

Realising she was special, she'd thought it was a wondrous thing. Back then!

But now? It was ordinary.

She watched the horseman.

So clear she could see his clothes.

He held his neck low, galloping, and the horses's head was stretched ahead, reaching for the road, like it was food to be eaten quickly.

She watched this awhile, and then got up from the fire, and walked across the clerareing to the Storyteller.

'There is a horseman to the east,' she said, 'a horseman riding, fast.'

The Storyteller looked, to the east. And saw nothing.

'How can you see, girl?'

'My eyes are younger,' she said with a smile in her voice. And the Storyteller knew she did not see any horseman, not with her eyes, no, she was seeing it in her head and mocking him. But, even knowing that, he went along with the pretence and squinted, this way, that, held the corners of his eyes with the tips of his fingers the better to see. But, of course, no matter what he did he saw nothing. 'Is it a vision you see, girl?'

'Is there a difference between what I see? What if it's in front of my eyes or behind them? I tell you, husband, there is a horseman to the east. . . now. . . look at him there.'

The Storyteller peered. And yes, there was a tiny speck of a man on a horse. . . well. . . a tiny speck is what he saw, only knowing it was a man on a horse because the girl had told him.

'Where does he go?' wondered the Storyteller aloud.

'He follows us,' said the Wife.

'He follows our route,' said the Storyteller, 'but does that mean he follows us?'

'He follows us,' repeated the Wife, with certainty.

'Alright,' said the Storyteller, 'but why?'

'How do I know,' she said, 'we wait, we watch, we'll soon find out!'

HE WAS A SOLDIER.

His clothes a soldier's clothes, his horse a soldier's horse.

The charcoal burners gathered round him, curious.

They touched the sword that hung from his belt.

They fingered the harnesses and buckles and brasses on the horse.

They looked wide eyed at the skulls that swung from the bridles.

The soldier ignored them. He swung himself down. He was far taller than the charcoal burners, and they looked up at him in a wonder. He paid them no heed. Apart from handing his reins to the toothless man, he ignored them completely, looking right over their heads at the Storyteller.

'I caught you quicker than I thought,' he said.

'Caught us? Quicker?' replied the Storyteller.

'They sent me after you from Tara. . . I thought you'd be further west by now.'

'Ah,' said the Storyteller, 'we went east for awhile.'

'East?'

'To see the Neladoir of Slane.'

'By the gods. . . is he still alive?'

'Well he was. . . but that was hours ago. . . now what brings you here. . . why do you *catch* us?'

'There is a message from Tara,' he said.

'What message is this, and who sends it?'

'Our king sends the message.'

Oh. . . I better hear the king's message,' agreed the Storyteller.

'The witch. . .'

'What witch?'

'The witch we burnt. . .'

'Oh *that* witch. What of her?'

'In the morning, the old ones were raking the fire. . . for bones.'

'For spells. . .' the Storyteller explained, 'they powder the bones between stones, and make potions.'

'There *were* no bones,' said the soldier.

'Probably not. . . the fire was hot. . .'

'But. . . something else. . . those magicians she brought with her. . .'

'Yes, Laoghaire had their heads. . .'

'Yes he was angry, furious when he heard the news about his daughters. . . he had their heads. . . I myself took off the head of one. . . with this very sword at my side. . .'

He put his hand on the hilt.

The charcoal burners all stepped back slightly.

'So what do you tell me now?' asked the Storyteller.

'The heads were gone. . . there were no heads nor bodies where we left them either.' The soldier shrugged, and spread his hands, a gesture of mystification.

The Storyteller looked at him, wondering. The soldier looked right back, waiting for reaction. And round him too the charcoal burners looked at the Storyteller, waiting for reaction. The Wife too, she too looked at him. He felt trapped, surrounded by an audience, as if they were waiting for a song! And him with no music in him, not even the hint of a tune! 'Nonsense man,' he snorted at the soldier, 'what madness is this. . . I myself saw the old ones, I *saw* them collect the blood from the heads. . .'

'There was nothing. . .' the soldier shook his head, insisting, 'nothing. . . no blood in their bottles in the morning. . . there was nothing of the witch. . . nor of her magicians. . . not in the whole of Tara. . .'

'By the gods man. . . the whole of Tara saw the witch. . . I stood with the king myself. . . and we watched her burn.'

'I tell you Storyteller, there was nothing. As if it was all a dream.'

'A mighty strong dream for the whole of Tara,' the Storyteller mocked.

He didn't quite know what to do, or say, or think, other than mock.

He looked across at the Wife, and she was looking into herself, listening, but silent. And then, feeling the Storyteller's gaze, she spoke. 'What is the message then, and what does King Laoghaire say?'

'He is calling the druids together,' the soldier turned to her, 'the wise men, the poets, to discuss the matter.'

'Oh they're the right ones for discussion anyway, those boyos,' said the Storyteller, then added, morosely, 'if not for decision!'

'But what of the Storyteller?' said the Wife to the soldier, 'the Storyteller must be there for such a gathering.'

'Indeed,' agreed the Storyteller, vaguely pleased at her support. Some hint of wifely loyalty there? 'Indeed I must. Give a little commonsense to the proceedings.'

'Well not that,' said the Wife, 'it's the custom.'

'Oh,' said the Storyteller, thinking maybe it was a bit soon to be admiring her for the support and wifely loyalty! 'Oh so you're the great one for the custom, aren't you girl? All of a sudden too!'

'Without custom, what have you got?' She spread her hands, to show them empty, and she grinned.

Something about that grin got on his nerves.

She was playing a game with him.

What game he did not know, but some game it was anyway!

'By the gods girl,' he sneered, 'well *you* go back to Tara now, and discuss these things *yourself* with the druids and the wise men and the poets. Those buckos will make a week out of a word with you. Go on, go back, with this fine warrior here. . . and you can warm him on the way.'

The Wife lookeed the soldier up and down, as if to say well that I might, a handsome lad, why not!

The soldier stood stern, well trained, the words around him just so many spears or arrows. He wouldn't move until the order came. 'Well,' the Storyteller asked him, 'what do you offer for this wife, this talking wife, I'm tired of her. . . she is yours for. . . what have you got?'

'I have little, Storyteller.'

'That sword, that is a fine sword. . . a very fine sword. . . would you change that for this yapping female?'

'This sword was given me by Laoghaire's son. This sword is not mine to give.'

'Nor I his to give,' said the Wife.

'I paid for you.'

'That is just a custom.'

'A *hah*, girl, a *hah*. . . and what was that you said, a moment ago. . . without custom, what have you got. . .. ah hah. . . it is the custom that I can sell you. . . you're not a chief wife, nor even a minor wife, you're an ordinary concubine. . . remember that. . . and by the gods they don't come much more ordinary. . . would you look at the cut of you!'

'Do you love me less because the lawyers make me so? And anyway, you brought me to the Lag an Aenaigh!'

She smiled, triumphantly.

'By the gods,' he shook his head. Hadn't he known that would come back in his face, like a piss into a strong wind. 'By the gods. . . is this the time or the place to be discussing marriage matters? I am the Storyteller of Tara. An important man. I sit three places from the king. Do I want my own story bandied about the campfires of Laoghaire's armies? Am I to be the joke of drunken soldiers?'

Saying nothing, she smiled, twiddled her hair between finger and thumb.

The Storyteller sighed, turned back to the soldier. 'So what, young man, so what does my king send message that I do now?'

'Well he sends a question, not a message. He says do you go back to Tara, to discuss with the druids and the wise men and the poets. . .?'

'Oh a fine prospect that!'

'Or do you go on to Rathcroghan, to discover if the daughters are dead, or alive. He thinks they may be alive.'

'A father will think that. . . until the end. . . until the clay turns.'

'He thinks the witches and the magician were a dream, a storm, a moving of the gods. . .'

'He may be right.'

'And he has ordered that there be no more listening to the Roman and his preaching, and no more crosses in the sacred places of our gods. Not until the matter is decided, one way or the other.'

'So,' said the Storyteller, 'the king thinks this, and he says this, and he orders the order. . . but to me he sends a question? Can he not send *me* an order?'

'I'm only a soldier. I don't know how a king thinks.'

'With great difficulty sometimes,' laughed the Storyteller, 'with great difficulty, that's exactly how a king thinks.'

'We will go on to Rathcroghan,' said the wife, interrupting.

'Have you a wife?' said the Storyteller to the warrior, ignoring her contribution.

'I have.'

'Does she make decisions, order you about?'

'I'm not sure. Perhaps. But women have a way of ordering without a man noticing.'

'Have you no whip in your house, if your dog craps in the corner would you not whip him?'

'Surely.'

'And if your wife craps in the corner, her too?'

'I don't think my wife would crap in the corner.'

'But you let her crap in your ears?'

'You are clever with words, Storyteller. I am no match.'

'That's the way of it,' the Storyteller sighed again. 'Just as you are clever with that sword, and I no match with you.' He bowed, a courtly little bow. This is the way the world should be, he thought, where each man knew his place in the scheme of things, and made graceful exchanges, courtesies of conversation.

'Oh but a sword rusts,' said the Wife, 'and words change their meaning.'

The soldier and the Storyteller looked at her, at each other, then at her again, the way men will when a woman joins into a conversation. She spoke on, ignoring any messages in their looks. 'So enough of this. . . by the gods, men say that *women* chatter without reason! By the gods. . . enough of this. . . let's have decision. . . to Tara, or Rathcroghan? I say Rathcroghan.'

'Do you indeed?' said the Storyteller.

'Well we *are* half way there.'

'We are *not*. . . half way. . .'

'We've come a decent journey anyway. . .'

The Storyteller looked at her, carefully. 'Aren't you very determined. . . to get to Cruachan Ai. . . even if there's no purpose in the going. . .'

'I do think there's a purpose. And anyway it's my own place.'

'Your place is with me,' he snapped in a shout.

She looked at the ground.

Like a child, shouted at.

He remembered once, a year ago or so, he had to whip her, for something. A good whipping. She'd borne it well, and hadn't cried. But afterwards she'd looked at the ground, like a child, whipped. Looked at the ground, just like this. And he'd put his finger under her chin, and lifted her face to his, and looked into her eyes. And one was cold, the other cruel. And he'd loved her for all that darkness in her soul. And he'd never whipped her again. And now again he put his finger under her chin, and lifted her face to his, and looked into her eyes. And one was cold, the other cruel. And he loved her for the darkness in her soul.

'Sorry Wife,' he said, 'I shouldn't shout at you.'

She smiled. And turned to the soldier, still beside them, and more than a little embarassed. 'Learn from the Storyteller,' she said.

'What do I learn, my lady?'

'It's a strong man says sorry to a woman.'

The soldier nodded, but the Storyteller listening wasn't that sure he really understood. Not that it mattered. The best soldiers understand nothing. . . except that the enemy is over there, and how to get at them and kill them!

'Alright,' he said, decisively, 'we go to Rathcroghan.'

The Wife nodded, as if she agreed with the decision. As if the decision was his. And he had made a wise choice! As would be expected from such a wise man.

'You,' he spoke to the soldier, 'you bring that message back to Laoghaire. . . that I have gone on to Cruachan Ai. . . I'll find out one way or the other about Eithne and Fidelma. . . and I will return to him with the news. . .'

'I'll do that,' said the soldier, preparing to get back up on his horse. Efficiently. Glad to have a definite order.

'No, by the gods,' the Storyteller stopped him with a wave, 'stay, stay here, and rest. And rest your horse. . . you'll be no quicker leaving now than if you leave in the morning.'

'You're right.' The soldier stopped in his mounting of the horse, slid down again. Glad to have another definite order!

'These good people will give you food,' said the Storyteller.

'Probably lend you their woman,' muttered the Wife, 'if you're unlucky!'

'Oh I don't know about that,' said the Storyteller, watching the soldier lead his horse to the others. 'It might be lucky he'd be.'

'Would *you* stir her kettle?'

'Well. . . she looks like. . . she knows. . . what a man. . . might like. . . '

'You mean she looks like a whore!'

'But a man often needs a whore.'

'Hah,' said the Wife, 'men!' And then 'hey. . . did you notice. . .

the soldier called me *my lady*.'

'Probably because you're my wife.'

'I suppose so,' she nodded, mock sadly. 'Strange, isn't it?'

'What?'

'A man can make a woman whore or wife. . . and all the world agrees with his decision.'

⌒•

THE STORYTELLER WALKED IN THE WOODS.

He was tired.

Difficult woods these, for the walking, through undergrowth, coppices, small trees. He followed the line of the river, flowing from the north, from the hills, from Sliabh na Caillaige, he saw them on the horizon.

He knew that land, he went there once.

The graves of the old people are there, and a man can talk to them in his mind. But they don't say much, the old people. Except that these are our graves. We lived. But it was a long time ago. And now we are dead.

The Storyteller walked on, along the bank of the river, the little scrubby woods on either side.

Easy to cut, he supposed, those woods.

A good place for charcoal burning.

And does the charcoal care if it comes from a great tree, or a branch?

He swung his bone at thistles.

And does the bone care what leg it comes from, from a great man or a fool?

He sighed an answer to that question, and walked on, tired.

A walk now in the woods had seemed a good idea, to think on this latest development, this mysterious message from Tara. A walk to clear his mind. To clear his mind in the murky air. By the gods, he coughed. He'd walked upwind from the charcoal burners' fire, to get away from the smoke, but in truth there was little wind, and the smoke hung like a puff over a wide area, adding even more darkness to the darkness of the evening.

He sat, a rest.

He may have dozed.

He thought of Eithne and Fidelma.

And about what difference his finding out about anything would make to anything at all.

A man gets older.

And wiser, sometimes. And if he gets wiser he starts to realise how small he is, small in the scheme of things. Life is a garment on a ghost. A woolen garment? Perhaps, something like that. Knitted together from many strands. So that when it catches on a thorn, it leaves a piece of wool behind. But the ghost that wears the garment passes on, and the garment still keeps the wearer warm. While the piece of wool sits on the thorn in the rain. Then a bird picks it, knits it into a nest. The eggs are laid, the fledglings hatch, and fly away. And the nest falls to the ground in a storm. And is washed apart. And the piece of wool is trampled into the earth. . . and in the earth. . . oh. . . it goes on! And on! And anyway that's how small a man is. A piece of wool on a thorn. From someone else's garment, for someone else's nest!

The Storyteller though of this, and nursed it along into a little story, a story he might tell to some druid sometime over beer. . . always good to have a stock of stories for those boyos. . . meaningful stories! Keep one step ahead!

It was then that he saw her, creeping through the trees in his direction.

A slavegirl, wearing a slavegirl's cape, and the hood about her face. With one hand she held the cape closed at the neck, and in the other she carried a bag.

'Who are you?' he asked.

'I am a slavegirl. . .'

'I can see that! I asked *who* you were, not *what* you were.'

'I killed my master. . . they hunt me down with dogs. . . save me. . .'

The Storyteller reached out his hand, but her hand in his was smoke from charcoal burners' fires, a thing of shadow, and it slipped through his fingers without touching.

That was when he knew she was a wraith.

'Where will you run to?,' he asked the wraith.

'Ulster,' she said, 'my people are in Ulster.'

'Your people are my enemy. . . and the enemy of my people. . . why would I save you?'

'You met me yesterday morning, and I was pretty,' she said, and he recognised her. Irial's slavegirl! Irial the pig slaughterer's slavegirl! The attractive one, the one with dirty feet. The one he might think of doing a deal about. And here she was. A dream, a wraith.

'Is that a reason,' he asked, 'a reason to help you?'

'You watched me sway my hips.'

'Is that a reason either? Where have you run from?'

'Tara. Through bogs, and woods, and over hills. . . but I'm getting tired. . . and I might not make it to Ulster. . .'

'What will happen if you don't?'

'They'll hang me. . . as a lesson for the other slaves. . .'

The Storyteller reached out his hand, but her hand in his was smoke, a shadow, and it slipped through his fingers without touching.

'How can I help you? I go to Cruachan Ai, not Ulster?'

'Well take me there. . . yes take me there. . . across the big river. . . I'll go north from there to Ulster. . .'

'But you're a shadow, a dream, how can I take you there, I cannot touch you.'

'Take me as a dream.'

'Where will you hide.'

'In the folds of your cloak. . . and when you get across the river you can shake me out. . . and then I'll go north to Ulster. . .'

'Are you dead already, girl, have they hanged you already?'

'Does it matter to you?'

'You *are* dead already, girl,' he said, suddenly realising, 'they *have* hanged you already.'

'Take me as a dream,' she pleaded.

'I am weary with dreams, girl, worn down with dreams, tired with their heaviness.'

'Oh but I am pretty. . . and you like a pretty girl. . .'

'Where is the warmth in a woman who's a dream?'

'Take the slave girl across the river,' said another voice.

It was the witch.

The one they thought they'd burned at Tara.

She stood slightly to the north, Sliabh na Caillaige behind her as a horizon, as if she'd come from there, and as if the hills were hers.

He looked at her, and nodded. 'Ah,' he said, 'ah hah. . . I *thought* I'd be seeing *you* again!'

'You asked the girl about her warmth, and where was it, in a dream.'

'I did.'

'Well did you ask me of the weight in my breast, Storyteller,' she said, 'when you pressed me with that bone, did you, did you ask me anything at all?'

'What are you saying?'

'How can you feel the weight of my body. . . and not take the dream of the slavegirl to safety?'

'Her hand is smoke, she's a wraith. . . but I *think* I understand what you're saying, witch. . . but I'm tired, I've been travelling all day. . . though if it makes you feel better. . . I'll take her. . . but if she's hanged she's hanged! What use am I to her or her to me?'

'What use is a spade to a man with no field?' said the witch.

'Oh stop speaking like a druid,' said the Storyteller, 'haven't I enough of them in Tara?'

She laughed.

A very attractive woman, the Storyteller realised. How happy she seemed when she laughed. Her white teeth, her dark hair, her well formed meaty body. . . pity she was a witch, and a wraith, and ashes in Tara, and smoke in the woods near Sliabh na Caillaige.

'Do you know what your problem is?' she said.

'Oh yes, I know many of them,' he replied, 'but for sure I'm about to hear another!'

'Do you play dice?'

'Oh yes, I play dice.'

'Do you think the number that comes up is the same number on every side of the dice?'

'No. . . of course not. . .'

'Well don't be living your life like that. . . just because one number is there in front of you. . .'

'I've gambled on that number.'

'There are other numbers, on other sides of the dice. They may come up next time. They may have come up in the past. Just because you win or lose your bet doesn't mean the number stays the same for every throw.'

'By the gods, there's a terrible similarity between a witch and a druid. . . the preaching!'

'The tumble of the dice, the tumble of times, the spinning of lives. . . that bone you carry in your hand as a walking stick. . .'

'What of it?'

'It searches the country for my breast. . . and my breast. . .'

'What of it?'

'It travels through time, searching for that bone. . .'

'What of all that, we said all that, flesh clings to the bone. . . what of all that?'

'Don't be too clever and too quick. . . to say what use is this, what use is that. . . you do not know. . . remember the bird, I said watch that bird. . .'

'I wouldn't forget that bird,' said the Storyteller.

He thought of that bird as death.

'Think of that bird as life,' said the witch, reading his mind, contradicting him. 'As life. And its feathers as maybes. . . maybe this, and maybe that. . . maybe you *did* buy this slavegirl here. . . yes. . . live your life as if you bought her. . . from Irial the pig slaughterer. . .'

'After much haggling,' said the ghost of the slavegirl, mockingly.

'Maybe you bought her as a wife.'

'Oh I've enough of wives, believe you me!'

'Maybe she's a good wife. . . and has two sons. . . and three daughters. . .'

'Oh I've enough of children, believe you me!'

'But maybe that is all in another world, another time. Your clothes are different. You speak a different language. Everything you know is forgotten. And everything you have learned is not yet known.'

'There is no Meath,' said the slavegirl.

'No Connacht,' said the witch.

'No Ulster,' said the slavegirl.

'Everything has changed,' said the witch.

'I won't be happy there,' he said. And wondered. Why am I talking to witches and wraiths?

'You'll never be happy, Storyteller,' said the witch, 'no more that I'll be ever happy. . . it's not in us to be happy. . .'

'Us?' asked the Storyteller, 'who is this *us* you talk of? You are the witch and I am the storyteller. . . how now do you bring *us* together into an *us*? Firstly, I am a man. You are a woman. There is no *us* betwen a man and a woman! Secondly, I am a living man, and you are a wraith. . . you come and go, in and out of living. . . like. . . like I don't know what. . .'

'Like a slavegirl into a room,' said the slavegirl.

'Like a story into a storyteller,' said the witch.

'Hardly noticed, she brings this, takes away that,' said the slavegirl.

'Coming and going, in and out,' said the witch.

'In and out of living,' said the slavegirl.

'In and out of death,' said the witch, 'the story comes and goes.'

'But. . .' The Storyteller raised his hand to stop, to interrupt this litany which sounded like it might go on forever otherwise. 'But. . . the point. . . if not happiness. . . what am I living for then, witch?'

'As long as the story needs telling, you live. . .'

'How long does the story need telling?'

The witch smiled, her dark hair about her face, and she flicked it away.

Her hands were very old. He noticed that. He noticed how the bones of her fingers started from the wrist, and that is the sign of someone very old. But still, her smile was very young.

'How long,' she said, 'how long is a piece of string?'

And then she laughed.

And then the Storyteller saw, coming through the woods, a line of horses, eight horses. One horse was riderless, and on each of the seven others was a silent wizard. And all were grey and wraiths, horses and wizards alike, they were like the smoke from the charcoal burning fires, drifting through the trees. The witch mounted the riderless horse, and the line of eight horses went on, grey and wraiths, horses and wizards and witch alike, smoke in the trees, drifting away.

They moved to the west.

But the wraith of the slavegirl was still there.

'I will hide in your cloak,' she said, 'I won't be any trouble.'

'Well you'd better not,' he said, 'I've trouble enough on this journey.'

So she hid in his cloak, and he slapped it about him, and he walked back to the others.

⌒·

THE WIFE GIGGLED AT THE FIRE.

And beside her the charcoal burners' woman sat, giggling too.

What do they giggle at, wondered the Storyteller, looking over.

Strange, women in the company of men will damn another woman as a whore. But when there's no men around they'll come together, gossiping, giggling.

Strange.

He mooched about the camp.

The charcoal burners weren't great company, their conversation was limited, they didn't seem to know that many words.

And it was too early to lie down.

The dogs and the horses were fed, resting.

There was nothing much to do.

He was relieved when the soldier came up to him.

'I have something to tell you,' he said.

'Something?'

'Something I feel I should tell you.'

'Best go along with the feeling so. . . sit here. . . what is it, what is it you have to tell me?'

The soldier sat beside him on the log.

It was completely dark now.

Bats squeaked.

And one suddenly swooped right by the soldier's head.

He drew his sword, and waited.

'Oh you'll never kill a bat,' said the Storyteller. 'They catch insects in the dark, they'll see the blade of that sword a mile away!'

Another bat swooped by. The soldier swung the sword, and missed.

'See,' said the Storyteller, 'you'll never kill a bat.'

'Best to creep into barns,' said the soldier, 'and kill them in the day when they're asleep. They're flying rats you know.'

'If a man had a flying dog he could put it in the air, to catch them.'

'Are there flying dogs? I've never heard of flying dogs.'

'Probably in some far country, probably there there's flying dogs.'

'A man who'd go there. . . bring back a flying dog. . . or a breeding pair. . . he'd make good money.'

'He would, indeed. Particularly among people who wanted to catch bats.'

'Yes, that would be the place to make the money.'

'Yes it would.'

The two men looked at the bats for awhile, and each thought their own thoughts.

'Now,' the Storyteller said, when it was time to talk again, 'now what did you want to tell me? What is it I should know?'

'There is a soldier in our troop. . .'

'What is his name?'

'Fintan of Cualann.'

'That is a good place, Cualann. . . there is a mountain there. . . they call it the Ear of Cualann. . .'

'I know it. . .

'I climbed that mountain once,' said the Storyteller, remembering, a place of whin and wildness, wonder. What time of year was that? He thought. But the actual season was gone away from the remembering, faded, merged. Details of memories go that way. They trickle off.

'It's near the fort of Laoghaire. . . on the sea,' said the soldier.

'I know that place.'

'It guards the great white strand.'

'I know that place too,' said the Storyteller. 'Conor mac Nessa fought the birds there. . . in ancient times.' . .'

'Fought the birds?' said the soldier.

'Never mind. . . tell me what you have to tell me. . . of this soldier in your troop?'

'He guards the gates of Tara now at night. . . do you remember we burned the witch?'

'Will I forget? But didn't you just tell me. . . we didn't burn the damn witch. . . it was a dream. . . an illusion. . . a fog on all of Tara. . .'

'Yes. . . yes. . . but that night anyway. . . Fintan of Cualann guarded the gates. . . and he saw. . . or he dreamed. . . he does not know now. . . guard duty at night is like that. . . a man dozes. . .'

'What did he see, or what did he dream he saw. . .?'

'He saw eight horses passing, out from Tara. . . going to the West. . .'

'Along this road. . .?'

'Yes.'

'Who rode those horses?'

'The witch we burned. . .'

'Or did not burn!'

'She rode the first. . . she was naked. . . a woman to the waist. . . but her feet were the claws of birds. . .'

'Does Fintan of Cualann drink a lot?' said the Storyteller, but his smile was lost to the soldier in the darkness.

'Oh he drank a lot the day after this, I'll tell you that for nothing! I drank with him as he told me. . . his hands were shaking.'

'Who were on the other horses?'

'The seven wizards. . . the wizards whose heads Laoghaire had. . .'

'Or did *not* have.'

'Agreed. Or did not have. Anyway. They carried their heads beneath their arms. . . and their horses were like cats. . . huge cats. . .'

'The witches horse? Was that a cat?'

'No, that was a horse. . . because as it passed him Fintan of Cualann saw her feet against the side of a horse. . .'

'The feet that were birds' claws. . .'

'That were birds' claws, and they were cutting into the side of the horse as she drove it along. . . and blood was dripping. . .'

'Did she see him?'

'She didn't look to left, or right. . .'

'How did he know it was her, that particular witch? Could it not have been an apparition. . . any witch. . . there's lots of witches you know. . . the night is full of them.'

'No it was her. . . she had that black hair. . . shiny. . . like the feathers of a bird. . . and that white skin. . . and he remembered her breasts, they were very heavy. . .'

'Why would he remember them?'

'Because when she was on the fire before they burned her. . .'

'Or did *not* burn her. . .' the Storyteller muttered.

'Whatever. . . when she was there the young boys were taunting her, teasing her for her breasts, making cow noises, grabbing her, pretending to milk her. . . you know what boys are like. . .'

'Boys will be boys. . . but so. . . why would he remember her so well?'

'Because the boys annoyed one of the old men about the place. . .'

'Old men will be old men'

'And he sent Fintan of Cualann to chase away the boys, to guard the fire until it was lit. . .'

'Did he talk to the witch. . . while he was guarding her?'

'No, because the old men in charge of the fire had told him, pay no heed to the witch. . . do not talk to her. . . just chase away the boys.'

'A very obedient soldier. . . but did the witch talk to him?'

'She told him he would die an old man. . . in the Glen of The Sheep in Cualann. . . he would fight one more battle. . . and he would tell the story of the battle to the children of his children. . . and they to theirs. . . and they to theirs. . . forever. . .'

'Forever?'

'Yes forever.'

'What else did she tell him?'

The soldier did not answer.

The Storyteller waited. The bats swooped. And yes, he thought, yes, it would be good to have some flying dogs. . . if such a thing were possible!

He waited, and when he felt he'd waited long enough he repeated the question, expanding it slightly, for clarity. 'What else did the witch tell Fintan of Cualann? While she was on the fire, and he was guarding her?'

The soldier did not answer, immediately. And he turned and shrugged and made up some mind in his head and said 'oh alright. . . but you're probably not going to like this bit.'

'Try me!'

'Now I didn't remember this until I came. . . arrived here. . . on my horse. . . because it didn't seem that important. . .'

'What reminded you?'

'Your wife.'

'How?'

'Well. . . when I saw her. . . I thought she was a boy. . .'

'That's what you're meant to think. . . do you know she had lovely hair. . . but she cut it for the journey. . .'

'I like a woman with long hair.'
'I think all men do.'
'Why would that be?'
'Well,' the Storyteller thought, 'well there was a custom long ago. . . a man would tie a new wife to the bedpost by her hair. . . that might be it. . .'
'What? Be what?'
'The memory of the custom. . . why men like. . . oh never mind. . . what were you saying, what did she remind you of?'
'I thought she was a boy.'
'You said that.'
'Yes. . . now. . . going back a bit. . . Fintan of Cualann told me. . .'
'Yes?'
'Told me that after the witch had told him about him dying in Cualann as an old man. . .'
'Yes?'
'Well they'd talked about death then. . . generally speaking. . .'
'How *much* did you say Fintan of Cualann drank?'
'No this is true. . . this is what happened. . .'
'Go on. . .'
'Well he said to her aren't you afraid of death, witch? And you to be burnt soon. . . know what I mean?'
'Indeed. . . and her reply?'
'Yes. . . she said no matter. . . and she said a funny thing, a phrase. . .'
'Flesh clings to the bone?'
'Yes yes. . . how did you know?'
'She said the same to me. . . but tell me Soldier now. . . how and why did seeing my wife remind you of this. . .'
'Because. . . because the witch said. . . it was no matter. . . dying. . . because flesh clings to the bone. . . and there were many bones to cling to. . . and flesh comes in all shapes and sizes. . .'
'And?'
'You might not want to hear this.'
'Oh tell me, man, by the gods!'
'She said to Fintan of Cualann. . . how will you know, how will anyone know. . . tomorrow, or in a month or a year or a life. . . I may be a crone. . . or a child. . . disguised. . . like a girl dressed as a boy. . .'

The Soldier looked at the Storyteller.
The bats swooped, scooping up insects.
The Storyteller looked at the bats.
Life lives on life, he thought.
And death?
On death.

⁓•

THE WIFE STIRRED, in her dreams, restless.

The Storyteller stirred, in his dreams, restless too.

The charcoalburners' food had been awful. And the Storyteller had muttered to the Wife 'well I hope the sex she gives these men is better than the food.' And they'd laughed together.

And now they dreamed together.

Their bodies wrapped in bodies' arms.

Their minds in different worlds.

She dreamed she was a slavegirl.

She had killed her master, because he beat her. And now she was running away through the woods. But they were following her, with dogs. She could hear them baying. They would surely catch her. And when they caught her they would bring her back. And hang her by the arms from a tree. And put a hook up her hole and pull her innards. Because that was the punishment for a slave who killed a master.

She ran on.

Terrified.

And now she was a deer.

Still running, running through the forest, dogs after her.

She darted, this way, that. Very fast, using the trick of the trees, and something in her born, some skill, some knowing, using all of that to escape the baying dogs.

But she did not escape the dogs.

Their only skill was one, to chase and hunt her down.

And one skill will always conquer many.

They ploughed through undergrowth, and brambles. Caught her, pulled her down, and tore the flesh away.

She felt her legs being stripped of flesh.

And then her belly opened, and her innards pulled.

She died. And watched, the dogs, pulling her innards from mouth to mouth.

What is in me that watches now, she thought. . . where is the *I* and the *me* and the *my*?

Am I the slavegirl, am I the deer?

You are death, said a whispering voice.

I am death, she agreed.

But who are you, she asked.

I am life, said the voice, and I am your friend.

You are my friend, she agreed.

And then a man walked by with an axe. And it was the Storyteller, walking in his dream. But he was not the storyteller in the dream. He was a hermit, a Christian hermit, chopping trees and making logs for a hut. He expected other hermits to arrive, any day now. The plan was to build a monastery. Something along the lines of the monastery in Armorica. He had the memory of it in his mind. There would be cells for each hermit. And a dining hall, and a church, and a place to walk, a place that was sheltered from the rain. There would be fields, and vegetables and herbs, and a brewery too, yes they would drink beer.

Didn't God made beer, just as he made the stars?

Would a hermit not look at the stars in wonder?

He paused, his axe across a shoulder.

And he looked through the trees at the dead deer.

And the dogs tearing the flesh of the deer, they paused too, and looked at him.

And then they decided he was no danger and went back to their gnawing and tearing. And the whole body of the deer was torn to pieces, all except the head. And that lay there, sideways. With big brown eyes, looking wet, and crying. And the hermit thought, if a woman had those eyes, a man would reach out and touch her hair, to comfort her. In fact, he remembered once, he did know a woman with those eyes.

In Armorica.

The boat was leaving.

She didn't understand.

He was going away.

To preach the gospel where the gospel needed preaching.
She stood by the harbour wall.
She had brown hair.
She dressed in the Roman way.
A silver clasp on her shoulder.

The hermit stood on the boat, and sailors walked this way, and that. They prepared ropes, and sails, there was quite a fuss going on, quite a bustle. But a silence like a cloud was around him on the deck and around the girl on the wall of the harbour. She was beautiful. Yes now in his memory he remembered. A Roman girl, from the Roman people. She had a gentle graceful body. And her dresses fell across her body in that Roman way. He remembered looking, at the clasp on her shoulder, the clasp that held her dresses together. And he remembered looking down at his own feet, where his bag of things stood, and beside it a case with the holy books of God, a box with a clasp. And he had noticed how the pin on the clasp of the girl's dress was so similar to the pin on the box.

Either pin could be pulled by the grip of a finger to a thumb.

And if he pulled the pin on the girl's shoulder, her dress would fall. And she would be graceful, and gentle, and beautiful.

He thought of this.

But the ship moved from the harbour.

And her big brown eyes were wet with tears.

And then they were no longer to be seen.

He sat on the deck. And watched Armorica, fading. At first it was a mountain. Then a hill. Then a line across the horizon. And then it was gone, and gone forever. And when it was gone, gone forever, he sat on the deck and pulled the pin of his bible box. He took out the great book. And he read the word of God.

It never changed.

And through the years it never changed.

And sometimes in the years he thought of her, the Roman girl. And how of course she had changed. No longer a girl. A woman. A mother no doubt, perhaps a grandmother. And perhaps she still dressed in the Roman way, though that fashion was fading. But no matter the fashion, whatever dress she wore, it would not fall away to show a gentle graceful body. It would be a woman, well worn, the flesh tired from children, from the bearing them, feeding them.

That is the way of things. Just as his own body was not that young man now. No, he was worn, tired too. Sometimes the logs he dragged through the forest were too heavy for his strength.

He was getting old.

But the word of God was still the same.

It was neither young, nor old.

It would not die.

It would not lie like a deer dead on the forest floor.

He waved his axe, and sighed, and waved his axe again. And the dogs got anxious, scattered into the trees, trailing guts and pieces of flesh. They would hide there til he was gone. He walked to the head of the deer.

The eyes of the deer looked at him.

The eyes of the long ago girl in Armorica looked at him.

He reached out and touched the head of the deer.

It was warm.

He reached out and touched the head of the girl in Armorica.

It was cold.

Cold.

Cold.

THE STORYTELLER STIRRED from the cold, and woke.

The wife was warm in his arms, but not warm enough.

A fatter woman would be better.

But he wrapped her body to himself, making the most of what was there. And as he wrapped her round him she herself stirred and woke, and she complained 'you woke me.'

'I dreamed I was a hermit,' he said, 'and the dream woke me.'

'I dreamed I was death,' she said, 'and my friend was life.'

'Tell me of that dream.'

'Tomorrow.'

'No, you will forget.'

'We met in the forest. I was death, and my friend was life. And we were wandering, looking for people.'

'What for?'

'To show them death, and show them life.'

'What for?'

'Because until they saw us we were not there. . . do you understand that. . . I don't. . .'

'Vaguely. . . did you find people?'

'I can't remember.'

'What did you look like, when you were death?'

'I was beautiful. . . I was dark, not fair. . . I had heavy breasts, not skinny, not like a boy. . . and I'd meat on my behind, all curvey. . . you would have liked me. . .'

'You'd have kept me warmer anyway. And what did life, your friend, what did life look like?'

'Old. . . very old. . .'

'Isn't that strange. . . I'd have thought that death was old, and life was young. . .'

'Yes, I remember that, thinking that.'

'And there was no-one in the forest, no people?'

'No, just trees. . . and graves. . .'

'Graves? Were you afraid?'

'I wonder sometimes if I'll ever return to Tara now.'

'Why do you say that, so suddenly.'

'We are not far from the river.'

'What of the river?'

'In the old days they would drown girls in the river, to make the water sweet.'

'No-one will drown the wife of the Storyteller.' He held her tight.

'In the old days they would hang girls from the trees, to make the seasons turn.'

'No-one will hang the wife of the Storyteller.' He held her tighter. 'And anyway, these are not the old days.'

'They are,' she said, 'in Connacht.'

'Go to sleep, girl,' he said, 'and don't you be brooding.'

'Death never sleeps,' she said.

He held his hand across her chest. 'Death would fill my hands with flesh, you barely tickle my fingers.'

She shrugged.

'I am hidden in me.'

'Go to sleep, wife, go to sleep.'

'Do you love me?'

'Of course I do,' he said, surprised he didn't have to lie.
'Will you love me, when we've lived the story through?'
'What will be the difference?'
'Everything. Go to sleep, husband, go to sleep.'

'THEY ARE COMING soon,' said Eithne, by the well.
'They're near the river,' said Fidelma, looking into the water of Ogulla Well.
'They sleep in woods.'
'In each others' arms.'
'In smoky woods, the camp of charcoal burners.'
'They dream.'
'But not of us.'
'When will they dream of us?'
'When they come across the river.'
'Across the river. . . does he know. . . does he know he sleeps with death, in his arms?'
'Does he care? Of all his wives he loves her.'

7

THE CHARCOALBURNERS' WOMAN stirred a pot. The Storyteller looked over her shoulder.

'It'll be ready soon,' she said.

That's what I'm afraid of, thought the Storyteller, but he held his peace, and muttered things polite instead. The polite phrases piled up around them. Shifting together, uneasily, like leaves trapped in a corner by a breeze. Dry phrases, each one dead, and their rustling together their only meaning. Better to go now. Eat later in the day. But thank you very much. Get an early start. Soon as the Wife is ready.

'Whatever pleases you,' said the charcoalburners' woman, kneeling on her knees, stirring the pot.

'It's for the best,' said the Storyteller, looking down the front of her dress, and thinking of the heavy breasted witch.

Flesh clings to the bone.

He tapped the ancient bone he'd brought from Tara against his leg, absentmindedly. His eyes followed the stirring, absentmindedly, and he noticed something.

'You always stir from left to right?' he said, thinking of the absent minded eye, and how it sees things hidden. And it's the eye that strains to look clearly sees far less!

'Oh yes, that's the way for a wife to stir,' she said. And stopped, looked up at him. Her big eyes the eyes of a whore. 'Watch a woman stirs the other way.'

'And why is that?'

'That's a witch, that woman... she puts a spell on you...'

'If she stirs from right to left?'

'Oh yes... watch a woman stirs that way...'

'Well I'll certainly remember... what's that you cook?'

'Deer meat...'

'The deer my dogs eat the head of?'

'The very same...' The woman dipped in to the murk and raised a little bit of meat from the liquid. It looked rather like a rag in a washtub. 'That'll be nice,' she said.

'Yes it's a pity I can't stay,' said the Storyteller.

He looked down the front of her dress, and thought of the witch.

He looked at the ragged piece of meat hanging from the woman's stick.

He felt the bone from Tara at his hand, and it tapping at his leg.

He remembered poking the witch at the fire.

And the way her meat clung to his bone.

Flesh clings to the bone.

'That soldier left early,' said the woman, dropping the ragged grey lump back into the stew.

It sank, like something drowning, slowly. But not with a struggle, no, that lump was tired of life, it welcomed oblivion.

'Left? The soldier has left?' The Storyteller looked about. And over beyond there was two horses only, no sign of a third. 'Did you see him leave?'

'No he was gone... and I rise early...'

'You didn't see him at all, this morning?'

'No, not him nor his horse. Gone back to Tara I suppose.'

'I suppose.'

He looked down the front of her dress, and thought of the heavy breasted witch.

The woman knelt there, stirring, slowly.

He knew she knew he was looking down the front of her dress.

The stick she stirred was round and smooth, well worn from many horrible stews. She held it the way a whore might hold a man's prick, fondling strength into him. Up, and down, gripping, tight, and soft and slowly, stirring.

Her dirty hair hung down about her shoulders.

I'll bet there's insects in that hair, thought the Storyteller. Living their own lives. Safe from water anyway!

'You'd have thought he would say goodbye' she said.

'Who?' said the Storyteller, half listening.

'The soldier. He got a good meal here. And food for his horse. You'd have thought he would say goodbye.'

'Maybe he didn't want to wake people.'

'Maybe that's it.' She stirred on awhile. He looked down her dress awhile.

Their minds had unspoken sex with each other.

The steam from the stew smelled of sweat.

Or a woman's crotch, whatever.

Something shagable, perhaps, but certainly nothing edible.

She stirred, she squeezed her stirring stick. And with every stir and every squeeze he felt the strength in his prick, stiffening. This is a game, he thought, a silly game. And she and I are playing. Or. . . he thought then. . . or is it that she and I are not the players at all, but merely pieces in some game, dumb pieces on a fidchell board?

And if we are, whose fingers think to move us next?

He shook his head, pondering that. And then she looked up, suddenly. The wondering wideness of her whorish eyes. She's got nice eyes, he realised. Deep, and wise, and knowing. How can a woman with eyes like that cook so badly?

'What're you thinking?' he asked her.

'Maybe,' she said, 'maybe he wasn't here at all.'

'What do you mean?'

She stood up.

She wiped her cooking stick on the end of her dress.

She brushed her dirty hair away from her dirty face with dirty hands.

Her eyes were clean and clear. Whorish, yes, but clean and clear.

What colour are those eyes?

'Maybe,' she repeated, 'maybe he was a ghost, come to haunt us.'

'On a ghost horse?'

'How can we know?'

'Well you can have a pretty good idea. . . for example. . . tell me this. . . when I am gone. . . and my wife. . . and my two dogs. . . and my two horses. . . when we're all gone will you be thinking we were ghosts?'

She didn't answer that. Just looked at him, thoughtfully. But her look said 'perhaps'. She ran the tip of her red tongue across her red lips. And again he was reminded of that small tongue a woman keeps between her legs. A little prick that is, that tongue. A person decides to grow into a man or a woman when it's a baby in the womb. And there's useless bits and pieces left over from the decision. A man with his dry nipples. And a woman with her tiny prick.

'Your wife told me,' said the woman, 'when we were talking yesterday...'

'What did she tell you?'

'That your black dog you call Night... and your white dog you call Day...'

'I do.'

'Why do you call them that?'

'Well it seems... pretty... obvious?'

'Not if you live in the forest.'

'What do you mean?'

'Sometimes here the days are dark... and the nights are bright...'

'Well... I suppose...'

'Sometimes here the ghosts are people... and the people ghosts... sometimes here you dream, and that's your life. Sometimes here you live, but it's a dream... do you hear what I'm saying, Storyteller?'

'Why do you live in the forest... with these ignorant men... you're an intelligent woman...'

She smiled.

Sadly? A little,

'Perhaps that's the very reason I live here.' And then she walked away, and the Storyteller noticed how she was banging her cooking stick against her leg as she walked. In exactly the same way he had the habit of banging his bone against his own leg. And he thought that strange, the pattern, the similarity.

Is her mind mine, he thought?

Am I the whore?

And she the Storyteller?

He sighed away the other questions, the other questions that a dark morning stirs. And he walked to the horses, and he called *gaddup yadogs* to the dogs.

⌒•

'DIRECTLY WEST,' the Storyteller said, 'we ride directly west now.'

'Yes, I noticed that,' agreed the Wife.

'A long straight road.'

'Yes, a long straight road, I noticed that.'

'Well ask me a question.'

'What question would that be?'

'Ask me why the road is straight, sometimes, and sometimes not.'

'I bet you know the answer!'

'I might,' the Storyteller grinned.

'Alright,' she said, 'why *is* the road straight, sometimes, and sometimes not?'

'Rivers,' he said, 'rivers and hills.'

'Rivers,' she asked, 'rivers and hills?'

'When Asail built the road, he followed the rivers. . . almost. . . if they were going nearly in his direction. . . he followed the rivers because the old paths went along the rivers. . . yesterday from the hill of Slane we followed the Boyne. . .'

'Did we?'

'Oh yes, it was there, on our left.'

'I didn't see it. . . well. . . I saw it. . . now and then. . .'

'Well it flows quite well without your seeing it.'

'Or your knowing it?'

'That's a different question. There's them that say without a knowing or a story, things will change.'

'You've lost me there.'

'I think I've lost myself! But anyway. . . as I was saying. . . the Boyne was on our left. We were moving west, or nearly so. And then at Nuachongbail the Boyne would have led us south. . . and led Asail south too! He realised that. . . so he made the road to follow another river, the Bright River. . . we followed that. . .'

'Going north?'

'Yes, going north. . . but still to the west. . . more or less. . . but then, at that hill where you had the vision. . .'

'I've visions in lots of places!'

'That *particular* vision. . . there Asail decided it was time to leave the rivers, to move directly west. . . he followed the hills. . . he was already on a hill. . . the hill where you had the vision. . . and he saw another hill. . .'

'The hill behind us?'

'Yes the hill behind us now. . . so he built the road from hill to hill. . . straight across the land. . . down one hill and up the next. . .'

'Where does he go now, Asail?'

'To the lakes. . . there are lakes ahead. . . and to get around the lakes he built the road going north, and south, and east, and west, to wriggle round the waters. . .'

'Its simple when you explain it. . . like that.'

'The sign of a good teacher, simplicity!'

'And what would be the sign of an arrogant man?' asked the Wife.

The Storyteller didn't answer, didn't have to answer. Because at that point they were curving alongside some homesteads, a group of raths, and people looking around at them, curious.

'What place is this?' he called out.

'Galmoystown,' came the answer, 'Galmoystown.'

Twice, the answer came. Once from a man on one side of the road, and once from a man on the other. And both in a hurry to get the word in first. As if being the person with the answer would give some meaning to their day.

⁓•

'THAT HILL THERE,' said the Storyteller, 'there to our north. . .'

'You asked me about that. . . yesterday. . . leaving Tara.'

'Oh no I didn't, I never saw that hill before in my life.'

'That's not what I said. . . you asked me if I believed the sun was a god. . .'

'I did. . . so?'

'That hill there. . . it's Greenan Hill. . . up there is a fort where the old people worshipped the sun.'

'Does that answer my question?'

'No, just general information,' said the Storyteller, 'and if you want more. . .'

'*General* information?' interrupted the Wife.

'Yes, if you want more, well you're going to get it anyway. . . there's dozens of hills called Greenan round the place. . . where the old people worshipped the sun!'

'Well that's very interesting,' said the Wife, 'in a *general* sort of way!'

The Storyteller laughed.

Time to change the subject.

But to what?

Personal things, perhaps. Like most women the Wife was more interested in personal things. Trying to get history into her head was hopeless, he admitted, but nonetheless a useful excuse for hearing the sound of his own voice!

'What did you mean,' asked the Storyteller, thinking of something personal to mention, 'yesterday. . . when you said you'd sooner die screaming?'

'A hook up my hole and my innards pulled?' She gave a little start. 'Oh funny that. . .' She paused.

'Oh funny what?'

'Reminds me. . . last night I dreamed. . . I was a runaway slave-girl. . . they hung me from a tree.'

'From a tree?'

'Yes,' said the Wife, quietly.

'Yes,' said the wraith in the Storyteller's cloak, even more quietly.

'Oh don't trouble me with dreams,' said the Storyteller, 'haven't I enough of my own in my own head.'

'By the wrists,' said the Wife, quietly.

'I swung there,' said the wraith in the Storyteller's cloak, even more quietly, 'and my innards streaming from my hole, like the tail of some beautiful bird.'

'I said don't trouble me with dreams, your gruesome dreams. . . just tell me this. . . why wouldn't you die peaceful?'

'I just have the feeling. . . better to let life know you're going. . . and let death know that you're coming. . . wouldn't a howl be better than a silence for that purpose?'

'I suppose it would,' said the Storyteller, and then, remembering something. 'Did you know the old warriors in the old days had a weapon, the Gae Bolga they called it?'

'No, I didn't. . . what of it?'

'Don't sound bored, it's very interesting. . . the Gae Bolga was a little spear, with lots of little hooks on it. . . they shot it out of a little bag. . . right into you. . . pulled your innards to bits'

'Yukhh,' said the Wife.

'Gaddup yadogs!' said the Storyteller, and rode on.

'WHAT PLACE IS this'? said the Wife.

'That fort there? Tubbrid,' said the Storyteller, 'it guards the crossing between the lakes.'

'Are they our soldiers there?'

'I hope so. . . unless the Ulstermen have taken over the fort!'

'What if they're Ulstermen?'

'Oh they'll kill me and rape you. . .'

'But I'm a boy.'

'Oh that wouldn't bother the Ulstermen. . . you're a pretty enough boy. . . you'll be upended pretty quick, and up your arse they'll go! Remember what the Neladoir said. . . and he was right. . . all foreigners are very fond of using boys as girls. It's a sickness in them.'

'You sound very calm about this whole matter.'

'Only because I know quite well that these are Laoghaire's soldiers here. . . the Ulstermen won't come this far south again. . . not for a few years anyway. . . they got their lesson the last time. . .'

'Will they always be our enemies?'

'Will a rat always be a rat?'

'Is that your answer so?'

'That's my answer.'

They rode on. The huge fort of Tubbrid was to the right of them, and there were lakes to the right and left of them. The roadway led between the lakes. Soldiers looked down on them from the fort.

The Storyteller noticed the Wife looking up at them, thoughtfully.

'Tell me,' he said to her, 'had you ever seen him before?'

'Who?'

'That soldier. The one who came last night.'

'Or didn't come!'

'Yes him.'

'Tara is full of soldiers. How would I know one from the other?'

'Well you might. Women are always eyeing the soldiers. . .'

'I'm a respectable married woman! Just because you chase slave-girls doesn't mean I'm going round with my tongue hanging out after soldiers.'

'I don't chase slavegirls!' said the Storyteller, the words chasing a vision into his mind.

A slavegirl in the woods.

A frightened slavegirl.

But still with a cheeky sexy grin.
And still with dirty pretty feet.
A girl like that would brighten the darkest day.
Even here, a day like this.
Dark, more thunder, rumbling, in the west.
Yes she'd be the girl to brighten a man's day... or... or would she?
Does a woman take on a man's gloom?
Is a woman a mirror or a window?

Questions, questions, interrupted by the Wife who suddenly asked him another. 'Why did you ask, had I ever seen him before, that soldier?'

'I was trying to work out if he was real or not.'

'Ah,' said the Wife.

'Ah' said the wraith of the slavegirl, hidden in his cloak.

'Shush,' said the Storyteller.

'What did you say?' asked the Wife.

'Nothing.'

'I thought you said shush...'

'No... just whistling.'

'Whistling? By the gods... whistling in the rain.' She shook her reins, and cantered on. And when she was out of hearing the Storyteller said to the wraith 'I told you to cause no trouble...'

'Sorry,' she said, leaning against his back, her head on his shoulder. 'I'll be quiet, ever so quiet.' And she was. But still, he knew she was there, hiding in his cloak. It was no trouble, but it was a complication, and one he could have done without!

˜•

'NOW,' SAID THE WIFE, 'that's a lake, that's a big lake, that's what I call a lake!'

'Lough Derravaragh,' said the Storyteller. 'Did I ever tell you the story of the children of Lir?'

'Was it about swans?'

'Well yes and no.'

'People turning into swans?'

'Yes and no.'

'Well you told me that.'

'Do you want to hear it again?'

'Why would I want to hear it again?'

'Well it would sound different. . . beside the lake. . .'

'Would it still be about people turning into swans?' asked the Wife, carefully.

'Well. . . more or less,' agreed the Storyteller, reluctantly.

'Well I don't want to hear it again so.'

'More fool you,' said the Storyteller, 'many's a wench would like to hear the story. . . right here beside the lake. . . the very lake, where the happenings happened. . . told by a famous Storyteller too. . . many a wench. . .'

'Well manys the wench is a fool,' said the Wife. 'Which reminds me. . . that woman. . .'

'What woman?'

'How many women have we met. . . that charcoal burners' woman. . .'

'What about her. . .

'I saw you talking to her at her cooking pot. . . I could see what you were thinking. . .'

'And what was I thinking?'

'You were thinking that after a night of my skinniness it'd be fine to get a grip of the meat on her.'

'Maybe so. . . I was certainly not admiring the meat in her pot! What about her anyway?'

'Just wondering what you were talking about.'

'She said to me about the soldier. . . the one who brought the message. . . that maybe he was a ghost. . .'

'He brought us story of ghosts in Tara. . .'

'Yes and that's what I'm thinking now myself. . . how do we know. . . if he was a ghost. . . and tricking us with his story from Tara. . .'

'Well we could go back. . . and find out what other people are saying in Tara. . .'

'I suppose we could.'

'But we won't go back, will we?' said the Wife.

'No. Not now. We ride on,' said the Storyteller.

'THEY RIDE THE lonely road,' said Eithne.

'Yes,' agreed Fidelma, 'it gets more lonesome now.'

'This is the empty country, the Plain of Asail.'

'They pass through Coole.'

'Yes, and they cross the river named for me.'

'Named for you?'

'Yes, the River Eithne!'

'It wasn't named for you. . .'

'Well maybe I was named for it!'

'You think so!'

'Well at least there is that chance. . . of it for me or I for it! But we'll have a long way of travelling to find a river called Fidelma!'

'Fidelma means the faithful one, did you know that?'

'Yes, and Eithne means the seed'

'So the seed is fair and the faith is dark?'

'Something like that. . . oh look, they pass near Templefanum.'

'Yes and the Storyteller doesn't know it's there, it's hidden in the woods.'

'A temple to the old gods.'

'A tiny cell, no priest there now.'

'Overgrown.'

'Tumbling down.'

'Are the old gods dead, or are they taking back their own?'

⌒•

'WHAT PLACE IS THIS?' asked the Wife.

'Nowhere in particular,' he replied.

'Nowhere in particular? Is there no story in this place?'

'Oh I'm sure there is. . . but I'm not the one to tell it!'

'Is this not the country of King Laoghaire. . . and you not his Storyteller?'

'Do I have to have a story for every inch of ground?'

'No. . . but. . .' the Wife shrugged. 'Up there. . . what's up there. . . to our north. . .'

'Ulstermen,' he said. And the black dog and the white dog snarled at the word. 'Ulstermen,' he repeated. The dogs snarled again.

'Stop saying that,' said the Wife, 'it upsets the dogs.'

'Upset the dogs,' he muttered, in a low sarcastic voice. And then it came to him. 'Oh yes. . . up there. . . to the north. . . there's two lakes up there. Gowna. And Kinale. Gowna to the west.' He pointed. 'And Kinale to the east.' He pointed.

'And?' asked the Wife.

'And what?'

'The story?'

'Well I'll tell you this. . . between them there's a ditch, a dyke. . . Duncla it's called. . . it's there to keep out the Ulstermen.'

The dogs snarled.

'Good lads,' said the Storyteller.

'How would a ditch keep out Ulstermen?' asked the Wife. 'Couldn't they climb into and out of it as soon as look at you!'

'That'd be my thinking too. . . of course the ditch was actually built by a pig!'

'A pig?'

'Yes, a giant pig. . . there's ditches like that all round the country. . . they're all called after pigs! Pigs this and pigs that! Black pigs this and black pigs that!'

'Oh yes there's one in Cruachan Ai. . . the Mucklaghs it's called. . .'

'Sure I know it is. . . a giant pig built that too!'

'Why would a giant pig dig ditches all over the country?'

'Well it probably wasn't meaning to dig ditches. . . it was rooting along. . . you know the way pigs root. . . well it was rooting along. . . looking for giant acorns probably. . .'

'It's all ridiculous,' said the Wife.

'Oh there's many strange things,' said the Storyteller, 'and many strange things are true.'

'Yes,' said the Wife, 'but that's not one of them!'

⌒•

THEY STRUNG OUT along the road.

Well apart from each other, as if all tired with each other's company.

The Wife was far ahead.

The black dog followed her, but not closely.

Then came the white dog, but again, not too close to the black dog.

Lastly came the Storyteller, a good way back from the white dog.
I am alone, he thought, the way I like it!

'Oh no you're not,' he heard, the voice of the wraith that was hidden in his cloak, the slavegirl from Tara.

'You be quiet there girl,' he said, 'I told you not to be disturbing me.'

'I was thinking,' she said, 'I could go north from here. . . I heard you say to the Wife. . . that Ulster is just over those hills.'

'Dangerous country this,' he said, 'you'd be better to go from Connacht.'

'When will we cross the river?'

'Late, today. Tonight I'll sleep in Connacht.'

'So not much longer so.'

'Not much longer.'

'Will you miss me, when I'm gone?'

'Does a man miss a ghost?'

'Does he?' she said, throwing the question back at him.

The Storyteller wondered.

The past was a ghost. Yesterday was a ghost, and all the people in it. All the happenings, ghosts, in the memory. And tomorrow too, that was ghosts, ghosts in the planning, and in the dreams. When it got right down to it, most of life was ghosts! There was only one moment, and that was the now, this breath, this heartbeat, this was not a ghost. But how short was that moment? Half a breath, half a heartbeat? Whatever. Very short indeed anyway! Yes, when it got right down to it, most of life was merely ghosts and ghostly things, memories and dreams.

And does a man miss a ghost?

Well if he didn't he'd be missing all of life.

'Yes, of course I'll miss you, when you're gone,' he told the wraith.

She giggled. And then she said to him 'my name is Ranait. . . you never asked, but I'm telling you anyway.'

'A graceful name.'

⌣•

THEY RODE TOGETHER along the road.
Close together, as if needing with other's company.

The Wife to the Storyteller's left, and the black dog at the heels of her horse. And the white dog by the Storyteller's.

I am with my dogs, he thought, the way I like it! My dogs and my Wife and the world.

'Last night I dreamed I was a deer,' said the Wife.

'I saw a deer in my dream last night,' said the Storyteller.

'Was it me, or another deer you saw?'

'I saw a deer in the cooking pot this morning.'

'Was it me, or another deer you saw?'

He didn't answer, too busy watching the dream reappear in his mind. 'I dreamed I was a hermit, a Christian hermit.'

'That'll be the day. You! A Christian!'

'I left a girl behind, in Armorica.'

'Have you ever been to Armorica?'

'Only in a dream.'

'What's it like there, in Armorica?'

'Oh it's a fair country. Or so I've heard and so I've dreamed. They grow the vines for wine. And there are villas, and temples, and marble statues of strange gods.'

'What is marble?'

'It's a stone. . . smooth. . . they polish it. . . they carve statues of gods and girls and boys from it, so real and so well you'd think they were real gods, real girls, real boys. . . it's the Romans taught them that. . .'

'Where is Rome?'

'Very far away.'

'Further than Armorica?'

'Much further than Armorica.'

'What was the girl like, the one you left behind, in Armorica, in your dream?'

'A gentle girl. Graceful, the way the Romans are. Civilised. Sophisticated.'

'Are Connacht women not the same?'

'Not quite, not quite,' said the Storyteller, thinking it better to break that fact to her gently!

'What did she wear?'

'A dress, a Roman dress, they fall from the shoulders. . . so's a man can hardly see the form of the woman. . . except in his imagination. . .'

'A man would need a good imagination so.'

'Oh the dresses give little hints. . . of a curve here. . . and a softness there. . .'

'What colour was the dress?'

'It was blue. . . a pale blue. . . yes I remember that now, it was a pale blue, because the sea was a dark blue. . . and I remember noticing the differences. . .'

'What did she wear on her feet?'

'Snakes,' said the Storyteller, 'snakes.'

'Snakes. . . that's a very strange thing to be wearing. . . very strange dream. . .'

'No. . . not wearing. . . that's not what I mean. . . her feet were bare. . . but she was standing on snakes. . . and they were curled about her feet and ankles. . .'

'Were they alive. . . or dead?'

'Alive. . . they moved. . . they moved their heads. . . they were looking up at her. . . up her legs. . .'

'And if she lifted her foot, would a snake curl up her leg, around her knee. . . and up her thigh. . .'

'Yes. . . that's why she was standing on them. . . to stop them doing that. . . from getting up into her.'

'Yukkhh!' said the Wife.

8

'How much to cross the river, ferryman?'
'I see by your clothes you are from Tara, a learned man from Tara.' He looked him up, and down. 'A poet? A man of law?'

'I am the Storyteller of Tara, and Laoghaire is my king.'

'Laoghaire is a great king. . . what story has his Storyteller?'

'How much to cross the river, ferryman?'

'You travel with your page, a pretty boy.'

'I need no warriors to guard me. I travel in Laoghaire's shadow.'

'I have heard there are armies gathering, Storyteller. Have you heard there are armies gathering?'

'I have heard nothing. . . how much to cross the river?'

'You travel with your dogs, a black dog, and a white dog. . . what are your dogs' names?'

'Night. And Day.'

'What do they know, your dogs that are Night and Day?'

'My dogs know nothing.'

'What does your page know?'

'My page knows nothing.'

'What do *you* know, Storyteller?'

'I know that I want to cross the river, but I don't know yet the price!'

'Ah,' said the ferryman, 'I will tell you about that. Because my father the ferryman told me, and his father the ferryman told him before that. . .'

'Is the history of your family long?' interrupted the Storyteller.

'Let him talk,' said the Wife they called the daughter of the moon. He felt her fingers touch his arm, so weak, so strong. The Storyteller looked at them and thought, the way one thought borrows the next, he thought of bees, so small, but strong. Sometimes strong men die from their sting. He thought of that, and wondered what was strength, and what was weakness.

'Tell me of your father, ferryman,' he murmured.

'My father the ferryman told me. . . when I was a boy. . . do you see those bullrushes there?'

'I see them.'

'When I was no higher than those bullrushes. . .'

'Oh by all the gods,' whispered the Storyteller to the Wife.

'Shush your shush,' she whispered back.

'When I was no higher than those bullrushes. . .' the ferryman leaned on his oar, and looked into the river like a man seeing yesterday's water flowing. 'My father told me, charge them well, the travellers. Because they go on journies, from fine house to fine house, and they forget you when their feet touch the ground. Charge them well, the champions, the warriors, the princes and the sons of princes, the traders, the farmers, and the men looking for a bride. And the woman flying from the husband who beats her, charge her well too. All of them. Because they have their lives, and care nothing for yours. That's what my father said.'

'A father's words should not be forgotten,' said the Storyteller.

'But,' the ferryman grinned, 'but he also told me. . . when poets and druids and priests and that class of person. . . and the mad and the hermit and the drunken wanderers, when they come, they travel free.'

'Your father was a generous man.'

'Not particularly. But he said that the poets and the druids and the priests, not to mention the mad and the hermit and the drunken wanderer. . . he said that they were the river too. . . and without them they're be no flowing. . . no water. . . no job for a ferryman.'

'Your father was a man of learning.'

'Well,' said the ferryman, 'perhaps because the father of my father's father was not *actually* a ferryman.'

'Indeed?' said the Storyteller, with great feigned interest, but through his teeth he whispered to his wife 'how well can you swim?'

'Shush your shush,' she whispered back.

'He went to the school at Imleach Ono,' said the ferryman.

'And a good schooling to be had there.'

'But there were problems with a woman.'

'Women,' the Storyteller spat into the water, 'best in the bed or at the cooking pot.'

The Wife made a little snorting noise, and kicked him in the ankle. But her feet were small and her sandals light, and it didn't hurt, except in his heart, where he loved her.

'The problem with the woman at Imleach Ono,' said the ferryman, 'was particularly complicated, and perhaps you do not have the time to hear it.'

'Unfortunately. . .' the Storyteller murmured, looking up at the sun.

'On your return, perhaps, perhaps you will have more time.'

'Perhaps,' the Storyteller agreed, thinking 'if I return!'

'Enough to say now that the problem was serious enough for him to have to flee the school. . . he came this way. . . and was lucky enough to be taken in by the chief of this place. . . and given the job of ferryman. It was vacant.'

'Vacant?'

'At that time it was not at all peaceful. Much like the recent wars in fact. There were bandits and marauders about the country. And the ferrymen here were killed, frequently. Sometimes a ferryman lasted a week, but rarely more than a month.'

'Still,' said the Storyteller, 'that chief was generous enough to give him the job. A week's work is not to be sneezed at!'

'Well the father of my father wasn't given a choice, not really. The chief said to the father of my father, so. So, you are in flight from the druids of Imleach Ono, so it seems to me that I have two options. And you have none. I could send your head to the druids. And it will stand me in good stead with their gods. Or, I could make you the ferryman, a dangerous job, for you. . . but an advantage for me. . . people will be able to travel about my country again, and I will be able to tax them.'

'That chief was no daw.'

'He was the father of the father of my own chief now.'

'A wise man, I'll warrant, your chief now, a man who keeps a quiet country for his king.'

'Who *is* his king?' said the Wife, her voice a surprise after her silence.

'Well. . . this side of the river is King Laoghaire's. . . and that side of the river is King Daithi's. . . but my chief has this part of this side of the river, and that part of that side of the river.'

'He's in a delicate situation, your chief.'

'Does the river divide the kingdoms, or seal them together?' asked the Wife.

'Well right now,' said the Storyteller, tired of words, 'right now it divides them. . . how much to cross the river, ferryman?'

The ferryman smiled, and he held his hands out, and looked at the sky, like there might be rain, and he'd feel it soon on his palms. . . and then he looked with raised eyes at his hands, as if he were surprised not to see any drops there.

'Sure the river is free to the Storyteller. . . free to the man who carries the story. . . just as it is to the mad. . . and the crazy!'

The ferryman laughed, the Storyteller didn't.

The ferryman gestured, politely. 'Get in my boat. . . you're most welcome to my boat. . . the horses can swim behind. . . your page can hold the reins. . . he has pretty hands, your page.'

'He is a musician.'

'Will he sing as we cross the river?'

'He will sing.'

The Storyteller turned to the Wife.

'Sing for us, boy,' he said.

'Would my master like a sad song. . . or a happy?'

'The river is beautiful today,' said the ferryman.

'So I will sing a happy song?'

'There are no happy songs on this river,' said the ferryman, 'the waters are too deep. . . for happiness.'

'So I will sing a sad song ?'

'Sing the Song of Clothra. . . do you know the Song of Clothra?'

'All singers know her song.'

'That is her island there, beyond,' pointed the ferryman.

'Which one where?'

'That one there. . . do you see the trees, and them crying into the river?'

'Yes.'

'That island there is hers. . . I hear the Romans plan to build a church there.'

'Let's hope it keeps fine for them,' said the Storyteller.

'Oh it will,' said the ferryman, 'for awhile. But the church will be gone in its time. . . and the trees will still be crying into the river.'

'That is the way of things,' agreed the Storyteller.

'Well let us go then,' said the Ferryman, dipping his oars in the water, 'and sing, boy, sing.'

And so she sang, the Wife they called the daughter of the moon. She sang of two sisters, Clothra and Maeve, and how both would be queen of Connacht. And how both were pregnant, both planning to give birth to the king of Connacht. But only one could be queen, and only one could give birth to the king. So Maeve killed Clothra. And cut open her belly with a sword. And killed the baby there. And Maeve became queen, and Clothra forgotten. Except in the name of an island. And the story is a song, the Song of Clothra, the song of the river. The song that can only be sung on the river, or there'd be no music in it, and no meaning. But on the river there was music, and meaning.

And the Storyteller listened, to the words, thinking.

Yes of course he knew the words. But he'd never heard them singing on the river. . . except once. . . before. . . when he was bringing the girl from Connacht. . . and she hadn't been his wife then, and he hadn't known or loved her then, so that was different too. He listened, and he thought. And he remembered the Neladoir of Slane. . . what had he said. . . what *exactly* had he said? About the children, cut from the bellies of mothers, and the land dying, and the story dying. . . the Neladoir had seen that in the clouds.

The Storyteller looked to the clouds. And now in the evening they were darkening to the east. . . darkening, as the wife sang, and the ferryman rowed, and the oars splashed, and the horses kicked in the water behind. He felt the pull of the reins in his hands, easing and tightening as they swam. Easing, tightening, in his hands. The feel of it reminded him of when he had held the bone to the witch's breast, and the weight of the flesh on the bone, and the weight of the bone in his hand, and how she had said that the flesh clings to the bone. Because the bone loves the flesh, and the flesh loves the bone.

What did she mean?

That one is life, and one is death, and life and death are one?

Perhaps.

Perhaps.

The Storyteller listened to the song. Strange, he thought, strange that it didn't mention the third sister, because there *was* a third, yes, as well as Maeve and Clothra there had been Eithne. Yes, she bore the same name as the daughter of Laoghaire. But that was surely coincidence. Because Eithne is a common name. Eithne, and it was a word too as well as a woman's name, a word meaning seed, or source, or the kernel of things.

Was there a meaning in that, he wondered.

But even if there were no meaning, why had the songwriter left her out of the song?

Is there always someone left out of a song, or a story?

Is there always some feeling left out of a poem?

Is that what makes a song, a story, or a poem, that emptiness? That feeling of *almost* complete. But not complete! That reminder that nothing in life is complete. And cannot be. . . without death. Is that the art in a song, or a story, or a poem, that little space of emptiness?

The Storyteller brooded.

The Wife sang.

The ferryman rowed, and then they were suddenly there, and he lifted his oars from the water. And the boat slid into reeds, and stuck in mud. And the ferryman got out and pulled it further in. And the black dog and the white dog jumped out, and splashed onto the firm ground. And the horses kicked themselves to their standing, and followed the dogs.

'Welcome to Connacht,' said the ferryman. And he held out an arm to the Wife, and she took it, and jumped out onto the earth of her own place, and the Storyteller felt her feeling, knew her thinking, I am home. And he felt a little happiness for her. But a sadness too, because it made part of her a stranger. Then he watched as the ferryman bent down, and picked a clod of mud from the shore. And held it up and squeezed, so the water dripped. 'If I had hands. . . hands strong enough. . .'

'What then, Ferryman?' said the Wife.

'I could squeeze the blood from the earth of Connacht,' he said. And the Storyteller saw them smile, together. And he knew they shared that blood of Connacht, the blood that ran in the veins, and the blood that soaked the earth. And, when he knew that, a little more of her was a stranger. But still he watched, and listened. And he heard their voices different, that Connacht accent that they shared. That Connacht accent that he didn't have. And he felt a stranger in a different land. But still he watched. And the ferryman reached out and touched the Wife's face with his muddied hands. 'Welcome home,' he said, 'welcome home. . . wizard woman.'

'How did you know?' she asked.

'The song. . . no boy could sing that song.'

'Touch me, touch me with that mud, ferryman.'

The ferryman smeared her face, and her hair and her throat with the mud from his muddied hands. And still the Storyteller watched, the wizardy mud of Connacht on her face, and her one eye cold, and her one eye cruel, watching him. And then he saw her close her eyes, and sigh, and shiver like a woman sucking a man's seed into her womb, and shake that way a woman shakes, and then be still.

The Storyteller turned away, and lifted the legbone from Tara off the seat of the boat where it lay. It felt heavy, suddenly. And was that the tiredness in his wrist from the travelling of the day? Or was it the flesh that clings to the bone?

He looked out over the river, and he saw a diving bird suddenly dive, and the water whispered, but not to him.

⌒•

'DO YOU SEE the lunadán?' said Eithne to Fidelma.

'Yes I see him there, beyond the reeds.'

'Well watch, and wait, he'll dive.'

'The country people think he changes, from bird to fish, and back to bird again.'

'Oh the country people will believe anything. . . you and I know he's always a bird, swimming on top of the water, or under it. . .'

'Yes but you and I went to school. . . there. . . he's gone. . .'

'Where will he come up?'

'I don't know. . . he never comes up where you think. . .'

'Always surprises. . .'

'Watch the water.'

'I'm watching, sister, I'm watching!'

'How can he see, in the darkness of the water?'

'I don't know, how can we see in dreams, in death, our eyes closed. . .'

'Or in death, our eyes rotted.'

'I don't know. . . he's a long time down, that lunadán. . . what does he do in the darkness. . .'

'Searches.'

'What do we do, in the darkness?'

'Wait.'

'How long more of waiting?'

'They're in Connacht now.'

'Her face is streaked with wizard's mud.'

'She sang so well.'

'Of death. . . oh look. . . there's the lunadán. . .'

'I didn't expect to see him over there at all.'

'No, me neither. . . I was looking completely in the other direction.'

'Does he do it deliberately?'

'Who?'

'The lunadán. . . to confuse. . .'

'Perhaps.'

⌒·

THE STORYTELLER GATHERED the horses. It was time to go, move on. 'How did you know?' he asked the ferryman, 'how did you know about the Wife?'

'The song. . . no boy could sing that song.'

'No, that's not what I ask. How did you know she was a wizard woman?'

'How do you know that dog is black, and that one white, Storyteller?'

The ferryman laughed, and said no more. He stepped back into his boat, and pushed it away from the shore. And it moved over the reeds at the shoreline, like a hand on a child's hair, smoothing them. And ducks flappered away from the prow of the boat, and settled again in its wake like they knew nothing of its passing.

'We'll stay here tonight,' said the Storyteller, looking at the birds bobbing, a brown bird and a green.

'There is light in the day,' said the Wife.

'Yes, but there's houses here, over there, behind that hill, if I remember. And I wouldn't like another night of camping, I've had my fill of living like a charcoal burner!'

'How long since you passed this way?'

'Not since last time with you. . . but I don't suppose much has changed.'

'Nothing much changes in Connacht. . . or so I've heard. . .'

'The ferryman knew you were a woman.'

'When I sang.'

'A wizard woman of Connacht. How did he know that?'

'There is mud on my face, mud in my hair.'

'No. . . before. . . before the mud was on your face. . . he knew. . . oh no matter. . . no matter how he knew. . . are you going to wash it off?'

'In the morning.'

'Why in the morning, girl? There's a huge river here, water beyond wanting. . . why wait 'til morning when you may have no water?'

'I will wash it,' she paused, 'in the morning.'

'Oh.' The Storyteller looked her, up and down. She was wearing brown, the very colour of that female duck, but apart from that there was no knowing she was a woman. He looked her up, and down, and she looked back, defiantly.

'So,' he said, 'do Connacht women not obey their husbands?'

'Betimes,' she shrugged, 'and other times they don't.'

'So now that you're in Connacht you will wash your face when you will?'

'Is it important?'

'Perhaps not. . . it's just that it reminds me of those magicians. . . Laoghaire had their heads. . .'

'The soldier said differently,' said the Wife.

'I think that soldier was a ghost, he went suspiciously early in the morning.'

'Why would a ghost tell us such a story?'

'Well why would a witch come to Tara. . . with ghostly magicians?'

'Maybe ghosts have their own reasons.'

'Maybe they do. . . anyway. . . ghosts or real. . . those wizards had mud on their faces. . . and now you remind me of them. . . and I don't like to see your head on a stick. . . in my mind.'

'Because you love me.'

'Because I love you.'

'Why do you love me?'

'Why does that river flow?'
'I have no breasts, you mock me in the bed.'
'There's breasts aplenty in the world.'
'I'm skinny, like a boy.'
'There's fat women everywhere.'
'I'm troublesome. I remember you said you'd send me back to my people.'
'I would have. But they refused to return the cow I paid for you.'
'One cow. . . you couldn't call me expensive.'
'The best things in life are free.'
'Why do you love me?'
'Why do the reeds flatten to the passing of the boat, like the hair of a child to the passing of a mother's hand?'
'It is the way of things.'
'It is the way of things. . . now come on girl, enough of chatter. . . get on that horse. . . to those houses. . . let's put a test on the hospitality of your Connacht people.' He scooped a hand into the shape of a hook and she stepped in it and he whooshed her onto the back of the horse. And he slapped the backside of the animal with the bone he still carried, the legbone from Tara. And it made a twack. And he remembered the sound of it hitting the thigh of the witch before she was burned. And he remembered the witch. And then the horse trotted away, and he swung up onto his own horse and followed the Wife. And following him behind came his dogs, at first the one called Day, and then the one called Night.

Were the witch and the Wife the one?

He wondered.

∽•

'KING LAOGHAIRE'S STORYTELLER passes this way,' said the crone to the crone. 'He stays the night in our headman's house.'

'Where does he go, what brings him here to our village?' said the crone to the crone.

'He goes to Daithi in Rathcroghan.'

'I have seen no foreign warriors, heard no clatter of horses, nor seen any poets or princes. And where are the fine women in chariots, and the servants with gifts for Daithi? I've seen none of that.'

'The Storyteller travels alone,' said the crone to the crone. 'Except for a woman dressed as a boy. And two dogs, one black, one white.'

'Who is the woman, the woman dressed as a boy?'

'One of our people.'

'Which one of our people, who is her father?'

'I don't know. Except that she is one of our people. She has mud on her face.'

'A magician? A wizard?'

'I think so.'

'I know who she is,' said a third crone, to the first crone and to the second crone. 'I know who she is.'

'How do you know this?'

'Last night I dreamed.'

'What did you dream?'

'I went to the woman's mountain. I was young. And all the young girls round me.'

'I remember those days.'

'We were picking berries. My hair was red. We carried baskets on our arms. Our feet were bare. The grass was soft. My fingers were blue from the berries.'

'And now they're blue from the cold!'

The crones chortled, and then fell silent. Maybe it wasn't that funny.

'I remember those days,' said one, to get the talking going again.

'And in my dream,' said the other, to keep it going, 'in my dream there was a stranger girl there. Not from our village.'

'What was her name, her tuath, who were her people?'

'We asked her that. We clustered around her, the way girls do.'

'I remember that, the way girls do.'

'What colour was her hair, the stranger girl?'

'Fair, a yellowey colour, with streaks of red.'

'Who was she, did she tell?'

'Yes, she said. . . she said I am the one they call the daughter of the moon.'

'What did she mean?'

'I do not know.'

'What happened then?'

'The dream changed. Into another dream.'
'The way dreams do.'
'And in this other dream I was married to Donal the Wright.'
'How long is he dead?'
'Oh it must be twenty years.'
'He was a fine man.'
'I was a young girl married in the dream. He tied me by the hair to the post of the marriage bed. The way they did. In those days.'
'Tell us more.'
The crones chortled.
'Would you ask a woman about her married bed?'
The crones chortled.
'But it was all a dream,' said one, 'and Donal the Wright is dead.'
'For you. . . perhaps. . . but not for me,' said the dreamer of the dream.

The fire smouldered. And the three crones stared into the embers. And passed from hand to hand a jug of beer. And they sipped, and stared, and sipped, and stared. And all the dead men and all the grown children gone walked in that room. And a particular man long dead danced on the flag at the hearth, and his feet clacketing, echoing, there's a horse's skull beneath that stone, that makes the echo, everyone knows that. . . but no-one knows how a man's feet can move so fast, and him dancing.

The sound filled the silence.
The old women and their memories.
The stones of the house and its memories too.
The earth of the floor, hardened by dead feet.
Memories.
The flag at the hearth, polished by dancing feet.
Memories.
And the dancing feet, dead in the earth of the land, memories.

'So,' said the second crone to the third crone after a long silence, 'so what of your dream?'
'Yes what of your dream?' said the first crone.
'What dream?'
'About the stranger girl. . . on the mountain.'
'Ah yes. . . that is her.'
'Who, who is her?'

'The woman dressed as a boy. Who travels with Laoghaire's Storyteller. They are going to Rathcroghan. That is her. I'd know her anywhere.'

'What was that she called herself?'

'The daughter of the moon.'

━•

THE FIRE BURNS, not for warmth, but for the memory of warmth that is in it. There is no real need for a fire, thought the Storyteller, looking into the flames and remembering a great book he had seen once, a book where the scribe had drawn a letter like a flame at the head of each page, a huge capital letter, blue, and red, and yellow, the colour of flame.

Where had he seen that book?

He could not remember now.

He sorted through his mind, his thinking moving like the fingers of a man looking for weevils in flour, sifting. Then his thinking found the memory and yes. . . that book was in a box. . . the box was held together with a pin. . . the box was on a ship. . . and the ship was leaving a girl behind in Armorica.

He was someone else!

It was a dream of someone else!

A dream about a girl, she stood on snakes.

They would slide up her legs. And wrap her thighs. . . if she let them.

But her feet were firm on their tails.

It was a dream.

The snakes tongues flicker, upwards. They would kiss the little tongue the girl has between her legs. If they could reach. But they cannot reach.

Her feet are firm on their tails.

It was in a dream he saw those.

It was in a dream he saw the book, and the words were the colour of flames.

Red, yellow, blue.

The fire burns.

There is no need for a fire, in summer, he mused, but the fire is there to tell the people of the house that when they need it, when they need it, here there'll be warmth, and light, and friendly conversation.

Even if there won't!

It gives a good impression.

'More beer, Storyteller?' The headman held a jug. And the Storyteller looked at the shape of the jug, and saw that it was all belly, much like the headman himself. And he looked at the headman and he thought it strange, how a man who likes his beer too much becomes a jug of beer himself.

'No more beer, not for me, I have a long journey tomorrow.'

'There's a good bed ready for you.'

'You are a generous host.'

'And a settle for your page at the foot of it.'

'Ah sure him,' said the Storyteller, 'sure he can sleep on the floor.'

The Wife said nothing, sitting, quietly, hugging her knees to her chest, what was she thinking?

'It's no trouble,' said the headman, 'a settle bed will have him rested for your day ahead.'

'Well if it pleases you. . . but. . .' The Storyteller looked moodily at the Wife, nodding his head, and wondering, what was she thinking, 'but in Tara we feel that servants are better suited to the floor.'

'Do we indeed,' muttered the Wife, 'do we indeed.'

'Perhaps you're right,' said the headman. 'They expect too much. . . servants. . . these days. . . not like in our father's time eh?'

'Not at all,' agreed the Storyteller, wondering what does he mean, *our* father's time. Sure the man himself could be *my* father!

'Sure those were the days, better ordered.' The headman drank an almighty draft of beer from the jug. 'The servants knew their place. And the wives too. And if they forgot there was the whip to remind them.'

'We won't see those days again.'

'We surely won't. And. . .' the Storyteller stood. . . 'we won't see this day again either.'

'You're to bed?'

'Yes. . . and your advice is good. . . I'll put my dogs on the settle. The boy can do with the floor. The more they get the more they want. Is that not so, boy?'

'Whatever my master says.'

'You'd actually prefer to sleep on the floor, wouldn't you?'
'Whatever pleases my master.'
'Come, to bed.'
'Your horses will be ready in the morning.'
'You are a generous host. Your name will travel back to Tara.'
'My men guard the river here,' said the headman. He paused. And then added, 'for King Daithi.'
'And guard it well, as will be rightly mentioned in Rathcroghan.'
'That is good,' said the headman, a sinister man, untrusting, not to be trusted. He watched the Storyteller and his companion leave. And then looked over the room at the silent fat woman who was a wife and who sat there twisting yarn. He looked at her to meet her eyes, to share an opinion.

'That is no boy,' she said, as soon as the others were gone, and the yarn twisting in her hands, and a heap of it on her knees like her belly was split and her guts had spilled.

'I know that, woman. Have I no eyes in my head?'
'Well why then this pretence?'
'Do you want me to call my guest a liar?'
'No but. . .'
'If a man does honour to my house, an important man. . . should I insult him with argument?'
'No but. . .'
'No but but, woman. If he tells me those dogs are his wives then, so far as I'm concerned, those dogs *are* his wives.'
'She is one of our people. . . a wizard. . . I can see it in her. . . why does he travel with her?'
'There are strange things happening. My men are not in their beds tonight.'
'What have you heard?'
'They are along the river, to the north, and to the south. I have heard enough to watch for Laoghaire's army.'
'That Storyteller. . . perhaps he is a spy? Perhaps you should kill him, send his head to Daithi?'
'Storytellers must pass, unharmed. It is the custom.'
'Well I would kill him, custom or not. *And* the girl who dresses as a boy!'
'But she is one of our people. You said so yourself.'

'Yes but she's a magician, a wizard.'

'How can you tell?'

'I can feel it.' The fat woman twisted her yarn, and the gut-like lengths of it on her knees stirred. 'You should drown her in the river.'

'The Storyteller must pass, unharmed. And those with him, the like!'

'The river hasn't had a girl drowned it it for too long. . . that's why it runs brackish. . . everyone is talking. . .'

'Talking?'

'About the water quality. . . and how when we were young it was sweet, and clear. . .'

'The weather is changing.'

'Yes but why?'

'Because that's the way of things, woman.' Exasperated, he looked at the fat woman, and the yarn in her lap like her guts spilled. Like her belly split and her guts spilled. A sow at the slaughter. Yes, he thought, that'd be the doing for her! He saw it in his mind, and a pleasant sight it was. The knife goes in, and slices through the fat, and the guts spill. Yes, that'd be the right ending for her, squealing like the pig she is. Oh yes. A pig must squeal, say the slaughtermen. The longer it squeals, the better the meat. The slower it bleeds, the better the meat. The trick is to keep the pig alive as its butchered. Alive as long as possible. Oh yes, keep her alive. Skin her alive. It's a bad slaughterman lets a pig die too soon!

'Well the water is brackish,' she insisted, 'whatever you say!'

'There's always an explanation,' he snapped.

The fat woman twisted the yarn, her fat fingers ten surprises in their nimbleness. 'And there's always a solution,' she insisted.

The headman laughed. 'And your solution, woman, yours is to drown the Storyteller's girl? Which will leave me here, with one great king to the west, one great king to the east, and both looking for my head. . . pssaw.'

He spat into the fire.

The spit sizzled.

It was the sizzle of a pig on a spit.

Or the sizzle of a nagging fat woman on a spit.

The headman chuckled.

The fat woman twisted her yarn.

The smoke from the fire drifted into the sky, slowly.

It drifted in the way of smoke, first high, then falling again, across the village, getting lower all the while. And on the banks of the river it almost touched the ground. But only almost. It drifted on, across the water. And out on the dark water it lay, like a man on a woman, and the water moved slowly, and the smoke moved slowly, and in the dark there was no knowing which was smoke, and which was water. And in the headman's guest house the Storyteller lay on the girl, and looked into her eyes, the eyes of the Wife they called the daughter of the moon. And there was no knowing there either... there was only darkness, mystery.

Is there light beyond this darkness, he wondered?

Or just more darkness?

He lay awake and wondered.

Wondered, his mind a stew of thoughts, a simmering stew in the bucket of his head. His mind was a grey stew, made of the old meat of long dead things. His mind was a grey stew being stirred by a slattern, she had the eyes of a whore. Her skin was streaked with ash. Her face, her throat, her chest, all streaked with ash and she stirred from left to right.

Watch a woman stirs from left to right!

He could not sleep. And then he heard a creaking and a squeaking out beyond. He left the bed of the Wife and went to the door, and looked across the way. And there in the headman's street he saw the coming of a cart he recognised, they had passed it on the road the day before. A hag on a horse had drawn that cart, a hag with an evil eye.

9

THE MORNING MIST came up from the morning river. And that disc there is the sun, realised the Storyteller, though in the mist it looks a lot more like the moon.

He saddled up the horses.

A enjoyable sort of job, didn't get much chance to do it back in Tara. Back home there was always a stableboy doing this, and that. Just as there was always a servant bringing food, or another servant, digging a garden. Servants, slaves, they steal the work from a man, and leave him empty handed. And foolishly he helps them to steal his work away. In fact he goes out deliberately looking for them. . . which is a sort of a madness. . . a man might just as well search out robbers to take his gold!

The horses stood, calm, as he went about the belts and buckles, the straps and leathers. Each belt, each buckle, each strap and each leather taking away another little bit of their freedom. They didn't seem to mind. In fact, if they did mind, the Storyteller realised, they could trample him to death, and that'd be the end of the matter. But horses seem to like being horses, to like their servitude.

And slaves?

Perhaps the same.

And women?

Definitely the same!

He finished the horses' bridling up, looked up at the day, felt the air, shook out his cloak and laid it neat across the horse's back behind his saddle. There was a warmth in the air. A damp enough warmth, a sort of heavy breathing warmth, the between time of angry showers, a heavy breathing time, like the between time of a man's anger.

'Some slaves may like their slavery,' she said, 'and some women. But not all of us!'

The slavegirl of Tara stood beside him.

'Some of us must be free,' she added.

He remembered.

Her name was Ranait, and she'd been hiding in his cloak.

And now they were in Connacht, they had crossed the river, and he had shook out his cloak, and she was free, to go to Ulster, to her own people in Ulster.

He reached out a hand, to touch her, but she was the mist from the river, drifting in the air of the early morning. And then he remembered walking through Tara, and how it was misty then too, the cattle's legs were hidden in the mist. . . that was when he saw her.

He could have touched her then.

But now she was a wraith.

She had killed her master, and escaped. But they'd run her down with dogs. And hung her, horribly, from a tree. And now she was a wraith, a ghost, drifting through time, from time to dream and dream to time.

'Don't be sad,' she said, 'I'm happy, I go to Ulster.'

'What is Ulster like?' he asked.

'Ulster is beautiful.'

'How do you remember?'

'I was captured in the wars. . . ten years ago. . . or so. . . I was ten. . . or so. . .'

'Those were bad times.'

'Is it me you're telling!'

'The country is still poor from those times. . . did you see the land we passed. . . empty. . . houses burned. . . no cattle in the fields. . . no-one there at all. . . few travellers on the road. . . and the roads grown over. . . bandits in the woods. . . and charcoal burners in the woods. . . and not much difference between the bandits and the burners. . . the country is still poor. . . from the wars. . .'

'Those were bad times,' said the slavegirl.

'Is it me you're telling,' said the Storyteller.

'Have you never been to Ulster?'

'Never. . . they're my enemies there, and my people's enemies.'

'Am I your enemy?'

'Did I bring you across the river, hidden in my cloak?'

She smiled, nodded, a thanks. 'It's beautiful in Ulster,' she said.

'Or is it beautiful in a girl child's mind, when she was ten?'

'What's the difference?'

'Don't you think there's a difference? Between the dream in the mind, and the place on the ground?'

'Your wife. . . the one they call the daughter of the moon. . .'

'She's over there. . . getting ready. . . for the journey. . .'

'Yes. . . I see her. . . a scraggy little one. . . dressed as a boy. . . with harsh coloured hair. . . no-one could call her beautiful. . .'

'What're you saying?'

'You love her, of all your wives. . .'

'What're you saying?'

'To you she is what Ulster is to me!'

The Storyteller laughed, and the slavegirl laughed too. He reached out a hand, to touch her, but she was the mist from the river, drifting in the air of the early morning. And he remembered her in Tara. He could have touched her then. But now she was a wraith. And he would never touch her now. Not until the dice rolled, and a different number tumbled up a different life.

'You must be going now,' he said, 'to the north. . . and I to the west. . .'

'Yes.' She picked up her bag with one hand. She held her slave-girl's cape at her throat with the other, and looked at him.

'Don't be sad for me,' she said.

'It's a long journey ahead of you.'

'It's where I'm going makes it short.'

'Into your past?'

'And your future, Storyteller.' And before he could ask her what she meant by that she held up a hand to quiet him. A hand that was a wraith's hand, with fingers of mist, fading now in the warmth of the sun. 'Nothing dies,' she said, 'nothing dies but time. Remember that.'

And then she was gone.

⌒•

'KING LAOGHAIRE'S STORYTELLER passes this way,' said the one-legged man.

'I have heard no tell of that,' said the warrior.

'Well I have. But then, a one-legged man is in the way of hearing things,' said the one-legged man.

'And why is that?' asked the warrior.

'He stays in the same place longer, longer than a man with two legs. Oh yes, it's true as I'm sitting here. King Laoghaire's Storyteller passes this way. . . along this very road, we'll see him soon.'

'You're very sure of that.'

'I'm telling you, a one-legged man is in the way of hearing things. News is like water, it will not fill a moving bucket.'

'By the gods you're like a storyteller yourself, with your sayings.'

'Yes I was probably born with a bit of the storyteller in me,' mused the one-legged man.

'Was that the bit they cut off with your other leg?'

'Oh you may mock, brave warrior. But remember, I was a warrior too, once. . . listen, now listen, do you hear horses?'

'No.'

'Ah well a one-legged man has better ears than a two-legged man. Listen, do you not hear that?'

'No, yes, oh alright maybe I do. . .'

'And look, there, around that bend, below that hollow, do you not see them?'

'No.'

'Ah well a one-legged man has better eyes than a two-legged man. Surely you see them, look.'

'Yes, yes yes, alright, you're right.'

'Of course I'm right. One horse there. . . and look. . . another.'

'Yes, and there's another.'

'Oh. Another. Only it should be two horses, from what I've heard.'

'Well you heard wrong, because there's another. And another and another and another.'

'How many is that. . . there's one two three there's eight. . . eight horses.'

Eight horses passed the two men. And each of the two men raised a hand in greeting as they passed. But they got no greeting in return. Not from the rider of the first horse, nor from the riders of any of the others. They didn't even get a look or a glance in their direction. No rider turned their head. Not the dark and meaty woman on the first dark horse, nor any one of the seven thin men on the seven thin horses that followed her.

'Well that's a gloomy bunch,' said the one-legged man.

'Certainly is,' said the warrior.

'You'd be minded to draw a sword, and challenge them, for the insult.'

'You certainly would,' agreed the warrior, 'but maybe your challenging days are done.'

'Why do you tell me that? Sure didn't I fight the Ulstermen with you. I'm still a warrior too, even though a one-legged man. Sure a warrior's legs and arms are only temporary attachments.' The one-legged man stuck a stick into the ground, in an idle fashion. 'Only temporary,' he repeated, 'and his head too.'

'All jobs have their good points, bad points.'

'A king seems a fair enough position. With land. And cattle. And servants. Fine clothes. Gold. Wives and concubines.'

'Aaachh,' the one-legged man spat with a dry spit that lay on the ground like a snail had passed and the sun had shone awhile, 'aach, sure the cattle can be stolen. And the wives fight all the time.'

'But a poor man's cattle can be stolen too. And a poor man's wives fight the same as a rich man's.'

'So what do you mean?'

'If a man has to be a man, he might as well be a king at the same time.'

'There is that,' said the warrior, watching the one-legged man, and him sitting on the ground, with a stick driven in beside him, and now fiddling about with another. 'What're you doing with those sticks?'

'I'm making a cross.'

'Like the Roman makes?'

'The very same.'

'He sticks them on hills. And beside wells.'

'The very same.'

'You'd be wondering how his head stays on his body, that Roman. . . and him going round telling folks their gods are dead.'

'People don't care enough, I suppose.'

'I suppose.'

'The priests and storytellers care.'

'Ah sure they're old. . . who listens to them?'

'King Laoghaire's Storyteller, he who passes this way. . . he's not old. He has a black beard on him.'

'Where does he go, what brings him through our country?'

'He goes to Rathcroghan. To the king.'

'Has he a message?'

'Well if he has it's not for the likes of you and me.'

'Who goes with him, many horsemen?'

'He travels alone, except for a woman dressed as a boy. And two battle dogs, one black, one white. He calls them Night, and Day.'

'Why is the woman dressed as a boy?'

'I have no idea.' The one-legged man tightened the string holding the cross piece of the cross to the upright. Straightened the bar so it was horizontal. Sat back. Admired. 'I have no idea,' he repeated. 'But it's not me that'll be asking her. She's a witch.'

'Ah sure they've no proper witches in Tara. . . or the whole of the kingdom of Meath. . . none to be afraid of anyway.'

'She's one of our people.'

'Oh. . .' said the warrior, thoughtfullly, 'that's a different matter entirely.'

'She's the one they call the daughter of the moon.'

'What one? I've never heard of anyone called that.'

'Ah sure what have you heard. What have you heard but the whore asking for her money, or the innkeeper telling you to get out of his house.'

'You were a warrior too, you're talking your insults to yourself,' the warrior laughed. 'But tell me. . . about this witch. . . how do you know of her?'

'Sure you'll soon know as much as me yourself, isn't that them coming now?' The one-legged man pointed down the road.

'Two horses, yes, could be, and two dogs. Look like battle dogs to me. Tell you what, I don't like the look of those two dogs.' The warrior drew his sword, and placed it on the grass beside him. 'Just in case,' he said, 'those dogs would have your throat as soon as look at you!'

The two men watched, carefully. First to come up to them was the black dog. It stopped, a little way away. And then the white dog, and it stopped, a little way away. Dogs and men looked at each other, calculating.

'I don't like the look of those dogs,' said the warrior.

'It's what they think of us that counts,' said the one-legged man.

'True for you,' said the warrior, his hand on the hilt of his sword. He and his companion watched, and then a horse drew up behind the dogs. The man on the horse was rich, well dressed, with a great cloak, and a black beard. 'Would you take a sword to a storyteller's dogs?' he said, in the accent of a rich man, a rich foreign man.

'A dog's a dog,' said the warrior.

'And a throat's a throat,' said the one-legged man, 'no matter whose dog tears it!'

'Indeed,' said the Storyteller, a smile in his voice. And then, to the dogs, 'geddup yadogs.'

The animals ran ahead. And then a second horse drew up alongside the first. And this one was ridden by a small and slender person, obviously a woman, but dressed in a boy's clothes. Her legs were bare. She had a streak of mud across her forehead. And her very short hair was a dirty yellow red.

'I am the Storyteller of Tara,' said the rich man on the horse, 'and this is my wife.'

'I know,' said the warrior, 'and you are welcome in our country.'

'How do you know who I am?'

'They talk about you on the road,' said the one-legged man.

'And what do they say, about me on the road?' asked the Storyteller.

'They say you go to Daithi in Rathcroghan.'

'They say right.'

'They say you travel with two dogs.'

'You saw the dogs.'

'And they say you travel with a wizard woman, one of our own people, and she is a wife to you.'

'You see the wife. What else do they say?'

'They know no more to say,' said the one-legged man.

'They know enough,' said the Storyteller. And he raised his right hand in a salute, and moved his horse on, on and away up the road. But the girl dressed as a boy paused and stayed for a moment, looking thoughtfully down at the men.

'Who else passed this way?' she asked.

'Oh many people pass this way,' said the warrior.

'That's why we sit by the road, to watch them, and chat, and meet our friends, and hear the news,' said the one-legged man.

'I mean what other strangers passed this way, to-day?'

'There was a dark woman on a dark horse,' said the warrior.

'With seven men companions,' added the one-legged man.

'What did they say?'

'Nothing, not a word. They were a very gloomy group.'

'What was she like, the dark woman on the dark horse, was she beautiful?'

'Her head was veiled, I couldn't see. But she was a fine big hold of a woman, that's for sure.'

'Not like me then, not like me.' The girl dressed as a boy turned her horse and kicked its flanks with her sandalled heels. And the horse gave a whinny and trotted away, and the whinny of the horse was their only goodbye.

'What did you think of her?' said the warrior.

'Oh a witch and a wizard, no doubt about it. Sure they're talking of her at the village by the river. . . the village. . . you know. . . where the ferryman lives.'

'That ferryman? Has he done talking yet? He knows everything.'

'Ferrymen always know everything. Or think they do. Anyway, yes, that village. . . well. . . it seems that the Storyteller stayed there. . . at the house of the headman. . .'

'The one with the fat wife.'

'The same.'

'How could a man bed a wife like that. . . wouldn't you sooner have a pig. . .'

'Sure in the dark what's the difference. . . hasn't a pig the same parts as a woman?'

'There is that. But I think we're moving from the point. . . why do you think she's a witch and a wizard?'

'Why are you so interested?'

'Well I'm not interested. . . it's just when I become a one-legged man, and sitting here with nothing to do but make silly crosses, I'll be wanting to know how to get the news. . . how to know things. . . I'm relying on you for the teaching!'

'It may not be your leg, it may be your head that'll be missing. Or your prick.'

The warrior laughed. 'Do you remember Tadgh, he who fought with us against the Ulstermen.'

'Oh I do indeed, a sword took his testicles.'
'A bad blow.'
'He went home to his people.'
'Unlike his testicles.'
'And after a while he started dressing in his wife's clothes.'
'Yes yes, I remember.'
'So she went home to her people.'
'Yes. And Tadgh was left alone. . . a sort of half man and half woman.'
'Sure some are born like that.'
'Who're you telling. . . there's them that say. . . about those men you wouldn't want to sleep in a tent with. . . they should be hung. . .'
'Sure what tree could you hang them from? It minds me. . . not far from here there was a woman had a baby with a big head. I mean a *big* big head. And it got bigger as it grew.'
'Sure you'd drown a child like that. That's a witch's doing.'
'Yes, that's what they said to her, to this woman.'
'So she drowned it?'
'No.'
'Because of her mother's liking for the child?'
'Not a bit of it. . . because she was afraid of the water. . . and the goddess in the water. . . she said if I'm going to drown anyone in the river or the stream, or the well, or the water from the river or the stream or the well, if I'm going to do that it'll have to be a perfect baby. . .'
'Bit of a witch herself, I'm thinking.'
'But you do see her point. . . and the same about the tree. . . you'd want to be careful who you'd hang on a tree.'
'Without a doubt! If you're going to be hanging someone from a tree it'd want to be someone perfect.' The one-legged man lifted his cross from the ground and he looked at it carefully. 'The Roman, and the followers of the Roman, they say their god was perfect. . . and he was hung from a cross. . . and what's a cross but a tree?'
'Will you follow the Roman?'
'How far can a one-legged man follow anyone?'
'I mean in your mind.'
'I'll wait to see. . . to see which way the crumbs fall from the table. . . I'm thinking Daithi may decide to have done with the Roman

and his followers. . . and may be sending soldiers for their heads. . .'

'I'm a soldier of Daithi.'

'Don't I know you are!'

'Well it'll be a clean blow I'll give you.'

'Oh I'm grateful!' snorted the one-legged man. 'But would you look now there. . . coming along. . .'

'This is a busy morning on the road.'

'Certainly is. . . and they say it'll get busier.'

'Busier?'

'With armies. They say that Laoghaire is thinking of war. . . against Daithi.'

'Laoghaire is always thinking of war against someone!'

'No. . . they say. . . this time. . .' the one-legged man nodded, the nod of a man who knows.

'Oh they they they, who is this *they?*'

'Never mind them, who is this here?'

They watched the passers-by. Come from east and moving west, it was an old man leading an old woman on an old horse. The horse drew a slatted cart. And the old man and the old woman and the old horse passed quietly, with not a sound but the squeaking and creaking of the cart.

'Another gloomy bunch,' said the warrior, watching them go.

'You're right there,' agreed the one-legged man. 'Come, help me up. I've seen enough. Even though it's raining it's my throat that's dry with the talking.'

'It'll rain beer in the otherworld,' said the warrior.

'Yes it may, and then again it may not. But in the meantime I'll settle for a tavern!'

The two friends laughed, and the warrior helped the other up, and handed him his crutch, and the two walked away, two men with three legs between them, close together, no light between them, so they seemed like the one, like an animal seen in a dream. And behind them in the grass the cross made of two sticks lay there, forgotten.

⁘

'THEY MOVE IN our direction,' said Eithne.

'But slowly,' said Fidelma. 'The weather has been bad, and the roads are washed away. What is *wrong* with the weather these days?'

'There's a change come over it certainly.'

'Does the weather change when times change?'

'Why ask me that, Fidelma? Didn't we go to the same schools, don't we know the same things? Wait your questions for the Storyteller of Tara!'

'Will he answer? In my experience storytellers answer questions with more questions.'

'Look, they've stopped. . . they shelter.'

'Already?'

'His horse is lame, he tends its hoof.'

'And she goes off, where is she going?'

'To that herders' hut? '

'Perhaps. . . for help with the horse, perhaps.'

'At this rate they'll be forever getting here.'

'Well we must wait, we have no choice.'

'And what is time to us?'

'A dress we do not wear!'

'It hangs unused in the closet.'

'It doesn't fit.'

'The colour doesn't suit.'

'We slide it aside, and wonder how we ever wore it!'

'Time!'

⁓•

'NEVER HERD CATTLE,' said the old man to the boy, 'never herd cattle with an interesting man.'

'Why is that, old man?' said the boy at the boley door, a stick in his hand and the watery sun in his watching eyes as he peered down the slope of the field to where the cattle grazed. Where is that brown beast gone, he wondered, the one with one horn longer than the other?

'An interesting man has much to talk about,' said the old man.

'But wouldn't there be learning in that, in the listening?'

'For the first week!' snapped the old man. 'But how long is the summer?'

'Three moons,' the boy muttered, calculating, numbers not his strongest point, 'three and so and four weeks in each and that's. . .'

The boy paused, calculating, and the old man looked skywards, waiting, sighing like the life was going out of him.

'Twelve,' said the boy, 'twelve weeks.'

'Yes twelve, and another. . . now listen close.'

The boy whisked the head off a nettle with his stick, and listened.

'The thing about an interesting man,' said the old herder, 'the thing is he goes on and on. . . and on. . . and no matter how interesting. . . no man's life can last longer than a week in the telling. . . so what will happen then?'

'What?' said the boy, whisking the head off another nettle with his stick, but this time with a backhand swing, 'what will happen then?'

'I'll tell you what. . . when he's done talking for the week, he'll start all over again. . . for the second week, that's what. And when that week is done. . .' The old man sighed again, like he'd found more breath deep inside and he needed to get rid of it before he died. 'When the second week is done he'll start all over for the third. . .'

'Where is the brown beast gone,' the boy interrupted, bored with all this, 'the one with one horn longer than the other?'

'Oh lost, I'd say.'

'You're very easy about it.'

'I knew a man with a short leg once.'

'If the beast is lost we'll be the poorer.'

'The man with a short leg I knew. . . the thing about him was. . . he kept getting lost. . .'

'Why was that, old man?'

'He couldn't walk in a straight line,' said the old man, chortling.

'So you're telling me?' The boy asked, walking away from the boley door to find a nettle with a head.

'That cow with the one horn longer than the other. . . she gets lost too. . . because of her head. . . like it's heavy on one side.'

'Would that be the reason?'

'Perhaps. Though there could be another reason. . .'

'And what would that be?'

'Because the herdsboy wasn't watching?'

'Maybe I'll go looking?'

'Maybe you should. . . and while you're down that way would you check the rabbit traps. . . I'm hungry.'

'We have bread. And buttermilk.'

'What am I, boy? Am I a wench with a baby on the tit? Bread!' The old man hawked a spit from deep inside, and spat. 'Buttermilk!' The second part of the spit followed the first. 'Meat, I want to eat meat.'

'I'll be looking,' said the boy, walking away, whisking nettles with his stick, whistling. And the old man watching him, and another boy in the memory that was his eyes.

Himself, that was!

Yes once he whisked at nettles with a stick.

And once he whistled too.

⌒·

THE HARE SAT.

Watching.

Her leg held firm in the trap.

Waiting.

Watching.

Feeling.

The pain in her leg.

Knowing.

There was nothing to do but wait.

Hearing.

The sound of whistling.

And a boy in the field at the corner there, how he suddenly stopped, stopped whistling, stopped walking, stood, watching her. And a stick in his hand as he came running over.

The hare jumped.

But the string about her leg held her firm in the trap. And she fell back into the grass, panting. And the boy suddenly said 'shit it's a hare.' And stood there with his disappointment. Because there's no killing or eating a hare. Because a hare could be a witch, that is the way of them. And if he killed a hare, (who could really be a witch), there'd be a hex on him and worse. . . the other witches would be looking out revenge. . . and he'd have no life worth living.

Not that life was much worth living anyway, he thought, taking his knife from his tunic. Stuck up here all summer with an old man for company, his thoughts ran on, holding the hare with one hand, twisting the knife into the string around it's leg with the other. Stuck up here and the old man talking talking talking.

His knife sliced through the string. And the hare was free. Or would be free when he let it go. He held it tight for a moment, and its heart thumping. And then he let it go and it sprang away, and ran, to the far side of the field. And stopped, and looked back for a moment. And then it was gone. And the boy walked on, but not too far away he reached the great road that goes from the east to the west along the side of the slope of the mountain. And he paused there, wondering. If the lopsided cow had come down this far then there was no knowing which way she had gone. To the east, or the west, or ruffians might have taken her. There's travellers on the road would take the eye out of your head if you weren't looking.

'Shit,' said the boy, dithering.

And then he heard a horse, snorting. And he followed the sound of the horse up the road a way, to the opposite side, where a stream ran across the road into a tangle of trees, and the ground lower there and hidden from the road unless you had a reason for looking.

The herdsboy had a reason for looking.

He peered over, through the tangle of whin and bushes and trees.

And down there there were two horses, and, much more importantly, his cow, yes that was certainly his cow... he'd know her anywhere... not many animals have one horn shorter than the other.

He clambered down.

There was a man tending the hoof of one of the horses, and a boy, sitting on a hummock, tying sandals to bare legs, watching the man. And there were bits and pieces about, as if they had been resting here. And the man tending the horse wore the sort of cloak a great man wears. No herdsman he! But the boy with him was dressed in an ordinary brown tunic, bare legs, sandals.

The great man in the cloak had the look of a stranger. But the boy looked like one of the herdsboy's own people.

'I am the Storyteller of Tara, and my king is Laoghaire,' said the man who dressed in the cloak of a great man.

'I am honoured you pass this way,' said the boy, politely.

'Is that your cow, lad?' asked the great man, the Storyteller.

'I mind that cow for Fraoch.'

'Fraoch? A well known name in these parts.'

'There are many Fraochs. . . I mind that cow for Fraoch the Black.'

'Why do they call him black?'

'There is a black rock near his house.'

'I see. . . simple as that. . . well. . . tell me boy, do you know why there are many men called Fraoch in these parts?'

'No. . . not really. . . it is the custom, I suppose.'

'Aye,' sighed the Storyteller, 'aye. . . it is the custom.'

Two very large dogs suddenly bounded out of the whin. . . and when they saw the herdsboy they snarled. . . and he held his stick the tighter.

'They are my dogs,' said the Storyteller, 'have no heed of them. They're very friendly.'

'They don't look friendly to me.'

'Looks in a dog can be deceptive,' said the Storyteller, 'as, indeed, they can be in a man, or a woman.'

'What are their names, your dogs?' asked the boy.

But the Storyteller ignored the question, and turned instead to the pageboy to talk. 'Many a man puts on a show,' he said, 'of being someone else. And many a woman has a gentle air. . . but in reality she may be driving her man to an early grave. . . is that not so, page?'

'Your words are wise, master. . . as ever,' murmured the boy on the hummock, not looking up from the tying of his sandals.

'What are their names, your dogs?' the herdsboy repeated, slightly louder, feeling a bit forgotten in the others' exchange of conversation.

'Oh, sorry,' said the Storyteller, 'my mind drifts. . . their names are Night and Day.'

'Which is which?'

'Which is which?' the Storyteller looked at him, bemused. And then decided to make nothing of it. 'The black is Night, the white is Day.'

'Oh,' said the herdsboy. 'What class of dogs are they, are they hunting dogs?'

'Oh no, they're battle dogs, these dogs. . . trained to tear the throat.'

'You said they were friendly.'

'To their friends. . . sure who would be friendly to an enemy?'

'Don't mind his words,' said the page, interrupting, 'he plays with your mind.'

The Storyteller laughed, and fiddled now with his horse's bridles. 'Move on, page, the day is half over.'

The page did not move, remained on his hummock of earth, looking up, at the herdsboy.

'I milked your cow,' he said.

'You milked the cow?'

'My master needed milk.'

'The cow of Fraoch the Black, you milked?'

'She came out of the whin, we thought she was a lost cow.'

'All cows have owners.'

'Oh boys, boys,' interrupted the Storyteller, 'leave it be, forget the argument.' He walked over to the cow, his bone in his hand. 'By the time the son goes down,' he said, 'your argument will be pointless.' He poked the udder of the cow. And the saggy flesh dripped around the bone, like a garment being lifted from a washing tub on a stick. And a memory in his arm suddenly felt the weight of the witch's breast, the witch they burned at Tara. And he heard her in his head. And he saw her in his head like a picture painted on the back of his eyes.

'Flesh clings to the bone,' she said, in the tone of a woman who will open her legs to the right man, her head to the side and her eyes looking down at her own shoulder. 'Indeed,' he said back to her, silently in his head, remembering the fair amount of flesh clinging to the witch's bones herself! Eating and drinking on her, as men say round campfires. And then he blinked the vision of the witch away and said aloud, 'Life goes on, boys, and there'll be more milk there by the time the sun goes down.'

'That's not the point,' said the boy, like a lawyer bringing a case to a king. 'The cow belongs to Fraoch the Black. We bring all Fraoch the Black's cattle to the mountain pasture in the summer. And the cows we milk. And we have a churn in the boley. And we make butter. And we bury the butter in wooden casks. This is our work.'

'Are you arguing with me boy?'

'Sorry sir.'

'No matter, you are right to. To protect your master. And to look after the cow of your master. But think this way. . . would not Fraoch the Black give me that cow if I asked.'

'He might,' said the boy, very doubtfully.

'Might?'

'Fraoch the Black is not known for his generous ways.'

'What is he known for?' asked the Storyteller's page.

'The strength of his sword arm. And the heads that hang at his door.'

'Oh, I see.' said the Storyteller.

'Are they the heads of those who milked his cow?' asked the page, grinning.

'No,' said the herdsboy, 'they're from great battles that he fought when he was young. He fought the men of Ulster.'

'And them boyos take some fighting,' said the Storyteller, 'but listen. . . listen. . . this is all well and good, but we must away.'

'Where are you going?'

'To Rathcroghan, to your king, Daithi.'

'Oh,' said the herdsboy, very impressed.

The Storyteller gripped into a bag that hung from his horse, and held out a small coin, small but gold. . . and handed it to the herdsboy.

'For the milk.'

'This would buy the cow.'

'Tell Fraoch the Black to keep the change,' said the Storyteller. 'Well. . . that is. . . that is if you tell Fraoch the Black anything about the matter.'

'If I keep the coin myself I am rich.'

'But if you don't tell Fraoch the Black about it,' grinned the Storyteller, 'you have stolen his money, and you are poor.'

'Don't be heeding him, herdsboy,' said the page, 'he plays with your mind.'

'What should I do?' the herdsboy asked, looking over.

The page stood up, and walked towards him. And as he came towards him the herdsboy saw two things, first, that this was no boy, but that it was a girl, dressed as a boy, and second, that this girl dressed as a boy was limping, ever so slightly.

He turned to the Storyteller.

'Why is your page a girl, a girl dressed as a boy?'

'Why,' said the Storyteller, without a question in his voice, 'why,' but apart from that he took no heed, busy with his horse.

'I am no page,' said the girl, 'I am a wife to him. I am the wife they call the daughter of the moon.'

'You have mud on your face. . . like certain ones of our people.'

'What would be the reason for that, boy?'

'You *are* one of our people?'

'Indeed. . . now take the cow of Fraoch the Black. . . and go. . . and bring the coin with you. . . but keep it for yourself. . .'

'Myself?'

'A reward,' she grinned, and turned, and walked away, limping.

⌒•

'SEE HOW SHE GRINS,' said Eithne to Fidelma.

'She grows much stronger, here in the air of Connacht.'

'Here on the earth of Connacht.'

'A witch, a wizard girl.'

'Does he see her growing stronger?'

'What does a man see. . . in a woman? Does a man ever see *anything* of a woman?'

'Particularly one he loves,' said Fidelma.

10

A ROAD IS A DANGEROUS PLACE for a man bored easily, the Storyteller realised. And a road is a place where a man gets to know the laws of the gods in unhappy detail. One of these laws says that the bores are always going in your direction, while the interesting ones are coming the other way, and the meeting with them is short. But the bores are on the same journey as yourself, and you're stuck with them.

For ten miles now an elderly horse dealing man on a very fine horse had been alongside, talking. And the Storyteller had nearly had his fill. They had reached a place to camp, but the horse dealer had decided that yes, that'd be a good place for him to camp too. And he too had got off his horse, and arranged his things, and was still talking.

'As a man gets older,' he continued, 'he has a choice.'

'And what choice would that be?' asked the Storyteller, wondering about his own choices!

'Well, he can walk up a hill, or climb down into a well.'

'And what would this riddle mean, old man?' asked the Storyteller, not too patiently.

'He can walk up a hill, into the light, where he will have a view of the countryside around. . . or he can climb down into a well. . . where it is dark. . . and there is no seeing the countryside around.'

'Sometimes,' said the Storyteller, 'sometimes it is easier for an old man to walk downhill.'

'But this is the way of it,' said the old man. . . 'so before he gets old he must be moving up the hill. . . a day at a time. . . because when he is too old he will be tired. . . and there'll be no strength in his legs.'

'Aye,' said the Storyteller, losing first the thread and then the interest.

He looked over towards the fire, and to the Wife and her wreathed in smoke.

'What does with the food, woman?'

'Not good,' came the reply, 'the fire won't take, the sticks are wet.'

'This is a wet country,' said the old horse dealing man.

'Is it you who are telling me this,' snorted the Storyteller. 'Does it never stop raining here?'

'Oh you can get lovely weather here,' said the old man.

'I'm sure you can,' said the Storyteller, rain trickling off his nose into his beard.

'It'd be hard to beat, the weather you can get here... I am minded of a lovely day not long ago... the sun splitting the heavens...'

'Indeed.' said the Storyteller, raising his eyes to the leaden skies.

'It was the day I met some Romans passing here.'

'Which way did they go?'

'To the West, why do you ask?'

'No reason. What of this day, this lovely day you met the Romans?'

'They were followers of Patrick the Roman... and they were from Armorica... do you know where that is?'

'Somewhere across the sea...'

'Somewhere there, yes. And a country known for its weather. And its wine. And do you know what these Romans said to me?'

'Not yet.'

'They said you'd be hard put to get this weather in Armorica... isn't that a thing?'

'What?'

'Well, that our weather is better than theirs...'

'What of it, old man, what is their weather to me? This rain or this sun falls on this head here. What do I care about them?'

'Well... they were complimenting us...'

'Oh you foolish old man... have no heed of these foreigners... their compliments are of a man coming into your house... he listens to your stories... and thanks your wife for her cooking... but he wants to bed your daughter... take it from me, the best foreigners are either dead or getting into their boats to go home!' The Storyteller stood up, annoyed, and walked over to the ball of smoke that was a long time from a fire.

'This is not looking good,' he said grumpily.

'No,' agreed the Wife, 'not good at all.'

'We will eat raw food tonight.'

'When I was a little girl my grandmother would talk to the sticks, and they'd burst into flame.'

'Talk to the sticks, or to the fire?'

'Well, probably the fire. . . she'd talk to the fire. . . it was from her own grandmother she learned the skill. . .'

'Well did she not pass it on to you? What did she say to the fire, to make it burn?'

'Words. . . in the old language.'

'What words?'

'I don't know, I don't know the old language. . .'

'More's the pity.'

'Where do languages go, Storyteller?'

'*Go*? How do you mean go?'

'Go. Like when the wind stops blowing here, it blows somewhere else. . . so when the sound of a language stops, where does it sound?'

'That I do not know,' said the Storyteller, looking back at the horse dealer who had now taken offence and, seeing him looking, called out angrily 'I'll eat by myself.'

'Whatever makes you happy.' He turned to the Wife, 'are the sticks the enemy of the fire, or is the fire their friend?'

'But surely they're the one. . . they need each other. . .'

'But does the fire need the sticks more than the sticks need the fire?'

'Tell me.'

'I will,' he said, sensing a satisfactory little lesson forming in his head. 'The sticks are old and tired. . . dead wood. . . after the fire they are ash. . . turn that ash into the soil and new things grow, and grow well. . .'

'And what are you saying?'

'Bury an unburnt stick in the soil? Nothing much grows from that.'

'True.'

'So the fire is the friend of the sticks. But a fool passing by, a fool will see the sticks turn to ash. . . and a fool will think the fire is no friend to the sticks. . .'

'They are the one, the fire and the sticks.'

'Yes,' said the Storyteller, the lesson over, and now bored with this conversation too. He looked out into the darkening of the evening. And the dark hump of a hill over there, not a great hill, but a big hump nonetheless. 'Yes, and the old language that the old people spoke. . . it was the one too. . . there was the words and the fire and the sticks. . . and your grandmother stirred the words into the fire. . . and the fire burned. . . and now the words are gone, wherever the words go. . .'

'Tell me where the words go. . . you surely know. . .'

'The words seep into the soil. And when a man passing, a man with ears to hear, when his feet presses the ground the words are squeezed out again, like water from a cloak. And sometimes the sounds come out in words, single words, like single drops of water squeezed from a cloak,. But sometimes they come in sentences, like a whole run of water that you could wash your hands in, that you could drink, a whole run of water that would be cool on your eyes, and clear your sight. . . that happens. . . sometimes. . .'

'Yes Storyteller,' said the Wife. And then she laughed. 'And isn't it the strangest thing. . .'

'What?'

'That we have this conversation here.'

'Why here, what is strange about here. . . other than any of the strangeness of your savage country.'

'Do you know that mountain there?'

'That is not a mountain, woman, that's a hill. In the kingdom of Meath we have *mountains*. Here in this boggy place you have *hills*.'

'Oh mock our land, Storyteller. . . it will live longer than your mockery, and long enough to mock you.'

'Alright. . . tell me of that hill. . . oh. . . my apologies. . . tell me of that *mountain*?'

'That is Slievebaghna.'

'Is it. . . I've heard of that. . .'

'Of course you have. . . you're an educated man. . .'

'But I needed you, the uneducated you, to put the place onto the story.'

'A man needs a woman.'

'Is the woman the place, and the man the story.'

'Something like that.' She fiddled with the fire. There was

smoke. But no flames. And the only colour near it was the harsh yellow of her hair and the streaks of red.

'Baghna.' he said, 'he was the chief of the old people. And so that was his mountain? Well well, you learn something new every day! Tell you something for nothing, *he* would know the words to fan the fire.'

'If he was here.'

'But he's not here. That mountain was the last place of the old people. They fought their last battle there.'

'Are they gone?'

'They're gone.'

'Are they not in the new people, who took their women, bred with them. . .'

'What colour is the calf of a black bull and a white cow?'

'Sometimes the colour of the black bull's mother.'

'White. . . or black. . . or brown. . . come girl, give up that fire.'

'Maybe you're right,' she stood up, reluctantly, and walked over to him.

'You're limping, girl.'

'I turned my ankle on a tuft, this morning.'

'It looks more like you caught it in a briar.'

'No, I turned it on a tuft.'

'No matter what, you're limping anyway.' The Storyteller knelt, and held the Wife's foot in his hands, and the toes were the toes of a child and he remembered tying the sandals on his own children.

She sat on a rock and he held her ankles. And he thought of the dirty feet of the slavegirl he'd seen at Tara, the day before this journey. And the sameness of feet. But the different paths they walked. That slavegirl was now a wraith, and on her way to Ulster. But still, despite the paths they travel, there is a sameness of legs, and bodies and heads and all the parts of a person. . . how much the same. . . but how different the spirit in them. . . and why would that be?

'You caress my feet,' she said.

'You have lovely feet.'

'But have you a cure for my foot, my lovely foot, in your hands,' she murmured, maybe mockingly.

'Not in my hands. . . I cure with words. . . but there's a man I know in Fingall. . . he would touch you well in minutes. . .'

'It's a fair walk to Fingall. . . and in the wrong direction. . . I'll cure myself. . . go pick that moss there, by the stone. . . and bring me mud from that puddle. . . and string from our saddles. . .'

The Storyteller did as she said. And watched as she rolled the moss and mud into a paste, a stiff paste, and coated it round her ankle, and tied it with the string.

'There,' she said, 'that's cured.'

'Get away with you, girl, will you ever get up the yard. . .' said the Storyteller. . . 'come on. . . stand up. . . walk to me if it's cured. . .'

She stood, and put a weight on the foot, but the pain made her hop, and she stumbled, and would have fallen but for him catching her.

'Some cure that,' he said.

'Give it time,' she said.

And he put his arms around her, and she felt like a child. But she was not a child. She cut a man's throat in Cruachan Ai. And that's why they called her the daughter of the moon. Because the man's throat she cut was the son of an important man in that country. And they would have hanged her but her father, Anluan of Ardakillen, he talked to Daithi. And they went back a long way. Anluan of Ardakillen drove chariots for Daithi in wars that were not forgotten. And a man and his charioteer have a closeness.

And Anluan told Daithi that the girl was mad, a daughter of the moon. That she was a wizard girl, and the wizards watched her for omens.

And Daithi, a very religious man, he agreed not to hang the girl, but he told Anluan that he must get her out of his country, and sell her as a wife to Meath or Munster. . . but not Ulster. . . because Daithi wasn't very keen on Ulstermen and wouldn't sell a wife to any of them, not even if there was a fair chance she'd cut the man's throat!

And so Anluan of Ardakillen talked to a man, who talked to a man, who talked to a man.

And that man knew another man who'd been selling hides in Tara.

And one evening after selling hides he had met the Storyteller at a fire. And the Storyteller was telling the idle men round the fire, and anyone else who would listen, telling them the story of a dream he dreamed. How in this dream he went to Connacht to buy a young wife. And he bought her cheap, because the Connacht people called her the daughter of the moon, and they were trying to get rid of her. And that was all of the dream.

The man who had been selling hides thought nothing of this.

Except that maybe Tara's storytellers told poor stories!

But then the hide seller went home to his own country and met the man he knew, who knew the man who knew the man who had talked to Anluan of Ardakillen. And so it came known generally that the Storyteller of Tara had dreamed of the girl they called the daughter of the moon. And there was no getting away from this now. There was a geis on them all, on Anluan, on his daughter, and on the Storyteller, a geis on them to do a deal and bring the dream to the world, to give it life, to put a feeling that could be felt upon it.

So, messengers went back, and forth, and the arrangement was made.

A cow was agreed.

Anluan would actually have given away the girl free, because there was pressure on him to get her out of the place. But there would have been tut tutting from women, about tradition, and people saying hasn't a woman got her own dignity? And doesn't every woman deserve a price on herself? And what sort of man would give away a woman free? And what sort of man would take a wife without paying for her?

So, for the look of the thing, the price of a cow was exchanged. And the Storyteller went to Connacht to collect the girl.

'Do you remember I came here to Connacht to get you?' he said to her now in his arms.

'It's not two years. . . of course I remember.'

'I don't mean that. . . I mean do you remember the feeling of being collected?'

'Yes.'

And what was that feeling?'

'Well. . . that marrying you was better than being hanged.'

'I hope that's a joke.'

She giggled. 'Alright it's a joke.'

'How old were you then?'

'Nineteen. . .'

'Very old to be getting married.'

'Marry in haste, repent in leisure,' said the wife, hopping out of his arms.

The Storyteller looked at her, loving her, too much. Knowing that she didn't love him, very much. But then, she was not a loving woman. She was touched. A daughter of the moon. With her one eye cold, and her other cruel. A man can't ask a woman like that to love him. All he can ask is that his throat will be safe when he sleeps.

'We'll stop here awhile, and rest,' he said, 'but I think then we'll ride on awhile, and sleep somewhere drier. And get away from old . . .' He nodded his head towards the horse dealer. 'And then a thought occurred. He stood there, thoughtfully stroking the beard on his neck, touching his throat, looking at her, in her tunic the colour of a deer, and the dark band of the belt around her waist, and on one side hanging the purse she carried, the purse made from the skin of a sow's dug, and on the other side her knife. She read his mind.

'Your throat is safe.'

'Because you need me to help you on the horse in the morning?'

'My foot will be cured before the morning.'

'You seem very sure.'

'You must learn to have faith in people, Storyteller, it's a great failing of yours. . . this doubting. . .'

'Indeed, is it? Maybe it's the witches and the wizards of Cruachan Ai that I don't have much faith in.'

'Maybe magic belongs to a people, and is born in them, like the colour of their hair. . . and there's no way a foreigner can learn.'

'You are the foreigner.'

The wife grinned. And looked around. And the Storyteller looked around too. And there was a whispering wind. And a splatter of thin rain. And the smell of the earth, and the smell of things that rot on the earth. Corpses of animals that no animal will eat. And the mulch of leaves where beetles run. The smell of Connacht, thought the Storyteller, a place where even the shadows smell. He looked at the shadows, and them falling on the country. One by one. Like the day was an old woman, undressing. And she was dropping black clothes, one after the other, one upon the other. Stripping, undressing, revealing nothing except more layers of blackness to drop on the ground.

Darkness, leading to darkness.

The day is the mother of night.

And the night is the father of the day.

And the wife is the daughter of the moon.

He looked at her, and she at him. And she said 'here, it's you, it's *you* that are the foreigner, not I.'

'I bring my story with me,' he said.

'And I. . .' she took the knife from her belt and held it up so it glinted, 'and I bring mine.'

'Are you the woman who cannot light a fire,' said the old and boring horse dealing man, suddenly reappearing. 'If you dressed as a woman maybe you'd have the knack.'

'I wouldn't be rude to her,' said the Storyteller, 'not with that knife in her hand.'

'Ah I know her type,' said the old man, with all the irritating confidence of a horse dealer.

'What type is that?' she said, sweetly.

'I knew you by that bag at your waist. . . soon as I saw you. . .'

The old man came closer to the Storyteller, closer, so that the distance between himself and the girl was more than the distance between himself and the Storyteller.

'This is a wizard you have here, do you know that?'

'She's a good wife to me.'

'May be. . . may be. . . but I'll tell you this. . .'

'Of that I have no doubt. . .'

'I'll tell you this. . . I was in Rathcroghan once. . . as a young man. . . and I met a wizard girl. . . and she too had a purse like that around her waist. . .'

'It's the skin of a sow's dug,' said the Storyteller.

'Hmmnn,' said the old man, mysteriously. And then he shrugged. 'Yes. . . when the sow is being slaughtered. . . the wizard girls go into the slaughterhouse. . . and slice off the dugs while the sow is still squealing. . . make purses of them. . .'

'Not a custom I know of,' said the Storyteller.

'Aachh what do you know, man from Tara, what do you know of people here?'

'What *should* I know?' asked the Storyteller.

'They have a place called the Mucklaghs,' said the old man. 'They sacrifice pigs. And. . .' He paused, looked over at the wife, carefully. 'And people too, or so I've heard.' He tapped his finger against his nose. As if to say no more. And then he walked away. And stood so that the distance between him and the wife was smaller than the distance between him and the Storyteller.

'If I light your fire will you lie with me?' he said.

The Storyteller looked to the sky, but held his peace.

'Seems a fair bargain,' said the horse dealing man, now speaking to the Storyteller. 'you have a woman handy, and I am handy with a fire.'

The Storyteller sent a sigh to the sky.

'Sure what would you do with me,' said the Wife, 'I'd say that prick of yours is a stranger to a woman.'

'If you were a real woman there'd be life enough there.'

'These days I'm a boy,' said the Wife. . . she looked him up and down. . . 'and feeling more like a boy by the minute.'

The old man laughed.

The Storyteller laughed.

The Wife smiled.

'Oh alright,' said the horse dealer, 'I'll light the fire anyway.'

He hunkered down beside it, and muttered, and poked, and muttered, and shook, and muttered again. And the fire flamed.

The old horse dealing man stood up. 'There you are,' he said, 'What're we eating?'

'Pig,' said the Wife, limping to her saddlebags, kneeling, and taking out a long strip of meat. She flipped it onto a stone and the Storyteller watched, the knife in her hand, and it slicing through the flesh, expertly.

⌒•

'THE HORSE DEALER is surprised to see them go,' said Eithne.

'Yes,' agreed Fidelma, 'they've played a trick on him. . . they said they'd camp. . . and now they say they've changed their mind. . .'

'And ride on into the evening.'

'He sits alone by the fire.'

'Thinking of horse dealing.'

'And he sits on a bag of gold.'
'What use is a bag of gold to an old man?'
'An old man who sits with an old prick between his legs.'
'Weary.'
'Chewing meat off of the rib bones of a pig.'
'Throwing the bones into the fire.'
'Watching them burn.'
'Crackling.'
'Spitting.'
'Watching. . . listening.'
'Thinking. . . how much money is in the bag between his legs.'

⌒•

'LOOK AT THE SUN,' said the Wife, 'look at the sun setting, over there, look and tell me this. . .'
'Well?'
'Well we rode all day. . . sometimes we rode to the north, sometimes to the south, now directly to the west. . . why does the road weave so?'
'Didn't I tell you that already girl! The road follows rivers, or from hill to hill, or goes along the high ground. A long time ago this was the road of the chariots. And chariots are useless in the boggy places. So the road was built for them.'
'Did Asail actually *build* the road?'
'No, but it has his name. . . but it was there, before his time. . . the old people who used chariots built it. . . he brought it back to life. . . that's why it has his name. . . it was probably here in his father's time.'
'Who was his father?'
'Dordomblas.'
'Where do you learn. . . such history?'
'In the schools. . . Cathbad has a school in Rathcroghan. . . maybe you would go there. . . Eithne and Fidelma go there. . .'
'Not if they're dead!'
'No. . . not then. . .'
'That school. . . I might not be welcome. . . there are those that remember why I left Connacht. . .'
'You are my wife now. . .'

'There are those who don't care much about the Storyteller of Tara. . . and less about his wife!'

'A few, I suppose,' agreed the Storyteller of Tara.

And the Wife laughed, and pointed at the sun, going, directly ahead. . . 'the day is dying.'

'If we move west, as we are now, directly west,' said the Storyteller, 'move fast. . . then we will keep up with the setting sun. . . and have a longer day. . .'

'So a day is shorter for someone moving to the east?' said the Wife.
'It is shorter.'

'So if a man moves west all his life, he gets a longer life?'
'No, girl. . . he gets a longer light. . . his life is the same. . .'
'So if he's moving towards the darkness, then his light is longer?'
'You riddle with me girl, don't you?'

She laughed. And kicked her bare heels into the side of the horse. Her heels were bare because her sandals were off, and her sandals were off because that one ankle was still swathed in a mossy bandage of mud. The Storyteller hadn't seen her limping much anymore, but he was biding his time, to mock her cure if she did.

At first the bare heels kicking had no effect on the horse, so she kicked again, harder, and said 'gaddup yah.'. . . and the horse trotted ahead. And the black dog and the white dog followed her, so that the four of them, the two horses and their riders and the two dogs became strung out along the road. And ahead of them there was the sun setting, like they were going to a burning fort.

Silence for awhile.

The hooves of the horses.

Or a 'geddup yadog' call from the Storyteller to one or other of the dogs when they wandered off the roadway, their noses pointing at something interesting to them.

It was warm now, and it had stopped raining for awhile. But a man didn't have to be a nelladoir to see more rain in the sky, coming, tonight, tomorrow.

'The dark is catching us,' he called out to the girl.

'My horse is tired,' she replied, 'I can't ride any faster.'

'Is there nowhere along this road to stop or stay, no strong man's place, no bruidin, no house even. . . does no-one live in this place?'

'I don't know every road in Connacht,' she protested, 'do you know every road in Meath?'

'This is the Slighe Asail, the main road, by the gods. . . this is one of the great roads of Ireland. . . and would you look at its condition!'

'Sure a good road is only good to a restless man,' muttered the Wife.

'May be, may be so. . . but philosophy won't put a roof over our head tonight. . .'

'We'll sleep under the trees. . .'

'I don't want to sleep under the trees. . . I am the Storyteller of Tara. . . I have a dignity.'

'Sure you have me to keep you warm, and what's a warm man need of dignity!'

'A woman can't be mattress and blanket at the same time. And anyway it's a thin mattress and a light blanket you make too.'

She laughed. 'The horse dealer would've been happy enough to give me a shag.'

'Happy enough to give anyone, in my opinion,' responded the Storyteller, 'so don't be flattering yourself with that! Anyway. . .' He looked around, disgruntled. 'What're you talking about, trees, I see no trees. . . to sleep under. . . no shelter. By the gods what a grim place this is. Is it any wonder you're all mad in Connacht!'

'Oh yes there are. . . trees. . . look beyond. . .'

'That's just a crossroads on the road. . .'

'Should we ride on, to a house? It's not a road to ride at night, in my thinking,' she said.

'Alright, alright,' the Storyteller agreed.

They rode up to the trees. And immediately the dogs stopped, and snarled, and barked. And the Storyteller saw that the place was more than trees, it was in fact a little woods, with the four roads of the crossroads going into it, and emerging on the other sides.

An owl hooted. Something shuffled in the undergrowth. But the dogs weren't snarling at the owl. Nor at the something in the undergrowth.

'What's with the dogs?' he asked.

'They're your dogs,' came the reply.

He slid off his horse, walked carefully to the edge of the woods. And the dogs walked beside him, snarling. There was nothing to see, so he walked slightly in among the trees. And now he realised that the trees were not actually a woods, no, they were more like a ring of trees. And the place where the roads met was clear, and flat. And beside that place there was one huge tree, with huge branches spreading over the place the roads met. And hanging from the branches were hanged men, swaying, their feet only inches from the ground.

'By the gods,' he said, 'what place is this?'

The Wife beside him said 'there are hanged men hanging here.'

'Haven't I eyes in my head, woman. . . don't give me description, give me explanations.'

She walked forward. And the black dog went with her. 'Hanged women too,' she called back, 'this must be a hanging place.'

'I'm beginning to realise that,' said the Storyteller, 'we won't stop here tonight.'

'This is not good country to be travelling in,' she said.

'I'm beginning to get that impression myself,' he said.

'What I mean is. . . we're probably safer here than out on the road. . .'

'There's a logic there,' he had to agree. . . 'well look. . . we'll camp way over there. . . put some distance between ourselves and the corpses.'

'Sure what can the corpses harm,' said the wife, walking among them. . . 'look. . . here. . . this was a handsome man. . . his curly hair. . . strong hands. . . there's a woman lonely in her bed tonight for him. . .'

'Come away from the corpses girl.'

'And look. . . this was a pretty girl. . . her dark hair to her waist. . . would you be happy to love her, Storyteller?'

'Come away from the corpses girl.'

'And this, a clever looking man, a man of learning. . . perhaps another Storyteller. . .'

'Would you ever come away from the corpses girl.'

'The handsome. . . and the pretty. . . and the wise. . . all hanging. . . all smelling of shit. . .'

'Their bowels open when they hang them. If you don't come away from them you'll smell of shit too.'

'Sure why would I care. . . if I smelt of shit you'd still love me.'

'I might. . . but I wouldn't share your bed.'

'If I painted myself with shit like the witches on the islands in the west. . . you would love me. . .'

'Why are you so sure?'

'You love me with mud on my forehead and cheeks. . . these finger stripes of mud. . . you know it is the custom here. . .'

'I wouldn't love you in Tara with mud on your face. . .'

'But you love me more. . . when I'm here. . .'

'Perhaps. . . you're different. . . here. . .'

'I will get more different,' she said, mysteriously. 'The nearer to Rathcroghan. . . will you love me more then. . .'

'Perhaps,' said the Storyteller carefully. . . 'but I'm not going near the shitty islands with you. . . a man has limits. . .'

The Wife laughed, and the Storyteller laughed, and then she came out from among the corpses, her mood was changed, and lighter.

They gathered the dogs and the horses together, and made camp at the far corner of the trees, out of sight of the crossroads and the corpses hanging.

'Will we eat again?' she asked.

'No, I'm tired,' said the Storyteller, 'I will sleep.' And so he did.

And the dream he dreamed was home at Tara. And his Chief Wife and her son. And the silver bands on her ankles, and the silver bands on her thighs. And her red hair going grey. A red haired woman goes grey young. Of her he dreamed. And the stuff she put in her hair to keep away the grey. And how it stained her hands, like blood, for days after. He dreamed of her. And of his second wife the Quiet One who baked good bread, and her daughters and her son. And the pigs beyond. And the stableboys who slept in the shed above the pigs. And the field that he had bought from the widow of a man who had not come home from a long journey. Well, hopefully she was a widow, and hopefully her husband would never come home from the long journey! Because if he did they're be arguments for lawyers. And lawyers would strip a man bare as soon as look at him. Yes, yes, he dreamed and murmured yes in his dream. And all his life was there. He saw the hams of six pigs hanging in his house in twos, so that lying there you'd be looking up at the backsides of three women. And the rows of herrings hanging too, too many for the counting. But he would count them, he would try. One, two, three, four. . . he got to seven and he suddenly woke, to the banging of a drum.

'By the Gods,' he said, sitting up. . . 'what is this madness?'

The Wife sat up beside him.

'It's a drum.'

'I know it's a drum. But why is it a drum?'

'Why ask me?'

'This is your place, your country.'

'If you were woken by a drum in Meath, would you know the reason every time?'

'Don't start that argument again, girl,' he snapped, standing up. He looked around. 'By the gods, there's people here, gathering.'

'They dance at the crossroads,' she said, matter-of-factly, 'it's a custom, in these parts. . .'

'Dance? Dance?'

'Yes, dance,' said the Wife they called the daughter of the moon. 'Like this, dance.' She did a little jig to demonstrate. 'And look, my foot is cured, so mock me not!' She danced a little more, to demonstrate the cure.

'I know what a dance is. . . I mean why, why dance. . . here?'

'Because it's a crossroads.'

'But the trees are full of hanged men.'

'They hang people at the crossroads too.'

'At the same crossroads?'

'How many crossroads are there in the world,' she said, a mockery in her voice. . . and then she snapped her fingers, and danced a little jig again.

And then she stopped.

'This is the way of things, Storyteller. . . in these parts. . . the hanging and the dancing are the one, this morning they hanged these people bandits, robbers, unfaithful wives. . . sheep stealers. . . strangers. . . whoever they are. . .'

'Every country has people to hang, I know that.'

'Well, round here they hang in the morning, and dance in the evening.'

'I see,' said the Storyteller, looking gloomily at the gathering, 'how long will they be dancing?'

'Until we are tired,' said a young man suddenly come up to them, overhearing. He looked them up and down. 'You are strangers in these parts. Do you sell, or buy?'

'I do neither,' said the Storyteller.

'A stranger sells, or a stranger buys,' said the man. 'Or a stranger steals.'

'I do none of those,' said the Storyteller.

'If a stranger sells, we buy, if what he sells is good. If a stranger buys, we sell, if the price is right.'

'And if he steals?' interrupted the Wife.

'We hang him from a tree,' said the man, looking thoughtfully at the corpses.

'Enough of this,' said the Storyteller, 'I am King Laoghaire's Storyteller.'

'I know,' said the man.

'Why then did you ask?'

'It was not for me to ask, but for you to tell.' He grinned, a gap toothed grin. 'They talk about you on the road. You travel with a girl, dressed as a boy.'

'That's me,' said the Wife.

'You travel with a black dog, and a white dog.'

'They lie there, watching you,' said the Wife, 'they will kill you if I call.'

'Better not call so,' was the reply. 'You go to Cruachan Ai, to Rathcroghan. . . to the King. . .'

'How far is it now?'

'A day, two days, depends how fast your horses!'

'So you know all about me. Well do you know what I had for breakfast,' said the Storyteller, 'how old I am, and who was my father's mother?'

'No but I do know,' grinned the gap toothed man, 'I know that this girl, dressed as a boy, I know she is one of our people.'

'You can tell that by looking at her,' said the Storyteller, his tone meaning several things at once.

'They say she is the one they call the daughter of the moon.'

'Why do they say that?'

'I don't know, some story or other,' said the gap toothed man, 'I really don't know. . . maybe the druids in Cruachan Ai will tell you. . . if there are any druids left in Cruachan Ai. . .'

'How do you mean, left?'

'Oh they're all very old. . . and the Roman and his priests are preaching the new ways. . .'

'Do you follow the Roman?'

The gap toothed man grinned. 'Ask me that in an hour,' he said, and looked about to the sound of a jangling instrument which had now joined the beating of the drum. 'I'll dance now. . . will I dance with the girl, dressed as a boy?'

'She is a wife to me.'

'Well I don't mind.'

'I'm not concerned about what you might mind. . . I might mind.'

'Oh round here we're not fussy about that sort of thing. . . what's that they say. . . a woman was made round to go round. . .'

'Oh dance with her. . . if she will dance with you. . . be careful of your foot, girl.'

'Sure I won't let him near *that*,' she said, with a grin, a sexy grin. And the Storyteller saw again in a vision in his head that witch, and her grinning that sexy grin, looking down at her own shoulder.

Was the Wife the witch, he wondered, briefly. Then hurried the thought away. He shook the vision of the witch away with the thought, and watched as the gap toothed man held the wife by the hand, leading her off into the place where the people were gathering to dance. It was the exact place under the great tree where the roads met, where the corpses of the hanged ones swayed. . . and as they gathered over there the Storyteller noticed how the living and the dead in the dark were almost the one, indistinguishable.

He watched them for awhile, and listened to the jangling and banging of strange Connacht music. And then felt the tiredness coming over him. And even with the jangling and banging of the strange Connacht music in the air, he slept again. How long, no knowing.

⌒•

'HE SLEEPS,' said Fidelma.

'She dances,' said Eithne, 'dances with country people.'

'Among the dead.'

'This is a savage country.'

'A country of dance and death.'

'And death and dance.'
'Do the people know the difference?'
'Is there any difference?'
'Why ask me that. . . why tease. . . you know the answer.'
'I know the answer.'

⌒·

THE STORYTELLER WOKE suddenly, forgetting where he was. And he reached out for the wife in the habit he had. But she wasn't there, no wife there at all. No Chief Wife, nor other wife either, not the Quiet One who made good bread, nor the one they called the daughter of the moon. . . no. . . it was a cailleach by his side. A hag, with the lank grey hair of a hag.

Her skin felt like old rags bundled.

He reached for his bone to hit her away.

But the bone was gone. . . 'my bone,' he said, 'my bone from the sacred hill of Tara. . . what have you done with my bone?'

'Flesh clings to the bone,' she said, swinging a leg to the floor, and it was a thin shank like a piece of rope that had washed from a ship to a shore. And then another thin shank, and she stood.

'Is my sacred bone in that leg?' he asked.

But she did not reply.

'Do I dream?' he asked.

'What is dream and what is not,' she grinned, red gums for teeth.

'Where is my wife they call the daughter of the moon, what have you done with her?'

'For shush,' said the Cailleach, tipping her thin lips with a very thin finger. 'For shush and watch with me.'

The Cailleach pointed.

And then he saw the Wife, dancing in the moonlight, naked, the wife they called the daughter of the moon. Her hair was long, and she used it in her dancing, like a dancing girl might use a veil. He started to call out but the Cailleach said no, she cannot hear you. Between you and her there is a time. A time you can think across, but not reach.

And they stood there in the shadow of the trees, where the light of the moon could not reach, where the daughter of the moon could not see. But they saw her, dancing. And around her the other people dancing, in a hand holding circle. And then he saw her kneel, and bury her face in the grass, and stay that way. And the circle of circling dancers stopped, and stayed that way, still. And then the great black dog that the Storyteller called Night came bounding over. And sniffed about the Wife. And when he'd done with sniffing he mounted her, like she was a bitch dog. And like a bitch dog in heat she moved her backside to his movements, but did not raise her face from the grass where it was buried. And then he was done, and disconnected himself, and wandered off, vaguely, like there might be something of interest somewhere else.

'I'll kill that dog,' said the Storyteller.

The Cailleach laughed.

'That dog is the dog you called Night? Would you kill the night?'

'Don't riddle me, Cailleach.'

'If you kill the night, you'll only have the day.'

'I'll kill that dog.'

'You'll be a one-legged man, limping.'

'That dog will die.'

'You'll be a man than cannot turn his head, a man who can only see the way he's going, a man not knowing where he comes from.'

'It'll die. Oh yes. No doubt about that.'

'Would you not have the night make love to the child of the moon?'

'Oh don't riddle words with me, I'll kill that dog.'

'Would you rather she made love to the gap toothed man?'

'Any man. . .'

'But what is a dog, and what is a man?'

'One has four legs!'

'What is a pig, and what is a woman?'

'A pig squeals.'

'What is a squeal but a scream?'

'A scream is what a witch does on a fire.'

'All witches, storyteller, all witches, do all witches scream?'

'Not all, Cailleach, not all,' said the Storyteller, suddenly recognising her, and her voice. He turned back to her, and saw that dark hair heavy on her shoulders, and a blue dress falling from her breasts in a tumble of material to her waist, and there it was gathered in with a strap, or a belt, a strap or a belt weighted down with a sword, a sword like a warrior carries, a working sword.

'Why do you carry that sword?'

'Why do you carry that story in your head.'

'Are all questions to be answered with questions?'

'Do I know any answers?'

'You are a witch.'

'Am I? A witch screams on a fire. . . did I scream on that fire those days ago?'

'I didn't hear you. . . maybe I was too far away.'

'If you were in my arms, Storyteller, even then you would not have heard me. I do not scream.'

'But you laugh,' said the Storyteller, remembering, 'you laugh like a bird.'

The witch laughed. But not like a bird. Like a woman amused. And she reached in under her skirts and took out a bone and held it out to him, his legbone, his bone from the sacred hill at Tara.

'Your bone, Storyteller.'

He took the end of it, carefully. It felt heavy, like her weight was on it at the other end. And then it felt light. And it was in his hand and she was gone. And down among the corpses the dancers were still dancing, dancing, dancing.

He shook his head, like a man on a path will shake away a spider's web that catches him, he shook and shook until the last piece of the web of the dream was gone. . . if it was a dream. . .

He walked down among the dancers, and some were living, some were dead. And when he found the Wife she was dancing with a corpse, holding its arms out like she was teaching it. It was the corpse of a man. And beside her the gap toothed man was dancing with another corpse, the corpse of a woman. . .

'Come girl,' said the Storyteller, 'we must sleep now.'

'There'll be time enough for sleeping,' she said to him, and then, to the corpse, 'isn't that right, my friend?'

'Come. . . now,' said the Storyteller.

'Yes, my husband,' said the Wife. And she let go the hands of the corpse and it swayed away, its arms swinging, like it was looking for another partner. And at the same time the gap toothed man let go the arms of the woman corpse he danced with, and it swayed away, its arms searching. And the two corpses met each other, and their arms wrapped, for a moment, and then they parted, for another moment, and then they swayed together, and parted, and came together, and so on, and so on, like lovers saying goodbye.

'She dances well, your wife,' said the gap toothed man.

'Not from me she learned.'

'Not from no man, nor woman. . . it's in her feet. . . she was born dancing.'

'It must have been that.'

'Some women are born dancing. And some rutting. And some cooking. It's the way of them.'

'And some men are born talking,' said the Wife.

Both the Storyteller and the gap toothed man looked at her, neither sure which one of them she was mocking. And then, then they realised it was the both of them, the both of them that she was mocking. They looked at each other and laughed, the way men come together nervously at the mystery of a woman.

'Oh yes Storyteller. . .' said the gap toothed man, as if to break the silence between them. 'You asked me an hour ago. . . did I follow the Roman. . . and I said to ask me now.' The gap toothed man smiled a gap toothed smile. And in the background the dancers danced. The drums drummed and the jangles jangled. And the corpses swayed in the sound like it was wind.

The Storyteller smiled.

'The question is answered,' he murmured, and led the Wife away, and her hand in his was warm, warmer than his. . . as if he were the corpse, and she was the living.

11

'The road is bad,' said the Wife.
'The road is hard,' said the Storyteller.
'The road is muddy,' said the Wife, 'the horses slip.'
'We lead them by the bridles over boggy paths.'
'My sandals seep with water.'
'The trees drip more water on our heads.'
'We push through the whin, the hedges are overgrown, does no-one care for this road?'
'No-one. Few pass here now.'
'No-one, except the Storyteller, and the daughter of the moon.'
'And the daughter of the moon.'
'And two dogs, one black, one white.'
'The black called Night.'
'And the white called Day.'
'But both of them muddy with grey mud now, both are grey.'
'So we can't tell Night from Day.'
'Nor the dreams of night from the doings of day.'
'They are the same, now.'
'The road through dreams is hard.'
'We pick our way.'
'And at night along the way we pass them, people, sleeping.'
'We move by day along the edge of their dreams, like a man at the hedge of a field, and someone ploughing.'
'They see us out of the side of their eyes, but don't take heed, not too much heed. The ploughing is more important.'
'But they are in our dreams, and we in theirs.'
'Is it the same dream?'
'I don't know.' said the Storyteller, 'I just do not know.' He looked ahead, and he saw a house up there on the lonely road, and smoke from a chimney fighting against the rain to get at the sky. The front of the house glowed red, and sparks of fire arched through the glow, and died in the rain.

The banging he heard was the bang of a hammer on iron.

The dogs reached the house first, and stood, looking. Their fur glowed red from the fire within. Then the Storyteller and the Wife drew up, and stopped their horses.

'I am Daragh the Smith,' said the hammering man at the fire, 'and you are the Storyteller.'

'What else do you know?'

'I only know what the road tells me, and the passers-by on the road.'

'Do you know about dreams, Smith, we talk of dreams, my Wife and I. . .'

'What do you say?'

'The road is hard,' said the Storyteller, 'the road we travel by the day. . .'

'And the road of the night and dreams is harder still,' said the Wife.

'What of it?' said Daragh the Smith, banging the iron with a hammer.

'Nothing, really,' said the Storyteller, 'it's just what we talk about, to shorten the road. What do you make?'

'What do you need?'

'We need to know about our dreams,' said the Wife.

'People on this road,' said the Storyteller, 'they travel the same hard road, from east to west, from west to east.'

'And the question is, do people in their dreams travel the same road?' added the Wife.

'I only know what the road tells me, and the passers-by on the road.'

'And what do you know from them?'

'That they ask the same questions.'

'So people are all the same?'

'Iron is all the same,' said Daragh the Smith, hammering. 'And the hammer is always the same. But this is a shoe for a horse.' He pointed to his anvil. 'And that is a bar for a gate.' He pointed behind him. 'And that is a hinge for a door.' He pointed to one side.

'I understand,' said the Storyteller. 'Now tell me, what do you know of the Romans, do many pass by here?'

'I don't talk of the Romans. . . their leader annoyed me.'

'How?'

'He hexed against me. . . said his god would save the people, from the curses of women and smiths.'

'Not very pleasing to women, either, that hex,' said the Wife.

'Did he say anything rude about Storytellers?' asked the Storyteller.

'No. . . but he probably relied on others' opinions!'

The Storyteller laughed. . . and shook his reins. . . 'We ride on.'

'No time to stop for a drink,' said Daragh the Smith, putting down his hammer.

'No time, no time.'

'There's always time for a drink.'

'For a smith, perhaps,' said the Storyteller coldly, 'but not for me.' They rode on.

'The road is hard,' said the Wife, 'hard and muddy, the horses slip.'

'We lead them by the bridles over boggy paths.'

'My sandals seep with water.'

'The trees drip more water on our heads.'

'We push through the whin, the hedges are overgrown, does no-one care for this road?'

'No-one. Few pass here now.'

'Except the Storyteller!'

'And the daughter of the moon.'

'And two dogs, one black, one white.'

'The black called Night.'

'And the white called Day.'

'This is a poor country,' saaid the Storyteller and then, as if to echo his words, an almost naked child was playing there in the mud beside them, and a ragged man and a ragged woman sheltered by the hedge.

'The roof is off our house,' said the ragged man, 'we had no rent for the chief.'

'And now we have no house,' said the ragged woman.

'What do you do now?'

'We wait.'

'For what?'

'We don't know. . . will you buy the child, it's a healthy child, grow into a fine boy.'

'We have no place for a child on our journey.'

'Will you buy my wife, a healthy woman of this country. She can cook, and sew, and that child there is evidence of her healthy womb. . .'

'I have no place for a woman on the journey.'

'Wll you buy me, I can work, I am strong, I once fought against the Ulstermen and can use a sword, I could guard your horses during the night.'

'Do you not sleep and dream at night?'

'Not if I am guarding horses. And what would I know of dreams.'

'Should a poor man not know more of dreams than one who is rich?' asked the Storyteller. But the ragged man did not understand, and looked at him blankly. So the Storyteller changed the subject. 'You fought against the Ulstermen?'

'Yes.'

'For your Chief?'

'Yes.'

'And now there is peace he takes the roof off your house?'

'He has no need of me now.'

'Does he not know he might need you again?'

'There'll be other fools to fight.'

'There are always chiefs and there are always fools,' said the Wife.

'And always will be,' said the Storyteller, 'we ride on.'

'You will not buy the child,' pleaded the raggedy man, 'just look at that child. . . laugh and dance there, child,'

The small boy laughed, and danced in the rain, his small prick bouncing like it was a string, controlling him, and he a puppet.

'I told you, I have no place for a child on my journey.'

'You will not buy the woman, look at that woman, kneel there, woman.'

The woman knelt on hands and knees, arse in the air, the way a Connacht woman likes to take a man.

'Lift her skirts, your eyes will be well rewarded.'

'I have no need to lift her skirts, no need of a woman on the journey.'

'Watch me,' said the ragged man. He turned, and lifted a rock, a huge rock, and held it above his head.

'See, see how strong I am.'

'I have no need of a strong man. . .'

'Well if you don't buy us we'll have to join the tribe of the saint. . .'

'What is the tribe of the saint,' asked the Wife, her question not to the raggedy man, but to the Storyteller.

'It's a saying they have. . . in these poor parts. . .'

'What does it mean?'

'The chiefs have given a little land to some of the Romans. . . and they've built little churches on them. . . and slaves and outlaws and bastards of the clan go gather there. . . and form a little tribe. . .'

'Oh,' said the Wife, a crinkle of thinking on her muddy forehead. . . 'oh. . . oh we couldn't be having that. . . it's my thinking there's well and enough saints in this country. . . we will buy you so,' she said to the raggedy family, 'all three.' She reached into her saddle and took out coins, three gold coins. And handed them out, one to the child, one to the woman, and one to the ragged man.

'You have made a wise purchase,' said the ragged man, quickly taking the coins from the hands of the child and the woman. 'We'll follow behind your horses.'

'You'll do nothing of the sort,' said the Storyteller. 'You'll take that money, and go pay rent to a chief.'

'Pick a different chief,' said the Wife.' And not a Roman saint either!'

'Pay your rent and plant a field.'

'But when will you come for us?'

'A year. . . or twenty. . .'

'But the child will be grown in twenty years. . . and the wife withered. . . and I'll be weak. . .'

'It's not the laughter of the child that money buys,' said the Storyteller.

'Nor the plumpness of the woman,' said the Wife.

'Nor the strength of the man,' said the Storyteller.

'It's not them that money buys,' said the Storyteller and the Wife, together.

They rode on. And the shadows of trees were the shadows of wars in the Storyteller's mind. And the horses splashed through bloody pools, and the bone at his belt banged at his thigh, searching for flesh.

'WHAT LAKE IS THAT?' asked the Storyteller of the Wife, thinking that on this side of the river it was him with the questions and her with the answers. . . hopefully!

'Cloonfree, I think,' she said, 'yes, Cloonfree.'

'Ah, yes, of course,' he agreed, 'it takes its name from Fraoch.'

'I milked the cow of Fraoch, Fraoch the Black.'

'Not the same Fraoch. . . all these men called Fraoch. . . they and the lake all take their name from the one, from Queen Maeve's Fraoch.'

'I see one day,' said the Wife, suddenly. . . 'oh never mind.'

'What do you see?'

'It won't please you, what I see.'

'I can live with that!'

'Well I see one day when people are not called Fraoch. . . in memory of the great Fraoch. . .'

'Well I can see that too! By the gods is that the best your sight can do!'

'No but I can see them called Patrick. . . after the leader of the Romans. . .'

'You're right, that doesn't please me. . . but I'm probably not surprised.'

⌒•

'IT'S THE LONG straight road to Beal na Builli now,' said Eithne.

'Uphill, the horses plod.'

'There's nothing much to see, or talk about.'

'There's no-one on the road to meet,' said Fidelma.

'They look in on themselves.'

⌒•

'THE ROAD IS HARD.'

'And we have met no-one to answer our questions.'

'We are none the wiser.'

'But slightly poorer. . . you were generous with my money to the ragged family.'

'Isn't that what a good wife is for, to spend her husband's money.'

176

'What good is that for the husband?'

'He doesn't become mean and crotchety.'

'No but he becomes poor instead?'

The Wife laughed. And they rode on in silence for a while and then suddenly, suddenly another voice beside them. 'Ask me your question, Storyteller,' said the woman, the dark woman suddenly met on the road. She pushed a cart. And she wore clothes of a black that shone blacker as she moved. Like it caught the rain sodden dark of the day the way a mirror catches light.

'How do you know I am the Storyteller?'

'People along the road are talking of your passing.'

'They've little to be talking about.'

'Perhaps. . . so. . . ask me the question you asked this girl, this girl dressed as a boy. . . I may have a better answer. She is young. And you'll get no sense from a woman who hasn't suckled babies.'

'Is that so,' said the Wife, sarcastically.

'Well, alright, *is* it the same dream?' said the Storyteller, more to cut across a squabble than seek an answer.

'Yes, the road, and the sleep, and the man ploughing, and the girl who is dressed as a boy, and she leading her horse on the hard road, and the rain on your head and the whin scratching at your legs. . . and the memories and hopes in your mind. . . the memory of a fire and the memory of better times and the fears of worse. . . that is all the same. . .'

'And all a dream?'

'It is all a dream, like the cup of water from the stream is the stream. No matter that some day the stream runs dark, some days light. The cup dipped in the water will always quench your thirst.'

'You speak in riddles.'

The woman laughed, and pushed her cart, but slowly over the difficult ground, it creaked, an old dilapidated cart that had seen many difficult roads in all weathers, it creaked and bounced from rock to rock.

'What have you here, in your cart?' asked the Storyteller.

No reply from her, the woman too busy with the cart, steering the wheels between the rocks. The Storyteller noticed that the fingers she gripped tight on the handles were old fingers, bird's claw fingers, a lifetime older than the fullness of her body, than the skin of her face, and another lifetime older than the gleam of her hair.

'They are clothes.' said the wife, looking into the cart, 'nothing but clothes. . . clothes and garments. . . soaked with blood.'

'Don't touch those clothes,' said the Storyteller.

'As if I was going to,' said the Wife, looking at him, her eyes raised, 'as if!'

'Where do you go with the bloody clothes?' asked the Storyteller.

'To wash them, of course, to wash them in the stream.'

'Whose clothes are those?'

'They are not born, the owners of these clothes. . .'

'But they've all already died?'

'Aye, Storyteller, there's a wisdom in you. . . they've already died. . . this one here is a hundred years from now. . . and this one here. . .'

She poked among the clothes, picking up a corner of a garment, dropping it again. 'This one here a hundred years from then. . . and fifty years. . . and a hundred years more. . . and more. . . and two hundred years from then. . . and another ten. . . and another four hundred years. . . the wearers of all these clothes will be born. . .'

'But they've already died.'

'To be born is to die,' said the woman with the cart, 'isn't that so?'

'But why so bloodily, these ones?' said the Storyteller.

'Are they warriors, soldiers?' said the Wife.

'Many, most, perhaps. But I have all, all sorts of people, here in my cart. I have babies. . . this one. . .' she held up a tiny garment. . . 'This baby, skewered on a soldier's sword, five hundred years from now.' She dropped it back in to the heap. 'And these, soldiers, warriors, by the score, I have heaps of them, heaps! And I have women too. . . this one. . .' She held up a dress. . . 'Raped by rebels, hung from a tree with a rat in her womb. . . oh yes. . . I have them all here. . . this cart would scream if clothes could scream. . . if you die of the evil of man, or if you die of the carelessness of gods, your clothes lie in my cart. . . and so I have all, all sorts. . . all ages. . . I have the old, oh yes, I have a lot of the old. . .' She rummaged in the heap, her arms buried. 'These. . . old people. . . a thousand years and more from now. . .' She held up a swatch of rags.

'What killed them?'

'The hunger,' she replied, dropping the swatch of rags back into the cart, grabbing the handles with her bird's claws hands, and pushing on.

'You tell a story of bad times, woman,' said the Storyteller.

The woman did not speak.

'The road is bad,' said the girl, the Wife, the one they called the daughter of the moon.

The woman did not speak.

'The road is hard,' said the Storyteller.

'The road is muddy,' said the Wife, 'the horses slip.'

'We lead them by the bridles over boggy paths.'

'My sandals seep with water.'

'The trees drip more water on our heads.'

'We push through the whin, the hedges are overgrown, does no-one care for this road?'

'No-one. Few pass here now.'

'Except the Storyteller!'

'And the daughter of the moon.'

'And a woman with a cart of clothes.'

'Bloody clothes.'

'A cart that rattles over stones.'

'And two dogs running at its wheels.'

'One dog black, the other white.'

'The black called Night.'

'And the white called Day.'

'This is a hard road,' said the Storyteller.

'You were unlucky on the road,' the woman spoke at last, 'but it is not me who tells the story, Storyteller, it is written...'

'There is nothing can be done?'

'About?'

'About the future? The now, and the past? About the bad times there in your cart?'

'Nothing,' she said, and the road suddenly softened then, and led away more smooth and more grassy in a slope downwards, and the woman with the cart pushed onwards, drawing away from the Storyteller and his wife who had paused, gathering themselves to mount the horses.

'Wait for us,' he called out after her.

But she didn't, she ignored his call, and walked on faster, and faster, almost in a run.

'That is a strong woman with that cart,' said the Wife.

'If it *is* a woman,' said the Storyteller, watching the retreating figure, now a black shadow in the distant rain. And then the shadow being lost in the curve of the road, like the curve of the road was an edge of a tide, and the land was washing over her.

'Gloomy gloomy gloomy,' said the Wife, watching the empty road, and the place the woman had vanished, 'by the gods she was a gloomy one!'

'But isn't it strange,' said the Storyteller, noticing, 'the light is getting lighter, I think it's going to stop raining.'

'That one would be gloomy, no matter the weather!'

'Yes the sun is going to come out,' said the Storyteller, watching the sky, and the clouds breaking, dispersing, like they were in a hurry to rain on someplace else.

'Yes, definitely, the sun is going to come out.'

'And not before its time,' said the Wife, 'we'll rest awhile.'

～•

THE WIFE LAY on the grass, resting. And the black dog lay beside her, resting. Her hand ran idly through its hair. It was nearly dry. Her eyes were closed. Her sandals were kicked off, and the edge of her tunic drew a line across her knees, and her legs were bare. And the pink prick of the black dog glistened, twitching, touching the edge of her leg, and falling away. Her hand ran idly through its hair. And the pink prick twitched, and stretched along the side of her leg, and lay there, touching. Her hand ran idly down her leg and held it, pressing it against her.

A bee buzzed.

The horses chewed at grass nearby.

The Storyteller looked at the Wife, and the dog's prick in her hand. And he remembered the charcoal burners' woman, and her with the stirring stick in her hand, the way she held it. And he wondered about a woman's hand, and how it was born to squeeze strength into a man. . . or a dog for that matter!

The Storyteller looked at the dog.

And the dog looked at him.

And the Storyteller remembered that morning when the servant came into his room, back in Tara, with the king's message. And he'd stood there looking at the Chief Wife's thigh. Dog, Servant, Storyteller, all males, all on the one side of life. And the females on the other!

That was the way of it!

He looked at the sky, surprised that it was blue. . . and the sun shining, first time for days. It made a peaceful dozy hour of it. He closed his eyes. And the white dog dozed near the horses' feet. And a bird cheeped. And the white dog opened one eye. And looked. And closed the eye again.

A bee buzzed, or was it a fly?

'There are men on horses coming, and men and women walking with them,' said the Wife, her eyes still closed, and her hand still holding the dog's prick against her leg.

'I see nothing.'

'Coming from the west. . . I see them in my mind. . .'

'How far away?'

'Soon. Very soon.'

'Where do they come from?'

'They've come a long way. . .'

'From Cruachan Ai. . . ?'

'Further than that. . . do you see them now?'

The storyteller stood up, and looked. 'Perhaps,' he said.

'Perhaps, what do you mean perhaps?' She stood up beside him, suddenly, leaving the black dog looking up at her, mournfully. 'What do you mean *perhaps*?'

'Over there. Perhaps I see something.'

'Yes. . . of course you do. . . or are you blind. . . will I be spending my life leading a blind man. . . of course you see men on horses. . . and people walking. . .'

'Soldiers?'

'Perhaps.'

'What do you mean *perhaps*?' said the Storyteller.

And she smiled at him. And they waited, watching the group approach.

'I am Chief Coroticus,' said the man on the leading horse, 'who are you?'

The Storyteller looked at him, for a moment, silent. He knew this man, by reputation. A ruffian. Almost a bandit. His head on his shoulders only because he was useful to kings.

'I am the Storyteller of Tara.'

'King Laoghaire is my friend.'

'I'm sure he'll be pleased to hear that,' said the Storyteller.

Coroticus laughed, and swung down off his horse. 'Everyone rest,' he shouted back to his troop. And the four or five other horsemen dismounted too, and drifted together, talking. And the people walking sat down against ditches, waiting.

'I am Coroticus, I buy slaves, I sell slaves. Have you a slave to sell?'

'I have no slaves to sell.'

'Do you want to buy any? Look at them.' He pointed down the line of people on the banks. 'Strong boys. Good looking girls. This is an opportunity for you.'

'I have no need of slaves.'

'Oh alright. That girl there. . . dressed as a boy. . . do you want to sell her?'

'She is a wife to me.'

'Is she a free woman, or a bought wife?'

'She's a bought wife. . .'

'Well you can sell her to me so. . . or do a trade. . . she could be pretty. . . sort of. . . if she washed her face and grew her hair. . . there's a good market for girls like that. . .'

'Where?'

'The Romans like their girls to look like boys. Now I'll tell you what I'll do, Boss. And only because you're the Storyteller. A man of status. I like doing business with nobility. It's the sort of business I run. Now I wouldn't do this for everyone. . .'

'What will you do for me?'

'I'll give you two fine women for her. . . for that skinny one of yours. . . you can take your pick. I'm doing you a favour mind, I must be mad.'

'Your women look a dreary bunch.'

'They have walked far. They're tired. A day's rest and they'll be singing. I bought some of them in the islands. They're the dark ones.'

'I've no real need for a slave.'

'Get away with you. A dark woman like that will keep a man warm. . . and in bed. . . whoooaaa. . .' Coroticus sucked his teeth. 'Know what I mean, Boss. . . sure I dont have to tell you, we're both men of the world.'

'I don't want them.'

'Alright. . . I get it. . . you don't like island girls. . . I admit. . . they're not to everyone's taste. . . and they smell horrible. . . but wait a minute. . .' Coroticus stood up and shouted to his men. . . 'hey, one of you, bring up that Christian one.'

One of the men brought up a woman.

She was neither good looking nor ugly.

If a man met her one day he'd mistake her for her neighbour the next.

She had brown hair.

'Look at that,' said Coroticus. . .

'Look at what?' said the Storyteller.

'That here is a genuine baptised Christian girl. . . and a genuine legal bought slave too. . . lift your skirt woman.'

She didn't.

Her gaze stayed straight ahead, whatever she was seeing was in a private world.

'Oh by the gods,' said Coroticus. . . 'very modest, these Christians.' He walked over, lifted the woman's skirts and pointed at her thigh. 'See that. . . that brand. . .'

'Yes.'

'If you find any Christian girls without that brand. . . don't touch them with a twenty foot pole.'

'Why not?'

Coroticus laughed, and dropped the skirts, and made a cutting motion across his throat. 'Because old Daithi will have your head, that's why! The Romans got to him. . .'

'Got to him. . .'

'Too influential, those Romans. . . if you ask me. . . certain traders. . . not me mind you. . .' Coroticus winked. 'Certain traders were taking away the baptised girls. . . they live in little groups in lonely places. . . to pray. . . easy to collect, if you know what I mean. . . say no more. . . nod is as good as a wink to a blind horse. . . anyway the Romans got none too pleased. . . so they persuaded Daithi to put his foot down. . . and now only Christians with these brands are allowed to be sold. . .'

'Seems reasonable.'

'Thin edge of wedge if you ask me. . . but there you are. . . once a king starts interfering with honest men of business there's no knowing where it will end. . . just giving jobs for lawyers. . . but thats only my opinion. . . she's yours for the price of a cow.'

'A cow? Are you out of your mind?'

'Ah now. . . think of it Boss. . . the thing about these Christians. . . under the skirts they're exactly the same as real women, know what I mean. . . of course you do, say no more. . . plus. . . plus. . . they tend to be educated, clever, suit a man like you.'

'Does an educated man want an educated woman?'

'I don't know. I'm a simple trader. Didn't get to school. Went to the school of life, know what I mean? So. How much do you offer. Name your price, Boss. A man can't buy and sell at the same time.'

'I don't want her,' said the Storyteller, but beginning to think the opposite. An *if* ran through his mind, like a rat in a room, in little starts and stops and dashes. If, if that girl is a baptised Christian, well then she may be able to help, to tell, to give some information about Eithne and Fidelma. . . and about what happened to them. . . and if the Christians were involved. . . they're thick as thieves, these Christians. . . know each other. . . have their own network of gossip. . .

'She could help your wife here. . .' said Coroticus, sensing the Storyteller's dither, 'a great help, with the tasks on the road. . . firewood. . . the horses. . . cooking. . .'

'We're nearly at the end of our journey,' said the Storyteller, sighing inwardly at the salesman's patter. . . that old trick. . . get a man's wife on his side of the bargaining. . . 'Tell you what. . . I'll give you the price of half a cow.' Even if he kept her for a day, he thought, he could pick her mind, and sell her then. Surely get back his money. She wasn't *that* plain. Nice brown hair.

'Are you trying to make me a poor man, take the food out of my children's mouth?'

'Half a cow or nothing.'

'You're a hard man, Storyteller. Gold or coin?'

'I have some Saxon coin.'

'I'll take the gold thanks.'

'The deal is done?'

'The deal is done.'

Coroticus spat into his hand and slapped it into the Storyteller's. The deal was done.

'Now are you sure,' said Coroticus, 'sure you don't want to get rid of that skinny one.' He pointed to the Wife. She looked at him like he was still steaming after dropping from a horse's arse. But she said nothing. 'Sure that skinny one of yours doesn't look like she has any life in her at all. . .'

'She cut a man's throat when she was eighteen,' said the Storyteller, surreptitiously wiping his hand on the side of his tunic.

'Come again?'

'She cut a man's throat when she was eighteen. . . so her father sold her to me. . .'

Coroticus looked at the Storyteller, silently, thoughtfully.

'I'll give you a tip. For nothing. Take it from me, Boss. You wouldn't want to be telling men that about her. . . generally affects the value. . . know what I mean. . . I mean men like to be able to sleep knowing they're going to wake up. . .'

'But I'm not selling her. . . so it doesn't matter. . .'

'And, no offence mind, but I don't really think I'm buying her'. Coroticus shook his head. He looked around. 'Now tell me, Boss, how much do you want for that horse?'

⌒•

THE CHRISTIAN GIRL knelt on the ground, praying.

Coroticus and his band were almost out of sight.

A thrush bashed a snail on a stone and the Storyteller watched.

Bash, bash.

The thrush stopped, and looked at him.

The Storyteller did not move, so the thrush starting bashing again.

Bash, bash.

The thrush stopped, and looked at him.

The Storyteller did not move, so the thrush starting bashing again.

This went on for some time.

The Christian girl prayed in some foreign language, monotonously.

That went on some time too.

Latin, thought the Storyteller, Latin?

Most likely. It was no matter, he wouldn't understand the language even if he did know its name. He watched the thrush. And wondered how that thrush knew there was meat inside that shell.

Experience?

Knowledge?

Passed down from thrush generation to thrush generation. But a thrush does not speak, so how does it teach its young? Is it that the thrush is born with the knowledge in it? Are humans the same way? If a human child was not taught anything, would it know how to get food?

The Christian girl knelt on the ground, praying.

Would a human child know how to pray, if there was no language to teach it praying?

Bash, bash, the clicking noise of the snail shell on the stone.

Is praying as natural to the human child. . . as the need for meat of the snail?

Is it a thing, born in them, like the shape of a hand or a wing?

Bash, click, the shell broke and the thrush pulled a piece of the snail out, and swung it round so more came out of the shell. . . eating pieces and swinging at the same time so that the exposed piece of snail remained the same length.

A cruel world, thought the Storyteller.

Why pray to the God of a cruel world, thought the Storyteller, looking at the praying Christian girl.

'Will I beat her now?' said the Wife.

'Why beat her at all?'

'In Connacht it's the custom to beat a slave as soon as bought.'

'Even if the slave has done nothing wrong?'

'Better to beat before the wrong than after. The slave will be afraid of another beating, and work well.'

'We have no whip.'

'I could use my belt. . . or a branch. . .'

'Your belt. . . or a branch? Are you mad girl. . . I want to sell this slave as soon as possible. . . how can I sell a slave covered in bruises and cuts? What will anyone think? This is a troublesome slave, that's what they'll think. By the Gods, girl, sometimes I think you've no sense.'

'Why buy her, if you're going to sell her so quick?'

'How long does a man buy a harlot for? For as long as he needs her body. I have bought this slave for as long as I need her mind, for as long as it takes to find out about these Christians. . .'

'What's there to know?'

'That's what I want to know. . . but what I want to know right now is. . . how long is she going to pray?'

'She's giving thanks for being delivered from the slave dealer.'

'Bit soon isn't it? We might be going to eat her for all she knows.'

'We could eat her,' said the wife, thoughtfully.

Too thoughtfully, in the Storyteller's opinion.

'So you eat slaves in Connacht, do you?'

'In the old days, my father told me. . .'

'Anluan of Ardikillan. . . the charioteer of Daithi. . .'

'Yes. . . he told me. . . in his father's father's time. . . after a battle. . . they'd eat the brains of the enemy slain. . .'

'I know all that.'

'But only if the enemy had fought well.'

'I know, they thought the strength and bravery would come into them.'

'Well then,' said the Wife, 'if we eat the Christian girl. . . maybe we'll understand her god. . . and how she prays. . . and know all about Eithne and Fidelma. . .'

'How will we cook her?'

'On the fire.'

'She's very big to go on a fire. . . particularly the bad fires you light. By the Gods, is she going to pray all night?'

'She's no bigger than a pig. . . I've cleaned and cooked a pig,' said the Wife.

'Oh enough of this. . . we are *not* eating this slave, so stop being ridiculous. . . I am a civilised Storyteller from Tara, not some savage Connacht warrior of your father's father's father's time. . .'

'They weren't savages.'

'They ate the brains of the slain. . . to me that lacks a certain. . . civilisation?'

'The Connacht kingdom used rule all. . . in Queen Maeve's

time. . . but now we're small. . . and Laoghaire rules, really. . . Laoghaire rules all of Ireland, in reality. . .'

'Laoghaire is my king, I see no harm in that.'

'Maybe Connacht is weak now, because our warriors no longer eat the brains of the slain.'

'Connacht is weak because the people are stupid. . . because they talk to ghosts and witches, and listen to wizards. . . wizards like you. . . oh by the gods, tell that woman to stop praying, I would talk to her.'

The Wife went over and put her hand on the other woman's shoulder, and squeezed to stir her from her prayers. And then she squeezed again to feel the flesh, to find out how much meat there was on her. And feeling the meat on the woman put two sparkles in her eyes, one sparkle in her cold eye, and one sparkle in the cruel.

'Come,' she said gently, ' my husband will talk with you.'

'Talk to me?'

'He wants to know about you, and about the Christians.'

The Wife helped her to her feet. And turned her by the shoulders, gently, pointing her in a certain direction.

Plenty of meat on the shoulders, thought the Wife.

'He's over there, go on, don't keep him waiting.'

The Wife patted the Christian girl on the backside, friendly, hurrying her.

Plenty of meat on the buttocks, thought the Wife, watching her walking ahead. The tip of her tongue ran over her top lip, thoughtfully. The tip of her tongue was red, and wet, and her lip was pink, and dry. And the move of the wet red on the dry pink was like the touch of a dog's prick to a woman's thigh on a sunny afternoon.

⌒•

'THE ROMANS CAME preaching, and baptising, among the people. At first people laughed at their ideas. And then they got angry. There were fights. The Romans blessed the sacred wells with their blessings. The women who went to the wells attacked the Romans. But the headman of the place said that King Daithi ordered the Romans to be left in peace. So the Romans kept preaching.'

'What did they preach?'

'There is one god. He lives in heaven. He sent his son to the world to save everyone. To teach everyone. So that they could be baptised. And when they were baptised they could go to heaven. But some people didn't like this teaching. So they killed the son. They nailed him to a cross. That's why the Romans carry crosses. As a memory for that. The son died. But because he was the son of God he did not stay dead. He came alive again and went to heaven to his father. Because he is his father.'

'What does that mean?'

'No-one knows what that means. Only Patrick knows what that means.'

'Why won't Patrick tell anyone?'

'It's not for him to tell. The meaning will come when a person prays enough. God is the Father. And the Son. And the Spirit.'

'So there are three gods?'

'No, the father and the son and the spirit are all the one.'

'What does that mean?'

'Only Patrick knows what it means. When a person prays enough the meaning will come to them. That's why we must keep praying. And building churches. And baptising people. Because people can't pray properly unless they're baptised. Because the water washes their sins away.'

'What sins?'

'Everyone is born with sins. And they can't pray because of those sins. So they must be baptised.'

'Is it magic?'

'Magic is a sin.'

'Is god's magic a sin, the magic he uses to wash away the sins?'

'God has no sin, god is only good.'

'Who made the world?'

'God made the world.'

'Is the world good.'

'The world is full of sin.'

'So god made the sin?'

'People made the sin. God sent his son to save them from the sin. The only way that people can be saved from sin is by being baptised.'

'Do you know of Eithne and Fidelma?' the Storyteller asked the Christian girl, 'have you heard of them?'

She looked at him, but did not reply.

'Eithne the Fair, and Fidelma the Dark, the Auburn Haired. . . do you know of them?'

She still did not reply.

Her eyes were brown, the colour of a cow's eyes, and as hard to know about her thinking as a cow's.

'Why don't you answer?'

No reply.

'Will I tell my wife to beat you til you speak?'

The Christian girl shrugged. 'I have been beaten often, what matter.'

'Who beat you?'

'My father beat me when I told him I was going to be baptised. He beat me again when I was baptised. And he beat me again when I wouldn't stop praying the Christian prayers. He said he'd have no Christians in his house. Then he sold me to Coroticus. And Coroticus beat me. Then Coroticus brought me to the lawyers to be branded as a slave. And the lawyers beat me because I kicked out when the iron burnt my leg. So what do I care about beatings?'

'Are you a virgin?'

'Yes because Coroticus wanted to sell me to the Picts. And I'd be more valuable this way.'

'What do you know of the Picts?'

'Nothing. . . nothing much. . . they are blue men. . .'

'They're not really blue. . . they paint themselves blue. . .'

'Oh. . .'

'What do you know of Eithne, and Fidelma?' he tried once again.

She did not answer.

⌒•

'I KNOW SHE KNOWS. . . something,' said the Storyteller to the Wife, in the darkness, 'but no matter how I ask, she will not say, she will not talk of Eithne and Fidelma.'

'I'll beat it out of her.'

'You'd be wasting your strength. . . if she doesn't want to say, she won't say.'

'So what'll we do? You've wasted your money. Half the price of a cow! Oh won't your Chief Wife be pleased with you! Oh won't the Quiet One lose her quietness! Oh won't. . .'

'Oh won't you shut up, woman,' he interrupted, 'shut up with that keening. We'll be in Rathcroghan tomorrow. . . we'll sell her there. . . get the money back. . .'

'Might not be so easy. . .'

'Oh we'll do something with her. . . go to sleep. . .'

The Storyteller looked at the stars.

The Wife looked at the moon.

There are patterns in those stars, he thought, in the movement of those stars. Certain druids track them through the years. And then they die, those certain druids. And the stars move on, in patterns.

He reached out his right hand, and felt the bone from Tara, lying there beside him. He reached out his left hand, and felt the leg of the Wife from Tara, lying there beside him. He looked at the stars.

There are patterns in those stars, he thought, in the movement of those stars. They belong to no time. To the stars the bare bone is the same as the fleshy leg. Death is the same as life. Light as dark, and night as day. It's only here, on the earth where things rot, only here that the bone is the bone, and the flesh is the flesh. And only here on the earth where things rot, only here that the flesh clings to the bone.

He closed his eyes, and pulled the darkness over them, like a child going under a blanket. And the Wife stared at the moon. And the night moved across the earth, and the earth spun through the sky of dreams. But these were dreams that were not remembered.

⌒•

'THE STORYTELLER SLEEPS,' said Eithne.

'And the wizard girl beats the Christian girl,' said Fidelma.

'Her back is bare.'

'She beats her back with a cruel branch.'

'She wants to know of us, of Eithne and Fidelma.'

'But the Christian girl will not talk of us.'

'Her breasts and her belly are bare.'

'She beats them with the cruel branch.'

'But the Christian girl will not answer questions.'

'I think the wizard knows, knows she will not answer questions.'

'Of course, of course, she's beating her for the cruelty, not for answers!'

'They are very cruel, those wizards.'

'Very. . . they serve a cruel goddess.'

'Very. . . the Christian girl is very brave.'

'Very. . . and isn't it strange to see. . .'

'To see what?'

'The bravery and the cruelty together.'

'As if they're the one.'

'Maybe they are.'

'Maybe they are.'

⌒·

'WHY ARE SOME dreams not remembered?' said the Storyteller, first thing on waking.

'Perhaps that's best, to be not remembered,' the Wife said, sounding old, and distant.

'How will the day be?' he asked.

'Fine, until the afternoon. . . and then it will rain again.'

'We'd best be going so.' He looked around. 'Where's the Christian girl?'

The Wife looked around. 'I don't know. . .'

'Well go look for her . . . go look in the woods. . . I'll gather things and do the horses.'

He gathered things and did the horses. And the Wife came back from the woods about and said 'I don't know where she is. . . she must have ran away during the night.'

'Ran away?'

'Well she's not here. . . so I suppose she ran away. . .'

'Ran away, ran away.' The Storyteller paced up, and down. . . 'What. . . how. . . oh well. . . I'm at the loss. . . I'm at a loss now. . . how could. . . oh by the gods!'

'You're a rich man.'

'Not that rich. . . oh by the gods. . . ran away. . . how could. . . don't tell tales of this disaster to my Chief Wife. . .'

'What, you would have secrets from her, with me?' said the Wife, that flirty tone, and look, the eyes downcast. That look from a woman doesn't fool any man, but he likes it anyway.

'You know who I love,' said the Storyteller, playing his part, throwing his words into the pot of love. Like vegetables into a stew, he thought, brooding. . . ran away. . . how could they have been so foolish. . . to let the slave run away?

'Will you free me. . .' said the Wife, 'and make me your Chief Wife?'

'I can't afford a divorce.' And at this rate, he thought, what with buying slaves on the road and losing them. . . first the ragged family. . . then the Christian. . . at this rate I won't be able to afford a marriage either!

'You could sell your pigs. . . for the divorce. . . and that field you bought from the widow, you could sell that. . .'

'And then I starve?'

'Laoghaire will help you.'

'Not if I bring no news of his daughters!'

'Your Chief Wife's hair goes grey. . . she dyes it red. . .'

'Yes but at least she has breasts. . . and not the thighs of a boy!'

'Her breasts sag.'

'No danger of that with you!'

'Will you. . . will you free me. . . and make me your Chief Wife?'

'They're only words and lawyers' things. . . what difference does it make. . . what a woman is called. . .'

'A woman likes to be the Chief Wife. . .'

'I know she does. . . but it is not possible for them all. . .'

'Is it possible for me?'

'Do you enjoy talking in circles? We move now, pack up, come on. . . we'll be in Rathcroghan today. . . if we get going. . .'

⌒•

THE WIFE WAS RIGHT.

It was a fine day. And they made good time across the country.

They met a herder driving cattle.

He hoped to get a good price.

They passed through the settlement of Tulach Uisce, and were watched from windows by the daughter of a dying man.

'Who goes there?' said the dying man from his settle bed.

'It is that Storyteller, from Tara, there was news of him on the road.'

'What does he look like?'

'He has a black beard.'

'What does he wear.'

'A leather cloak, and leather leggings on his legs.'

'A rich man.'

'He dresses like a rich man.'

'Who goes with him?'

'That girl, the one who dresses as a boy. . . they call her. . .'

'I know what they call her,' snapped the dying man, interrupting. . . 'they call her the daughter of the moon.'

'Why ask me. . . if you know?'

'I know. . . but I cannot see. . . I am blind. . . and dying. . . what else is out that window?'

'Their dogs, they travel with two dogs. . . a black dog, and a white. . . great battle dogs. . . I would not like to be running from those dogs.'

'What is the weather like?'

'Fine. . . but it looks like rain. . . later. . .'

'What else is happening in Tulach Uisce?'

'Nothing else. . . today.'

'It's a quiet place.'

'A quiet place,' said the daughter, fingering her hair, watching the empty street, and the empty blue sky, and it filling with clouds. Yes, she knew the weathers well. It *did* look like rain, later. And it *would* rain, later. And yes, in the afternoon the rain did come, again, and the wind blew up a little, from the south. And leaves piled against ditches. And loose leaves tumbled over twigs.

And the daughter of the dying man sat in her window and watched.

She thought of the rain on all the countryside around.

She had an itch between her legs. That itch that only a man's prick could scratch. She fiddled her hair in her fingers.

She thought of the rain on all the countryside around.

And out in the country, back along the road, back near the place where the Storyteller and the Wife had stayed, back there in the rain there was a particular gust of the south wind, and it tumbled a particular pile of leaves. And the same particular gust reached out like a hand and tumbled brown hair from the face of the Christian girl, fingers of wind like a mother's fingers, like they were tidying a child.

She lay there, peaceful. Her mouth half open, almost like a smile. And her throat cut, almost like a mouth laughing. And her eyes stared at the sky, wide, open, like she was surprised her god was nowhere to be seen. And ants walked on her body, up and down the hills of her curves, looking for sweetness.

12

Coroticus sat by the road, angry, exhausted. How had it got to this? A dead man lay in front of him. And another dead man over there. How had it got to this? The arm of another man lay in the mud.

'How has it got to this?' he asked, nobody. And nobody answered. Neither people nor spirits nor gods would give him heed. And the only voice in his head was Cunneda, his father, dead, asking him, 'Son, what have you done?'

A one-armed man walked back and forth, still dripping blood, and roaring with the pain. Others tried to tend him, but he howled them away. Clutching his empty shoulder, he rolled in the mud, howling. And the blood from his wound stirred into the puddles, like the mud was meat, oozing.

'How has it got to this,' said Coroticus aloud.

Was it a curse, he wondered. . . that Roman. . . that Roman had cursed him. . .

Was it that?

What had he said?

He was a rebel against Christ.

He was selling baptised women?

Yes it was that, Coroticus decided, definitely that.

The Roman had raised his left hand against him, cursed him. . . yes. . . it was that. . . and all the day was part of the curse. . . and all the other days were there. . . just to lead him into the curse. . . to lead him and lull him. . . yes. . . yes. . . they'd met that Storyteller from Tara. . . and sold a slave to him. . . for a good price. . . a baptised slave.,. . .

Well it seemed to be a good price at the time!

But that was the waking of the curse.

A man can live with a curse for years, unharmed. But it's there in him, waiting to be woken.

The one armed man howled.

Coroticus chopped at the ground with his sword, tiredly.

He thought of the Storyteller, and his sinister wife, yes she was a wizard. And they were the coming of the curse! Yes but the curse was there before the Storyteller. But sleeping. It was the Storyteller was the stirring of the curse.

And now one man lost, thought Coroticus. . . and another dead in the road. . . lost. . . two men lost. . . and few left now to guard the slaves. . . how would he keep them together in the night?

'How has it got to this?' he said aloud.

The curse.

The Roman curse.

They'd sold the baptised woman to that storyteller. And they'd moved on happy. And then later on the road a spot of luck. They met a family. . . a man and a woman and a child. . . a ragged family. . . and talked to them. . . and the ragged family had no chief. . . so Coroticus had decided to take them as slaves. . . it was a strong man. . . and a fair enough woman. . . and a good looking child. . . and who would know the difference if he took them as slaves?

They had no chief.

A family with no chief are outlaws on the road.

He was doing the king a favour, really.

Too many outlaws on the road.

It was a good idea to take them as slaves.

Except for the curse.

The curse made it a very bad idea indeed.

The man was strong alright. Very strong. Too strong. He took a sword from his tunic and he fought like a warrior, a trained warrior. It took five men to overcome him. But he killed one and had the arm of another. And another had a gash on his leg, and would not walk for days.

'How had it come to this?'

Chaos. Out of control.

During the fighting the woman had screamed, continually.

And the boy child had vanished into the whin, and hadn't been seen since.

And after the fighting the woman had continued to scream. And Coroticus in a red fighting rage had hanged her from a tree. That was another loss. More of the curse. She wasn't dead, but nearly, gurgling on the rope, swinging.

Coroticus looked at the legs, above his head, kicking aimlessly around in the air, tiredly.

A waste.

Everything gone wrong.

A curse.

'How had it come to this?'

Coroticus looked at the ground, put his sword across his knees.

What to do now?

One man dead, one man with one arm, one man not walking. And the slaves restless. Oh yes they'd vanish in the night, he knew those slaves, they'd sneak away, one by one. They wouldn't be afraid now. Fear is the only thing that kept control.

He looked at the ground.

A rat. . . a rat was creeping towards the severed arm on the ground. . .

Coroticus watched. . .

His sword hand tightened on his sword.

He waited.

Swung.

And struck.

The head of the rat rolled one way, and the body another.

Coroticus cleaned his sword on grass to his side.

Blood of rat, blood of men, is it the same?

How had it come to this?

A dead man in front of him.

And another dead man over there.

The arm of another man in the mud.

The head of a rat there.

The body of a rat there.

And the legs of a hanged woman kicking in that tree.And the fuzz between her legs the echo of the dead rat. He looked up. The slowly twisting thighs above his head were white, soft and agreeable to a man's eyes, a waste. Her buttocks bounced against branches, and the branches moved in reply, like they were enjoying her.

'How had it come to this?' said Coroticus aloud. 'This. . . this shambles. . .'

'The curse!' said something else, around, a ghost, a voice in the air.

'Was that you?' said Coroticus, shouting at the hanged woman.

But it wasn't. Her face was purple, she was beyond talking. And what was left of her life was seeping into the tree, slowly, the hard branches and the soft flesh knowing, something, together. She would not talk again.

But Coroticus had to believe it was her, because otherwise it was a ghost, hanging in the air.

He stood up.

'You're a dead man now, Coroticus,' said the voice.

He looked around. There was no-one near. Only the hanged woman, swaying above him, beyond talking. And above her in the tree a dark bird, sitting, watching, silently.

'Come out of the air, ghost,' he called, pacing back, and forth, and looking, this way, that, his sword at the ready. 'Come out of the air, I'm not afraid of you.'

'Sure what has a dead man got to fear,' said the voice. And then it laughed. And the laughter washed around Coroticus like a wind. Coming from here, and coming from there, and driving him mad with a red anger. He turned to the swaying woman on the tree. He lashed out with his sword, cutting right through her leg at the foot. The foot fell to the ground. He picked it up with his free hand and threw it at the terrified group of slaves.

'Walk,' he roared, 'walk,'

They stepped back some paces, huddled.

He lashed out with his sword again, cutting through the other foot. He threw it at the slaves. 'Walk, I said, walk.'

They ran away some paces, and stopped, huddled, looking at him.

'I said walk I said walk I said walk,' he screamed, and hacked at the hanging woman's leg. The sword sliced through the flesh and crunched the bone, and the leg fell. He picked it up and, sword in one hand, leg in the other, he ran at the slaves.

They ran.

I am well cursed now, thought Coroticus, when thought came back into his head. I'm a dead man. I'm as dead as my dead father, Cunneda.

He threw the leg after the retreating slaves. It tumbled through the air, a white and fleshy thing, dripping blood drops through the dropping of the rain.

⌒•

THE HORSEMEN CAME out of smoke to meet them.

The Storyteller raised the legbone from Tara in salute. And in reply the leading horseman raised an empty hand in welcome.

The smoke was from a hundred household fires, from more, from many times a hundred times! Clouds of it covered the hills of Cruachan Ai. Wood smoke, it smelt of yew, and the Storyteller had the memory in him of being a child, and the child fiddling at a fire, and how the mother of his mother said 'take care'. Smells have that power, to stir forgotten places in the mind.

The horsemen wore strange clothes, and rode alongside them. Are we prisoners or guests, wondered the Storyteller. No answer. Obviously sent out to meet him, to lead him into Rathcroghan, this was a ragged bunch of guardians, no man wearing the same as the next, some in skins, other leather, other cloth. They were wild haired and wilder eyed, some seemed drunk and probably were. And others in that trance they get from certain mushrooms. Glassy eyed, they smiled, stupidly. And all wore talismans of luck around their necks or pinned to their clothes. These were the soldiers of King Daithi, and the talismans would save them from the enemy.

They hoped!

In vain, well knew the Storyteller, they hoped in vain. If Laoghaire's disciplined armies came, there'd be no battle here. If these were the defenders, Rathcroghan was defenceless.

'Is it an honour they do us,' said the Wife, 'riding alongside of us, or are they afraid?'

'A bit of both, perhaps,' said the Storyteller, 'honour is the child of a mother that's called fear.'

He looked around.

His black dog and his white dog ran alongside.

The rain drenched fields were full of cattle.

He had never seen so many cattle in the one place. . . well, not since the last time he visited Rathcroghan!

They love their cattle here, he knew. And they watch them endlessly. And men walk in the fields in the morning, counting. And in the evening they walk there too, counting, watching. They'd ask a naked woman to get out of the way of their counting!

A gathering up ahead.

The horsemen slowed, and paused, and it was to watch a huge brown bull mount a small brown heifer. The animals were tethered in a pen, and men sat on a wall, watching. And others stood around, watching.

'That is a mighty beast,' said one of the soldiers, approvingly.

'That prick will come out her mouth,' said another.

'That's the way to do it,' said a third.

'Up ya boyo,' said a fourth.

But then with a crash the heifer's knees collapsed and the huge brown bull fell on top of her in a commotion. The wind whoofed out of her and she lay there, looking dead. But, still connected, the bull rutted away at the corpse. . . if it was a corpse. . .

'He's shagging meat,' said the Wife to the Storyteller, shaking her head disapprovingly.

'He'll do what he has to do,' said the Storyteller, vaguely remembering having sex with his other wife, The Quiet One, the one who was good at making bread. But not that great in bed!

'My cow is dead,' suddenly yelled a small man in the group that stood around. 'Your bull has killed my cow.'

'If she can't take the bull she's better on a fire,' said a large man in the group that stood around, 'my bull is the test of a good cow.'

'You'll pay me,' said the small man.

'I'll pay you nothing,' said the large man, 'it's you who'll pay me for waste of my bull's seed.'

'I'll pay you this,' said the small man, taking an axe from his belt and rushing at the other.

The larger man fell back, and stumbled, and the small man swung the axe. But the larger man rolled aside in time, just in time, and the axe buried itself in the ground, inches from his head. He grabbed the small man by the throat. And the two grappled on the ground, rolling and kicking and punching. And the group around shouted encouragement. And the soldiers on the horses joined in.

'By the balls, get his balls.'

'Bite his ear.'

'In the gut, in the gut.'

'Up ya boyo.'

And in the background to the fighting the great brown bull still rutted away at the corpse of the heifer. . . if it was a corpse.

'By the gods,' said the Storyteller, 'what sort of people are these!'

'Connacht people,' said the Wife, proudly, 'my people.'

'I wouldn't be spreading that boast around,' he muttered. Then the soldiers escorting them lost interest in the spectacle and, laughing, spurred their horses on. And the Storyteller and the Wife and the black dog and the white dog rode on among them.

Smoke from many times a hundred fires blanketed the hills. And smoke from hundreds more on the lower slopes drifted up to join that smoke. It rained. And rainy clouds hung over all, like a lid on a smokey pot.

'The air is bad,' said the Storyteller, sniffing, the smell of yew, and damp, and dung, and rotten hay.

'Not that bad,' said the Wife, defensively, as if it was her air, and she was responsible for the quality.

'And would you look at the rubbish,' said the Storyteller, nodding at the side of the road. . . 'have they no pits for their rubbish?'

'A lot of people live here.'

'A lot of very dirty people. . . look at them. . . and that lot. . . what by the gods are they up to?' he pointed towards a group, scavenging, bags on their backs.

Bare legged men and women. Almost naked children.

'They pick for things to sell,' said one of the soldiers alongside.

'It's a poor place,' said the Storyteller.

'Depends how you look at it,' said the soldier, obviously eager to test his skill, his conversational skill, and when better than against a famous Storyteller.

'Explain that to me,' the Storyteller encouraged.

'Well, if this was a poor place, there'd be nothing to pick in the rubbish. But the more to be picked in the rubbish, the richer the place.'

He smiled at the Storyteller, like a man just placed a bet on a sure thing.

The Storyteller paused before he answered.

An almost naked girl child carried firewood past the feet of his horse.

There was mud in her hair.

The black dog sniffed at her female parts.

'Geddup yadog,' snapped the Storyteller, moving him along. 'And so,' he said to the talkative soldier, 'so the richer the place, the more poor rubbish pickers. . . is that what you're saying. . .'

'Well,' said the soldier, carefully, 'it's one way of looking at it. . .'

'So,' said the Storyteller, remorselessly, 'the richer the place, the more poor people?'

'Well,' said the soldier, thinking, 'well. . .' He gave up. 'Oh you're too good with the words for me. . .' And he spurred his horse away.

'You're too hard on that man,' said the wife.

'Hah,' said the Storyteller, 'if a man bangs his head on a rock, is the rock too hard on the man? Or is the man a fool?'

The Wife laughed. But the laughing filled her lungs with smoke and she started coughing. At which the Storyteller laughed. And that filled *his* lungs with smoke so that *he* started coughing. And so it was that, when the soldier said 'we're here,' and stopped, they were both coughing.

'By all the gods,' thought the Storyteller, sliding from his horse, its curvey rump reminding him of his Chief Wife's curvey rump at home. . . and why wasn't he there, where he belonged. . . instead of here. . . where he didn't!

⌣·

'A BODY SWINGS from a tree,' said Eithne.

'It was a woman once,' said Fidelma.

'Another body lies in the mud.'

'It was a man, once. . . and another man lies over there, look. . .'

'Yes, that was another man.'

'And there's an arm. . . it held a sword. . . once.'

'And a foot.'

'It danced, once.'

'And the head of a rat, and the body of a rat.'

'It chewed at the dead, once.'

'Now other rats will come and chew at him.'

'And at the bodies on the ground. . . and the arm. . . and the foot. . .'

'And the body in the tree will dance, a footless dancer at the feast, a one-legged dancer in the wind.'

'For awhile. . . but the weight of the body will break the neck. . . in time. . .'

'And it will fall.'

'And become part of the feast itself.'

'That is the way of dancers,' said Eithne. 'And look now, there's a hag with a handcart, she picks the clothes from the dead.'

'And there,' said Fidelma, 'there's that crone with the evil eye.'

'She comes with a cart to gather the flesh.'

'The flesh of the dead.'

'And the flesh of the living too.'

'It's all the one in her slatted cart.'

'It squirms and squeals like a pig.'

'And the cart moves on, squeaking and creaking on the lonely road. And the crone with the evil eye rides on, her skirts the colour of her horse. She looks neither right nor left, but straight ahead.'

'She follows the living.'

'And the living follow the dead.'

⌒•

A SMALL BOY sat, wide-eyed.

And an old man told him of a foreign land.

It was far in the west.

It was way past where the sun goes down, way past!

It was ruled by a great king, a king so great he was married to the earth itself. Because the earth is a woman, of course. . . and it's a woman who is queen of everything. . . and a man who marries the earth will naturally be king.

'How can that be?' asked the small boy, of the old man, long ago. Long ago when the Storyteller was a small boy, and the old man was an old storyteller, teaching him. 'How can it be?'

'Never mind how it can be,' was the reply, 'it just is!'

'Oh,' said the small boy, in a wonder. He was satisfied with that answer, because he was small. And he listened on.

In this foreign land, in the west, the great king, who had married the earth, lived in a great palace, on a huge mound, and the huge mound was surrounded on all sides for miles by other mounds. And in all those mounds. . .

The old man paused, dramatically.

'What were in all those mounds?' asked the small boy.

'The dead,' came the reply, dramatically.

'Oohhh,' said the small boy, in a wonder.

And the old man continued the story.

The dead were the dead kings, and their wives, and all of their people and their slaves, the dead kings and their wives and their people and their slaves for thousands and thousands of years. Which makes an awful lot of dead people.

'But,' said the old man, and stopped.

'But?' prompted the small boy.

'They were not really dead.'

'Oooohhh,' said the small boy, in a wonder.

'No. . . they were in the Otherworld.'

'The Otherworld?'

'Yes, the Otherworld. Because. . .'

'Because?'

Because this great city, where this great king, who had married the earth, where he lived and ruled. . . he had a hundred wives, five hundred concubines. . .

'I thought he was married to the earth?'

'Don't interrupt, boy.'

This great city was built about the entrance to the Otherworld. And the people in the city were the guardians of the Otherworld, the guards at the gate, the gate between time and time, reality and reality. . .

'I don't understand,' the small boy interrupted.

'You will,' said the old man.

And that story was told to him by the dead storyteller of Tara, long ago when he was a small boy. And now the small boy had given his childhood away to the years, and had hid himself in the body of a grown man, like someone dressing heavily for winter. Now he himself was the Storyteller of Tara. Now he himself was a great man, visiting Rathcroghan, standing outside the great palace of the great king. Oh yes, of course, he had been here before. But each time he'd visited he had felt like a small boy again, remembering the lessons of childhood. And particularly the old man telling him that one day he would understand. And each time he visited he wondered when, when would that day be. . . because he didn't understand!

But that was a secret, in his heart.

A Storyteller must look like he always knows the story.

Because when he slips, or doubts, or pauses, the king will have his head, and will surely find another Storyteller, another story.

A Storyteller must stand tall!

The Storyteller got off his horse, and he clapped his cloak about him, and he stood tall!

The Wife got off her horse, and she smoothed her boy's hair, and she straightened her boy's tunic, and she stood small, beside him.

Ahead of them was an avenue, leading upwards towards gates, an avenue lined by posts that were the height of a man. And all up along the avenue were groups of people, on both sides, waiting, silently, some sitting, some leaning against the posts. There were men, and women, and men and women together, and women alone with children. All waiting to see the king. They seemed to be making no effort to shelter from the drizzley rain. Not that there was any shelter anyhow.

'My name is Erc,' said one of the soldiers who had escorted them in, 'you will come with me.' And so they walked along the avenue, and the people waiting watched them pass, some of them silent, some of them whispering.

'That is the Storyteller of King Laoghaire.'

'He comes to see our king.'

'That boy with him is no page, no boy.'

'That boy is a woman.'

'She is a wife to him, the one they call the daughter of the moon.'

'She is one of our people.'

'I know, I knew her father.'

'I knew her father's cousin.'

'Was he the charioteer?'

'No, the father was the charioteer. . . the cousin was the hangman in the old king's time.'

'Yes, I remember now.'

'They're talking about us,' whispered the Wife to the Storyteller.

'Will that slow our path? Do we have to carry their words in a sack on our back?'

'No but. . .'

'Oh don't fret about their talking. . . worry about those watching ones?' he pointed, and the Wife followed his fingers and saw the skulls that hung from the posts, and the empty sockets of their eyes, and she thought it strange how the eyes of skulls look deeper into a person than the eyes of the living. And how the empty skull knows more.

'Who are all these people anyway?'

'The skulls. . . or the people?'

'Both. . .'

'The skulls. . . oh. . . the dead from old battles. . . sons who rebelled. . . unfaithful wives. . . wizards who failed. . . all sorts of people. . . and the living, they are much the same. . . a farmer in dispute with his chief, come for a judgement. . . widows with children, their husband's brothers haven't done their duty by her. . . all sorts. . . sure haven't you seen the same at Tara?'

'Yes but they don't line up. . . in an avenue of skulls. . .'

'Do you know what it is, wife?'

'What is it, husband?'

'There's them that say you can't move back in time. . . but you can. . . if you move west. . .'

'Are you mocking me. . . and my people?'

'Mock? Do they need me to mock them? Are they not mocking themselves, with their naked children on rubbish dumps?'

The Wife said nothing.

She looked at the ground.

But was about to speak when she was interrupted by Erc, 'Come this way,' he said, and led them through the gates. And around a building. Grass grew from the thatch. He led them alongside another. A hole in the wall had a patch. And a boy child walked past with a line of ducks in his path. And a girl sat on a stone, her fingers picking lichen, and her head nodding. . . she was talking to someone that only she could see.

'She's mad,' said Erc.

'I can see that,' said the Storyteller.

'Wife to a wizard.'

'Oh,' said the Storyteller, 'no wonder she's mad.'

'Oh no,' said Erc, 'she was mad when he married her. . . all the wizards marry one mad wife, the custom here, did you not know that?'

'I didn't, actually,' said the Storyteller.

'Oh yes,' said Erc. . . 'if you have a mad daughter, bring her here, a wizard will marry her.'

'I'll bear it in mind,' said the Storyteller.

'Why do they marry the mad?' said the Wife, to Erc.

'Well,' said Erc, 'a normal man. . .'

'A normal man?' asked the Storyteller.

'A man who is not a wizard, I mean.'

'Oh,' said the Storyteller.

'Well he will marry a fat wife. . . and a thin wife. . . and a quiet wife.'

'Will he?'

'Oh yeah, look around you. . . if he has three wives they'll be all three different. . . you know what it is. . . like with his different wives he's marrying a sort of huge one woman, with all the different types of a woman. . . in the three. . . in one. . . know what I mean?'

'I think so.'

'But your wizards. . . they believe that madness is also another part of the woman. . . so. . . to get a full woman. . . in the one woman that's all the wives, know what I mean. . .'

'I'm right there with you.'

'Well they've got to marry a mad one. . . anyway. . . they all do. . .'

'Do the mad wives have mad children?' asked the Wife.

'Not that you'd notice. . . in fact some of the wives who aren't mad have madder children. . . than the mad ones do, know what I mean. . . we're here. . . go in.'

And, with that, Erc was gone, his job done.

13

'I COME IN PEACE in search of truth,' said the Storyteller.

'This is a peaceful country,' said Daithi, a watchful man with watchful eyes. 'All who come in peace are welcome here.'

'This is a country where peace is kept,' said the wise man at the king's left.

'This is a country where the truth is told,' said the wise man at his right.

Both wise men had grey beards.

Two cats tumbled in a cage.

A naked woman lay asleep on her back in a corner. Her arms by her side held a sword across her belly. The weight of the flat of the sword divided the belly, so that there was one belly below, and another above. The Storyteller noticed that detail, his eyes like fingers on a quill, recording. He also noticed a quiet woman in a red dress, sitting near the king, looking quietly at the visitors. That woman's hair was very short. She was pretty enough. He wondered who she was.

The hall smelt of cooking, old food, and older sweat, and of smoke and damp and the mouldering droppings of animals. It was a poor enough place, for a king. No sign of richness here. The only decoration seemed to be some old brown skulls, watching. And that, the Storyteller noticed, that was more than a lot of the living people around the place were doing! Many of them seemed to be going about their own business, whatever that was. Groups in huddles, bargaining cattle? Who could tell. And over there in the corner some other people eating in a circle, two chickens circling the circle for scraps.

'I bring you the greetings of King Laoghaire, son of Niall, greatest of kings.'

'Yes yes yes,' said Daithi, 'but what does he want?'

'He wants to know the truth,' said the Storyteller, 'the truth about Eithne the Fair and Fidelma the Dark.'

'They are dead,' said King Daithi, shortly.

'That is not good news for my king.'

'Would he prefer a lie?' muttered Daithi, coldly, looking at the Storyteller like he'd come from under a stone. . . and come with the added disadvantage that there was a geis on himself not to crush him!

The Storyteller thought about what to say next.

A small boy opened a small door in the cats' cage.

He popped in a small bird, closed the door again.

The bird fluttered to the roof of the cage.

The cats pulled it down with their claws.

'King Laoghhaire expects the truth,' said the Storyteller, 'the truth from his good friend King Daithi.'

'Well he has it now!' snapped Daithi.

'These were the dearest daughters of Tara, sent here in peace, to study with your druids.'

Daithi nodded his head, sombrely. 'It is not good news, I'll grant you that.' He looked moodily towards the cats' cage. One wing of the bird was in the mouth of one cat, the other in the other.

'It is very bad news indeed,' said the Storyteller. 'Behind me there are armies. gathering. King Laoghaire talks to his sons. And they to the chiefs. And the chiefs gather the warriors. And the warriors are saying goodbye to their wives as we speak.'

'There will be dark times so.' said Daithi, still nodding his head, but not sounding particularly concerned.

He gazed at the cats' cage.

The bird was dead.

The cats chewed at its body.

'How did the daughters of Tara die, and why?' asked the Storyteller.

'At the well of Clebach,' said the wise man who sat at the left of the king.

The naked woman in the corner suddenly woke, sat up, and listened. She had the tattoo of a necklace round her neck. And now she sat with that sword across her knees.

'They went there to bathe,' said the wise man on the left.

'In the early morning,' said the one on the right.

'And there they met the followers of the Roman,' said the man to the left.

'Who ravished them and killed them,' interrupted the one to the right.

'Who told them of their God, who took their souls to him,' contradicted the man to the left.

The king held up a hand to the wise men, silencing them. 'There is some slight disagreement in the tale,' he said to the Storyteller.

'That I see,' said the Storyteller. 'But I come here to learn the truth. King Laoghaire doesn't want to hear of disagreement at the court of Daithi. He has enough disagreement himself in Tara. He wants the truth.'

'I will tell you the truth,' said the wise man to the right.

'Your truth,' muttered the man to the left.

'Let one man speak, one voice, in turn,' said Daithi.

The wise men at each side of him started speaking together.

'By the Gods,' roared Daithi, suddenly standing up, 'my sword,' he roared, 'where is the keeper of my sword?'

'Tetchy,' whispered the Wife to the Storyteller.

The naked woman at the wall stood up, and carried the sword to Daithi, and handed it to him, silently. Then she walked back to the wall again. Her breasts were blue veined bags. They swung to her waist, and her belly hung like an apron, hiding her private parts. And when she noticed the Storyteller watching her she curled her lips in a toothless sneer. And then sat down, and watched King Daithi.

Her head was shaved.

A whorl was tattooed across her skull.

That probably meant something, realised the Storyteller. But what that something was, he did not know. Except that it was strange, and old, very old, and it reached back into the darkness of the past. A fat woman guards the king's sword in that darkness. The king owns all the wealth of the people. All the women. Owns and protects them. And in return the women guard his sword, protecting him. That was the way of it, mused the Storyteller, but this pleasant historical musing was suddenly interrupted by a mad roar from Daithi.

'Now by the gods,' he shouted, waving the sword around his head, 'must I have all your heads before I have sense spoken in this house.' He brought the sword crashing down on a wooden stool beside him. The stool split, and the pieces tumbled, and the small sound of the small tumbling pieces filled the silence.

'Tetchy, very tetchy,' whispered the Wife.

'Shush,' whispered the Storyteller, 'or it's our heads he'll be having.'

'Where are those damn Romans,' roared Daithi, looking around the hall.

'We are here, O King,' came a voice in a foreign accent from behind.

'Well come forward then you skulkers. . . stop lurking there in the back with the riff and the raff of my kingdom.'

He sat down. 'Why do I rule this country?' he sighed, to no-one in particular. And no-one answered.

The cats in the cage started fighting over the last bit of the dead bird.

The keeper of the king's sword chewed on a bone in the corner. She held the bone steady in both hands, both hands unmoving. To tear the meat from the bone she moved her head, back and forth, and sideways. And all the time she watched the king, as if waiting for a sign. The wise men on each side of the king watched him too, as if waiting for advantage. But the quiet woman in the red dress watched the Storyteller, learning.

Two foreign men and a foreign woman came forward. They wore the clothes of foreigners, their tunics to their ankles. And the two men had their hair shaved in the style of the Christian priests. But they were young, quite young indeed, much younger than the wizards and the wise men and the druids of Rathcroghan who sat about the place.

'This,' Daithi waved his hand, vaguely, suddenly tired, 'this is the Storyteller of Tara, he comes from my good friend. . .' He paused, meaningfully, and he examined the roof for a moment. . . 'from my *very* good friend. . . King Laoghaire.'

The two foreign men and the foreign woman nodded.

'And this,' Daithi leaned forward, suddenly cunning. He pointed at the Wife. 'This boy, this page beside the Storyteller. . . this is no page, this is no boy. . . oh no. . . is that not so, woman?'

'That is so, my king.'

'Are you not the one they call the daughter of the moon?'

'I am.'

'Are you not the daughter of Anluan of Ardikillan, my faithful charioteer?'

'I am.'

'Was not your uncle Ir, my father's hangman?'

'He was.'

'Well. . .' Daithi leaned back in his chair. 'One more question then. . . what're you doing in my country?'

'It is *my* country too,' she said, quietly.

Daithi stood up, picked up his sword and roared, 'you whelp I'll have your head. . .'

'She is wife to me,' said the Storyteller, protesting, 'I bought her legally.'

'I am the law here,' roared Daithi. . . 'I'll have your head too. . .' He looked around, like a man hearing voices. 'Where's my stool, to have their heads?' He waved his sword about, erratically.

'You smashed it with your sword, O King,' said the wise man to his left.

'Shall I get another?' asked the wise man to the right.

'Oh . . . oh never mind. . .' Daithi sat again. . . 'well you're lucky, you from Tara. . .'

'I could get another stool,' said the wise man to the left.

'Oh never mind I said,' said Daithi. . .

'Yes, never mind,' whispered the Wife, 'you keep your own counsel!'

Daithi slumped in his chair for a moment, his breathing heavy. He stared at the Wife. 'Your father Anluan was a great charioteer.'

'That is good to hear, my king.'

'And your uncle Ir a better hangman.'

'That too is good to hear, my king.'

'A country can't have a good enough hangman.'

'Very true,' agreed the Wife.

'But you were sent from this country. . . banished. . . for cutting a man's throat. . . tell me. . .' He leaned forward. . . again that cunning. . . 'did you not dance with the wizards as a girl?'

'I did, my king,' she said, and the Storyteller listened, carefully. What did he mean, exactly, dance with the wizards?

'At the Mucklaghs. . .' said Daithi, 'are you not a wizard girl?'

'I am, my king.'

'Hah,' he laughed, 'and the Storyteller married you. . . hah. . . the great Storyteller of Tara. . . you married a wizard girl. . . hah, you fool, hah. . .' He pointed at him, laughing. And he looked a signal to the wise man on his right, and he started laughing. Then he looked a signal to the wizard on the left, and he started laughing. Then he looked generally out into the hall, and all the hangers-on of the place started laughing.

'I know nothing of the magic of this kingdom,' said the Storyteller.

'And you're better off for that,' muttered Daithi, his laughter forgotten in a flash. Then he waved at the waiting foreigners. 'Tell them the story. Of Eithne. And Fidelma.'

'I would know your names,' said the Storyteller to the foreigners.

'I am Bernicius the Bishop,' said the first man.

'I am Hernicius the Bishop,' said the second man.

'I am Nitria the Bishop,' said the third, the woman.

'And we would know *your* names,' said the first.

'I am the Storyteller of Tara,' said the Storyteller.

'And I am his wife, the one they call the daughter of the moon,' said the Wife.

'And those are my dogs,' said the Storyteller.

'But the names?' said the Hernicius the Bishop.

'The white dog is called Day,' said the Storyteller.

'And the black dog is called Night,' said the Wife.

'By all the gods of Rathcroghan,' roared Daithi, 'by my ancestors in the graves. . .' He stopped. And leaned forward. And whispered, ominously. 'Everyone.Get.On.With.It.'

'I will tell the Storyteller what happened,' said Bernicius.

'And I,' said Hernicius.

'And I,' said Nitria.

Daithi sighed, and fingered his sword.

An unstable man, thought the Storyteller. But a weak tree in the strong winds of the times. He bends, this way, that, but does not break.

'Our leader Patrick went at sunrise to the well,' said Bernicius.

'That was the Well of Clebach,' said Hernicius.

'By the side of Rathcroghan,' said Nitria.

'We were not there,' said Hernicius, 'but he was with some other followers. And this is what we heard from them.'

'These clerics sat down by the well,' said Nitria, 'And two daughters of Laoghaire...'

'Who is the Son of Niall,' said Hernicius.

'I know quite well who he is,' interrupted the Storyteller, 'Laoghaire is my king.' Something annoying about hearing Christians tell his story, he felt. Half a chance and they'd grab it for their own!

'Of course, of course you do,' agreed Hernicius, and continued. 'These daughters went early to the well to wash their hands, as was a custom of theirs, and they were Eithne the Fair, and Fidelma, the Dark, sometimes called the Auburn Haired.'

'Only wash their *hands*?' murmured the Wife, but no-one heard her, or if they did, they ignored the question.

'The maidens found beside the well the assembly of the clerics in white garments, with their books before them,' continued Bernicius, 'and they wondered at the shape of the clerics, and thought that they were men of the elves or apparitions.'

'They spoke to Patrick,' said Nitria, 'and asked him "whence are ye, and whence have you come? Are ye of the elves or of the gods?"'

'And Patrick answered,' said Hernicius, 'it were better for you to believe in god than to inquire about our race.'

'And the older of the girls asked him,' said Nitria, 'Who is your god? And where is he? Is he in heaven, or in earth, or under earth, or on earth? Is he in seas or in streams, or in mountains or in glens? Hath he sons and daughters? Is there gold and silver, is there abundance of every good thing in his kingdom? Tell us about him, how he is seen, how he is loved, how he is found? If he is in youth, or if he is in age? If he is everliving, if he is beautiful? If many have fostered his son? If his daughters are dear and beautiful to the men of the world?'

'Yes, that is what she asked him,' agreed Bernicius, and Hernicius nodded his head and said 'then answered holy Patrick, filled with the Holy Spirit, "our god is the god of all things, the god of heaven and earth and sea and river, the god of sun and moon and all the stars, the god of high mountains and lowly valleys, the god over heaven and in heaven and under heaven. He hath a dwelling both in heaven and earth and sea and all that are therein."'

'Yes yes,' said Bernicius, 'that was the answer of holy Patrick.'

'God inspires all things,' continued Hernicius, 'he quickens all things, he surpasses all things, he sustains all things. He kindles the light of the sun and the light of the moon. He made springs in arid land and dry islands in the sea, and stars he appointed to minister to the greater lights.'

'Yes.' said Nitria. 'And He hath a Son coeternal with Himself, and like unto Him. But the Son is not younger than the Father, nor is the Father older than the Son. And the Holy Spirit breathes in them. Father and Son and Holy Spirit are not divided.'

'What in the name of all the gods are they talking about,' whispered the Wife, 'it's gobbleydegook!'

'Shush,' whispered the Storyteller.

'And then he told the girls,' said Hernicius, 'he told them "I desire to unite you to the Son of the Heavenly King, for ye are daughters of a king of earth."'

'And the maidens said. . .' started Bernicius.

'As it were with one mouth and with one heart,' interrupted Nitria, 'they said "how shall we be able to believe in that king? Teach us most diligently that we may see the Lord face to face. Teach us the way, and we will do whatsoever thou shalt say unto us." And Patrick replied to them, "Believe ye that through baptism your mother's sin and your father's is put away from you?"'

'And they answered,' interrupted Bernicius, 'they answered "we believe."'

'And Patrick then asked them,' said Nitria, looking sternly at Bernicius, "Believe ye in repentance after sin?"'

'"We believe" said the girls,' said Hernicius.

'And they were baptized,' said Nitria, looking sternly at Bernicius for his interruption, 'and Patrick blessed a white veil on their heads. And they asked to see Christ, face to face. But Patrick said to them "ye cannot see Christ unless ye first taste of death, and unless ye receive Christ's Body and his Blood."'

'And what did the girls say then?' asked the Storyteller.

'They said "give us the sacrifice that we may be able to see the god",' replied Nitria.

'And what happened then?' asked the Wife.

'Then they received the sacrifice, and fell asleep in death,' said Bernicius.

'And Patrick put them under one mantle in one bed,' said Hernicius.

'And their friends bewailed them greatly,' said Nitria.

'Bewailed them greatly?' said the Wife.

'Yes,' said Nitria.

'That's a funny way of putting it,' said the Wife.

'Well. . .' started Nitria, but she was interrupted by Daithi who suddenly stood, raised his hand. 'That's the story, everybody,' he said, 'like it or leave it.'

'I'm thinking I'll be leaving it,' muttered the Storyteller.

'What's that you say, Storyteller?'

'It's a most interesting story.'

'Yes, isn't it. No doubt my good friend Laoghaire will find it equally so.'

'Oh he will, he will.'

The king moved down from where he sat.

The boy with the cats in the cage stood up.

The shaven headed sword carrier came over, and she silently took the king's sword.

The king walked out.

The sword carrier followed him.

The boy with the cage of cats followed her.

The wizards and wise men followed him.

The girl in the red dress with short hair followed the wizards.

The hangers-on followed the girl.

The Storyteller and the Wife watched, the silent procession leaving.

They looked at each other, and shrugged. And then one of the wise men drifted over, he had held himself back. It was the one who had sat on the king's right when they came in. 'Don't believe a word of it,' he said.

'Well I must admit I was having a certain difficulty anyway,' said the Storyteller.

'What *really* happened?' asked the Wife.

The wise man looked over his shoulder, as if for eavesdroppers. But the hall was empty now apart from they themselves, and apart from the skulls on the walls. And no-one was listening, though the skulls *seemed* to be listening, to the Storyteller's eyes. Just as they had seemed to be laughing when the king was mocking him marrying a wizard girl.

Skulls have that way with them.

They echo the goings-on in a place.

'What really happened,' said the Wise Man... 'I will tell you... what really happened is this...'

The Storyteller and the Wife listened.

The skulls listened.

'The girls went to the well,' said the Wise Man, 'there was a group of Romans there... riff raff... baggage handlers... stable-hands... cooks... accountants... that class of person...'

'And?' said the Storyteller.

'They ravished the girls and drowned them in the well.'

'Why would they do that?' said the Wife.

The Wise Man looked at her, looked at the Storyteller, looked at the Wife again. He shrugged. 'Because that's what they do, that class of riff raff... they have no respect for women... if they feel they won't be caught they will do as they please...'

'Were they caught?'

'Oh yes... Daithi had their innards pulled. Their corpses hang at Cloghannagorp.'

'There,' said the Wife, 'there... I told you!'

'Told me what?' said the Storyteller.

'Told you about pulling innards... for executions... you didn't believe me...'

'Well only in special cases,' said the Wise Man, 'Daithi felt this was a special case.'

'I see,' said the Storyteller, 'but tell me this, Wise Man...'

'Tell you what?'

'Why does Daithi now let the bishops tell their tale?'

'He feels it's a better solution.'

'Solution?'

'Yes there are a lot of Christians in this country now...'

'But you're not among them!'

'I follow the old ways.'

'I see,' said the Storyteller, 'but tell me this... why should I believe you and not the bishops?'

'Because you are a storyteller... and the old ways are part of your story. . .'

'But if what the bishops say is true?'

'Well. . .' The Wise Man looked at him, slantways, cunning. 'Well in that case you'd best be learning to herd cattle. . . because your story and your storytelling will have no purpose. . .'

⌒•

IT WAS STILL RAINING when they came out of the hall of King Daithi.

Not that that surprised the Storyteller, this was a rainy country.

Still raining, and the air still smokey with fires. . . if not smokier!

Nothing much seemed to have changed.

He stood there with the Wife beside him, the two of them watching the back of the Wise Man walking away until it was gone.

The boy with the ducks was still hanging around here, but now some of the ducks were dead. He was busy strangling. The live ones were in a coop, and the dead ones in a heap outside. The Storyteller and the Wife watched him, his methods. The boy reached into the coop, grabbed a duck, twisted its neck like he was squeezing water from a towel, and threw it on the heap of the dead.

'Quack,' said the Wife.

'Quack?' asked the Storyteller.

'Does a duck know which quack is its last?' she asked.

He looked at her, wondering.

'What will we do now?' asked the Wife.

'Go back to the horses, I suppose,' said the Storyteller. 'Everyone seems to have forgotten us.'

'Would you like to buy a duck?' the duck boy asked.

'Buy? A duck?'

'For your meal. . .'

'Am I not getting a meal from the king? Did I come across the country to buy my own dinner?'

'Which duck would you like?' asked the boy, ignoring that.

'I want no duck,' said the Storyteller.

'We may go hungry,' said the Wife.

'Would you pluck the duck?'

'I'll pluck the duck if I'm hungry enough,' she agreed.

'Do you want it live or dead?' said the boy.

'Well I'm not going to eat an alive duck,' said the Storyteller.

'But if we buy it live,' said the Wife, 'and if we are invited for a meal, then we could sell the duck back.'

'True,' said the Storyteller. . . 'and isn't it a pity you weren't being so economical when you bought the ragged family on the road. . . or gave the money to that herdsboy. . .'

'We'll take it live,' said the Wife to the boy, ignoring her husband. She took a coin from her purse. 'Have you a string for its neck?'

The boy tied a string around the neck, and the Storyteller and the Wife walked on, leading the duck.

The mad girl was still sitting on the stone. And she raised her hand as they passed, to halt them. There were six fingers on the hand she raised, the Storyteller noticed, six, not including the thumb. And then two men came along with a pig, and she raised her six fingered hand to halt them, and they did. Then the mad girl spoke.

They all listened.

'There were great kings here. . . in the old days. . . and every year they cleaned the stone of death with blood. . . beyond, at a particular place. . . a place they call Basleac still. . . a warrior was sacrificed. . . and cut into six parts. . . two arms, two legs, his body and his head. . . and the king sent an arm or a leg to each of the four corners, to the fighting men of the north, to the farmers of the south, to the monkey men of the western islands, and to the idle men of the east. . . and that was a message to them. . . and the message said we have warriors to spare.'

'That sort of thing keeps the neighbours quiet,' said the Storyteller.

The mad girl ignored him.

'She's really speaking to the duck,' said the Wife. And she was, her eyes distant, though seeming to be looking towards the duck. And the duck seeming to be looking at her.

'The body was buried in one of the ancestors' mounds,' said the mad girl to the duck, ' and the head was hung in a place of honour in the great hall of the king.'

'A fitting tribute,' said the Storyteller, walking on, the Wife beside him, she leading the duck. And beside them now the two men with the pig. One leading it, the other encouraging it along with a whip to the rear.

'So, I have questions for you good men of Rathcroghan. What are your names, and where go you now with your pig?'

'I am Fruich,' replied the man leading the pig.

'And I am Rucht,' said the man with the whip.

'And where do you go?'

'We go to run her through the Mucklaghs,' they both said together.

'It is an old custom,' said the Wife.

'Yes, I've heard of this,' said the Storyteller, 'and I thought it a custom long forgotten.'

'Not by the wise. . .' said Fruich.

And Rucht nodded his agreement.

'What do you think of this, Wife,' said the Storyteller, 'this running of the pigs?'

'I think it wise.'

The Storyteller nodded. 'I imagine the Romans mightn't have the same idea.'

Fruich spat on the ground.

Rucht spat also, but not on the ground. He misfired his spit and the glob of it landed on the pig's back, rested there a moment. Then slid, slowly, down the flank of the animal.

'So you don't think much of the Romans,' said the Storyteller, watching the travel of the spit. It looked like a slug, sliding.

'They have no respect for the old ways,' said Fruich.

'No respect at all,' agreed Rucht.

The slug that was the spit slid on, along down the side of the dug of the pig.

'And it's well they weren't here in the really old days,' said Fruich. And Rucht laughed.

'Why is that,' asked the Storyteller, 'and why are you laughing?'

'In the old days, the really old days, before my time, before my father's time, and before his father's too, and before. . .'

'Yes,' interrupted the Storyteller, 'I understand. . . very *very* long ago. . .'

The spit dangled from the pig's teat. Like a slug, a slug that might be escaping from a dug full of slugs. The Storyteller watched. a picture in his mind. He saw the woman who guarded Daithi's sword walk across the hall. She had the tattoo of a necklace round her neck. She had dugs like that, sow's dugs.

'In those days they ran the sacrifices with the pigs, and the druids would wait around where the boars were. . . and choose the sacrifices. . .'

'What boars?'

'Well the boars would be waiting for the pigs. . . and the druids would be waiting for the sacrifices.'

'Naturally,' said the Storyteller, trying to remove a picture from his mind. It was of a sow, asleep in the hall of the king, a sword across its knees.

'What of the sows not chosen. . . by the boars?'

'Oh they were sent to the magicians. . . and they'd choose some for sacrifices and ceremonies. . .'

'And the sacrifices?'

'They were sent to the keeper of the cave. . . and chosen for a journey there to the Otherworld. . . the cave would be sealed with boulders until Samhain. . . so they couldn't come back.'

'And what of the sacrifices not chosen?'

'Oh the same, the same. . .' said Fruich. 'They'd go to the wizards.'

'To the cave or the sacrifice,' said Rucht.

'I see,' said the Storyteller, seeing nothing but rain in a place of smoky shacks and poverty, hungry looking children, scrawney looking dogs and cats the colour of dung, looking. They reached a muddy lane, and a parting of their paths. Fruich and Rucht would take this lane, it led them to the Mucklaghs, or so they said in saying goodbye. The Storyteller watched them go. One leading the pig, and the other whipping it along. It didn't want to go. Fruich hauled on its halter. It struggled. Rucht lashed it with the whip. It squealed, but still did not move.

'Hit it harder,' called out the Wife.

Rucht hit it harder.

The pig squealed louder.

'Harder, harder,' called the Wife. The Storyteller watched her, sensed her breathing in the squealing, like it was good clean air.

'Come on,' he said. So they moved on, and as they moved the pig did too, as if their stopping had been its order. It moved away into the rain, calmly. And its haunches going reminded the Storyteller of the hams on his roof at home in Tara, and how they hung there, two by two, like the backsides of three women.

'What think you of all that?' asked the Storyteller of his wife. 'Running pigs through Mucklaghs?'

'I think it the way things are rightly done,' she said.

'What are the Mucklaghs anyway,' he asked. He knew the answer. But not hers, not what she knew.

'They're a pathway in the earth. . . in the old times there was a monstrous sow. . . she was a goddess. . . she carved the path in the earth with her snout. . .'

'Oh, I see,' said the Storyteller. 'Well I'm thinking the Romans wouldn't be liking any of this at all. . . at all at all. . .' said the Storyteller.

The Wife laughed, coldly.

The Storyteller thought of the witch, and how she laughed.

There was a sameness in the two of them.

Were they the same, the witch and the Wife?

He shrugged the thought away.

They were now at the edge of the King's enclosure, and their horses were there, and a young man watched them, and the Storyteller's dogs lay on the ground nearby, watching the young man. He sheltered in the vague shelter of a bent ash tree, the bend of the tree grown pointed away from the wind. And in the fork of the tree there was a ragged windblown nest.

A long time since a chick cheeped there, thought the Storyteller.

'I am your servant,' said the young man, 'I take you to the guest house.'

'Good,' said the Storyteller.

There were two slatterns lolling by the trunk of the ash tree, watching the dogs, and the horses, and the young man.

They chewed on sticks.

Their skirts were too short.

They looked the Storyteller up and down, insolently.

He ignored them.

They looked the Wife up and down, insolently.

'You'll know me the next time,' she said.

'Sure we'd know a slut from Tara anytime,' said one. And the other giggled. And spat a bit of chewed stick onto the ground.

'Ah,' said the Wife, 'is that the way of it.'

She handed the string of the duck to the Storyteller. Then she lept at the slattern's throat, and wrestled her to the ground. The second slattern came to the aid of the first, and the three women rolled around in a heap, arms and legs aflying so that it was hard to see where one woman began and the other ended.

They shrieked and punched and screamed and scratched and squealed.

'By all the gods,' said the Storyteller, handing the string of the duck to the young man. He went over to the rolling heap of women and watched their thrashing thighs. . . for a moment. The squeals coming out of the heap were the squeals of that pig gone down the road. I am Fruich, the Storyteller thought. And I'm Lucht too. And these three fighting women are all squashed into the shape of that one pig, squealing.

By all the gods!

He shook his head. What a world, what a mess! He gazed in at the squealing mass. One young slattern's tit was exposed from the rip of a shirt. . . and it couldn't be denied that all the nice young thighs and that nice young tit were good things to see. . . for a moment!

But only for a moment!

By all the gods!

Isn't the tit of the slattern the same as the tit of the woman poet, he thought. But, not sure of the meaning of that particular thought, he put the matter aside, reached in and grabbed the hair of one girl's head, and pulled her away. She scratched and punched but he managed to drag her over to the young man and said to him 'hold her'. The young man let go of the string of the duck and pinioned the girl. The Storyteller went back to the other two. The duck waddled away, trailing the string from its neck. The Storyteller reached into the remaining wrestling two and grabbed the second slattern. He held her arms from behind. She brought up a heel and kicked him in the testicles. He let her go, but as he let her go she fell forward to the ground. And before she could get up the Wife kicked her in the belly. She doubled up. The Wife kicked her in the backside. She rolled over. The Wife kicked her in the back. The Slattern rolled over again. The Wife stamped her in the chest. The slattern moaned. The Wife took her knife from her belt and the Storyteller, seeing that, hobbled to her quickly and held her wrist. . . so slim and gentle like a child, a naughty child. . . he felt that, loving her. . . then he took the knife from her hand.

'I'll finish her off,' said the Wife, panting.

'You'll do nothing of the sort,' he said.

'Would you have your wife called a slut?'

'Sooner that than have her hanged by Daithi,' he said.

'Daithi wouldn't hang me,' she said.

'Oh would he not? He looks the type of man would hang his mother for a bad mood.'

'Yes but not me. . . he knows what he knows. . .'

'What does he know?'

'Oh no matter. . .' the Wife waved her arm. . . first at the Storyteller, then at the slattern who was creeping away on the ground. 'Never matter. . .'

She looked around.

'Where's the duck?'

14

T̲ʜᴇ ʏᴏᴜɴɢ ᴍᴀɴ brought them to a small hillock, with a small house upon it. Two thorn trees marked the path to the door, more dead than alive, more thorns than leaves on their rickety branches. Between these trees sat an old and leprous man, begging. His skin was silvery, his fingers stumps.

The servant kicked him to his feet, and pushed him away. 'This is the Tullach Oichre,' he said to the Storyteller, 'and you are guests of Daithi here. And I am to be your servant.'

'What sort of servant loses my duck?' asked the wife.

The servant looked helplessly at the Storyteller.

The Storyteller smiled a peacemaker's smile, and said some peacemaker's words. 'There are other ducks, we won't go hungry.'

'Oh fetch me water,' said the Wife then, sounding tired. 'I would wash.'

The servant moved away, and when he was ten paces gone the Wife called after him. He looked over his shoulder, half turned. 'Be sure and you don't lose that bucket on the way back,' she said.

The servant smiled, weakly. The Storyteller laughed, slightly more than the joke warranted, but he calculated he had to do the laughing for two men. 'Would you not be better to go to the woman's well, to wash?' he asked the Wife.

'After hearing about Eithne and Fidelma?' she snorted, 'is it tired of me you are!'

'Oh that. . . I wouldn't worry about that. I don't believe a word of it,' said the Storyteller.

'Of what?'

'Of either story. . . of the wise man or of the Romans. . . particularly them. . . a shifty bunch, those Romans. . . Bernicius. . . Hernicius. . . and Nitria. . . would you say she sleeps between them?'

'It is said that they keep themselves chaste, those Romans.'

'Chaste my foot! I'll bet their pricks find shelter in her harbours!'

'Would you drop your anchor there?'

'Well I'd want to be pretty near the rocks,' said the Storyteller.

And so it was the Wife's turn to laugh. He liked the sound of that, a strangely warm and happy laugh, a sound which made it easy to forget her cold and cruel eyes. And a man would want to forget that, betimes. But other times, of course, he would need to remember.

'Well what do *you* think of the stories?' he asked her.

'Why ask me?'

'You have the sight.'

'It's not that that I see,' she murmured, her expression changing, becoming vague, inattentive. Well, inattentive to him, but very attentive to something else in her mind.

'What do you see?'

The daughter of the moon put her finger to her lips, and closed her eyes, and the Storyteller saw the trance coming over her, and he thought of the veil of a dancing girl, how that hides a woman from a man, but shows her clearer than clear at the same time.

'I see nothing in my mind but the names of men. Muredach,' she said, 'the son of Erc. I see the name of Fergus, they call him Wrymouth, and he is son of Conall. I see Fiachra the harsh, and he is son of Caelbad, and he is king of Dalariada. And I see Crimthann, son of Enna, and he is to be king of Leinster.'

'What else do you see?'

She put her finger to her lips, and was silent.

And then the young servant was back, standing in the door with a bucket of water. She sensed him there, and opened her eyes, and looked, and closed her eyes again. And then, her eyes still closed, she raised her fingers to her throat, and loosened her tunic. And then, her eyes still closed, she unfastened her belt. It slipped down her legs, and lay round her ankles like. . . like something brown and leathery and thin. . . like? The Storyteller wondered, and then remembered the dream he had of the Armorican woman, and how she had stood on snakes. And now the belt around the Wife's ankles on the floor was like a snake. But a pretty dead one, it must be admitted!

The Wife, her eyes still closed, then shrugged her arms out of her tunic, and it fell away from her. And she said 'wash me, my cuts and bruises and my blood.'

The Storyteller and the servant washed her, silently. And she said nothing at all. Except once, 'the water is very cold.' It wasn't a complaint. Just the saying of how it was. And then they dried her, and dressed her in the same tunic, and her eyes had stayed closed all of the while. And when she was dressed she said 'who is Aillill, Aillill Wether?'

And the young man, the servant said 'he is the son of Daithi.'

And the Wife said 'oh, I see,' and opened her eyes, and the veil that was the trance was lifted, and the Storyteller could see her clearly again, but not so clearly as before.

'Is it to starve to death we are?' she asked the servant in a businesslike voice.

'I'll go for food,' he said, and off he went.

They watched him go. And the Storyteller thought of servants, and how content they are, to come, and go.

⁓•

'WOULD YOU BELIEVE the Wise Man, and his story?' the Wife asked.

'Sooner than those bishops anyway,' said the Storyteller.

'Does a man believe what he already believes?' she mused.

'What do you mean by that, girl?'

'I mean, do you *prefer* to believe the Wise Man. . . because it's his story that suits your mind?'

'I prefer to believe what is logical and rational. . .'

'Is the real truth logical and rational. . . or is it magic?'

'Are you trying to riddle words with me girl?'

'Me?' she said, sweetly.

'You.' he said. 'Better you stick to your wifey things, to your visions and your wizardy. . . let me be dealing with the important stuff. . .'

'Important?'

'Well, the answer to the whole matter of Eithne and Fidelma. . . that will surely be pretty important to this country. . . it's my words might save the lives of all these people.'

'Ah,' she said, 'would you pick the words to save the lives, or would you pick the words to save the truth?'

'When I know the truth I'll decide that.'

'What do you mean?'

'If the truth's worth saving, I'll save it. . . otherwise I'll save the lives.'

'You're a hard man, husband.'

'And you are cold and cruel, Wife.'

'We're well matched so.'

'Well matched.'

He paused, thinking. 'Why did you mention Ailill. . . in your vision?'

'Those others I mentioned. . . those names with no faces,' she replied, and paused.

'Yes?' he prompted.

'They will kill him.'

⁓•

'SHEEP,' SAID THE STORYTELLER, 'we dine on sheep?'

'There isn't a pig to be had in all Rathcroghan,' said the servant, tending the pot on the fire. 'It's the time of year. . . they're being run in the Mucklaghs.'

The Storyteller looked over the young man's shoulder, peered in. 'Well I don't like the look of this,' he said. 'No I don't like the look of this at all. Not at all at all at all. What are those grey things, there, floating? Those things there?'

'Roots.'

'Roots,' the Storyteller shook his head, acting out a drama of disbelief. 'Roots, what am I now. . . some grubbing animal of the dark. . . roots? I don't eat *roots*. By the gods. . .' He turned to the Wife. 'And I thought those charcoal burners ate bad food!'

'This is a hungry country,' she replied.

'We had a duck, once,' said the Storyteller, tellingly.

The servant said nothing, he poked at the stew with a stick.

The Wife laughed. Still lying on a settle bed, her hands were behind her head, and one bare ankle was turned over the other. She gazed up into the roof, watching spiders, and their dusty webs, and the oars of a boat that someone had laid across the rafters there. Years ago, by the look of them. Forgotten. Dusty, rotten maybe, but still with the memory of strength in them, and the memory of a glisten of water along them, and the way it runs to the blade and the way it drips as the boat is rowed.

That's what she saw in the dusty oars.

She twiddled her ankles and hummed the tune of the Song of Clothra.

'Do you sing?' said the servant at the stew.

'Uh huh,' she said, breaking into her hum, but humming on.

'Oh she sings,' said the Storyteller, 'and she dances too. . . she has the sight to see like a neladoir. . . she can carve meat like a slaughterman. . . all in all, she is an amazing woman.'

'Aren't I just,' she said, breaking into her hum, and humming on.

'Oh by the gods,' sighed the Storyteller, 'how long would that stew be?'

'An hour,' said the servant, banging at a root with his spoon.

'An hour? An hour?' snapped the Storyteller.

'Sure when the gods made time,' interrupted the Wife, 'they made plenty of it.'

He looked at her, his look trying to convey his opinion on that remark. But, her hands still behind her head, and her eyes still on the ceiling, she didn't notice. The cut of her, he thought, looking at her, lying there, her ankles playing with each other. For a few seconds he saw in them the feet of the slavegirl from Tara, the grubby feet. And he thought of her then for a few seconds, that slavegirl from Tara. Dead now but on her way to Ulster. Where are you now, he called out to the wraith, silently. But he got no answer.

'Time?' he snorted at the Wife, 'what on earth are you talking about? Is it more like a druid you're getting by the minute, with these idiot sayings and meaningless remarks!'

'Ah now,' she said, 'ah now!' And that was the end of it as far as she was concerned.

'Well,' said the Storyteller, 'whatever about the gods making time. . . when they made women and servants they were obviously tired from the making of all the time.'

The Wife laughed, but she was still looking at the roof, and the Storyteller felt a question forming in her mind.

'Why,' she asked, not of him nor of the servant, just to the room, 'why are there oars in the roof here?'

'I have no idea,' said the Storyteller.

'I do,' said the Servant.

He stirred his pot.

'Well,' asked the Storyteller, 'well are you going to tell us?'

'Oh yes. . . well. . . well before I was the servant here in this guesthouse there was another servant. . . he taught me the job. . . he was Flidais of the Gamanrad. . . and he'd had enough. . .'

'Had enough?' said the Storyteller, recognising the feeling!

'Well,' said the Servant, 'enough of working here. . . he was going home to the Crich Airtigh country. . . that's to the west of here. . .'

'Indeed. . . and about the oars?'

'Well as I said. . . Flidais of the Gamanrad taught me the job, how to care for the guests, and that.'

'And the cooking?' asked the Wife, innocently.

'Yes, that too,' agreed the Servant.

'So,' said the Storyteller, 'the Gamanrad eat roots?'

'Oh yes, they'll eat anything, the Gamanrad.'

'Alright,' said the Storyteller, sighing, 'now fascinating as all this is, the diets of the savage tribes, but what about the oars?'

'Oh yes,' said the Servant, 'well when I came here I asked him the same very question. The oars were in the roof then too. And he told me that he himself had asked the same question of the previous servant. . .'

'How speedy came the answer?' muttered the Storyteller.

'Well,' said the Servant, immune to sarcasm or subtlety, 'it seems the story is that in the old days, which would be before the previous servant to me, and before the previous servant to him, and before. . .'

'Yes yes, I get the picture,' said the Storyteller.

'Well those oars were there then. For the use of the guests. Because in those old days it was the custom to bring gifts. . . to the gods. . .'

'Well why the oars?' asked the Wife.

'Because the gods were in the lough. . . Lough Shad they call it, over there. . .' The Servant waved his arm, vaguely to the south. 'And on the shore of the lake a little boat was kept. . . and the guests would come here, get the oars, go down to the lake, and row the boat out into the middle.'

'With the gifts for the gods?' said the Storyteller.

'Yes, they'd drop them in the water. Jewels and precious things.'

'Which is why the lough is called *shad*, a precious place,' murmured the Storyteller.

'Yes,' said the Servant, 'I suppose. Anyway then they'd come back here and put the oars back up in the roof.'

'For the next guests,' said the Wife.

'That was the way of it,' said the Servant, stirring his pot.

The Storyteller looked at the oars, and wondered. Who was the last guest to use those oars, and who was the first not to? And what happened between that last and that first, what happened to change the custom?

The Wife was also looking at the roof, and the Storyteller could see her also wondering. He could feel a question forming in her mind.

'Do spiders have an Otherworld?' she asked.

'Spiders? Otherworld?'

'Yes. . . when they die. . . where do they go?'

'Oh by the gods,' said the Storyteller, standing up and flapping on his cloak, 'spiders. . . otherworld. . . I can't be doing with this nonsense. . . I'm off. . .' He walked to the door. 'I'll be back in an hour,' he said to the Wife. And then, to the Servant, 'will there be wine, with the sheep?'

'Not a drop of wine to be had in Rathcroghan,' said the servant, 'not these days. But I might be able to get beer.'

'Do your best, young man, do your very very best.'

⁓•

THERE ARE MANY STORIES. There are as many stories as people. And they are all as different as different people. But. . . of course. . . the Storyteller calculated as he wandered. . . of course all those different stories are really all the same story.

Look at it this way, he told an imaginary pupil in some corner of his mind. Just imagine ten children playing in the mud. And that's not difficult, here, to imagine that. Because everywhere here was mud, and everywhere raggedy children were playing in it.

So, imagine, these children, ten of them, and them making mud balls, animals, shapes.

Different balls, different animals, different shapes. . . all from the same mud.

The mud is the story! The children are the people! And they come up with ten versions of the same story!

The Storyteller nodded, wisely, yes that'd be a good way to put it to a pupil!

He wandered on. And his black dog and his white dog walked beside him. They didn't have to snarl, the beggars kept their distance from the sheer look of them!

His mind moved on to other calculations. Wondering how. . . how to find out about Eithne and Fidelma.

What did he know?

Not much, to be honest. Except that *something* happened to them.

And that something was a story.

But, told by two different people, that story was two different stories. And neither of those were the truth. No, the truth in this case was obviously many different stories. And in each one of the many there was perhaps one glimmer of truth, and that could be added to the next, and so on, and so on. . .

The Storyteller calculated this as he wandered.

Then the white dog saw a rat, and chased it, but the rat ran under a house, and was lost to the dog. Then the black dog walked ahead, leading the white dog and the Storyteller. He followed, because he might as well as not! It was the direction of his thinking he was interested in, not that of his feet.

To find out, he thought, to find out about Eithne and Fidelma, he would have to talk to many people, not just to the Roman priests and the wizards of Daithi, no, each of those groups had their own story. . . and a man faced with two completely different versions of events should be careful of choosing one.

The black dog led them through houses, down lanes.

The white dog saw a hen, and chased it, but it ran through a door and a woman came out with a waving brush, and roared obscenities.

The storyteller made a friendly gesture in her direction. And she made a very unfriendly one back at him. So he shrugged, and moved on. The black dog was definitely and deliberately leading them now, and it led them to the edge of the rickety houses. And there on some scrubby waste ground was a small bitch dog in heat, and a queue of dogs waiting their turn at her. The queue was orderly, gossipy, good humoured, like soldiers waiting for their pay.

Oh by the gods, thought the Storyteller, my dog has led me to a bitch to shag! Has it come to this! But but but. . . moral of that? Don't be following dogs if you don't want to shag bitches!

'Listen, Night,' he said aloud to the black dog, 'you're far too big for her.' And then he remembered the night and the Wife dancing with the hanged, and her with the black dog called Night, the vision or the dream. Wondering, was it a vision or a dream?

The truth?

A question for these times!

Because there were two truths in this country now. The Christian truth, and the truth of the old ways. And one was a vision, and the other a dream for all the difference it made. And in these circumstances a man's mind was rotting oars in a roof, gathering dust for the want of a boat! But always there, waiting for the water!

The Storyteller shrugged.

Which part of his mind told one truth, which another?

Which part of his mind was like that of a Christian bishop, saying this is the way. . . and which was a Wise Man of the old ways, contradicting?

Oh the which and the where and the why!

He shrugged.

He watched the copulating dogs.

He remembered other copulations.

Himself and the Chief Wife.

Himself and The Quiet One.

Himself and the daughter of the moon.

And then earlier in this day, the farce of the great brown bull and the small brown heifer! He wondered what the upshot of that fight had been, which man had won. . . sometimes a small man will overcome the larger. . . a small man builds cunning in himself as he grows. Or *doesn't* grow, to be more precise!

He walked on, his mind above him in the air, watching. It hovered about an arm's length above his right ear, attached to him, but separate. It saw a storyteller leading a white dog, and a black dog bringing up the rear, reluctantly trailing. And then suddenly there was an old man and an old woman, they were walking the same path. Where the path went, the Storyteller had no idea. And it didn't really matter. He was killing time before his dinner. His sheep dinner! But still, seeing the old couple on the path ahead was a relief, a sign that the path led somewhere. No-one likes to walk an aimless path. And even if the aim of a path is meaningless to a particular man, at least it belongs to someone. And that gives it some sort of meaning!

His mind came down from above and settled in his head.

'It's good to see the rain has stopped,' he said, by way of introduction.

'It'll start again,' said the old man, neither gloomy nor happy about the matter.

'Before dark,' said the old woman.

'That's why we came out now,' said the old man.

'It would have been more convenient later,' said the old woman.

'But we don't like being out in the rain,' said the old man.

Their sentences merged, blended, stitched together by their years, together.

They carried a basket between them, a two handled basket. The old man gripped one handle, and the woman the other. And it swung as they walked. And the Storyteller looked at it, and thought.

Isn't that their life together, swinging between them.

Isn't that the reason they talk as one, a long life between them.

And when one of them dies, and the handle is slipped, won't the basket spill, and the life between them toss on the ground? And when that happens, won't the one that lives on be left with an empty life? The empty creel of an empty life.

And isn't that the way of things?

Emptiness. Loneliness. And death.

'Where do you go, good people?' he asked, cheerfully.

'We go to the cave,' said the old man.

'We bring food for our son,' said the old woman.

'Food and wine,' said the old man.

'Wine?' said the Storyteller, with a perk of interest. 'I hear wine is very hard to get in Rathcroghan. . . these days. . .'

The old man tipped his nose with his finger tip, tapping, nodding. 'It's where you look,' he said. 'And who you ask,' said the woman.

They walked on.

The country opened out, as if once it had been folded. And the folds and the creases and the crumples of it were gentle ups and downs, a generally gentle looking place, of woods that weren't very big, and fields with lots of sheep. Lots and *lots* of sheep. The Storyteller looked at them moodily, and saw them floating in a grey and greasey stew, and sighed. 'So what do you call this place?' he asked.

'Magh Seilig,' said the man.

'Because there is a view for miles,' said the woman.

'And a good view it is too,' agreed the Storyteller. 'I'll walk with you a ways,' he said, and he did. And the old couple told him their story. Or, more exactly, the story of their son, Fiachra, Fiachra the Happy. A warrior, he went to fight in the wars against the Ulstermen. They saw him go in the morning. They saw him kiss a pretty girl, and they wondered who she was, because he hadn't told them of any romance. But then, sons don't. They don't tell their parents until the girl is well wo'ed.

'The same all over,' said the Storyteller, 'they don't want to tell their parents of any failures.'

'Sons,' said the old man, smiling.

'Sons,' said the old woman, smiling.

The weeks went past, and Fiachra the Happy gone to the war.

And then the armies started to return. In groups, and bands. Some with cattle. Some with prisoners. Some with heads, some with wounded. But none with news of Fiachra the Happy.

'He went in the morning,' said the old woman, 'and the sun was shining.'

'Yes do you remember the spears and the shields, and them glinting in the light?'

'Yes, I remember that.'

'And then a wizard came in the moonless dark of the night, a wizard with a limpy leg,' said the old man, 'and he said that he was dead.'

'But he died bravely,' said the old woman.

'At Eamhain Macha,' said the old man.

'And now he is in the Otherworld,' said the old woman.

'And we bring him food and wine,' the old couple said together, 'at this time of year.'

They walked on. Down a warren of lanes, earth banks on each side, not much stone in this country. They passed a cabin, and there was a man carving wood at the door. Nods were exchanged, but no words. And then they were there, at the mouth of a cave. The Storyteller had been there before, as a pilgrimage, as a learning. But at the other times there had been great boulders rolled across the entrance. Now those boulders were rolled to one side, and the darkness of the cavemouth was there.

'They've moved the boulders,' he said.

'At this time of year,' said the old man, 'before Samhain. . . they open the cave. . . to put the sacrifices in. . .'

'Did you not know that,' said the old woman, 'I would have thought a great Storyteller would've known that. . .' There was a twinkle in her eyes for a moment. As if the young woman who had died in her was glancing through a window.

'Of course I know that,' the Storyteller lied. . . 'but I live a long way away. . . don't know the exact details. . . of every happening in this country. . .'

'And wouldn't be expected to,' said the old man, politely.

They placed the basket on the ground, stood back, and looked, thinking, remembering. And the hands that had held the basket now held each other, the fingers moving, slightly. No man would notice those fingers moving, slightly, no man but a Storyteller. He followed the eyes of the old couple, and their remembering. And he saw Fiachra the Happy. A baby in their arms. A little boy. A lad, a youth, a young man. And a warrior with a sword that glinted in the sunlight.

How many, wondered the Storyteller, how many babies and lads and youths and young men, how many have gone to the Otherworld? How many swords are rusty now? How many old people turn from graves, go home, alone? How long will this all go on, the endless wars, the foolishness of men, and the suffering, and the horror of it all. . . how long?

Forever, came the answer from the land beneath his feet. Forever, came the answer from the sky above his head. And the two answers seeped through him, and beat like a truth in his heart.

The old couple looked at the sky for rain, and it wasn't far away. They would go now. He bid them well, and watched them, hand in bony hand.

Flesh clings to the bone.

When they were gone he peered into the cave. The Cave of the Cats they call it, the cave, the cave that is the path that leads to the Otherworld. But the path is not easy. Not easy for the travelling, nor easy for a man's mind. This path leads from life to death, thought the Storyteller, and it leads from death, to life. At Samhain a great cat comes out of here, oh yes, that he knew, and it scours the countryside.

It is a storm of a cat, it flattens any crops that remain unharvested.
It scatters any hay that is left in the open.
It scratches the life out of the old, they will not live the winter.
It softens an old man's prick, he won't have weak children.
Yes, it is a storm of a cat, scouring, cleaning.
It is the brush of a woman that chases a dog from her house. . .
It is. . . it is. . . it is. . . it is whatever it is!

He sat there, thinking on these things, tired in the evening.

And with the thinking and the tiredness he became distracted, and did not see her, coming up on him. A pretty girl, her hair was blonde, she carried flowers of yellow gorse and yellow broom. And the strong yellow of the gorse and the lighter yellow of the broom and the pale blonde of her hair were a haze of the one colour. But her dress was of many different colours, the colours of the feni, and she was obviously the daughter of a rich man. No Rathcroghan slattern she!

'I am Eithne the Fair,' she said, 'you search for me.'

'What do you do here?'

'I wait for my sister. . . she sleeps late. Well, later than I. So I wait for her outside the house. And as I wait I watch the sun rise in the east. And I think of my home there at Tara.'

'But the sun is setting now. . . in the west.'

'No matter,' the girl shrugged.

'What is your sister's name?'

'Fidelma.'

'The Dark, the Auburn Haired,' the Storyteller added.

'How do you know?'

'I knew you as little girls in Tara. Maol and Caplait fostered you.'

'They did. . .' The girl looked into distances.

'You had ribbons in your hair. Dark ribbons in your light hair.'

'I did.' She looked into distances.

'And Fidelma had ribbons in her hair, but they were light, bright, bright ribbons in her dark hair.'

'She did.' Eithne looked into distances, then directly at the Storyteller. 'Did you hear about the darkness?' she asked.

'What darkness?'

'When we died. . .'

'How did you die, I am here to find out how you died?'

The girl shrugged away the question. 'When we died,' she repeated, 'Maol and Caplait were angry. . . and they brought a darkness of three days onto Cruachan Ai. . .'

'Three days. . .'

'And in the dark they conjured up a witch, out of the darkness. . . they did that on the first day. . .'

'And on the second day?'

'On the second day they conjured up seven wizards, for the witch.'

'And on the third day?'

'On the third day they conjured up eight horses, one for the witch, and one each for the seven wizards.'

'And then?'

'And then the light came back. And the witch and her wizards were in the light of the day and the light of the world. And they went to Tara with the news. . .'

'How did you die, I am here to find out how you died?'

'Have you met the Romans?' she said, ignoring the question again. 'Bernicius. . . Hernicius. . . and Nitria. . .'

'I have. . . and a gloomy trio they are too.'

She giggled. But then looked at him, thoughtful. 'They preach to the people. . . they have a Christ. . . the son of their God. . . he died and he was dead for three days. . .'

'They say,' shrugged the Storyteller.

'And when we died, Fidelma and I, when we died there was a darkness over Cruachan Ai for three days. . . is it the same three days?'

'Why do you ask me?'

'You asked me how I died.'

'Is it the same question you answer?'

'Or the same answer that I question?' She giggled again. And was silent, looking around, waiting for her sister. The sun was going down. But for her, the Storyteller knew, for her the sun was coming up.

There was a slip of time between them.

'Where do you go when you leave me?' he asked.

'I go to the Well of Clebach.'

'And what do you do there?'

'I sink down into the waters of the Well of Clebach. And the waters wash away my blood. And I feel the waters cleaning me. And I know I will go clean into the Otherworld. . . but where is my sister, Fidelma?' She looked around, anxious, nervously.

'She will come,' said the Storyteller, 'the sun is not half risen yet.'

He watched the sun go down.

'She is very late,' said Eithne, a little frightened.

'It is early yet,' said the Storyteller, 'there's the whole of the day ahead.'

He watched the last rays of the sun. And he saw them as spears of fire, spears that stabbed the belly of the sky. He remembered the wars against the Ulstermen. And the spears in the bellies of the dead. Dead men, dead women, dead children. Dead men no longer men. Dead women no longer women. Dead children no longer children. Just all the same in death. He remembered that. And the blood that was the colour of sunsets.

He remembered, all that.

And did not want to remember.

What gods make a man remember?

What gods make a man forget?

And where do those gods fight, on what field of battle?

'Very late,' said Eithne, interrupting his thoughts.

'Don't fret, it's early yet,' he said.

'I suppose you're right,' said Eithne, looking around. 'But all the same I wish she was here. . .'

'She will come,' said the Storyteller, 'the sun is not half risen yet.'

He watched it fall, and the darkness fall on the land. On Magh Seilig, on Rathcroghan, and on all of Cruachan Ai. And on all the road he'd travelled, he saw it, darkness, falling. On the bogs, the woods, the hilly places and the low, darkness. On the charcoal burners, and their woman, they shared her sooty flesh, in the darkness, grunting.

Darkness on the land.

Darkness, on beloved Tara far away. On Laoghaire, the greatest of kings. On the Storyteller's house in Tara. On the Chief Wife and her children. On The Quiet One and hers. On the hens. On the pigs. On the apple trees by the path to the widow's field.

Darkness.

On the great river between Connacht and the kingdom of Meath. On that ferryman, asleep. Does he sleep in his boat? Perhaps.

Darkness, on the headman in that house in the village by the river, on his fat and sinister wife. And on Ranait, the slavegirl of Irial. She ran as a wraith in the woods. In the darkness. And in the same darkness sleeping now, all the people who pass through a journey like footsteps, too many for the counting, but the sum of them the journey. That boy, the boy with the cow they had met on the road, sleeping in his herder's hut. A boy like that, that age, he'd dream of a girl like Ranait, in the darkness. And so, the Storyteller thought, the dream and the wraith are one. And I am in the middle, the Storyteller.

Do I make them the one, the dream and the wraith?

Or *are* they the one, already, before the story tells the story?

And if they are the one, already, what then? How many other dreams and wraiths and ghosts and stories wisp together, in this darkness?

How many?

Maybe there is no number.

Maybe it *is* all the one, the dreams and the wraiths and the ghosts and the stories, all the one, like the one darkness over this dark country. All the one. Just as the many roads are all the one. Asail. Cualann, Midluachra. Mor and Dala too, all the great roads of the country. What is a great road but a hacking away of the woods? And what is that but a small man's journey, cut into the land? And what is his journey but the digging of his grave? And what does he see in the end but the clay in his eyes.

In the darkness.

How it falls.

On everyone.

On the Storyteller. On the Wife. On the Neladoir of Slane. On the cailleach with the cart, on the witch they did not burn. . . and on the dream of the witch they did not burn!

Did she come from Rathcroghan at all, that witch, from Daithi, did she come as a messenger? Or was she always in Tara, hidden away? What magic was that, and where was she now, that witch?

A thought came to him. Were the witch and the Wife the one? And was the witch here, in the guest house at Tulach Oichre, hidden away in the Wife?

The Storyteller looked around, as if expecting an answer.

No answer.

His thoughts moved on. And he looked around him again, this time in search of Eithne. And where was she now?

Gone, off into the whispering night.

He looked at his hands, his empty hands.

He could plant a crop, with those hands. Milk a cow and tend a horse. Eat a meal, and turn the pages of a book. He could swing a sword. Hold a woman. But never hold the truth. It slipped through his fingers, like water. But no, not like water. Because water leaves wetness behind, as a sign of its passing. And the truth leaves no sign, of its passing.

The Storyteller shrugged, and he clicked his fingers at his dogs and walked the lanes to the guesthouse at Tullach Oichre. And the lanes in their dark earth banks were like darker tunnels through the night.

Through the night.

The hours had gone away from him, and now it was the very heart of night. The guesthouse was quiet. And lit by the faint glow of a fire, dying. And beside the fire a pot. He lifted the lid. He saw a layer of grease like ice on a winter turlough. It covered whatever was in the pot, but not completely. Through the grease stuck stumps and lumps and bits of things that were dead. Yes, just like the reeds and the tufts and the humps that stick through the ice on a winter turlough. 'Uch,' he said, and closed the lid. He didn't want to know any more about whatever was in that pot!

The Wife was asleep, and the servant boy was asleep. Near her, but not beside her. A servant's distance from a woman. The Storyteller lay down on the other side, a husband's distance from a woman. He looked up into the ceiling, and thought of Eithne, the vision he had met at the cave. And wondered where his hours had gone. Who had stolen them? Had something happened during them, something he did not now remember?

He thought of that. Then his eyes got better in the dark and he noticed those oars that were left in the rafters. The dusty oars. And they reminded him of the river, and the ferry, and the Wife singing the Song of Clothra.

And he heard it in his mind as he fell asleep, thinking.

Thinking about how on the river she had become the song, as she sang.

And how on the river the song became the river.

So that she was the river, flowing.

Between the kingdom of Meath and the kingdom of Connacht.

Between the known, the unknown.

Between the dark, and the light.

She was the river.

How much to cross that river, Ferryman?

Free, free to the Storyteller.

And no charge at all for the mad.

⌒·

'I MET HIM at the cave,' said Eithne to Fidelma. 'I thought you were lost, and I was worried, wandering round, looking for you.'

'What was he doing at the cave?'

'Walking, talking to an old couple. . . thinking. . . you know the way a person does.'

'And now he sleeps. . . with the Wife, and the servant in the guest house at Tullach Oichre.'

'The Wife sleeps in the middle.'

'See how they creep closer to her. . . in their sleep.'

'As if she draws them in.'

'But she sleeps too. How is it she draws them in?'

'Why ask me? What would I know of lying with a man... with *one* man, let alone two!'

'As much as I,' said Fidelma, 'as much as I!'

⌒•

THE STORYTELLER DREAMED of holding the Wife, from the one side, and the servant holding her from the other. And their hands wrapped round her, sharing her body. And their hands doing little deals, unspoken negotiations, you hold her here, I like this bit. He dreamed of that.

Or was it a dream?

No matter.

He would call it a dream in the morning.

And then the page of the dream, the page of the dream that might not have been a dream, he saw it turn, and change. And now he was Bernicius. But also Hernicius! And he was both at the same time! And Nitria lay between his two selves on the bed. Her front faced Bernicius, and her back was to Hernicius. And at a secret signal between them, the two selves plunged their pricks into her passages. And each prick could feel the other through a thin layer of flesh. They poked about, to get their bearings. Then they thrusted in a rhythm, so that the front prick was moving in as the back moved out, and the back moved in as the front retreated.

She moaned.

It was painful for her.

They adjusted their rhythm to the moans.

Not to ease them, no, but to make the most of them.

She moaned some more, and her body twisted. The curve of her body was like the hard bit of a harp, and the strings of the harp was the pain, and the moans was the music. And there was a tune there, very familiar, somewhere heard before, but not remembered where.

The woman moaned, and gasped, and every so often gave a little screech.

But that wasn't enough.

The tune needed more music.

So they reached about her body, grabbing, twisting limbs, and getting grips of flesh. She screeched, she screamed, she struggled. The pain was too much for her now, but not for them. They adjusted their rhythm, moving as one now, in and out, in and out together, opening, stretching the thin flesh between her passages. So that soon it was as if there was only one passage, and one prick pounding.

She screamed.

And the Storyteller turned in his sleep, and as he turned the page of his dream turned too. And now he was somewhere else entirely. Now he was watching, and listening, and nothing of the first page of the dream remained but the screaming and the screeching, but now it was the screeching of cats, the howling of cats in a darkness.

He squinted his eyes to see, and the skin around his eyes stretched like a woman's flesh will stretch to take two men. And he saw. The cats were on poles, spears, spears stuck in the ground by their blades, the cats impaled on the blunt ends, screeching, howling. . . except for some that were dead. Their heads lolled. Blood seeped from their arses round the thickness of the spears. And trickled down, but didn't quite reach the ground. There wasn't enough blood, or the spears were too tight in their holes, whatever reason!

The screeching cats on the poles were ranged around the entrance to the cave.

The Cave of Cats.

The entrance to the Otherworld.

But not an easy way to journey.

The boulders had been rolled back. And a group of wizards waited. And among them the Storyteller saw the Witch. . . she held a burning brand. . . and the light of it glowed her face, and she looked ahead at the entrance of the cave.

This was Samhain now, he knew.

He watched the cave.

And then he saw an eye, looking out. And it glowing in the light of the burning brands the wizards carried.

A cruel eye.

And then he saw another eye, looking out. And it glowing in the light of the burning brands the wizards carried.

A cold eye.

A cruel eye and a cold eye of some large animal.

Then a huge cat suddenly, half cat, half what, it bounded out. . . half cat, half woman, half what. . . it paced around, snarling, spitting. . . the wizards held their burning brands at it, holding it away. . . it bounded, and lept, and looked for an opening. . . but the wizards held firm, and then held it away. . .

It howled.

The cats on the spears howled.

And somewhere over the country there was another howl, like a mate, waiting.

And then other howls, like all the cats of Cruachan Ai were howling.

And then there was silence. And the great cat from the cave bounded away over the countryside, and was gone.

Half cat. . . half woman. . . half what?

The Storyteller watched the wizards walk to the spears. And the cats that weren't already dead they killed with knives, hacking them, slicing them, slowly, squeezing the last squeal out of them. And the last squeal from the last cat was a moan.

And the page of the dream turned.

And the Storyteller woke.

And the moan was the Wife beside him in the bed, moaning, turning, twisting in her dreams. What were her dreams? He touched her, calming, and she sighed, like she'd been loved.

15

It wasn't the rain on the roof that woke him in the morning. It was the rain dripping from the roof on to his head.

He moved slightly. . . but the drip seemed to follow him. Not a great drip, no flood this, he wasn't in danger of drowning. But nonetheless it was a slow and steady drip. And, in the way of drips, the slower the drip the more irritating. The wait between drips, that is the bad time. Not the actual drip itself. But the wait!

He turned his head to one side.

The Wife was there, a wife's distance away.

No drip bothering her.

He turned his head to the other side.

The Servant was there, a servant's distance away.

No drip bothering him.

Both wife and servant fast asleep. He listened to their breathing. He watched the grey light of another grey day coming under the door, and down the chimney too. A circle of pale light lay on the grey ashes of the dead fire, like a watery sun in a wintry sky. And that, through the door and down the chimney, that was all the light there was. The guest house at Tullach Oichre didn't stretch to a window!

He waited.

For what, he did not know.

Maybe a messenger would come. . . maybe not.

He remembered the messenger who had come at Tara, how many days ago was that? Three. . . or was it four or five? Whatever. A messenger *had* come at Tara. And he had been lying in bed with his Chief Wife. And the messenger had stood there and had spoken, all the while watching the Chief Wife's leg.

The Storyteller thought of the Chief Wife's legs. The bangles on her ankles glinting. And the bangles above her knees glinting too. That woman, he realised, that woman has the best thighs in Tara!

Or, perhaps to be more precise, the best thighs in Tara that he was likely to get his hands on!

He sighed.

That was all three or four or five days ago.

Or was it?

Was this all a dream?

Was he still in bed in Tara?

How could he know?

The fact that he was obviously here, with another wife, and another young man, well. . . that might just be the doings of some witch. Some magic, to confuse him. A man can never be sure. A wife, a bed, a servant, a dream or not a dream. He sighed. All a man can be sure of is that there's a pattern in these things. As if life is a tree. And every day and every year it grows anew. The same, but different.

Something like that anyway!

Though maybe the other way around.

Because every spring we see the tree the same. . . but it is different.

Whilst every day we see the life as different. . . but it is the same.

Who sets that pattern?

What god is that?

And where does that god live? In a palace, or a cave?

The Storyteller shrugged.

One thing for sure, that god wouldn't live in a damp guest house in Tullach Oichre!

He climbed to his feet.

His prick and balls were sore. That slattern girl, he remembered, she kicked me. . . a place of slattern girls, this Rathcroghan. . . and louts and layabouts. . . and mad women married to wizards, and them talking memories and prophecies to ducks!

He rubbed his prick and balls, putting them back into their right hanging.

He remembered the dream. If it was a dream! Did himself and the servant boy shag the Wife in the night. . . one to each passage. . . was that the way of it?

Hard to tell, now.

No-one would speak of it anyway, even if it was there to tell.

Oh well.

He mooched around, deliberately getting louder in his mooching. To wake someone else is always a good idea on an aimless morning. He succeeded, and the Wife and the Servant woke. And the Wife lay there grumbling, because she was a wife, and the servant got sharply to his feet, because he was a servant. The Storyteller looked at him carefully. But there was no hint or suggestion between them that they had shared the passages of the Wife in the night.

Not that that put any certainty on the matter!

'What would be the plans for breakfast?' he asked, casually.

'I'd be thinking to heat up the leftovers of the stew,' said the servant.

'For me, or the dogs?' said the Storyteller.

'Sure there'll be enough there for the all of us,' said the servant, immune to sarcasm. This lad, thought the Storyteller, is either very stupid or very clever. And the evidence for the first explanation was mounting by the minute.

'What about eggs?' asked the Storyteller.

'Eggs?'

'Yes. . . round things. . . they come out of a hen's passage. . . a hen's *female* passage,' he emphasised.

'Ooohhh. . . hard to get an egg in Rathcroghan,' said the servant, solemnly.

Hmmmnn, thought the Storyteller, his carefully cunning mention of the *female passage* didn't seem to have any effect on the lad. Hmmmnnn, he thought, again, not sure what conclusions could be drawn from the blankness of the servant. Sometimes with certain people dumbness is not a sign of anything but dumbness.

'Yesterday,' he said, 'yesterday I did see a hen. . . and where there's hens there's eggs. . .'

'Or *duck* eggs would do,' said the Wife, stirring herself up. '*Duck* eggs are nice. . . bigger than hen's eggs. . . stronger taste. . . which do you prefer?'

'We have neither,' he reminded her, watching her, was she limping? Does a woman who has been rightly shagged in both passages limp like that?

'What're you stareing at me for?'

'I thought you were limping.'

'My sore ankle has come back.'

'So much for the magical cure! How did you get that sore ankle anyway?'

'I turned myself into a hare. . . to get the milk from Fraoch's cow. . .'

'Fraoch the Black?'

'The very man. . . and coming back I got caught in a trap. . . but a boy released me from the trap. . .'

'You were very lucky so.'

'You don't believe me?'

' 'Course I believe you. . . I believe everything. . . tell you what. . . why don't you turn yourself into a hare now and I can eat you. . .' He turned to the servant. 'Can you skin a hare?'

'I suppose it's much like a rabbit. . . but I wouldn't be eating a hare. . .'

'Why not lad?'

'They're witches.'

'Aye,' said the Storyteller, thinking, 'aye.' And then, for some reason to do with the mysterious working of the mind, he then remembered the boy back in Tara who couldn't kill a bird because his name was Conor. Geiseanna, superstitions! Fragments of old beliefs, forgotten ways.

He nodded his head.

All that's left is pieces now, the gloomy thought nodded his head in a gloomy way, pieces, of some great truth that no-one remembers what it was like when it was whole. Or *was* it ever whole? Or is it *becoming* whole? Do we live in the fragments of the past, or of the future?

The Storyteller stopped nodding, shrugged instead.

Whatever the truth, the path we walk in life is stubbled with fragments anyway! Fragments, dusty oars in leaky roofs! Sure what're beliefs but dusty oars in leaky roofs. In the house of a man who has no boat!

Now, more importantly, the Wife, and that question?

Was she limping because she'd been rightly shagged in both passages?

Or was she limping because she'd turned herself into a hare and got caught in a trap?

All things considered, the first seemed slightly more likely.

But then, maybe there were other things that had not been considered!

The questions were similar in relation to Eithne and Fidelma.

Had the Romans killed them, in a lustful attack?

Or had they died peacefully to see the Roman God?

All things considered, the first seemed more likely.

But then, maybe there were other things that had not been considered!

'Aye,' said the Storyteller, thinking another thought, 'aye.'

Was the similarity so similar? If the Wife *had* been shagged in both passages, was this the same as a lustful attack on Eithne and Fidelma? And was her turning herself into a hare the same as dieing to go to see the Roman God?

Might not these two things cross over... might not the shagging be the same as going to that heaven place the Romans had... and might not the lustful attack be the same as the turning to the hare?

Oh, too early in the morning for all that... he shrugged all thoughts about anything away. Because those are the things that a man needs a good breakfast inside himself to consider. A good breakfast or a few jugs of beer! 'By the gods,' he shouted, 'will.someone.do.something.about.getting.some.food.in.this.place?'

'I'll look for eggs,' the servant said, and hurried out.

'And milk,' the Wife called after him.

'This is an awful place,' said the Storyteller, 'I wish I was at home.'

'With your wives and your children.'

'Yes.'

'And your pigs in the widow's field.'

'Yes.'

'And the hams hanging up in your ceiling.'

'Yes, six hams, like three women's backsides.'

'And your herring hanging there too.'

'Yes, too many for the counting.'

'And your barrels of beer and your skins of wine.'

'Don't touch my wine.'

'And your bones and your spells and your curses and your stories.'

'Yes.'

'And me.'

'And you.'

He reached out, and touched her fingers. And their fingers moved together. And he was minded of the old, that old couple at the cave, and how their fingers moved together when they held their hands. And how he had thought that such a movement comes from a long life lived together. In this moment now he knew he was wrong, or partly wrong. Because that touching of hands reaches into the future, just as it clings to the past. Fragments, moments. Coming together into a thing called day, or night. Light, or darkness. Life, or death. The fragments and the moments are always the same. Like the iron in the forge of the smith, it is always the same, but can make whatever is needed. It's who does the hammering decides. . . who *does* the hammering?

⌒•

THE SERVANT RETURNED with eggs, and milk, and bread, and some pretty bad news.

Bernicius, Hernicius, and their sister Nitria were outside the door!

The Storyteller listened, none too happily, to this bad news. What was worse, they wanted to see him, to take him to Duma Seilig, to meet someone important.

'Where is Duma Seilig?' he asked.

'Not many miles. . . they have a church there.'

'Miles. . . miles. . . I haven't had my breakfast yet. . . go tell them to wait. . .'

The servant went out. There was a mutter of voices. The servant came back in.

'They're not particularly happy,' he reported.

'Well who would be, in this weather?' said the Storyteller.

'I mean about the wait,' the servant stooped to the fire.

'Oh I know what you mean,' the Storyteller murmured. 'Well we could send them out that stew. . . cheer them up. . .'

'I don't think they eat meat,' the servant reported, straightfaced.

'Hmmmnn,' murmured the Storyteller, wondering. Whatever about anything else, he decided, this servant has absolutely no sense of humour. Takes everything literally. Only laughs when a man sends out strong joke-making signals!. . . 'Tell me,' he asked the kneeling servant, 'Tell me, where do you come from?'

'Oh Cruachan Ai. . . a place called Tulach Uisce. . . nearby here. . .'
'Were you born there?'
'No, my parents and me were captured in the wars, and brought as slaves to Tulach Uisce. . . a man called Nar, he had us there.'
'Was he a good man?' the Storyteller watched the fire take hold. And that was something new he'd learned. . . a sense of humour wasn't necessary to have a way with fires. A way with women, yes, of course, everyone knew that. Women like a man who makes them laugh. Perhaps because that way they don't have to take sex too seriously?
Perhaps.
'Oh,' said the servant, 'Nar was a good man. A very good man. When my parents were old he gave them a plot of land. And no festival time of year came round without a chicken in a basket at the door.'
'So they'd no thought of going back. . .,' said the Storyteller, thinking that Nar and his chicken would be well welcome right at the moment, 'they'd no thought of going back to where they were captured. . . where *were* they captured anyway?'
'In Ulster.'
'Oh, so you're an Ulsterman?' said the Storyteller, realising the explanation for the servant's sense of humour!
'Oh no, I'm from Tulach Uisce.'
'But but. . . but you and your parents and their parents too I suppose were all of Ulster. . .'
'So?'
'So if I take a duck egg and put it in with the hens, what will hatch?'
'A duck, of course. . .'
'So,' said the Storyteller, thinking wearily of more pointless argument, 'so. . .'
The Wife interrupted.
'Oh leave the lad alone,' she said, 'sure isn't it enough for him to be cooking eggs without riddling words with you.'
'A good conversation is food for the brain,' said the Storyteller.
'My father was good with the conversation,' said the servant, 'he had many stories.'
'Was he indeed. . . what story do you remember?'

'Oh I don't remember many, I was very young. How do you like your eggs done?'

'No matter, just done as far away as possible from that stew.'

'Though I do remember about Macha. . . she was the king's wife. . . in Ulster. . .'

'She was indeed. . . what do you remember about her?'

'She put a curse on the men of Ulster. . .'

'Oh she did indeed. . . wasn't the first to curse that lot. . . and probably won't be the last!'

'She was a horse.'

'What?' the Storyteller spluttered, 'a horse? She was in her arse!'

'Oh yes she was a horse,' the servant was quite positive.

'She was *not* a horse. . . the story's addled in your mind. . . hopefully the eggs are not going the same way!'

'That egg looks fine,' said the Wife.

'Well I hope you're watching,' he said to her, 'a wife who can cook well is a very useful person. And now that you're getting older you'd want to be learning that sort of thing. A woman has a time for rutting and a time for cooking, and many's a bad marriage has confused those two times.'

'Sure haven't you the Quiet One,' said the Wife, 'doesn't she cook for you?'

'Bread, she cooks bread. . . not very good at anything else.'

'They say that about women. . .' said the servant.

'What do *they* say about women?' said the Wife, in a flirty way, 'what do you know about women.'

'Oh,' he said, solemnly, 'a bit.'

'Well what *do* they say,' said the Storyteller, 'about them? Is this something they say in Tulach Uisce, because if so I'll be wanting to know! Tulach Uisce, the centre of civilisation. . . the Rome of Connacht! Yes, I'll be wanting the wisdom of Tulach Uisce to add to my knowledge!'

'They say women who can cook bread aren't very good at cooking other things,' said the servant, deaf to sarcasm.

'Ah don't be ridiculous,' said the Wife, 'bet it was a man said that!'

'Oh no,' said the Storyteller, his mouth now full of egg, 'not ridiculous at all. You know what they say. Horses for courses!'

'A woman is not a horse,' said the Wife.

'Unless she's the queen of Ulster,' said the Storyteller.

The wife laughed.

The Storyteller laughed.

The servant looked at them blankly.

～·

BERNICIUS, HERNICIUS AND NITRIA had made themselves a little covered place, a tent, to shelter from the rain.

But they were far from happy campers!

Moodily, they watched the Storyteller come out the door of the guest house.

He saw them, grinned, and slapped his belly with both open hands, a man with a good breakfast inside himself. He noticed the position of the tent, slung over the half dead thorn trees at the entrance, precisely in the place where the leprous beggar had sat the day before. One day a beggar, he thought, and the next three Christian bishops. And the same sodden sods of earth beneath their arses. What does the earth know of the difference of an arse? Sure isn't it only waiting for the arse to become earth itself!

Of course it is.

The thought added new cheer to the cheerfulness of a man with a good breakfast inside of himself.

'So, friends,' he said.

Saying nothing in reply, they stood. And wrapped their tent into a roll.

Bernicius slung it over the back of a horse.

Or, perhaps, the Storyteller pondered, perhaps that was Hernicius. They were very similar. Peas from pods. Clean cut young men. To them the truth was soap, and they washed with it in the morning. Intense, they dressed the same. And they both had that silly Christian haircut.

Nitria was different.

Not *very* different, it must be said, but recognisably a woman. And she didn't have that silly haircut. She had *another* silly haircut. Cut very short, in a circular fashion, a fringe across her forehead and over her ears. Rather like a child whose mother is worried about lice.

'Raining again, I see,' said the Storyteller, in jovial tones.

'The blessings of God on you,' said Bernicius, or Hernicius.

Nitria smiled, like she was seeing a vision.

Well, thought the Storyteller, well you weren't smiling like that when we were sweeping your chimneys in the dream. . . if it was a dream. . . hoh no, that was a different Nitria entirely!

'Where are my horses?' said the Storyteller, looking about, 'my dogs?'

'He's gone for them,' said the Wife.

'He?'

'The servant.'

'Well why hasn't he got them waiting?'

'Because he was cooking the breakfast.'

'You'd think Daithi would give us two servants. . . one for the food, the other for the horses. . .'

'I think he's making a point,' said the Wife.

'No doubt, no doubt. . . putting us in this falling down guest-house . . .'

'Sure his own halls are falling down.'

'True, true. . . but anyway . . . old Daithi wants us to know that he's not beholden to any Meath men. . . hah. . . would you look at the place. . . wouldn't Laoghaire be right to burn it to the ground?'

'Most of Rathcroghan is too wet to burn!'

'Sure you know what I mean. Burn it to the ground. Get rid of these people. Look at those louts over there. What use are they to man or beast? Sell them to the Picts. . .'

'If the Picts would have them. . .'

'And their women. . . did you ever see anything like their women?'

'They're pretty rough.'

'Rough,' the Storyteller raised his eyes to heaven.

'Here are the horses,' said the Wife.

The Servant walked between their heads. And the dogs walked between their legs.

'Good Morning, Night,' said the Storyteller, 'and Good Morning Day.' Then, to the servant, 'have my doogs eaten?'

'A sheep's head,' came the reply.

'That'll keep them going,' said the Storyteller, taking the reins of his horse and swinging up onto it. He settled his cloak about him.

And watched the servant help the Wife up onto her horse.

Did he *have* to hold her leg like that?

Did *she* have to grin that flirty grin as she settled her boy's tunic about her girl's thighs?

Are my dreams their dreams now?

Is there a world of dreams we all share?

What did the old woman on the road say, the woman with the cart of clothes?

Was she a woman, was she a witch?

Are there any answers at all to a man's questions?

He spurred his horse, not knowing where, but just to move.

'Come on, you Romans,' he called, 'you say you take me to someone important. . . well *I* am important. . . so waiting here is keeping *two* important people waiting!'

⸺•

THE PATH WAS only wide enough for one horse.

And even with that, bracken brushed the flanks. And briars twisted in and out the bracken, knitting a wall for the years ahead. The Storyteller noticed red berries on the briars. And thought of times in stories when the sky rained blood. And he thought of the sunset the night before, and his thoughts then.

Nitria led the way.

He followed.

Hernicius, or maybe that was Bernicius, behind him.

Next the Wife.

Then Bernicius. Or Hernicius.

Then the white dog called Day.

And the black dog called Night.

The trail of five horses and two dogs stretched quite a way.

Gentle country this. More sheep, more cattle, few people. A tumbled house. A cairn. A mound. A tree. A patch of water. Two white swans with three brown young. They marry for life, swans. They take one wife.

Must be Christians, muttered the Storyteller to himself.

Nitria rode a filly mare.

Her silly hairstyle bobbed up and down.

The mare's buttocks moved like she was chewing something in her arse.

The Storyteller thought of Macha, the queen of Ulster who was *not* a horse!

By the gods, that silly servant lad!

Macha was a human queen.

But the story was that her husband forced her to race against horses.

Ludicrous, laughable stuff.

Why would a husband force his wife to race against horses?

Perhaps he didn't.

Certainly he didn't, it was a damn silly story among lots of other damn silly stories. But but but. . .

The Storyteller thought. And watched Nitria's silly hairstyle bobbing up and down. And watched the filly mare's buttocks moving. And it was no leap of the mind to see the woman and the horse as one in front of him, the one animal.

The Storyteller brooded.

He remembered that woman they'd met on the road. The one who had sat on the horse which drew a cart. What was in that cart anyway? Something, moving, flesh between the boards, glimpsed. A pig, perhaps. And was it important, perhaps not. The point was that herself on the horse was a miserable old crone, she'd given them the evil eye. And *she* had been the same colour as *her* horse, hard to tell where she began and the horse ended.

Women and horses!

The Storyteller brooded.

Just like women and pigs!

In the stories they're the same animals. And in the past they very much were, the same. In the very old times, he had learned, the very old times before the times that were the past. . . back then the chief of a place had owned all the women and all the pigs. And he distributed them around as took his fancy.

And maybe he owned all the horses too!

But why would that be?

Who knows. . .

The Storyteller brooded.

If I were to be king, he remembered yet another story, to be king of this country in the old days... the good old days! If I were to be king I'd have to have sex with that horse... well, maybe not *that* horse... but with some white horse... after which I'd have to slaughter her, cook her, take a bath in the cooking water, and eat the horse. Or bits of it!

So says the story!

Another damn silly story among the damn silly stories.

What sort of a character wants to have sex with a horse?

Sure the prick would be floating around like a stick stirring a bucket, no joy in that!

More importantly, what sort of people would make such a man their king?

Wouldn't they be more likely to hang him from a tree? Or laugh him out of the place into the woods as a lunatic?

But...

The Storyteller brooded...

Why do people choose their kings, their leaders anyway? What do they look for in them? Someone strong? Oh surely that... but do they care if the king is good or bad or mad? Perhaps not. People have it in them to be good or bad or mad. And the king is there for the mood of the moment!

Ridiculous, the whole thing!

Ridiculous, ridiculous... ridiculous!

'There are many things are strange, ridiculous,' said the woman, beside him on a horse, another woman, another horse. Not Nitria, not the Wife, this was someone else, ridden out of the bracken from another path. He looked around, and behind. But there was no other path, no gap in the bracken. Bounded together by twisting briars, it made a fence along the sides of the path.

This woman beside him was a spirit of the place, he realised. And it was only he could see her, he realised as well, noticing the other's ignoring her presence entirely.

'How can you read my mind?' the Storyteller asked the newcomer, 'what woman are you, and where do you come from?'

'I am Fidelma.'

'The dark, the auburn haired?'

'So they call me... you search for me... well now you have found me... but my own search goes on.'

'Where do you go, for whom do you search?'

'For my sister Eithne, the night comes, I am worried about her.'

'But the sun is barely up,' said the Storyteller. 'I've only had my breakfast. The taste of eggs is still in my mouth.'

'It's late, and getting dark. I don't like to think of her alone in the dark.'

'She's safe.'

'How can you tell?' The auburn haired woman had big brown eyes, worried. And a tiny mole on her left cheek. And that was the step of a fairy when she was a child.

'Your sister is safe, I can tell, I know.'

'How can you know?'

'Believe me,' said the Storyteller, assuringly. If he knew anything about wraiths and ghosts and visions and spirits he knew one thing. . . keep them happy, content.

Silence but for the sound of horses for awhile. . . the sound of five horses. . . no sound from the horse of Fidelma. . . because that was a wraith, a shadowy thing, a memory of a horse.

'It grows dark,' said Fidelma. 'I worry.'

'It's only the rain that makes it dark. . . can you see the sun. . . there. . . there. . . that ball of light. . . it shines through the clouds. . .'

'But it is sinking in the west. . . soon it will be very dark. . .'

'It rises, it rises in the east. . .'

Fidelma laughed, nervously. 'Why do you tease me, Storyteller?'

'How do you know who I am?'

'You come in search of me and my sister.'

'Where will I find you?'

'At the Well of Clebach.'

'What do you do there?'

'We bathe in the waters. We wash away our woman's blood. We sink into the waters. Forgetting, remembering.'

'What do you forget, and what do you remember?'

'I remember as a child in Tara, a woodworker made us wooden toys, a cart, with little wooden wheels. . . I pushed my sister Eithne along in it. . . she was younger. . . but not by much. . . we were happy then. . .'

'Are you happy now?'

'I forget, I forget,' she said sadly. And was gone.

The Storyteller looked around, and up and down the path. And there was no gap in the bracken and briars. In fact they were higher here, if anything, growing now on raised banks along the edge. The path here was wider, but deeper, no longer possible to see across the rainy countryside.

'Where are we going, Nitria?' he called out to the horse's arse in front of him.

'Duma Seilig,' it replied.

'Who are we going to see?'

'Somebody important.'

'When will we get there?'

'Soon.'

They rode on, watched by a shepherd on a knoll, a knoll called Reilig na Ri. He leaned on his crook and watched. He had seen them come from quite a way, from off across the rainy fields of Magh Seilig, in the rain. He had seen them come out of the rain, led by a dark woman on a dark horse, and then seven thin men on seven thin horses. And then a huge black battle dog. And then a girl on a horse. . . or was it a boy? Hard to see in the rain, from this distance. No matter. The girl who might be a boy was followed by another dog, another battle dog, a white one. And then a man on a horse, a man with a black beard and a leather cloak which shone in the rain. And every so often it flashed, like a light, and that was the flash of yellow gorse, reflecting in the mirror of the shiny wet leather. That is a great man, on that horse, thought the shepherd. It is probably that storyteller from Tara. There'd been talk of him in the tavern. Yes, that was probably him. And these were his people.

The shepherd leaned on his crook. His own cloth cloak was soaked. But he stood there, doing what he did. The sheep around him were all wet too, but they ate on, nibbling at the wet grass, doing what they did. The lambs around the sheep were wet, but still they suckled at the teats of the grazing sheep, doing what they did. And life came up from the earth through the grass, through the mouths of the sheep and into them, and out through the teats and into the lambs, who suckled as they shat, and shat life into the ground as they suckled, and life was a circle in the rain.

The shepherd leaned on his crook, and watched the passing of the Storyteller's people. And last of all, quite far behind, last of all in the cavalcade came another group. A man on foot. He led an old horse. And on the old horse there was an old woman. And her skirts were the colour of the horse, hard to tell where horse began and woman ended. The horse she sat on pulled a slatted cart which creaked and squeaked. And the creak and the squeak came through the rain, strangely, in a surprise, like the sound of a bird on a birdless day.

The shepherd leaned on his crook, and the point of the staff dug slightly into the grass of the grassy knoll. And it pointed into the earth, like a reminder. Deep down there in the knoll, this is the grave of kings. Bones lie among jewels. And beside the bones of a warrior's arm lies a rusted sword, quietly, together like lovers in a morning. This is the grave of queens. Bones lie among jewels. The rotted fabric of a dress is the skin of a rotted breast. And the dark clammy earth is the hand of death, caressing.

⌒•

THE CLATTER OF A BAD BELL, a soggy dead sound, tired and tuneless in the rain. An irritating sound, thought the Storyteller, a lump in the pillow of a restless man. He turned about, to complain, to anyone. And now it was the Wife who rode alongside him, and she exactly on the side and in the place where he'd seen Fidelma. He thought that strange, slightly. But her talking interrupted his thinking. 'There's no music in that bell,' she said, reading his mind.

'No, none at all,' he agreed. 'Is that the bell of Duma Seilig?' he called out to Nitria's horse's arse in front.

'That is the bell,' said the horse's arse.

'Well there's no music in it. . . can't you Christians make a decent bell?'

'Sure isn't it the devil has all the best tunes,' said the horse's arse.

By the gods, thought the Storyteller, was that a smile in the voice?

'The Song of Clothra is a lovely tune,' said the Wife, quietly to him and not to Nitria, 'is that a devil's tune?'

'Don't be minding these Romans, sure how can a devil make a good tune? Does a duck come out of a hen's egg?'

'That would be my thinking.'

'If it's a good tune it comes from the good gods,' said the Storyteller.

But what is a good tune, and what is a bad? The Storyteller considered this. And considered how, when the woman in the dream, the woman with a man in each passage... when she screeched in pain, that was a good tune to play on her body... she was part of that tune, and she enjoyed playing it.

Pain, pleasure, just more words to the gods, like all the things of men and women... mere words. Pain, and pleasure, suffering and laughter, just words to the gods. They mean the same, they feel the same.

'I don't believe in good gods,' said the Wife.

'I have grave doubts myself,' agreed the Storyteller.

'Or in bad gods either,' she continued, 'I think they're all the one, and there's neither good nor bad in them...'

'The good and bad are people's things?'

'Exactly.'

'Did they teach you that... when you danced with the wizards... when you were a wizard girl?'

'Did they teach my breasts to grow?'

'They didn't grow much!'

'You know what I mean... for me to become a woman... did they teach my woman's blood to flow? Wasn't there a woman in me all the time? Like a tree in a seed...'

'So what you're saying... the wizardy is in you?'

'Born in me... aren't I the good wife for a Storyteller?'

'If a man wants to bed a boy! A skinny boy... never knew how much like a boy you were... until you cut your hair and dressed in boy's clothes.'

'Maybe I am a boy. And bandits cut off my balls when I was young... sold them to witches in the mountains... the Druids made me woman's parts?'

'Sold them to witches?'

'Yes, in those mountains over there on the far horizon... Sliabh Gamh they call those mountains... well there's witches there... they buy the balls of boys...'

'Who told you that?'

'Oh it's a well known fact... around Rathcroghan... boys round here are very careful of their balls... bandits will have them off as soon as look at them.'

'Oh,' said the Storyteller. 'I see. . . but whatever about that. . . I wouldn't really be believing that you're a boy. . . done up by druids into a girl.'

'You're right not to. . . isn't there more to a man or a woman than hanging pricks or dark damp cracks in the body?'

'Oh there is, there is. . .'

'Isn't it that every piece of skin and flesh is a woman's skin or flesh, or a man's skin or flesh?'

'Oh it is, it is. . .'

'Stop saying that.'

'What?'

'There is, there is, or it is it is. . .'

'I *am* agreeing with you.'

'You agreeing with me is a sign you're not listening. . . didn't you hear what I said. . . amn't I the good wife for a Storyteller?'

'Of course. . . of course.'

'Oh you may mock. . . but the wizardy in me. . . and the fact that I have the sight. . . that makes me a good wife. . . for a Storyteller. . . but. . .'

'But what?'

'When you heard of me. . . first. . . and came to Connacht to collect me from my father. . .'

'Yes?'

'Well you didn't know that I would make a good wife. . .'

'I was following a dream. . . a geis. . . I had no choice.'

'And because of that I'm a better wife than your Chief Wife. . . or The Quiet One. . .'

'They are fine women and I won't hear anything against them.'

'I know they're fine women. . . bossy, but fine. . . but what I mean is. . . I'm more suited to you. . . my wizardy and my sight. . .'

'The Chief Wife has a great pair of thighs. . . and the Quiet One cooks good bread.'

'Yes and you married them for that. . . you saw the thighs and heard about the cooking. . . you didn't marry them for the dream. . .'

'Ah hah what do you know girl. . . a man dreams of thighs like that. . . and a man has an appetite for good bread. . . gives him strength for the heavy thighs.' The Storyteller laughed.But only to put an end to the conversation. He knew what the Wife meant.

'You know what I mean,' she said.

'I do,' he agreed.

He loved her. And there was no words to hide that love, no laughter would silence it.

'We're arriving,' he said.

'Where?'

'No idea. . . but we're definitely arriving.'

The bell was louder now, and sounded none the better for its nearness.

The path opened out, and the banks about it faded, and now there was no path, they were on a flat open place, a plain, of gorse, and whin, and over there a mound, the height of three men. He spurred his horse alongside Nitria.

'Is that Duma Seilig?' he asked her.

'It is.'

'And who is buried there?'

'Some pagan king. . . long forgotten. . . as all pagans are,' she added, rather coldly.

'Will the Christians be remembered?' asked the Wife, sweetly.

The Storyteller knew that sweet tone, knew that it could lead anywhere, to argument, even to that knife at her belt appearing in her hand.

'Whoever is buried here,' he said, quickly, to avoid any unpleasantness, 'it's not Fraoch anyway. He's not buried here. . . he's buried over there, beyond, at that stone caiseal. . . Carn Fraoch they call it. . . I remember this place now. . . was here when I was studying. . .'

'What did you learn?' asked Nitria. She had a gentle face. But the gentleness was moss on a stone, it covered strength, and hardness.

'I studied with Cathbad.'

'At Rathcroghan? He's a pagan druid. . .'

'Well I'm a pagan Storyteller. . .'

'You must be saved.'

'Oh let me get lost first, woman. . . where is your church?'

'It's over here. . . we'll walk. . .'

She swung down from her horse. And the rest of them did likewise. And a young man in a long skirt and a funny haircut came wandering over and gathered all the horses' reins, and he led them away in a bunch.

'I hope we see our horses again,' said the Storyteller grumpily.

Nitria smiled. 'We do not steal,' she said, 'it is the commandment.'

'The what?'

'The commandment. . . the rules of god. . . Moses went up the mountain. . .'

'Who is Moses.'

'A holy man.'

'A Druid. . . what mountain?'

'Mount Sinai.'

'What for, why did he go up the mountain?'

'To get the commandments.'

'How did he know they were up there?'

'He was called by God.'

'How many commandments are there?'

'Ten. . .'

'That's not that many. . . we have thousands of laws in Tara. . .'

'Yes but they are the laws of man. . . God has simpler laws. . .'

'Like what. . .'

'First I am the Lord Thy God. . . Thou shalt have no strange gods before me.'

'But to me he's a strange God,' said the Storyteller, watching, Bernicius and Hernicius passing them out, hurrying ahead. And a tall man there, standing. And Bernicius and Hernicius kneeling in front of him, and the tall man touching each of their heads, and them standing up again.

'Who is he?' asked the Storyteller.

Nitria did not reply.

They walked on.

'I am the man they call the Roman,' said the tall man, 'but my name is Patrick.'

'You are well known in both names,' said the Storyteller.

'And your name?'

'Storyteller.'

'But you must have a name?'

'I do have a name. . . Storyteller. . .'

'That is not a name. . .'

'Not a name? Go ask. . . talk to anyone. . . ask where is the Storyteller of Tara. . . say lead me to his house. . . I tell you this. . .

there is no man will not lead you to my door!'

'What did your mother call you?'

'Son.'

'And what did you call your father?'

'Storyteller. . . he was the storyteller before me!'

'What does your wife call you?'

'Husband. Or Storyteller. Depends on their moods. You know women. They have moods.'

'Their? Them? How many wives have you?'

'I haven't counted lately.'

'You must know. . . you mock.'

'Yes I do know, and I do mock. . . because I have heard that you preach one wife.'

'It is the way of god.'

'What god?'

'God.'

'Does he have no name?'

'He does have a name. . . god. . . just as you have a name. . . Storyteller.'

Both men laughed. But it was the laughter of men about to pick up stronger swords.

16

THE MEN TALK. Well let them talk! Men have need of women when their talking's done! Patience is all that's needed. It's the still flower attracts the bee.

The Wife sat alone, brooding on such things. And brooding on other things too. She hugged her knees and imagined herself to be a chicken, bound for the pot. Or a duck, for that matter, a duck that had *not* escaped. She fingered the thongs of her sandals, felt how they cut into her bare legs, how the little red channels marked in the flesh beneath them. These are my bindings, she thought, I cannot escape. My mother is death in the kitchen, cooking! The water is coming to the boil. The flesh will fall from my bones. And they'll eat me, they'll pick the Y of my witch bone clean, and make a spell on that!

Look at them talking!

Patrick and the Storyteller over there, talking! Well let them talk! Men have need of women when their talking's done!

The Wife took out her knife, and stabbed the earth.

What was it the ferryman had said? If he had strength enough, he could squeeze the blood out of the earth? Yes, that.

She stabbed the earth. And remembered stabbing flesh, the feel of it. That Christian girl, ever so white, the flesh, and rather beautiful. Yes the gods of the road would be pleased at that, that sacrifice. The journey home would be safe now. On a dangerous road like that in these dangerous times. . . if you don't have the gods of the road on your side!

The Wife looked across at Nitria. And thought about stabbing her. . . a sacrifice. . . for the goddess.

THE BUILDERS PLINKED at stones with iron chisels.

A picky, irritating sound. What with that and the bell, not to mention Patrick's foreign accent! Irritating sounds, each one, and the sum of them worse, getting on the Storyteller's nerves. 'What do they build, your builders?' he asked.

'A bigger church. . .'

'Why do you need a bigger church?'

'To fit more people in.'

'Would you not leave them out in the world. . . with their own gods?'

'Their gods are devils.'

'Is all the world made up of devils then?'

'Most of it,' said Patrick.

'I see,' said the Storyteller, nodding, thinking, listening to the plinking of the builders' chisels. Those stones, he noticed, those stones they cut and shaped were older stones, from some older building. These were not new stones, not wild raw stones from the earth. No, these were long tamed, these stones. They had been cut and shaped for many uses, many buildings, graves, monuments, shelters. And these builders here had found them, tumbled, forgotten in briars, overgrown. These were the bones of the past. Coming alive again. Because bones cry out for flesh. And flesh clings to the bone.

'So,' he turned to his companion, 'so about this god of yours, Patrick. . .'

'Your god too, Storyteller.'

'Does a man pick his god, or does god pick a man?'

'Man must follow the one true god.'

'Why would a man follow a false god, what foolishness would that be?'

'A man knows the true god,' said Patrick.

'Yes,' agreed the Storyteller, 'but the god he knows is always true. . . and in different places, different times, though men know many different gods. And each one of them is true.'

'No, there is only one true god,' said Patrick, in the manner of someone who had said the phrase many times before. And was a bit tired of saying it. . . but unfortunately found it necessary!

'But doesn't everyone say that? About their gods?'

'Everyone *may* say that, but everyone is wrong!'

'And you're right?' the Storyteller grinned.

'It's not a question of *me* being right, it's a question of me preaching the right god.'

'What happened to Eithne and Fidelma?' asked the Storyteller, suddenly, throwing in the question to catch Patrick unawares.

'Didn't my bishops tell you,' Patrick replied, calmly, not caught unawares at all. 'Nitria, Hernicius, and Bernicius. . . I understood they told you.'

'Oh they did. . . but I didn't believe a word of it.'

'You have a problem with belief, I feel. What *do* you believe?'

'It's not my job to believe.'

'What *is* your job, exactly?'

'I keep the story. Of the people. I tell the king. And I tell younger storytellers. So they may tell the king in their time.'

'But it's a story of false gods!'

'They got us this far!' snapped the Storyteller, annoyed, wondering why he was bothering to argue with the Roman. In the old days, he realised, there would have been no argument. The kings would have had the Romans' heads, and that would have been the end of the matter. What was it now, he wondered, what was it now that made people listen? Was it something in the message of the Romans, this Christian message? Or was it something in the times of the old ways?

Were the old ways done for?

And if they were, what was to become of him?

What king would have him in his house?

He'd wander the roads, a man with a snatch of a story in him. Oh yes, they'd give him charity. And a bed for the night. But he'd have no place in the scheme of things. They'd allow him wander, give him charity, but hardly listen. He'd be an entertainer. A singer. Juggler.

Sing that song, singer!

Juggle those balls, juggler!

Tell us that old story, storyteller! Oh yes, that'd be the call! But would they hear it through the music of their own times? And what was the point of one story, when men are living by the words of another?

'You look gloomy,' said Patrick, 'you think on gloomy things.'

'Did you know,' said the Storyteller, perking up, knowing that what he was about to say would irritate the other, 'do you know that in the hills not far from here they dress their female pigs as women on a certain day, and chase them through the Mucklaghs to the boars.'

'Why do they do that?'

'Why not?'

'What god does it please?'

'Who knows. . . but the pigs look pretty in their ribbons and dresses. . . some of them a lot prettier than the women round there, let me tell you.'

'It is a dreadful pagan thing, and must be stopped.'

'The boars are not going to like that. . . but tell me Patrick. . . this word *stopped*. . . it comes up a lot. . . your god seems very keen on *stopping* things?'

'This country is full of devils, devilish things.'

'One man's devil is another's god! Anyway, we like it, the way it is. Or *was*, before your preaching. Tell me this, Patrick, what gives you the right to come into another man's country, *stopping* things! I have heard you even stopped the old ones grinding bones in bullaun stones. . .'

'A pagan thing.'

'But it was our ancestors carved the bullaun holes in rock. . . for just that purpose. We must do what our ancestors told us to do. It's in us. And now we can't.'

'So?'

'Well when your children's children turn away from *your* god, what will you feel then?'

'They won't.'

'Oh yes they will. . . because I'll tell you this, Patrick. . . gods may be true or gods may be false. . . but one thing they have in common, they come and go, they ebb and flow. . . your stonemasons there. . . look at them, picking at stones. . . so carefully. . . fitting them together. . . look at the door jamb there, neat and square. . .'

'What of it? They build well.'

'But not well enough. Those stones themselves come from other well built buildings. . . which have fallen. Those stones will fall again. And not to the wind or the rain. They'll fall to the move of the story, to the ebb and the flow of the gods, the true ones and the false.'

'We build a church eternal.'

'You do in your arse! But no. . .' The Storyteller paused, raised both arms in mock surrender. 'No, I'm wrong, you're right. . . I've just thought, just noticed there. . . your stonemasons, they build that doorjamb, facing east. . .'

'And so? East is to Jerusalem. Where Christ our saviour lived.'

'That's very convenient. Don't you find it strange that the old people also built their temples to the east, to the rising of the sun. The old people knew no Jerusalem!'

'Not strange at all, coincidence.'

'Hah,' said the Storyteller, 'don't insult me with that! You're a clever man. You build your churches just like the temples of the old days. If the doors of the old pointed to the west you'd build to the west! It's a trap. . . to lure the people in.'

'To guide, to *guide*, not lure!'

'Ah sure it's all for nothing,' the Storyteller sighed, tired of argument. 'I'll wager you this, Patrick. Your childrern's children will turn away from your foreign god. . . and come back to mine. . . I'll wager that!'

'Well wager on! Neither of us will be here to collect or pay the debt. . . I'll be with god.'

'What does that mean?'

'In the presence of god.'

'And are you not here, in the presence of the gods, with the grass that grows and the children playing.'

' This is a world of suffering, and disease, and war.'

'And a world of stars that move in the sky. . . and the world that knows the strength of men, the nobility of men, and the gentleness of women, and their beauty.'

'A world of old age, and death, and cruelty and slaughter.'

'You talk of the dark, Patrick, and I of the light. Isn't it that they are both god, the light and the dark. And your god is half a god.'

'My God has conquered darkness.'

'Well he didn't do a very good job of it,' said the Storyteller, looking thoughtfully over at the Wife. She was sitting there, quietly, idly, stabbing and slicing the earth. Idle, yes, there was an idleness in her manner, but the knife went in and out of the damp flesh of the earth, methodically.

The earth was Nitria, the sacrifice, for the goddess. This bit here her legs. The Wife carved at a thigh, slicing the flesh. Meat for the goddess, eat it while it screams.

The Wife giggled.

Yes, and this bit here's her shin. The Wife scraped the skin from the shin. It was a piece of grass. She bared the bone. It was a stone.

The Wife giggled.

A bird squawked, a sheep baa'ed, and Nitria screamed to the twist of the knife. Oh scream away, said the Wife to the clay beneath the knife. You've a day of screaming left to do. Half that day afraid of death, screaming for life. Then half a day afraid of life, screaming for death. . .

The Wife giggled. She came across a worm, and cut it neatly. The two halfs wriggled off. Half that worm is afraid of life, she thought, and half that worm is afraid of death. And both halfs wriggle in the same earth. The same goddess watches them, wriggling. Watches, with still cold eyes that see in circles, sideways, up and down. Not like the eyes of any person, those goddess eyes. No, more like the eyes of a bird. A scrawny black bird, with feathers like jagged knives.

It stood on a branch of leafless thorn, that bird, watching a slender girl with scraggy yellow hair. A bare legged girl, dressed as a boy, carving the earth for food.

⁘

'THAT WIZARD GIRL of yours?' said Patrick.

'My wife?'

'Well, whatever you choose to call her. . . what is she doing there, stabbing the earth?'

'What are your bishops there, Bernicius. . . Hernicius. . . Nitria. . . what're they doing over there?'

'Praying. . . they pray at this time of day. . .'

'Well my wife is doing the same. . . she often sits like that in a trance, stabbing the earth. . . for her it's a prayer. . . thinking of her goddess. . . at this time of day. . . and isn't her prayer as good as yours?'

'It's the god we pray to, not the prayer.'

'Is it not the same god? The goddess earth beneath the knife?

And this man god of yours in heaven?'

'You blaspheme.'

'What does that mean?'

'You speak against god.'

'What does that mean, what'll happen to me?'

'Your soul will be cast into hell, unless you repent.'

'Ah get up the yard, Patrick, I have no time for this. Things to do, people to see. . .' The Storyteller closed his eyes in a sigh, and listened to the baa of sheep and the squawk of birds.

The soggy bell bonged, like there was bad news in these parts.

Hernicius, Bernicius and Nitria prayed, their prayers the sound of humming bees.

Patrick gazed thoughtfully at his stonemasons, wondering if the church was going to be big enough. It was all a question of expense. God will provide, surely, but only if man acted in a sensible manner.

The Storyteller sat, his eyes closed, listening to the baa of sheep.

He planned to stand, in a moment, and go. He'd get no news of Eithne and Fidelma here, not from Patrick, that was sure. Maybe down at the well, he thought, maybe there'd be people there, in that locality. They might have news, gossip, whatever. Even if they had little to say it would be surely be better than listening to the lot to say that Patrick had! Sure that was just the baa'ing of a sheep!

Yes. Eithne and Fidelma, that was why he was here, after all, not to be arguing gods with the likes of the Romans.

Eithne. Funny that she bore that name, he thought. Eithne, the name of the sister of Queen Maeve of Connacht. . . the other sister apart from Clothra. Three sisters. Eithne, Maeve, and Clothra. Clothra who got pregnant by her three brothers. They fell on her in a drunkenness, so no-one knew who was the father of the child. Three, everything comes in threes.

For why? For who can tell!

Clothra. . . yes. . . he recited the story in his mind, one of the few places a man would get a good audience for the old stories these days! Clothra was an interesting person, rarely spoken of, unfashionable. She had a hard life. Was she unfashionable because she had a hard life? Who knows! All that anyone knows is that, after being shagged by her three drunken brothers, all called Fionn. . . after that she bore another son to her son!

What was his name?

The Storyteller searched his mind.

Criomthann Nia Nar, yes, that was the name.

He opened his eyes.

'What do you think of, Storyteller?' asked Patrick.

'Of the three sisters, queens of Connacht... and were they the one, like your three gods, your father god, your son god, your spirit god?'

'I know nothing of your pagan gods,' said Patrick, dismissively.

'Or perhaps you do,' murmured the Storyteller, 'and it's just that you give them different names?'

'There is one god.'

'Well tell me this, how can the one god be both god of life and death, love and hate, peace and war?'

'It is a mystery,' said Patrick.

'It surely is,' agreed the Storyteller, absentmindedly, following Patrick's eyes.

The Wife was coming over to them. Her knife now back in her belt, but her eyes sharp. She was looking past them, and through them... in one of her trances.

'Eithne and Fidelma,' she said, 'would you see them now?'

'I would see them now, Wife,' he said.

She raised her right hand to them, the flat of it, facing them. 'Look at the lines on my hand,' she said.

Patrick and the Storyteller looked.

'Do you know what it is about the lines on my hand?' she asked.

Patrick and the Storyteller shook their heads, they didn't know what it was about the lines on her hand.

'They say nothing about me, nothing. But look at your own hands?'

Patrick and the Storyteller looked at their own hands.

'Do you see the lines on your hands?'

They nodded, yes.

'Do you know what it is about the lines on your hands?'

They looked at her, waiting.

Her voice had no music in it, no lilt nor movement. It was flat, and still, but not unpleasant... calming... relaxing...

'The lines on your hands... they say... everything.'

They looked at the lines on their hands.

'Everything,' she said, 'everything.'

A trance came over them.

And the Storyteller looked up from his hand, and he knew there was a trance over him. And over her too, it was there, like the veil of a dancing girl. It hid her, and showed her clear as clear.

And a silence came over the place.

The bell stopped ringing.

The sound of the stonemasons silenced.

The sudden silernce came as a shock. And Patrick in his trance looked around, carefully. 'What magic is this,' he said, 'what devilish thing?'

'She is a wizard,' said the Storyteller, 'just as you said. . . but you said it as a word, without believing. . . now watch, and wait.'

'Who are these women now,' said Patrick, 'these women here. . . where did they come from?'

'This is Eithne,' said the Storyteller, 'they call her Eithne the Fair.'

'Because she has fair hair,' said the Wife.

'I can see that,' said Patrick.

'And this is Fidelma,' said the Storyteller. 'They call her Fidelma the Ruddy.'

'Because she has red brown hair,' said the Wife.

'I can see that,' said Patrick. 'But who are they, and why do they come. . . where have they come from. . . ?'

'It is dark,' said Eithne.

'Very dark,' said Fidelma.

'What are they talking about,' said Patrick, 'it is not dark, these women are mad. . . why do you bring them to me?'

'I am glad I found you,' said Eithne, to Fidelma. . . 'I was looking all day. . .'

'I am glad I found *you*,' said Fidelma, 'it's not good to be alone. . . in the dark. . .'

'They rant,' said Patrick.

'Do they,' said the Storyteller, 'would you not let them speak?'

'What will they say to me?'

'Eithne has a story. . . speak, Eithne, speak to the great man. What is the story?'

Eithne spoke. But not to Patrick, nor to anyone there. Just into the air, she dropped her words, one by one, and in little flutters then.

Much like a tree drops leaves, on a quiet day, after the summer.

'The Goddess of this place. . .' she said, and paused. 'The Goddess of this place. . . she went as a a witch to Tara. . . they stripped her clothes. . . they tied her to a stake. . . the brats of the place mocked her. . . they pulled on her breasts, pretending to milk them like a cow. . .'

'What is this pagan story?' said Patrick.

'Would you prefer a Christian one?' said the Wife, softly. 'Speak to him, Fidelma'.

'The Son of God of Heaven. . .' said Fidelma, and paused, and started again. 'The son of the God of Heaven, he went to earth as a man. . . he was nailed to a cross. . . they raffled his clothes. . . they mocked him . . . told him to get down off the cross if he was really the son of God.'

'That is the book,' said Patrick, excited. 'Yes I have a book. Where is my book? I will read you from my book.' Patrick looked around.

'Is it here?' said Eithne, bending down, trickling soil through her fingers. 'Is your book here?'

'Is it here?' said Fidelma, blowing a breath from her mouth, 'is your book here?'

'Who are these spirits?' said Patrick.

'I am Eithne,' said Eithne. 'And I have a question. . . for the axe headed man from Armorica. . .

'I am Fidelma,' said Fidelma. 'And I too have a question. . . for the axe headed man from Armorica. . .

'Ask him your questions,' said the Wife from her trance.

'Why,' said Eithne, 'why would the Goddess stay on her fire with the brats around her?'

'And why,' said Fidelma, 'why would the Son of God stay on his cross?'

'Why?' repeated the Storyteller, and fell silent.

'Yes why?' said Patrick, wondering, and fell silent.

And their silence became a small part of the huge silence of that place.

Magh Seilig stretched about them.

And it was called that for the view, of the open country. This was an ancient spot, the Storyteller knew. The old people *before* the old people, they had their kingdom here. The Carn of Fraoch was their Tara, their Rathcroghan. Deep down there in the earth, this is the grave of kings. Bones lie among jewels. And beside the bones of an arm lies a sword, quietly, like lovers in a morning. This is the grave of queens. Bones lie among jewels. The fabric of a dress is the skin of a breast. And the dark clammy earth is the hand of death, caressing.

The Storyteller looked into himself, and knew all this.

He looked around, the countryside, and knew the world.

Over there in the hills, the witches of Sliabh Gamh, they boil the testicles of boys, for potions. And over there, the lepers of Rathcroghan, they hold out fingerless hands, for charity. And back beyond, the wise men of Tara argue, endlessly. And everywhere slatterns squabble, and drinkers drink and fight in taverns. And soldiers wait for wars, while mothers wait for peace. The hanged rot in the trees, the rain falls, and the innards of animals are dragged from their bellies by the beaks of birds. And the innards of a slave-girl are dragged on the hooks of men. And all the while the wise men of Tara argue, endlessly. They write, poetry, law, philosophy. And still the slatterns squabble. Lepers hold out fingerless hands. Witches chop testicles, looking for life. . . and finding death. And still the wise men of Tara argue, endlessly.

It goes on, and why?

Why?

Why, said Eithne and Fidelma, why is the goddess on her fire, and why the god upon his cross?

That is the question.

The Storyteller looked into empty silent space and wondered for an answer, and Patrick looked into empty space and wondered too, both listening in their heads for an answer to that question. But inside their heads was silence too.

And in the silernce Eithne and Fidelma slipped away, hand in hand and hardly noticed. And then Patrick and the Storyteller and the Wife heard, somewhere in the countryside, the creaking of a cart, and it coming in their direction.

'I know that cart,' said the Storyteller, 'that creaking of that cart, and I know who pushes it?'

'How do you know?'

'The gods tell me,' smiled the Storyteller.

'Well you tell me. . .' said Patrick, 'so I know that you know when it arrives.'

'There'll be a crone pushing that cart.'

'Many crones push many carts.'

'She'll be wearing black.'

'Most crones wear black. . . in my experience.'

'Here she comes now. . . yes. . . I was right. . . a crone wearing black. . .'

'Ah get away with you. . .' said Patrick, 'enough of your cheap trickery, your tawdry wizardry.'

'Tawdry,' said the Wife, coming out of her trance, 'tawdry, what does that word mean?'

'It's not that much of a compliment,' the Storyteller told her, and then he called out aloud to the crone, 'where do you go with the cart?' Then he added in a whisper to Patrick, 'she brings clothes to wash in the stream.'

'I bring clothes to wash in the stream,' replied the crone.

'What clothes are those?' asked the Storyteller, aloud, and then in a whisper, 'the clothes of the dead.'

'These are the clothes of the dead,' said the crone, drawing her cart alongside.

She reached in.

'This is the dress of a witch. . . the goddess was in her. . . she went to Tara with a message. . . they stripped her of her dress. . . they tied her to a stake. . . boys stood around in a mockery. . . they burned her on a fire. . . and she died.'

She dropped the dress back in.

'And this is the cloak of a man in a distant country. . . the god was in him. . . he told prophecy. . . and he had a cure for the sick in his hands. . . and he said he was the son of god. . . so they nailed him to a cross and made him a mockery. . . and he died. . .'

'He didn't die,' said Patrick.

'Oh but these are his clothes,' insisted the crone, 'and these are the clothes of the dead, and I go to wash them in the stream.'

'He didn't die,' repeated Patrick, annoyed. 'Because he rose on the third day.'

'Where was he for the three days' asked the Wife, 'was he in the darkness?'

'That is not the point. . . the point is. . . he didn't die.'

'Oh but it *is* the point,' said the Wife. 'Because when Eithne and Fidelma died there was darkness here. . . for three days.'

'Mael and Caplait conjured up that darkness,' said the Storyteller.

'They are druids. . .' said Patrick, 'they work with devils.'

'They have a black bear, from the north,' said the Storyteller, 'and a black girl from the south.'

'Oh I know all about *them*,' said Patrick, 'they are druids, working with devils.'

'The land was dark here. . .' said the Wife, calmly, coldly. 'For three days. . . just as your god the son of your god was dead. . . for three days. . . and then he came back into his living. . . and the light came into the land here. . . tell me Patrick. . .' She leaned over, and touched his arm. . . 'tell me. . . is it the same darkness. . . and is it the same light?'

Patrick looked at the hand on his arm. And the Storyteller looked at the hand on the arm and wondered, how many women's hands had touched that man's arm? He wondered, and decided, probably not enough!

Then suddenly Patrick brushed the Wife's hand away. And stood tall. 'There is one God,' he said, 'and the people here must follow him, or die.'

'But the people here,' said the Crone, 'the people here are the children of the dead. They are dead already.' She laughed, and moved her cart, prepared to go.

'You, you crone, you are a devil,' said Patrick, 'and I'll cast you out of this country.'

'I'll take more casting than you think,' muttered the crone, and walked on, muttering, grumbling. And soon she was gone, off across the flat place of whin and gorse, past the Duma Seilig, and in between the banks of the path that led to Rathcroghan.

Patrick watched her go.

'It was you, Storyteller, wasn't it?'

'Wasn't it what?'

'It was you, you and this devil girl you go about with, you put a hex on me, you conjured up those girls. . . you conjured up that crone'.

'Why do you call her a devil girl?'

'I know a devil girl when I see one. And people tell me things. I keep my ear to the ground. Oh yes. I've been told. A priest of mine, he could not sleep last night. He walked in the moonlight by the place they call the Fort of Bulls. He saw her there. In the moonlight.'

'She is the daughter of the moon, that's what they call her?'

'What does that mean,' snapped Patrick, 'come, Storyteller, you are an educated man. . .'

'Thanks.'

'You mock. But you will answer to god, not me. . . you and your devil girl. . . my priest saw her. . . she had a bird on her shoulder. . .'

'She loves wild animals. . . and they love her. . .'

'And she walks with a black dog.'

'That's my dog, his name is Night. That's him there, he lies with my white dog, and she's called Day.'

Patrick looked at the Storyteller for a moment, shook his head. 'You are mad. . . mad. . . completely mad. . .'

'Can the daughter of the moon not walk with night?' said the Storyteller.

'Your priest was dreaming,' said the Wife, 'I did not stir from my husband's bed.'

'Oh yes you did,' said Patrick, 'it was you. You walked with that black dog, a bird on your shoulder. And I'm not going to argue anyway. You are mad. . . both mad.'

'And I am tired,' said the Wife, 'so tired.' And she sank to her knees, and then to her side on the earth, and slept. And as soon as she slept the life went out of the trance that she'd brought over them all, over herself, and Patrick, and the Storyteller. And when the life went out of the trance they heard the soggy bell again, ringing, no music in it, a sad sound in the rain. And then they heard the plinking of stonemasons, again.

The trance was gone, but not the memory.

Patrick and the Storyteller looked at each other's eyes, and looked away. And the Storyteller looked at the Wife, sleeping, and wondered. And Patrick sank to his knees. . . and prayed. 'Oh My God, why have I come to this country, this devil's country?'

He prayed.

He thought of the devil wizard girl beside him on the grass, sleeping. He knew he should have prayed for her. But he knew she was beyond the praying for. So he prayed for himself, and remembered, himself. And another woman, long ago, in another country.

IN ARMORICA.

 The boat was leaving.
 She didn't understand.
 He was going away.
 To preach the gospel where the gospel needed preaching.
 She stood by the harbour wall.
 She had brown hair.
 She dressed in the Roman way.
 A silver clasp on her shoulder.
 Patrick stood on the boat, and sailors walked this way, and that. They prepared ropes, and sails, there was quite a fuss going on, quite a bustle. But a silence like a cloud was around him on the deck and around the girl on the wall of the harbour. She was beautiful, now in his memory he remembered. A Roman girl, from the Roman people. She had a gentle graceful body. And her dresses fell across her body in that Roman way. He remembered looking, at the clasp on her shoulder, the clasp that held her dresses together. And he remembered looking down at his own feet, where his bag of things stood, and beside it a case with the holy books of god, a box with a clasp. And he had noticed how the pin on the clasp of the girl's dress was so similar to the pin on the box.
 Either pin could be pulled by the grip of a finger to a thumb.
 And if he pulled the pin on the girl's shoulder, her dress would fall. And she would be graceful, and gentle, and beautiful.
 He thought of this. But the ship moved from the harbour. And her big brown eyes were wet with tears.
 And then they were no longer to be seen.
 He sat on the deck. And watched Armorica. At first it was a mountain. Then a hill. Then a line across the horizon. And then it was gone, and gone forever. And when it was gone, gone forever, he sat on the deck and pulled the pin of his bible box. He took out the great book. And he read the word of god.
 It never changed.

And through the years it never changed.

And sometimes in the years he thought of her, the Roman girl. And how of course she had changed. No longer a girl. A woman. A mother no doubt, perhaps a grandmother. And perhaps she still dressed in the Roman way, though that fashion was fading. But no matter the fashion, whatever dress she wore, it would not fall away to show a gentle graceful body. It would be an older woman, well worn, the flesh tired from children, bearing them, feeding them. That is the way of things. Just as his own body was not that young man now. No, he was worn, tired too. Sometimes the journeys he travelled were too long for his strength.

He was getting old.

But the word of god was still the same.

It was neither young, nor old.

It would not die.

It was the truth.

And worth the bringing to these savage people.

With their druids, and their witches, and their poets, storytellers, wizards too.

Patrick glanced up from his prayers.

The Storyteller was there, over there, and his wizard girl had revived, and she stood quietly beside him.

Not a bad man, he thought, a clever man, with some goodness in him?

Perhaps.

But the wizard girl!

She reeked of evil.

Why would a good man go about with a devil girl like that?

What tied them together?

That is the question.

And to every question, there is an answer.

He felt better now, more confident. The prayer and the pleasant memory of the past had given him new strength. He rose from his knees.

'Time to eat,' he called over to the Storyteller, waving his arm.

'Eat?' said the Wife.

'Yes they have this magic. . . ' said the Storyteller, glad to see her out of the trance, recovered. 'They turn some bread into a man, and eat him. . .'

'You joke?' said the Wife.

'No they do, they really do...'

'Oh,' said the Wife, understanding. 'Yes in this country in the old days they would sacrifice a woman, and eat her as a pig in a feast.'

'Yes I know that,' said the Storyteller, looking at her. Of course he knew that, but he hadn't known that the Wife knew such historical things! In actual fact he had a pretty low opinion of her education generally. Her ignorance was breath taking. Oh yes she had the sight, and could conjure spells and visions... and hypnotise the unwary... but as for education! She just didn't seem to *know* very much.

The wizards, it was their fault!

The wizards taught these wizard girls.

But it wasn't facts they taught them.

It was something else.

Wizardy skills, useful, but no substitute for real education.

'Is Patrick going to turn bread into a man, now, right now?' she asked.

'No I think he's just going to give us a meal,' replied the Storyteller, looking ahead, seeing servants scurrying round a lowish building.

A lowish building with a lowish door.

They stooped to enter.

Most of the building was taken up with a table.

There were stools along both sides.

Light came from the lowish door, and from another equally lowish door at the far end.

In front of each stool on the table were loaves of bread.

Good smelling bread.

The Storyteller thought of his wife, The Quiet One, she who baked good bread. And always smelled of bread. A good healthy smell. Sometimes waking up beside her it was if he was with a huge loaf of bread in the bed. Mostly squashy dough, but with crusty bits at the edges.

A good woman that!

He wished he was at home, and sighed.

'Why do you sigh?' said the Wife.

'So far the meal doesn't look very appetising,' was his answer.

'There's a stew of old sheep in the guesthouse waiting.'

'We'll try our luck here.'

Patrick sat down, and waved to a seat beside him for the Storyteller.

Nitria sat down, and waved to a seat beside her for the Wife.

Then all the other seats were taken up by Patrick's followers, men and women, mostly young, all serious, solemn, silent.

'Your followers are quiet,' said the Storyteller.

'I don't encourage idle chatter.'

'Oh,' said the Storyteller, 'I'll hold my peace so.'

'No you may talk.'

'Thanks.'

'I'm interested in your opinions. . .'

'About?'

'About this country. . . you're a stranger here too, from Tara I believe. . .'

'But not so strange as you, from Armorica.'

'Is a stranger not a stranger, no matter where he comes from?'

'Perhaps. . . in a way. . .'

'Though of course there are degress of strangerness,' said Patrick, tearing a piece of bread off his loaf.

'Oh, no doubt,' said the Storyteller, tearing a similar sized piece of bread off his own loaf.

'This is a difficult country,' said Patrick, taking a bite out of his bread, 'I have learnt terrible things. . .'

'There are terrible things to be learnt,' agreed the Storeyteller, biting his own bread.

'Do you know, Storyteller, do you know how the king becomes the king in these parts?'

'Much like a king anywhere. . . he slaughters everyone else who would be king.'

'More than that. . . when he has done with the struggle. . . he must confirm himself. . . '

'Oh yes, that must be done. . . '

'So he has intercourse with a horse, a white mare. . .'

'I have heard this story. . . I suspect it spread by enemies. . .'

'Oh no, its true.'

'And you are not an enemy? You are the friend of the druids here?'

'I have heard it as true. . . after intercourse with the mare. . . he kills it. . . then boils it up and eats it while sitting in a bath of its cooking water.'

'How could a man eat a whole horse?' said the Storyteller, looking up and down the table at the bread. Wondering. Vaguely. Maybe a small bit of horse wouldn't go amiss here, might improve the meal!

'*Pieces* of the horse, and that is not the point, Storyteller. It is *evidence* of the barbarity of men in these parts.'

'Tell me, Patrick. . . does god not make the man, in your ideas?'

'He does.'

'So tell me this then. . . as man grows on, on through the generations, does he not become more like man and less like god?'

'Perhaps,' said Patrick, carefully.

'So the newer ideas are those of man and not of god? And you bring new ideas to this country. . . might not these ideas be those of man, and not of the gods?'

'Man falls. . . and god must make him pure again.'

'But man in the first place was not, as you say, he was not pure at all. . . is it not, in your ideas, that god made him one way, and then had to start all over again. . . like a potter with a leaky pot, a woman with a barrel of beer gone sour, a weaver with a broken thread?'

'Too many words in this country, Storyteller,' said Patrick. 'In the end your ease with words and argument will bring you all to hell.'

'But you have brought us god, to save us surely?'

'Oh,' Patrick sighed, 'this country sometimes tires me. . . but it is God's will I stay.'

'Well why did you come at all? Where do you come from anyway, who was your father?'

'My father was Calpornius, and his father Potitus. They were priests. And I was brought first to this country as servant to Milchu.'

'Milchu? My father knew him. A druid in the north, Milchu, the wizard king they called him. By the gods it's a small world!'

'He kept many pigs. . . and I was his pig keeper.'

'Not a great job for the son of a priest who was the son of a priest.'

'All work is the work of God. . . but I didn't do it for long. . . I went back. . . home. . . to Armorica. . . '

'And you came back again? You must like your punishment!'

'I came back to preach the word of god, to baptise the pagans, the Lord sent me.'

'What if my gods send me to Armorica? Or the goddess of my wizard wife sitting there, what if *she* sends *her*?'

'She'd probably be burned as a witch, in Armorica.'

'Probably?' laughed the Storyteller. 'I wouldn't say there'd be much doubt about that matter! But the thing is, Patrick, sometimes a witch does not burn. . . sometimes she laughs at the fire. . . and what do you do then?'

'I pray,' said Patrick.

He raised a hand.

It was a signal.

The tuneless bell started clappering away again outside. And the followers around the table started praying aloud. And to the Storyteller's ears it all added up to a mournful sound. And he picked idly at his bread like it was a doughy woman's flesh and he thought this truly is a mournful place, Magh Seilig, and why was Patrick here?

Why settle here?

Close to the grave of Fraoch.

King of the old people.

Lover of Queen Maeve. Lover of their daughter Findabair. And probably lover of her daughter too! Because in those old days a ruler married his way through the generations. His wife, their daughter, then his and her daughter, and so on and on until. . . well. . . until he was dead!

Why would Patrick come to such a place, to build a church, to pray? Is it ignorance or knowledge brings him here? Sure what can he know, even the people living here don't know their own story. What can a foreigner from Armorica know?

The Storyteller wondered, and picked idly at his bread like it was a doughy woman's flesh. Rolled pieces of it between his fingers, watched it change, a ball of sticky stuff.

'Flesh,' said the witch, a voice in his head. A man has another ear in his head, they say. A hidden ear, it listens to the dead. 'Flesh,' he heard her say, 'see how it clings. . .'

He rolled the doughy lump between his fingers.

'. . . to the bone.'

17

'W̲HAT HAPPENS TODAY in Tulach Uisce?' said the dying man to his daughter.
She sat at the window. So now I am eyes, she thought. All I am is eyes for a blind man. 'Nothing, today, Father.'

'No-one passes?'

'No-one passes.'

'You have heard no news?'

And I am ears, she thought, ears for a dying man. 'Where would I be hearing news, sitting here, tending you?'

'You go out. . . to collect the milk. . .'

'Does the cow talk to me?'

'No but women gather at the milking of cows. . .'

'Is that what you're thinking?'

'Women gossip. . . it's always been the way. . . and always will. . . it's in them. . .'

'Well we do get some work done as well. . .'

'Oh I'm not saying it's wrong, gossip. . . maybe it's even necessary. . . gossip. . . little tales and tattles, holding life together. . .'

'You worked for the druids too long, Father. . .'

'What do you mean?'

'Oh you with your druidy phrases. . . you picked them up from them. . . like *holding life together*. . .'

The dying man laughed, and coughed, and wheezed for breath.

'Don't laugh,' said the daughter, 'it's bad for you.'

'Would I cry?' he said, recovering his breath, struggling to sit in his bed, 'would you have me cry?'

'It's just that the laughing. . .'

'Oh I know what you mean. . . tell me Daughter. . . you reminded me. . . the talk of druids and the like. . . that Storyteller who passed yesterday. . . what news of him?'

'Well I heard. . .' she said.

'From the cow?'

'From another woman *working* at the milking...'

'Ah... what did you hear... while you were working... and she was working...'

'I hear why he is here.'

'And why is he here?'

'To find out about those girls... the daughters of Tara... the ones who died... Eithne and Fidelma...'

'Find out? Find out what?'

'How... and why... they died.'

'And why would he want to know that, this Storyteller?' said the dying man, cautiously.

'King Laoghaire sent him...'

'Ah,' said the dying man, and was silent.

The daughter looked out at the empty street of Tulach Uisce. Will I ever get a husband, she wondered. There are few enough men. Too many died in the wars against Ulster. And the men that are here, what do they want with the likes of me?

⌒•

EITHNE COMBED FIDELMA'S HAIR.

It was dark in the rain.

Fidelma combed Eithne's hair.

And it too was dark in the rain.

'Have you noticed,' said Eithne, 'how in the rain our hair is the same colour?'

'The colour of the rain?'

'But the rain itself has no colour.'

The comb ran through the hair, and water ran ahead of the teeth of the comb in a stream, and trickled from the ends of the hair. And as the comb ran the water out of the hair, so the hair got blonder. But the water that dripped from the ends of the hair was not black or dark or even coloured at all. It was clear, and it was the strangest thing to see.

'Isn't that the strangest thing?' added Eithne.

'Strange, yes.'

'But not so strange as the Storyteller's journey!'

'No,' laughed Fidelma, 'not so strange as that. And it'll get stranger!'
'They have left Patrick now.'
'I know.'
'They have ridden back to Rathcroghan.'
'I know, stop telling me things I know.'
'The Storyteller. . . and that wife they call the daughter of the moon.'
'And the dogs.'
'The black dog and the white dog, yes, the black called Night, and the white called Day'.
'They rode along that narrow path.'
'Through the yellow of the gorse, and the paler yellow of the broom, and the bracken closing in. It brushed against the horses as they passed.'
'The length of them, like a procession, they trailed across the countryside. Stretched out, no-one talking, none to the other. Like farmers coming home from a bad market. Each thinking their own thoughts.'
'First the witch. And her dark hair dripping rain. And her old woman's hands on her young woman's body, they held the reins, slackly.'
'Her horse knew the way, and needed no guiding.'
'Then her seven wizards, thin men on thin horses.'
'Their horses knew the way, they needed no guiding. And then the white dog, they call him Day. And then the Storyteller himself, he bends against the rain, muttering curses against Connacht.'
'And then the black dog, they call him Night.'
'And then the Wife, her bare legs wet, very wet, she hummed a tune.'
'What was that tune?'
'I forget, I forget.'
'And then, a long way behind, a slatted cart, creaking and squeaking. . . pulled by a horse that was led by a man on foot. A man on foot. He led an old horse. And on the old horse there was an old woman. And her skirts were the colour of the horse, hard to tell where horse began and woman ended.'
'She had an evil eye.'
'Would you want that cart behind you on a journey?'
'Not I, sister, not I!'

'Anyway. . . the Storyteller and the Wife are back in Rathcroghan now, in the guesthouse on Tulach Oichre.'

'It's the afternoon now. . .'

'But dark in the rain. . . no wonder we get confused about the time of day! This is a terrible country, for the weather!'

'Yes look at those, black clouds in the west. . . and listen to that, rumble of thunder. . . do you remember you were afraid of thunder Eithne?'

'Yes, when I was a child in Tara.'

'Do you remember once as children we went walking far away from Tara. . .'

'Yes, down the hill from Tara. . .'

'Too far for children.'

'We were playing in the rath they call Rath Maeve. . .'

'No-one lives there and it's ghostly. . .'

'Maybe Maeve lived there once?'

'Maybe she did. . . or maybe people only think she did, because the place is ghostly.'

'Oh she did. . . but not the Maeve of here, this place.'

'No? Who told you that?'

'I learn. I study. I remember. The Maeve of Tara was a wife of Art. And he was the father of Cormac.'

'Well that's useful to know,' giggled Fidelma.

'Well how would you like to be mixed up with some other Fidelma in the future? I wouldn't. . . what if people in the future think I'm the Eithne who was sister of the Maeve of here?'

'Whereas in reality you're the Eithne of Tara, sister of the Maeve of Tara!'

'Oh stop teasing me. . . what were we talking about. . . yes. . . at Rath Maeve. . . we were playing there. . . far from home. . . and the weather changed, and the thunder came. . . and we were frightened. . .'

'And we sheltered under a thorn.'

'And the thorn had no leaves.'

'But we stayed dry because the fairy in the thorn took pity in us. . . do you remember that?'

'I remember that.'

'And then the horsemen came, horsemen from our father,

looking for us in the rain.'

'And were relieved to find us.'

'But by that time we weren't frightened. . . because we knew the fairy in the thorn was protecting us. . . from the thunder and the rain.'

'We're alright, we said to the horsemen. . . we're good and dry. . . the fairy is looking after us. . .'

'Your father says you must come home they said.'

'And they swept us onto their horses.'

'One on one horse, and the other on the other.'

'They held us there between their arms, and brought us home.'

'I remember their arms, those young men. . . I suppose they were our father's soldiers.'

'Yes, I suppose.'

'Strong young men. . . with hairy arms.'

'I remember that too.'

'I looked at my own arms in bed that night. . . and they were the thin arms of a little girl. . . hairless. . . and weak. . . and I wished I had the arms of a strong young man. . .'

'Around you?'

'Around me.'

⁓·

'THERE'S A WOMAN HERE,' said the Servant, 'here from Tulach Uisce.'

'Tulach Uisce,' said the Storyteller, 'Tulach Uisce? Your home place? The Rome of Connacht?'

'What does she want?' said the Wife, cutting through the mockery.

'She brings a message, for the Storyteller.'

'Who do I know in Tulach Uisce?' said the Storyteller.

'What message does she bring?' asked the Wife.

'For the Storyteller, for him alone. She would not say any more.'

'Oh,' said the Wife, shrugging. 'Well I'll ask no more!'

'I know no-one in Tulach Uisce,' said the Storyteller, 'and I hadn't planned on changing that situation either.'

'What will I tell her?' asked the Servant, 'she waits outside.'

'Oh go to her,' said the Wife to the Storyteller, 'it's you she wants to talk to. . . you alone. . . not the likes of me!'

The Storyteller raised his eyes.

Women, he thought. Just the word, *women*. . . he didn't think anything *about* the word, just the word, *women*.

He went outside.

And the woman waiting there was huddled in the rain. She had no horse, or there was none to see, and she must have walked from Tulach Uisce with her message.

'How far is Tulach Uisce?' he asked.

'It's several miles, from there to here,' she said, and paused, 'uphill.'

'Your message must be important so. . . to walk so far. . . in the rain. . .' He paused. 'Uphill.'

'My Father sent me here, he wants to talk to you.'

'Why can't he come himself?'

'He's blind, and dying.'

'I am no doctor.'

'Oh he knows that. . . and he knows no doctor can help him. . . he's dying of the breath. . .'

'The breath?'

'He has none. . . the doctors say it's a drowning in him. . . and he has no breath. . .'

'I see. . . well I'm sorry to hear that. . .'

'People die,' she shrugged. 'Why are you sorry?'

'Well I'm not really sorry. . . it's just something we say. . . in Tara. . .'

'Why do you say things like that? Things you don't mean?'

'A good question, woman, a good question. I think we call it civilisation. . . in Tara. . .'

'In Connacht we might call it something else.'

'Indeed, you might, and you might be right. . . but. . . perhaps. . .' He looked at the sky, and rain fell on his face. 'Perhaps we should talk of more immediate things. . . we're both getting wet here.'

'I'm wet already, soaking through.'

'And you would be happy for me to be the same?'

'We'd have an equality then.'

'But I, I am a Storyteller from Tara. . . and you are a woman from Tulach Uisce. . .'

'And your point is?'

She looked at him, a challenge.

And he looked at her, and laughed.

'You're a woman of spirit,' he said, 'I like you.'

'So you will come to Tulach Uisce?'

'I'm not sure I like you that much.'

'But you must come. It's very important. My Father says it's very important.'

'And you are a loyal daughter?'

'Not particularly. . . he's a grouchy man. . . very demanding. . . and he says *everything* is important. . .'

'Ah. . . that's not very encouraging. . . that doesn't hurry me on my way to Tulach Uisce'.

'But,' she raised a finger, 'but I do know when things are *really* important. . .'

'You do?'

'Yes, and this is one of them. Would I walk in the rain. . . many miles. . .'

'Uphill. . .'

'Yes. . . for the whim of a grouchy man? No I wouldn't!'

The Storyteller looked at her, deciding, calculating.

She was definitely a woman of spirit. But, on the other hand, there are many women of spirit. And if a man were to be following the determination of each of them he'd have little life left for himself. But. . . on the other hand. . .

He decided.

'I go,' he said, and turned to the door. 'My cloak,' he called to the Servant, 'and my horse.'

'You go to Tulach Uisce?' said the Wife.

'I go to to Tulach Uisce.'

⁓•

HE GOES TO TULACH UISCE, thought the Wife, thinking, picking at her nails with the tip of her knife. To Tulach Uisce, with a woman come in from the rain.

A frumpy village woman, a total stranger.

She sits behind him on his horse, her arms about his waist.

The rain beats down on them.

She rests her head on his shoulder for shelter.

He himself has no shelter, and the rain is pebbles on his face. He looks out at the harsh land, where nothing lives, and nothing moves. And he hears the story of the land, whispering.

Whispering the message of a harsh land.

Do not forget, says the harsh land, Storyteller, do not forget... tell my story.

Ride on, Storyteller, to Tulach Uisce.

With the harsh rain in your face, and the cold wind in your face, and the soft meat of a frumpy village woman at your back. Warm at your back. Soft against your back. Ride on, thought the Wife, thinking, picking her nails with the tip of her knife. Thinking of the soft meat of the frumpy village woman. Thinking of the tip of her knife.

Ride on, she thought, ride on through the harsh land, husband.

Through my harsh land, my place, it'll be a learning.

The Wife smiled, knowing things. A man marries a woman like me, he finds her in a dream. Then he finds himself married to the rain, it beats like the pebbles on his face. And he finds himself married to the wind, clapping at his cloak. To the sound of the wind, and the cracking sound of the cloak in the wind. Married to Connacht, and to the soft meat of a Connacht woman at his back. Warm at his back, soft against his back.

Ride on, Storyteller, thought the Wife, to Tulach Uisce.

And then she smiled.

The Servant saw her smile, a cold and cruel smile, that was the smile of a wizard girl. He shivered a little, and went about his business in the guesthouse.

The Wife smiled, asking questions in her mind. But will you pause along the way, Storyteller, Husband, with some excuse about the weather? And lead the frumpy village woman under trees, and silently shag her?

She has it in her, she's a Connacht woman after all, and a Connacht woman hungry for a man!

What matter?

The Wife looked into her sight, and saw the answers to the questions in her mind.

The Father of that woman is dying.

Soon he will die, and she will be alone.

There are few men in these parts, particularly for a frumpy village woman.

She will grow old, alone, with a secret.

A great man shagged me once.

From Tara, he was, a Storyteller.

It was a rainy day, a very rainy day.

I mind it well.

I knelt in a little wood there, at Cnocavurrea, on the road to Rathcroghan from Tulach Uisce. The rain spattered on my back, on my arse, and a run of it ran down the crack of my arse like water in a drain.

And then he covered me, sheltering me.

Is that wood still there?

Or do I remember right, they've cut the trees for wood? No matter. It was there back then. I knelt there. My arse in the air for him. And he said something about Connacht women, always kneeling like that, to be shagged. And I said we like to see the earth at times like this. . . better to chew the leaves than a man's shoulder.

And he laughed.

And I said don't laugh at me.

So he didn't. But was very kind, and gentle.

Very civilised!

As you'd expect.

The people in Tara are very civilised.

Oh yes, they're not like us at all, us in Tulach Uisce.

The Wife smiled, seeing it all in her sight, hearing it in her hearing, ghosts talking, one to the other. 'What would I tell you, ghost in the shadows of Tulach Uisce?'

'Is that woods still there?'

'No they've burned it for wood. . . long ago. . .'

'So it's not even smoke anymore?'

'No, not even smoke.'

'Just a memory.'

'Just a memory. In the story of the land.'

'Whispering.'

The Wife smiled. Yes she saw in her sight the life of the woman from Tulach Uisce. One life that woman might live, if she lived, long enough.

She picked her fingernails with the tip of her knife. And then, done picking, she held out her nails to look. Claws of a cat, she thought, feet of a bird.

⁃

'CLOSE THE DOOR,' said the dying man, 'I would not have the daughter hear.'

'The door is closed,' said the Storyteller, 'though she's not even in your house. She's brought my horse to the yard.'

'A man can't be too careful. . . women gossip!'

'Is it me you're telling!'

'Come close, I cannot speak loud, it's the breath, I have no breath in me.'

The Storyteller moved closer.

The face of the man in the bed was grey.

'How close are you now?'

'Very close.'

The dying man reached out, and waved his hand, like he was saying a slow goodbye. But he wasn't saying a slow goodbye, he was reaching out to touch. Then his fingers found the Storyteller's face. And he tapped about. 'You have a beard like a druid on you,' he said.

'Don't be fooled by that,' said the Storyteller, 'beards hide more than they show.' He edged away from the feeling hands. Because perhaps they could see more than eyes, and he liked his privacy. 'Now what is it you have to say, why did you send for me?'

'I worked for Maol and Caplait, all my life, man and boy.'

'The druids? I know them by repute, two learned men.'

'Hmmmn,' said the dying man.

'So what of these learned men?'

'Well I talk of the girls. . . the ones there's all the fuss about. . . Eithne and Fidelma. . .'

'Yes of them I would be curious.'

'They came as students here. . . Maol and Caplait fostered them. . .'

'I know this much. . .'

'Let me tell the story. . . in my way.'

'Tell me. . .'

'First I will tell you of Patrick the Roman. . .'

'Ah. . . him!'

'Patrick the Roman came into this country, preaching his god. . . preaching his god to the people, and to the Chiefs, and the King. . . but mostly to the Chiefs. . . because if the Chiefs followed Patrick, then all the people ruled by those Chiefs would follow that god too. . .'

'Oh I know the way that boyo works.'

'A lot of Chiefs started following him. They thought it was a new strong magic that would help them. . . in wars with their neighbours. . . that sort of thing. . .'

'But if all the neighbours followed the same god, and had the same magic?'

'Aachh. . . Chiefs round here don't think very clearly. . . don't think at all to be truthful. . . cattle and women and fighting is all they think about really. . .'

'I know the sort!'

'But Maol and Caplait think.'

'Of that I have no doubt.'

'Patrick went to Maol and Caplait, preaching.'

'I'm sure he got his answer.'

'Indeed he did. But before they ran him from the place, he told them about Jesus Christ, his god, or son of his god, whatever he is. . .'

'It's complicated stuff. He's god, but also the son of god. And he's a man, but also god.'

'Complicated or not, Maol and Caplait were very interested in him. Particularly this idea. Of him being killed. And coming back in three days. They talked of it a lot.'

'Very impressive feat, that is!'

'Yes. . . and Maol and Caplait knew that this was very impressive to the Chiefs. . . even though it was only a story. . . even though no-one had actually seen that Jesus Christ dead, and coming back in three days. . . well no-one round here anyway. . . that all happened off somewhere in the Roman country. . . anyway. . . Maol and Caplait knew that this was one thing attracting the Chiefs to Patrick's god. . . so they decided to do something like it themselves. . . to show that they still had the power. . . to stop the Chiefs from leading the people to the new god.'

'What did they decide to do? Get killed and come back in three days?'

'No. . . but to kill someone. . . and bring them back in the three days. . .'

'How did it go, how did they manage the trick?'

'Well they did and they didn't. They killed someone. . . but. . .'

'Eithne and Fidelma?'

'How did you know?'

'Well I can tell the way the story's coming out. . . what you are saying. . . in a roundabout way. . . Maol and Caplait killed the girls. . .'

'Well. . . sort of. . .'

'What do you mean, sort of?'

'Well it was I that killed the girls. . . sort of. . . they told me to. . . to get some ruffians. . . to kill them. . .'

'Ruffians?'

'Rathcroghan is full of ruffians since the wars. . . soldiers. . . captives. . . slaves. . . foreigners. . . no-one knows who is who anymore. . . it's easy to hire ruffians. . .'

'I can well believe. . . I've seen the population of Rathcroghan. . . so. . . the druids told you to get the girls killed. . . you hired ruffians. . . how did they kill them?'

'They drowned them in the Well of Clebach. It was my idea. I knew the girls went there. . . because all the women go there. . . it's a sacred place to them. . . so I told the ruffians when to go. . . to drown them. . .'

'What happened then?'

'Maol and Caplait were planning to bring the girls back to life. . . after three days. . . just like that Jesus Christ. . . so they brought a big darkness over the place. . . for three days. . .'

'A big darkness?'

'So that it would be the same.'

'The same?'

'The same darkness as Jesus Christ. . . being dead. . . so they could show the people they were just as powerful. . . that their gods were just as good as the Romans'.'

'I see. . . so what then?'

'Well it was night here then. . . for three days. . . while they were doing the magic. . .'

'How did the magic go?'

'Not that well. . . not for Maol and Caplait. . . nor me neither. . . I never saw again. . .'

'Is that when you went blind?'

'Yes. . . when the darkness came, it got darker, and darker, and darker. . . and at first I thought it was the darkness. . . but then I realised that I was going blind too. . . everything getting darker, and darker. . . and when the darkness lifted I didn't know it had gone. . . because I was blind. . .'

'Had you trouble with your eyes before?'

'No, never. . . eyes like a hawk. . . before. . . the darkness.'

'There's many strange things. . . so. . . when the darkness lifted. . . for the rest of the people. . . what happened then. . .'

'Daithi was very angry. . . at the girls being dead. . . he was afraid of Laoghaire making war on him. . . so Maol and Caplait decided it would be best to blame the Christians. . . and they got it to Daithi about the ruffians who had killed them. . .'

'But they weren't Christian ruffians. . .'

'No matter, ruffians are ruffians. . . Daithi had their innards pulled.'

'A fearsome death.'

'But traditional.'

'Oh yes. . . tradition has its place,' murmured the Storyteller, thinking about all this for a moment, absorbing it. There was silence in the room, for that moment. Silence but for the bad breathing of the dying man. And the clucking of hens out there in the street. And was that the sound of a stream, trickling?

'But tell me this,' said the Storyteller then, 'why did the Christians start putting about their story. . . about the way the girls died. . . why did they bother getting involved in the matter at all?'

'That's how cunning they are.'

'Cunning?'

'Well it was the three days of darkness. . .'

'What about it?'

'Well the Christians weren't very happy about the power of the druids with that. . . so there was no way around. . .'

'No way around. . .'

'No they had to say they were involved from the start. . . that it was all a Christian thing. . . because if they wanted credit for the darkness then they had to take responsibility for the deaths of the girls too...'

'It seems to me that a lot of people round here were in danger of losing their innards!'

'Yes, they were... me included... that was it, so the Christians thought up that story of the girls dying by some magic... to see their god...'

'And Daithi believed them?'

'Whether he did or he didn't I don't know... by then I had my own problems... with sickness...'

'It came on you then?'

'Yes, I was well, a healthy man... but I got the drowning in me... and I couldn't breathe properly any more... I was far from worrying what Daithi believed, or what he didn't!'

'You didn't come well out of this, with your blindness, and your loss of breath...'

'No, but I still have my innards! Truth is, the girls put a curse on me... at the well of Clebach... I saw them naked... they put a curse on my eyes for that... that fair one...'

'Eithne.'

'Yes, she struggled to the surface... and her eyes caught mine... and she raised her left hand at me... I knew then...'

'You were cursed.'

'Yes... then one of the ruffians pushed her head back under the water... but her left hand was still over it, cursing me... he held her head down, and her legs were kicking and thrashing. She kicked an awful lot. I watched her thighs, they were white and pretty, kicking around, but the funny thing...'

'The funny thing?' asked the Storyteller, prompting.

'Yes the funny thing, with all the kicking, that left hand of hers held still all the while, over the surface of the water... cursing me... I tell you I didn't feel good at all!'

'A man wouldn't. But tell me this, are you sure of this... it was the fair one cursed you, not the dark?'

'No the dark one went quietly to her death.'

'Like she was death, herself,' mused the Storyteller.

'What do you say?'

'I say the things a storyteller says,' he replied, 'take no heed of them. So. . . anyway. . . it was you had them drowned. . .'

'Well. . . only carrying out orders. . . but still. . . the fair one put a drowning curse on me for that. . .'

'This is what you believe?'

'Well what do you believe?'

'The truth. . . when I find it,' said the Storyteller.

The dying man laughed, then coughed, then gasped for breath. His face went blue.

If he dies now, thought the Storyteller, what will I do?

He looked around, but the house was quiet. Hens clucked in the street. Was that the sound of a stream?

If he dies now, thought the Storyteller, what will I do?

But the blind man didn't die. Slowly he recovered. His face went a healthy grey again. 'I was nearly gone there,' he said.

'There's a time in you yet,' said the Storyteller, doubtfully.

'Aye,' said the blind man and then, suddenly, his fingers found the Storyteller's wrist, and clamped it there. 'Tell me,' he said, 'my daughter brought you here?'

'A good woman, she did indeed.'

'Have you a wife?'

'Three fine women.'

'A man in your position might need another?'

'He might, if he had the money, or the time, or the house to put her in.'

'My daughter would make a good wife. . . for the man who likes a mature woman. . . are you a man who likes a mature sort of woman?'

'Indeed. . . a giggling girl would have a man in an early grave.'

'A mature woman. . . and it's not for a father to say, but a fine good hold on her I'll bet.'

'Oh a good hold on her,' agreed the Storyteller, trying not to sound as if he was speaking from experience. 'A good hold, or at least that's what I should imagine.'

'A free woman, with a house of her own. . . and some good milking cows. . . and a patch of land over near Lissakirkea.'

'A right catch for a man, that woman.'

'Which would all go with her in a marriage. . . because her father would be dead. . . and there's no-one else belonging to her.'

'An attractive prospect. . . for the right man, I will agree. The Storyteller made to go. 'Well. . . I must. . .'

'You might bear it in mind. . . you know where I am. . .'

'I do indeed,' agreed the Storyteller.

He paused at the door. The way a visitor will, at the door of a dying man. 'Tell me,' he asked, 'why did you send for me, to tell me this story?'

'To clear the mind,' said the blind man, 'to clear the mind.'

'To clear the mind? Sure that's a Christian thing, before you go to see the Christian god. . .'

'Better safe than sorry,' said the blind man, with a cough that might have been a laugh.

⸺•

'THE RAIN HAS EASED,' the daughter said.

'It has,' the Storyteller agreed.

'You'll have an easier ride back so,' she said.

'But it is uphill,' he mentioned.

'Yes,' she said, 'downhill makes for an easier journey.'

'So long as the road is not too steep. A steep road is hard, either going up or down.'

'A man would want to rest. . . on any journey really. . .'

'Is it better to rest on the way of a journey. . . or before the start. . . or at the end?'

'I suppose it depends on the comforts to be had. . . a rest at the start might give him strength. . .'

'Yes, particularly if the journey ahead is uphill.'

'Well the journey to Rathcroghan is definitely uphill.'

'Maybe I should rest a little so. . .'

'I have a little room along here. . . you won't be disturbed here. . .'

'It's very quiet.'

'A quiet village, Tulach Usice.'

'Is that a stream I hear?'

'Yes. . . that stream flows from up the hill. . . from the Well of Clebach actually. . .'

'It makes a pretty sound.'

'What colour is your hair?'

'Sometimes brown, and sometimes black. . . when it rains it's black. . .'

'Yes I thought it lighter now. . .'

'It's had a chance to dry.'

'And soft, soft to the touch.'

'Soft, to a soft touch.'

∽•

'HE'S GETTING CLOSER NOW,' said Fidelma.

'Yes, he is,' agreed Eithne.

'He's with that village woman, in Tulach Uisce.'

'I see him, I see him, do you think me blind, sister?'

'It must be dark, being blind.'

'The father of the woman, he is blind.'

'And he drowns in his own breath.'

'He made his own curse, and lives it,' said Eithne, coldly.

'True true. . . look, look, see how she kneels, face in her pillow.'

'Connacht women!'

'Sshhh. . . they'll hear us giggling.'

'They'll think it the sound of the stream.'

'Is he going to mount her, or play with her buttocks all the afternoon?'

'He's thinking about it!'

'He's thinking of that sow, he saw with Frucht and Lucht, they were bringing to the Mucklaghs. He sees no great difference.'

'I don't either!'

'Ssshhh. . . don't giggle. . .'

'I tell you, I'm the sound of the stream.'

'You're more like a waterfall, with that giggling! But tell me sister, do you think he'll believe the blind man's story?'

'Will it bring him closer if he does?'

'Closer to us?'

'Yes. . . to us. . . is the blind man's story true?'

'Perhaps. . . oh look. . . he's mounting her. . .'

'She *is* just like a pig, isn't she?'

'Fat as one too!'

'Oh I think she's quite pretty. . . in a sad sort of way. . . see how her breasts swing?'

'Yes, they are pretty. . . in a sad sort of way. . .'

'Swinging, like a sow's dugs.'

'Remember the sows, running through the Mucklaghs. . . in their pretty dresses.'

'And pretty ribbons flying. Running on their little legs. And the boars beyond, waiting.'

'It's a wonderful thing to see.'

'It is indeed. Do you think the Storyteller will believe the blind man's story?'

'Do you think the Wife will believe his!'

Eithne and Fidelma laughed.

And the laughter was the sound of the stream from the Well of Clebach as it tumbled through the village of Tulach Uisce. Swollen with rain, it was almost a river today. The Storyteller drove himself into the blind man's daughter. Deeply. He was a man putting up the pole of a tent, and him looking for a holding in the softness of the ground. He put his weight behind his prick, and then in his mind he was a shepherd leaning on a crook. And his prick was a shepherd's crook in the ground, sinking, pointing, reminding.

Deep in the ground there are jewels and bones. They make no sound. They reach up from the darkness for a voice. And the sound of their voice today is the squirt and slurp of a fat woman's passage, squelching pleasantly. Squelching and gurgling, nicely, thought the Storyteller, a handful of ham in his left hand, and a handful of ham in his right. Or, he wondered, wondered suddenly, or were those watery noises the stream, and it laughing at him?

The fat woman moaned.

Or was that the sound of the blind man, dying?

She sighed.

Yes that was definitely a sigh. And the hens clucked in the street, suddenly excited, like someone was throwing them seed. And the sighs of the fat frumpy woman of Tulach Uisce were the shushes of seed in the air, scattering.

18

In Tara once there was an old slave. He worked silently, few talked to him, fewer knew who it was he worked for, or what precisely was his work. Some said he worked for no-one, in reality, and that he had no work. They said he just moved this way, and that, about the place, giving an illusion of being a slave, making an illusion of working. And that is all they said about him, because a slave is not important, and talking about one even less! There are many people like that, nothing about them is important, they fill the pauses between conversations. And so it was, any conversation about the old slave would pass quickly on to another subject. He was just part of the life that was there in Tara once. A busy place, with a complicated life, a life of threads, all tapestried together. And him just a loose thread, that old slave.

In Tara once, one morning, the Storyteller came across the same old slave. He carried two buckets on a shoulder yoke. He had red hair, gone thin on top and rusty over the ears, and long and lanky links of it curled on the bar of the yoke.

A tall man, the slave was, and so it wasn't possible to see whether the buckets were empty, or full. All that was possible to see was that they were balanced, evenly. The yoke leaned neither this way or that. It was an easy load.

'What do you carry in your buckets?' asked the Storyteller, taking this opportunity to satisfy some curiosity.

'Luck,' said the slave, mysteriously, looking this way, that. A man not wanting too many others knowing his business.

'Luck?' said the Storyteller, immediately thinking the slave was mad, and that that could be the answer to many questions about his life.

'Yes, luck,' said the slave.

'In each bucket?'

'Oh yes, each bucket carries luck.'

'Is it good luck, or bad luck?' asked the Storyteller.

'Good and bad,' said the slave.

'Good *and* bad?'

'Yes in this bucket here I carry the good. . . and in this bucket here I carry the bad. . .'

Yes, mad, thought the Storyteller, 'this man is quite mad.' Nonetheless, he encouraged him. 'So the buckets are equally loaded this morning. . .'

'Oh yes,' said the slave, 'that is the trick.'

'The trick?'

'To keep them equally loaded. . . because you see. . . if one is heavier than the other, the load will be awkward. . . and the thing is. . .'

'The thing is?'

'It doesn't matter which of the buckets is heavier, good luck or bad luck, the load will still be awkward. . .'

'I see,' said the Storyteller.

'Do you?' said the slave. 'Do you see that a man must have good luck, and bad luck. . . and if he's to travel easy he'd better have an equal share of each. . .'

'Yes I quite understand,' said the Storyteller, edging away.

He quite understood.

The slave was barking mad! But now, here, far away from Tara, with years gone, he suddenly remembered, that peculiar slave, and his theory of the nature of luck.

It held water!

He remembered all this, coming slowly up the hill from Tulach Uisce to Rathcroghan, his horse tired, and he himself likewise, but feeling reasonably relaxed, as a man does after an encounter with an agreeable woman. Frumpy and plain she may very well be, he thought, that blind man's daughter, but in a private arrangement such things do not really matter. It's a man unsure of himself needs glamorous women around him!

And so, all in all, coming up the hill, he felt his luck was evenly balanced.

His load was light!

There was a certain amount of bad luck, in being here in this desperate Connacht country, surrounded by savages. But, nonetheless, a fat woman who needed a man, and no questions asked or answered, that was good luck. The continuing problems of finding out about Eithne and Fidelma, that could be descibed as bad luck. But then, the story of a blind man, a story that might not or might be true, that was good luck. And now the rain had stopped, that was good luck.

He calculated on.

Then this sudden meeting, with Hernicius, Bernicius and Nitria on the road?

That was very bad luck.

The imaginary buckets of luck on his shoulder tilted wildly. His load grew heavier. He felt weighed down. He was suddenly very tired, tired of Bernicius, tired of Hernicius, and tired of their sister Nitria.

They grouped around him on their horses, all smiling in a saintly way.

'Well met,' said Bernicius. Or Hernicius.

'Nice to see a bit of blue sky,' said Nitria.

'I have the feeling we're in for a fine night,' said Hernicius. Or Bernicius.

The Storyteller made appropriate responses.

This endless optimism of Christians he found very depressing. Oh yes, long before the encounter with Patrick at Magh Seilig, long before that he'd come across them in Tara, knew them well, too well! Despite complete and overwhelming evidence to the opposite, they saw the world as good and kind, the creation of a friendly god. And they'd have no argument about the matter. Any problems in the world was the work of the devil. Who or what this devil was was never discussed. But to the Storyteller the same devil seemed a pretty powerful god in his own right, and should be kept happy!

The Christians didn't seem to see it that way!

'We're going to a prayer meeting,' said Hernicius. Or Bernicius.

'In Mullygollan,' added Bernicius. Or Hernicius.

'A prayer meeting,' said the Storyteller, 'in Mullygollan?'

'Yes,' said Nitria, 'you're most welcome to come along.'

'Most welcome?' said the Storyteller, aghast, 'to a Christian prayer meeting? In Mullygollan?'

'Yes, you'd be really welcome,' said Nitria.

The Storyteller looked her up, and down.

Not a bad looking woman at all, he thought. Take away those strange clothes, and that silly haircut, and that'd be a good looking woman for any man. A lot better looking than the daughter of the blind man in Tulach Uisce, that's for sure! But. . . but. . . the Storyteller considered, but looks aren't everything.

A man can be seriously led astray by a woman's looks.

Nitria smiled, at him examining her.

He smiled back.

Yes, he thought, her looks could lead me astray!

But a prayer meeting in Mullygollan was about as far astray as he wanted to be led. In fact, it was slightly further. 'Very unfortunately,' he said, 'I have an important arrangement, with important people.'

'Who?' said Nitria.

Who, he thought, who? What has it come to, an important man being interrogated about his movements by a blow-in foreigner of a wench from Armorica? Was a man not master in his own country anymore?

'Who,' he replied, aloud, politely. 'With Maol and Caplait, actually.'

'Maol?' said Hernicius. Or Bernicius.

'Caplait?' said Bernicius. Or Hernicius.

'But they're pagan druids,' said Nitria.

'And I a pagan storyteller,' said the Storyteller. He prepared himself for an onslaught. But it didn't come.

'Well,' she said, calmly, 'some other time.' She smiled, sweetly, patiently. And very irritatingly.

He rode away, away along the side track from the main route, looking nervously over his shoulder lest they follow. He passed whin bushes, and a crooked tree, and a clamp of purple heather flowers. But he didn't notice any of these things. Getting away from the preachy Romans was all that he had on his mind. It was good to put the bulk of the mound they called the little fort between himself and a prayer meeting in Mullygollan. They'd probably be discussing the mystery of the holy trinity!

He rode on, and as the distance between himself and the Christians increased, he relaxed. His load felt lighter!

He looked around.

I know this place, he thought, and remembered.

༄

'HE REMEMBERS,' said Eithne.

'Coming here as a student. . . years ago,' added Fidelma.

'He went to the house of the druids.'

'As we did too, we went to the house of the druids down that very path.'

'Near here, just there, beyond the little fort, and down that very path.'

'By that tree, that tree with a particular shape.'

'Yes, the shape of that tree, do you remember us talking about it?'

'Yes, the shape of it. . . like an old man bent to the wind. . .'

'And how when we came here in summer, strange because it was an like old man wearing a heavy cloak of leaves.'

'Yes, and in winter he was bare to the wind, a bony old man.'

'Bent to the wind. . . yes. . . look, the Storyteller. . . he remembers that too.'

'He thinks it strange, the memory, and that he should be here now, and that he should have just now mentioned Maol and Caplait to the Christians.'

'Before he quite realised he was near their house.'

'Yes, strange, how memories are there, before they're remembered.'

'How memories are there before the things remembered too!'

Eithne laughed. 'Sister you're confusing me,' she said, 'what do you mean, memories are there before the things remembered?'

'Well,' said Fidelma, 'he saw that pig, with Fruich and Lucht, and then he was mounting her, in Tulach Uisce.'

Eithne laughed. 'I still don't know what you mean.'

'Me neither,' laughed Fidelma. 'Look, he turns his horse.'

'He's going to the druids' house.'

'Now he knows the story of the blind man in Tulach Uisce.'

'But does he *believe* the story of the blind man in Tulach Uisce?'

'Perhaps, perhaps not. He is a cautious man.'

'Trusts nobody.'

༄

THE BEAR WAS STUFFED WITH STRAW.

It looked at the Storyteller with cold glass eyes.

The room was dark, rush candlelit. Dark, smokey, the candles giving out as much smoke as light. Whatever light they gave out was darkened by the smoke. So that if they were extinguished it'd be the same difference.

The glass eyes of the stuffed bear flickered, cold reflections.

'Where'd you get that bear?' he asked.

'From the north,' said Maol, 'a country to the north. There's lots of black bears there.'

'Was it alive when you got it?' he asked.

'Oh yes,' said Maol, 'but it died of the heat of the summer. They're used to a cold climate, those bears. So it died, and we stuffed it.'

'It's not just straw, you know,' said Caplait, 'there's herbs in that mixture, preserving.'

'That bear will be here long after our time,' said Maol.

'An ancient craft,' agreed the Storyteller. 'Where did you get that girl?' he nodded to the far side of the room.

The girl was stuffed with straw. She looked at the Storyteller with cold glass eyes. They flickered in the candlelight.

'From the south,' said Caplait, 'a country to the south, there's lots of black girls there.'

'Was she alive when you got her?'

'Oh yes,' said Caplait, 'but she died. The first winter, it killed her. The cold. And damp. They're used to a hot climate, those black girls.'

'So you stuffed her?'

'Yes,' said Maol. 'That girl will be here long after our time.'

'It's not just straw, you know,' said Caplait, 'there's herbs in that mixture, preserving.'

'An ancient craft,' repeated the Storyteller, 'where did you learn it?'

'Well do you know I'm not quite sure, I suppose it's something we always knew. . .' Maol nodded.

But Caplait shook his head, disagreeing.

'We learned it from our fathers,' he said, 'it's a very complicated craft, not the sort of thing a man would always know. I agree there's certain things a man *would* always know. Eating meals, drinking beer, shagging women, things natural to a man. Born in him like its born in a redhaired mother to have a redhaired child. But stuffing a bear or a girl? Well that's a different thing entirely!'

'Perhaps you're right,' said Maol. He was the older of the two, the Storyteller reckoned, and maybe a bit doddery. Not that there was much in it. Both were very old. And bent and shrunk, their backs in curves. They were barely the height of the bear, these druids, and far shorter than the tall black girl. And it was sad for the Storyteller to see them shrunk and old. And sad to see no younger druids around the place.

'When you are gone,' he asked, 'will there be anyone here who can stuff a bear, or a girl for that matter?'

'No,' said Caplait, 'the craft will die out with us.'

'Unless you want to learn,' said Maol.

'Learn? Me?'

'Well you *are* the Storyteller of Tara. . .'

'I don't think it's part of my job. . . to be stuffing things. . .'

'You could start with a rat,' said Maol.

'A rat?'

'Well there's a lot of insides in a bear, or a person. . . best to start with something small.'

'Oh yes,' agreed the other druid, 'you'd really be best to start with something small.'

'Oh,' said the Storyteller, 'oh, I see.' He didn't feel he wanted to start with anything at all, big or small!

The bear looked at him, eyes glinting.

The girl looked at him, eyes glinting.

The skin of the bear was black, furry, and the skin of the girl was black, glistening. The bear had monstrous paws with curvey claws, shining. The girl had elegant hands, silver rings on slender fingers, shining. The bear was fat and burly, built with a shamble, you could almost see him amble through a woods, somewhere. The girl was tall, and slender. And the fact that her big high bottom looked like it belonged to someone else didn't take from her beauty at all.

They were very different, bear and girl.

But the glints in their eyes, they were the same.

Cold. Glassy. Calm. Waiting.

Waiting for the Storyteller to say something.

'I HIDE IN THE BEAR,' said Eithne.

'I hide in the black girl,' said Fidelma.

'Our eyes are glass.'

'Our hearts are straw.'

'I look like a bear on the outside,' said Eithne.

'And I like a black girl,' said Fidelma.

'My skin is furry, the druids brush me, sometimes, to keep away the dust. They polish my claws with grease from the cooking pot.'

'My skin is shiny, the druids stroke me, sometimes, squeeze my nipples, to remember women. They buff up my skin with an oily cloth.'

'Do the druids know,' said Eithne, 'know that we hide?'

'Here in their house, watching them? Perhaps.'

'Perhaps. Druids know a lot, a lot more than you'd think.'

'WHAT DO YOU KNOW,' asked the Storyteller, 'what do you know of Eithne and Fidelma?' His eyes had got used to the gloom. He sat on a stool in the centre of the floor. He sipped a clear liquid from a small green glass.

'That'll put hairs on your chest,' said Maol.

'What do you know of Eithne and Fidelma?'

'They were lovely girls,' said Maol.

'Good learners too,' said Caplait.

'King Laoghaire is an angry man,' said the Storyteller.

The druids remained silent.

'And a powerful man, the greatest of kings.'

The druids remained silent.

'Anger and power is a dangerous combination in a man,' said the Storyteller.

He sipped the clear liquid from the green glass. He nodded. 'The next man at your door may have a sword in his hands, come looking for your heads.'

'Sure our lives are nearly done,' said Maol.

'What will happen to your bear, your stuffed bear, and your stuffed girl, when you are dead?'

'Hard to say,' said Maol.

'Maybe a king will have them,' said Caplait.

'Why on earth would a king want a stuffed bear or a stuffed black girl?'

'Kings collect such things,' said Maol. 'that's what makes them kings!'

'They collect things that are no use to them,' added Caplait.

'What do you know,' asked the Storyteller, 'what do you know of Eithne and Fidelma?'

'What do *you* know?' said Maol.

'I do not know yet, what I know. . . but when I know what I know, it must be news for Laoghaire. I must bring him the truth.'

'What is the truth?' said Maol, absent mindedly.

'One man's truth is another's lies,' said Caplait.

'Don't riddle words with me, old men,' said the Storyteller, 'we have druids too in Tara, I know your ways, the twisting and confusions.'

'We all know what we know,' said Caplait.

'I met a man in Tullach Uisce,' said the Storyteller. 'I'm lately come from his house.'

'A quiet village, Tullach Uisce,' said Maol.

'But not quiet enough, perhaps,' said the Storyteller. 'The man I met was a talkative man. He used to work for you. Man and boy he said, man and boy he worked for you.'

'A loyal servant.'

'Very loyal. But not quite as loyal as you might think.'

'And why would that be?'

'He told me, about drowning the girls in the Well of Clebach. . . so yes he was loyal enough to drown them, but not loyal enough to keep the secret.'

'Did you believe him?' asked Maol.

'Why did you drown those girls. . . they were lovely girls, you said yourself.'

'They were daughters of a king,' said Caplait.

'There were any amount of slaves or rogues or slatterns round the place, by the gods Rathcroghan is full of people could do with a drowning. . . why choose those lovely girls?'

'They were daughters of a king,' said Maol. 'The Christian god sent his son for sacrifice. How could we put an answer to that? With some rogue or slattern from Rathcroghan?'

'So the man in Tullach Uisce told the truth?'

'What is truth, and what is lies?'

'How did you bring the darkness on the land?'

'What is darkness, what is light?' said Caplait.

'Oh by the gods,' said the Storyteller, 'I'm not getting anywhere with you, am I? Well, when the soldiers are at that door, don't say you weren't warned. . . your heads will be in Tara. . .'

'A pleasant place to be,' said Caplait.

'A civilised place, I should imagine,' said Maol.

'Where men are civilised, and women civilised,' said Caplait, 'they lie on their backs to take a man.'

'They don't kneel like animals, like pigs,' said Caplait, 'in the woods of Knocavurrea.'

'Why do you say that, talk of that?' said the Storyteller, 'what do you know?'

'He has the sight,' said Maol. 'He sees you, rutting the blind man's daughter, and you thinking of the hams in your house in Tara.'

'How do you say that,' asked the Storyteller, 'what do you know?'

'I too have the sight,' said Maol. 'Just like that wife of yours, the wizard girl, the daughter of the moon.'

'What of her?'

'She knows, more than you think,' said Caplait.

The Storyteller stood to go. He remembered the Neladoir of Slane had said exactly the same thing about the Wife.

She knows, more than you think.

But what did she know, and what did he think?

'You go, so soon?' asked Maol, holding a green bottle containing a clear liquid, and his wrist mimicking a pour. Or was that just the shake of an old man's wrist?

'I know enough,' the Storyteller replied.

'Does that mean you know everything, or that you do not want to know any more?' asked Maol.

The Storyteller didn't answer. Her looked at Maol, and Caplait. He looked at the black bear, and the black girl. And he spun on his heel, and left. And in his mind as he left the black bear growled and the black girl cried.

'Take me home to the north,' the black bear growled.

'And me to the south and the sun,' the black girl cried. And the growl of the bear and the cries of the girl were one.

◠•

IT WAS GOOD to be on his horse. To feel the reality of the horse between his legs. There was no arguing with this reality. The horse was a horse, of that there was no doubt! A snorting breathing stamping thing. It wouldn't look at him with glassy eyes. It wouldn't growl like a stuffed bear might growl to shock a man, or cry like a stuffed girl might cry. A horse wouldn't read a man's mind, reveal his memories, like some old druid might. And it wouldn't change into a pig, like a Tullach Uisce woman might. No, the horse would just keep on being a horse, and take him where he wanted to go!

But where *did* he want to go?

He considered. But not in a precise manner. Tired from the shagging of the woman in Tulach Uisce, his mind moved slowly, like a water wheel in a dry summer. He *knew* it was moving slowly, so at least some part of his mind was still alert. But knowing is one thing, action is another. Tired. A woman sucks the strength out of a man. Be better off without them really, all things considered. Tired. And that drink of Maol and Caplait, that hadn't helped either. What was *in* that drink?

He licked his lips and explored the innards of his mouth with his tongue, looking for tastes, ingredients. The innards of his mouth felt like the innards of a woman's passage but, he reflected, that was probably only because of the day that was in it. In any event, the tastes and ingredients of the druids' mysterious concoction was long gone from his lips and his mouth. It was down in his gut now, for better or for worse.

Had they hexed him?

Was that why he felt doubly tired, and his mind working slowly like a waterwheel in a drought? Was that the reason?

'Geddup, yadogs,' he called. And Night and Day trotted alongside, one to his left, one to his right. He rode back up the pathway from the druid's house, considering! Back up to the fort they called the little fort. This little fort, he knew, it was only *little* in the sense that there was a much bigger fort further along the road to the west. The little fort was, in fact, a very big fort. A mound of earth, the height of two men, it was ringed with a ditch and topped with a wooden fence of upright posts and interwoven thorny branches. Some of these branches had taken root and grown into bushes, almost into trees. Perhaps a sign of neglect? Perhaps. It wouldn't be surprising. All of Rathcroghan showed signs of neglect, collapse, decay.

A place has a particular time.

There's hopes and dreams, first.

And then there's disappointment, memories.

And then there's ghosts, and the time of the place is done.

The Storyteller looked up the slope of the fort. Noticed how the ring of posts around the fort now interwove with a ring of trees, the two rings like two different necklaces round the same neck, overlapping, twisting into each other, the same but not the same. Almost like the mystery of the holy trinity, thought the Storyteller, sardonically, the mystery minus one! The holy twosome!

This double fence of posts and little trees was broken by a gateway, and on each side of this there were two much larger posts, each the thickness of a man's embrace, each holding an open gate. Inside there the Storyteller could see some huts, a cart parked, but no people. The cart was tipped back and the shafts of the cart pointed upwards like they were looking around for a horse. And on the left hand one of these shafts stood a huge black bird, watching him.

He stopped.

He knew that bird.

He had seen it hopping from head to head at Tara, and the boys chasing it vainly with their spears. This was the bird with ragged wings. The bird whose feathers were a bunch of jagged knives. He knew this bird! And he remembered hearing the witch at Tara saying about that bird, watch it!

So he watched.

It lifted off in a lazy way, and drifted out through the gateway of the fort, off ahead, and landed up in front of him on a post, this time by the path, a good way ahead, but by his path nonetheless.

He watched.

His horse watched.

Night on his left and Day on his right, they watched too.

The bird shook its feathers from itself, and as it shook a shower of feathers fell to the ground, some as if they were heavier, they fell straight, some as if lighter, drifting, so there was a darkness of feathers around the post, hiding it, a darkness in the air. And in the darkness of feathers the Storyteller saw the bird no longer a bird, but a woman now, a dark haired woman, dark hair on her white shoulders and a swatche of dark hair below her white belly .

That swatche of darkness was a warning to a man.

My whiteness isn't all I am!

The Storyteller watched.

Vaguely he wished the Christians were alongside him.

This sight would put some manners on their thinking!

But then, this sight was probably a hex from the druids, he'd drunk it up in that concoction, that clear liquid in the small green glass.

He looked up at the bird woman and clutched the bone he'd carried all the way from Tara. He clutched it for safety, in case she came at him in a fury. But the bone felt a weak weapon in his hand, a rusty sword, a broken spear.

The bird woman stooped, and she picked the feathers from the ground, and dressed herself in them. And then she reached out, and picked the floating feathers from the air, like a child at a game, and she dressed herself in these too. And they were no longer feathers when she put them on, but clothes of the finest. And then she bent to the ground and picked a handful of pebbles, and tumbled them in her hands and they were jewels, and she draped her neck and hair in these and then she picked some twigs from the thorn tree by her side, and twisted them into gold and silver, and the gold was bangles for her arms, and the silver bangles for her thighs.

Married women wear those bangles, the Storyteller thought, and he wondered, who is husband to this witch?

'What magic is this?' he called out.

But she didn't answer, only smiled. And beckoned, and walked, come follow me was the wordless message of her walk.

The Storyteller followed, and she led him to a field. And there there were horses, seven horses with seven grey men on them. The colour of the horses was that of the men, and it was hard to see where horses ended and riders began.

Each of the grey men carried a grey sack.

There was also a horse with no rider.

The Storyteller recognised it as the horse of the Wife, the one they called the daughter of the moon.

'Where do we go, witch, here in the lonely world of Cruachan Ai?' he asked.

'I go to build your world, Storyteller, my wizards are with me.'

'I see them. . . they've their heads on their shoulders now!'

The witch laughed. She mounted the horse of the Wife, and beckoned him to mount his own.

'Did that frightened soldier tell you otherwise?'

'He said they carried their heads in their hands.'

The witch laughed again. 'Sure that's ridiculous! But still, I suppose there's no story not improved by the telling. . . though of course you know that, it's the storyteller's trade. . . improvement of the story. . .'

'I only say what the soldier said.'

'No matter. . . their heads are on their shoulders now. . .' She kicked her horse and led away. The Storyteller kicked at his and followed her. And there was the sound of seven more horses coming along behind.

'What do they carry, your wizards?' asked the Storyteller.

'The first wizard carries an arm. . . from the shoulder to the hand. . . the fingers are closed. . . the skin of the elbow is torn away and you can see the workings of the bones. . .'

'Where did he get that arm?'

'From a wolf. . . the wolf was bringing it to her young. . .'

'Where did the wolf get the arm?'

'From a body in a wood. . .'

'What does the hand hold, the closed hand of the arm?'

'A cross.'

'A Christian cross. . . ?'

'Yes,' said the witch, 'if you like, call it a Christian cross. . . but does a tree belong to a field, or does it belong to the sky that gives it rain to grow?'

The Storyteller didn't answer that, and shrugged away the riddle. He'd had enough of that class of foolery with Bernicius, with Hernicius, and with their sister Nitria. 'What does the second wizard carry?' he asked.

'A bag of meat.'

'Where did he get that meat?'

'From a body in a wood. . . a one-legged body in the wood.'

'One-legged?'

'And one armed. . . the other had been taken by the wolf. . .'

'Who took the other leg?'

'That leg is lost,' said the witch.

'What will you do,' he asked her, 'with the meat your wizard carries?'

'I'll bring it to the Mucklaghs and feed my pigs.'

'And what will you do with the pigs?'

'I'll dress them in dresses. And run them through the Mucklaghs. They'll be pretty for the boars. Then all the new pigs that are born I'll feed to my people. To make strong children grow to strong warriors, healthy women.'

'And where will the warriors go?'

'To war.'

'And where will the women go?'

'To make more warriors, more women.'

'And so it goes on?' he asked.

The witched reined her horse. And stared at him. And he reined his horse and the seven wizards behind reined in theirs. And everyone waited while the witch stared at the Storyteller.

'And so it goes on,' she said, mimicking him. . . 'and so it goes on. . . well would you have it any different?'

'I only asked,' he said.

'Why should it not *go on*?' the witch pointed about. 'Does that ash there grow into a yew, and that oak, there, does that grow into a rowan?'

'No,' agreed the Storyteller.

'And is the child of that ash an ash or a yew?'

'An ash,' agreed the Storyteller.

'Well then,' she kicked her horse and moved, 'well then who shouldn't my world go on?'

'No reason, no reason,' agreed the Storyteller. Slow as his mind was working, he still knew enough not to be getting on the wrong side of a witch.

They rode on in silence for awhile.

'What does the third wizard carry?' asked the Storyteller then.

'A sack of innards. . . and before you ask, yes, they too come from the body in the woods.'

'What will you do with the bag of innards?'

'I'll sort through them. . . to find the bag of the womb. . .'

'And what will you do with that?'

'I'll plant a man's seed in the bag.'

'And where will you get the seed?'

'I'll tease it from a young boy in his bed. . . I'll press my breasts into his face, and him asleep. . . I'll excite his dreams. . . and the seed will seep from him.'

'And who will be born from the womb?'

'*I* will be born from the womb,' she laughed. And the sound of her laugh was the screech of a bird. And the dog called Night paused, and he looked this way and that for a bird. And the dog called Day, she stopped too, and she looked this way and that for a bird.

'Geddup yadogs,' said the Storyteller. And they moved on. Through mud and rain and dripping whin and thorny bushes plucking at the skin. Past houses made of mud and sticks, and hungry children with big eyes, watching. Through lanes all overgrown, half blocked with tumbled stone from tumbled walls, the horses picked their way, carefully. Dainty in the mud, their hooves moved like the delicate feet of dancers, the way they pick a place, a particular place to touch the earth.

'Will you die, to be born?'

The witch laughed, but this time with the laugh of a person. 'You've been talking to the Romans too much,' she said, 'to Bernicius, Hernicius, and their sister Nitria.'

'Why do you say that?'

'They talk of death, and resurrection. . . what do they know?'

'What do *you* know?'

'I know that Bernicius will die of the fever. . . soon. . . Hernicius will live on, and go to Rome to die as an old man. And Nitria will go to the land of Coirpre. Do you know that country?'

'I know it well.'

'There she'll join the Christian women at Cluain Bronaig, and she'll die there an old woman.'

'Will they be resurrected?'

The Witch laughed. 'Oh Storyteller,' she said, 'will you let the story write the story. . . ask me now, what does the fourth wizard carry in his bag?'

'What *does* the fourth wizard carry in his bag?'

'The head of a Christian girl.'

'What will you do with that head?'

'I will put it on a stake to guard my door.'

'Where is your door?'

'You'll have to die to see my door. . . do you want to see my door?'

'Not just at the moment,' he said, quite carefully.

The witch laughed. 'Oh there'll be maidens for you, beyond my door, and food and wine aplenty. And a place to hunt with your hunting dogs. . .'

'I'm in no hurry to get there. And anyway they're not hunting dogs, they're battle dogs, trained to kill.'

'Oh well then. . . there'll be battles for your battle dogs, that I can promise! Battles for them, and throats to tear 'til their teeth are ground to the gums.'

'It sounds like the heaven the Christian girl talked about. . .'

The witch laughed, again, and she stopped her horse again. And the Storyteller stopped his. But the seven wizards didn't, they rode past them in a line, each wizard looking ahead, each wizard holding his horse's reins in the right hand, each wizard holding a bag in the left.

'Where do they go?'

'You know this place.'

'I know this place.'

He did. It was the cave, the entrance to the Otherworld.

He knew it in a dream. And the dream returned to him.

Was it still a dream?

How could he tell, who was there to ask?

There was a hex on him from Maol and Caplait. And now they stood beside him in the rain. Maol held a chain, his black bear growling on the end of it. And Caplait held a chain, his black girl crying on the end of it. The rain pasted the hair of the bear to its body, and the rain glistened on the skin of the black girl.

Some idle men leaned against the shelter of a ditch. And among them the Storyteller recognised Fruich and Lucht. He'd met them in Rathcroghan with a pig. But now they had no pig. Now they were as idle as any idle men.

Nothing much at all seemed to be happening.

'What're we doing here, what're we waiting for?' asked the Storyteller of the witch. He got no answer. He turned to look at her, but she wasn't there. He was alone with Maol and Caplait. And a black bear and a black girl. And some idle men leaning against the shelter of a ditch. And no-one was moving, and no-one was talking. And he was tired, and he was cold, and getting colder. He banged the leg bone brought from Tara against the side of his own leg, in a rhythm like lovemaking, the living leg and the dead leg together.

Is this the legbone of a man or woman, he wondered for a moment.

But it probably didn't matter.

He thought of the daughter of the blind man. The agreeable squelch of her, how she gurgled like a stream. He listened for the gurgle of that stream in his memory, but couldn't find it now. There was no sound there but the growling of the bear, and the crying of the girl, and the moaning of wind and the lashing of rain and the creaking and the squeaking of a slatted cart.

It came up the lane, creaking and squeaking and swaying from side to side. It was drawn by a horse which was led by a man who looked ahead, silently. And on the back of the horse was a crone in grey, a withered hag with an evil eye.

'I know that hag,' said the Storyteller. But no-one replied. He sighed, watched, waited. The cart stopped. The black bear growled and the black girl cried.

Fruich and Lucht came out from the group of idle men. They went to the back of the cart and opened it, and took someone out, a woman, and they led her aside. She was fat and familiar.

'I know that one,' said the Storyteller.

'Yes you do,' said a voice beside him, 'yes you do.' A well known voice with a foreign Connacht accent. He looked, startled, yes it was the Wife.

'Who is she,' he asked, 'where have I seen her?'

'In the headman's house. . . on the river. . . she wanted to drown me. . .'

'How do you know?'

'I saw into her head... and in her head I saw a picture... like watching through a hole in the wall...'

'What did you see?'

'I saw another life, another life I lived, and it travelling alongside of me like a companion on a journey.'

'And?'

'And in that life they put me on a raft of rushes and sticks and branches... and there was four rocks tied to me... on this wrist...' She held out her right wrist to the Storyteller, 'there was tied a white rock... and on this wrist...' she held it out... 'there was a grey rock... and on each of my ankles there was another rock, and one of them was brown, and one of them was black...'

'Very colourful,' said the Storyteller.

'They cut me up and down with knives. Little cuts. So I bled but did not die. I was on the raft on my back, bleeding, and the blood seeping through the reeds of the raft into the water. They towed the raft out into the river with a boat... and the raft left a trail of blood in its wake... red blood near the raft... then pink, it faded into pink as the raft passed on... and then I could feel the water seeping through the reeds and the branches... and the raft became soaked and heavier and I could feel it gradually settle in the water... and then water washing about me so's I had to lift my head to breathe... and then when I sank lower I couldn't lift my head high enough anymore... and the water washed over my face...'

'Were you frightened?'

'No because I could hear the river whispering to me... and the moonlight shining through the water at me, like it was protecting.'

'They say drowning is very peaceful.'

'Very... for awhile... I sank lower... and lower and then it got dark... and I couldn't see the moonlight anymore, and then it wasn't peaceful anymore and I started to scream... but the river whispered to me... and told me its story...'

'What was the river's story?'

'I cannot say... to you,' said the wife. 'But haven't I sung for you the Song of Clothra?'

The Storyteller said nothing.

'I screamed and kicked,' continued the Wife, 'against the drowning. But the raft sunk, and there was no way away. But with the kicking and screaming and fighting against the drowning I managed to loose one hand, my left hand. . .'

'And?' prompted the Storyteller.

'And I held it up out of the water in a curse. . . against her.'

She pointed, and Fruich and Rucht were fiddling about the fat woman from the cart, stripping her bare. Then they put her on all fours, like an animal, a halter round her neck. And Fruich led her away, her backside moving like the hams of a pig, and Rucht followed behind, casually flicking at it with his whip, in a rhythm like he was thinking of something else.

'Where do they take her?'

'Where do you take a pig,' said the Wife they called the daughter of the moon. She drew her forefinger across her throat and made a gurgling strangled noise and laughed. . . and the Storyteller noted her eyes, how one was cold and the other cruel. He held his peace except to say 'but it's not a pig'.

'Oh yes it is'. The Wife raised her hand, and waved a vision across his eyes. 'Now what do you see?'

The Storyteller looked, and in the mist of the rain he saw two men leaving, one leading a pig, and the other whipping it along. It didn't want to go. Fruich hauled on its halter. It struggled. Rucht lashed it with the whip.

'Harder,' whispered the Wife beside the Storyteller, 'Beat her, harder, I want to hear her squeal.'

Rucht beat it harder, even though he could not have heard the whispering.

The pig squealed.

The Wife laughed. The black bear growled. The black girl cried. The wind blew and the rain fell. And then the laughter of the Wife faded, and the growl of the black bear grumbled away into the sounds of the night, and the cry of the black girl was only the wind. And the Storyteller stood in the rain, alone.

19

⌒.

THE WIND BLEW and the rain fell. 'The sounds of the night are all of death,' said a young man to a younger, long ago. As students of Imleach Ono, they came here, the Storyteller and his companion. They came at night, because that was the time to come, or so said the sorcerers of Imleach Ono.

That fellow student was a golden boy. There's always one or two. A handy scribe, he knew the Latin well, and those were times when many didn't. But he could drop his pen, take up a javelin, run a race. And there was always a clatter of girls around him, giggling. A golden boy. He went somewhere far and foreign then, and was never heard of again. Maybe he was a king. Maybe he was dead. Whatever. The sounds of the night are all of memories.

The Storyteller stood alone at the mouth of the cave, alone with the memory of younger days, and of himself and all the vanished others, gone. He stood there, wondering, thinking, calculating. Where was that damn witch? And her wizards? Gone into the cave?

He moved right up to the entrance of the cave, and listened.

He heard nothing.

How deep is this cave, he wondered, and where does it go?

'Where does the cave go?' he called back, thinking the Wife was there behind him, but he heard no answer. He glanced over his shoulder, but the Wife was no longer there. Hah, he thought, was the rain too much for her? Would she not wait for her husband before hurrying off?

Then he realised how ridiculous it was, thinking that. Because this was all a hex on him, and the Wife wasn't there at all. And whether he himself was there at all, well, that wasn't clear either!

He listened at the cave mouth.

And still he heard nothing.

And then he heard laughter.

Not from the cave, but from somewhere about. He looked around, but there was no-one about. No-one or nothing but that black bird again, its ragged wingtips like bunches of black knives, and it looking at him.

He knew that bird.

And he wasn't going to be caught out again! Quickly he drew a circle to protect himself, a circle about himself in the mud, with the tip of the bone he had carried from Tara. And the bird that the Storyteller knew, it watched. And the rain fell. And the Storyteller stood within his circle, safe!

The bird looked at him.

The Storyteller looked at the bird.

He waved the bone in its direction.

The bird hopped backwards.

The Storyteller felt the bone grow heavy in his hand, like it was lifting a heaviness, and he remembered lifting the flesh of the witch they burned at Tara.

Flesh clings to the bone, he thought, letting it swing to his side again.

The witch they burned at Tara? Or didn't! As that soldier had said, they didn't burn any witch that night, according to him. But was the soldier a dream, and the witch ashes?

That soldier had certainly left very early in the morning, and that's the way a dream will leave, like it's afraid of the light of the day. But, on the other hand, was it the witch that was the dream, and was the soldier at that moment safe home at Tara?

How could he tell?

Who was there to ask?

'Go away, bird,' he called, waving the heavy bone. . . and the bird squawked, and fluttered, and lifted itself into the air with a laziness of wings and drifted away and as it drifted the Storyteller felt the heaviness of the bone in his hand becoming lighter, like a weight was slipping from it. And suddenly there was the Wife again, calling to him.

'Are you coming or are you coming?' he heard her say.

'Alright,' he called back, 'alright.'

He stepped out of the circle to follow her.

But she wasn't there!

It was the witch, the witch who met him!

A trick, a trick to get him out of his circle.

A simple trick and he'd fallen for it!

And now everything was back the way it was. Himself and the witch were standing outside the cave, like time had slipped back and this was another chance at some day that hadn't gone quite right before. Yes here came those seven grey wizards again. Riding past... again... The first, followed by the second, again, and then the third, again. And so on until they'd all passed him for the second time.

But of course it wasn't them passing for a second time.

It was the first time, and he was seeing it all again.

He watched, the first horse rode through the narrow gap that was the entrance to the cave. Far too narrow that gap, for the passing of a horse. But the horse faded through the barrier of boulders that shaped the entranceway, like a fish through water. And then the second, the same, and then the third and so on until all the wizards had vanished into the cave.

'What magic is that?'

The witch didn't answer, instead she just swung down from her horse. And as she swung her skirt shifted in a flash from her thighs, and the flesh there looked young and strong. And the Storyteller noticed that she wore silver bangles just above the knee, those bangles a married woman wears. The flesh they pressed was in the full of health. He was a man who would notice such details. But then the hand she held out to him was very old. 'Come,' she said. And the hand that held his was dry as a bird's claw, and her bony fingers sprung straight from a bony wrist. She walked him through the boulders at the entrance of the cave.

'Who are you married to?' he asked, 'you wear the marriage bangles on your leg?'

She laughed. And did not answer that.

They walked on, deep into the darkness.

And as it got darker, the Storyteller noticed, so it got lighter. But lighter with a different light. As if it were a tube of light they were walking into. And gradually this tube of light became the light, so that the darkness had gone. And it was a normal world they were in.

They came to a doorway. And guarding the doorway was the head of the Christian girl, the Christian girl he'd bought from

Coroticus. That was her head here on a stake, watching with brown eyes. And as they passed she whispered.

'What does she say?' the Storyteller asked.

'Go close to her,' said the witch.

He went closer.

The head on the stake whispered again.

'I still can't hear her, can't make out what she says.'

'Closer, go closer.'

The Storyteller bent closer.

And the head on the stake kissed him on the cheek and whispered, 'flesh clings to the bone.'

The Storyteller pulled away, in a shock. And the witch laughed, and the head laughed, and when the head laughed her mouth was a cut throat, bloody with innards. The Storyteller looked, and shivered, then walked quickly ahead.

'Where do you lead me?' he called out to the witch.

'I lead where I lead.'

They came to a room, a hall, a great hall.

The room was draped with gold. And warriors stood around, with folded arms, guarding. And maidens walked on golden slippers, silently. And the slippers were threaded in blue, in patterns the Storyteller had once seen carved on stones.

The old people carved those patterns on their graves.

It was the sign of the sun, and the moon.

And those that understood those patterns understood the sun and the moon, and their movements. But no-one understood those patterns now. The Storyteller stared at the patterns, remembering, how it was back home in Tara, the discussions about them. The meanings, so many, and the conclusions, so few!

'Better to look at the maidens' feet,' he heard the witch, reading his mind, 'look at their feet and wonder. . . you won't find any meaning in their feet either. . . but they're prettier than patterns carved in stone!'

She laughed, that merry mocking laugh.

The Storyteller looked at the feet of the maidens, the golden slippers shushing back, and forth, and silently. And then in among them he saw bare feet. Cut and bruised and muddy. But pretty feet. And pretty ankles too. His eyes moved up the body of this particular maiden, knowing who he'd see. And yes it was Ranait the brown eyed slavegirl. She'd gone to Ulster as a wraith.

She grinned.

And raised one finger to her lips, as if to shush him. And then she was gone again, in among the throng.

Tricks, he thought, tricks and jokes and mockery!

He was tired of this witch, her tricks and her jokes and her mockery.

But then he suddenly felt her gone from beside him. And he was surrounded by people, who didn't seem to see him, but went about their business. Then the people moved aside, leaving him a path to walk among them. He walked the path, and there at the end of the room she sat, the Wife, the daughter of the moon. She sat like a queen on a throne, but not on a throne, on a simple chair you'd see in an ordinary house. She had the crown of a queen on her head. But the crown was made of leaves and reeds, with dabs of mud for jewels. And on her right hand sat a black dog. And on her left a white. Oh yes, those dogs were real enough, the Storyteller recognised them well. Because one was Night, the other Day.

The legs of the Wife were thin, and her bare feet sat on a cushion made of snakes. They writhed, wrapped around her legs like the straps of living sandals. Their tongues flickered towards her thighs, but her feet were on their tails. They could go no further, unless she let them.

The Storyteller tried to think where he had seen those snakes before, because he knew he had, but he was distracted from that thought by suddenly noticing that her hair was long, and he wondered, how has it grown so long?

She only cut it days ago.

And then he laughed.

It is long because this is a dream.

And times are different in a dream.

'Yes,' said Ranait the slavegirl, coming from somewhere, or from nowhere, reading his mind, 'this *is* a dream.'

'Well I want to wake up!'

Ranait laughed. 'There are dreams that have no waking.'

'Is this one of them, am I dead?'

'The Wife waits for you. . . would you go to her bed?'

'She is cold, and cruel. A wizard girl.'

'But you love her. And her bed is guarded by the dead. . . they protect her from the living.'

'I'll stay away so.'

'But she is warm. . . and loving. . . to the dead. . . watch some more.'

The Storyteller shook his head, and wondered at all this, and watched.

The cushion of snakes that rested the Wife's feet was sitting on a scatter of bones. And the black dog chewed one bone. And the white dog chewed another. And some of the bones were clean and bare, and others clung to ragged bits of meat. Half of a ribcage lay at an angle, like the wreck of a ship on a shore.

'Whose bones are those?' said the Storyteller.

Ranait didn't answer. But she bent down and picked from among them, and held out to him a piece of an arm, the hand end, and the hand was holding a silver cross.

'Would you hold her hand, Storyteller?' Ranait smiled, a pretty smile.

He backed away. 'I would not hold that hand.'

'Hold my hand, hold my hand,' he heard, and it was the head on the stake at the door, calling.

'I will not hold that hand, that Christian hand.'

Ranait scattered the hand into the bones. And she picked up the half of a ribcage, and held it out to the Storyteller.

'Would you sleep on her breasts, Storyteller?'

'I would not sleep on those breasts, those Christian breasts.'

'Rest on my breasts, rest on my breasts,' he heard, and it was the head on the stake at the door, calling.

'Rest on her breasts, rest on her breasts,' he heard, and it was the growl of the black bear, growling.

'Rest on her breasts, rest on her breasts,' he heard, and it was the cry of the black girl, crying.

'I am ribs and bones,' said Ranait then, 'me and the Christian girl. We are ribs and bones and part of the earth, we are dust and dirt and things that grow, and wriggle, slow, we are roots and worms, me and the Christian girl.'

'I will wake now,' said the Storyteller, backing away. 'Yes, definitely, now's the time, I want to wake!'

'Wait,' he heard, and it was the Wife, the daughter of the moon, holding out her hand to him.

'No,' said the Storyteller. He looked at the Wife, and knew she was warm and loving, but it was warm and loving to the dead she was. 'No,' he said, 'I will not wait. . . your bed is guarded by the dead. . . they protect you from the living.'

The Wife laughed, and he knew the sound of that laughter.

It was the laughter of the witch, the mocking witch.

They were the one, the Wife and the witch. They changed from shape to shape. The Storyteller knew this now, remembered. The Neladoir of Slane had known this too, but he had not said.

Why had he not said?

Had she hexed a warning on him, not to say? Perhaps. But definitely there on the hill of Slane she had been anxious, not happy to climb it, and in a hurry to go. And how she had run with relief into the woods as they left!

Yes, they *were* the one, the Wife and the witch.

He looked at her.

She nodded, as if she was tired. And then shook her head, as if to wake. Then she said 'close your eyes, Storyteller, close your eyes'. And she raised three fingers of her right hand, holding her little finger down with her thumb, the way the oldest of the oldest druids do. And she magicked his mind away.

⌒•

ONE HID IN THE BLACK BEAR, and the other in the black girl, watching.

'He knows her now,' said Eithne to Fidelma.

'She leads him from darkness to darkness.'

'She is death.'

'And he loves her.'

'That's why she can lead him.'

'The druids lead us by our chains.'

'But she leads him without a chain, she needs no chain at all.'

'Because she is death, or because he loves her?'

'A clever question, sister.'

'Have you a clever answer?'

'No. But then you're so much cleverer than I. . . at school don't you remember. . .'

'Not very well. . . I don't remember. . . school or things like that. . . sometimes I think it will all fade. . . the memories. . . and there'll be nothing of me. . . even of me myself. . .'

'Oh don't say that, you frighten me. . .'

'Hold me tight.'

'We have each other.'

'Yes, we'll have each other, always.'

'Even when we've forgotten, who each other is. . .'

―・

THE STORYTELLER CLOSED his eyes and a dream opened like a door. And this was a dream in a dream, he knew. Or maybe a dream in a dream in a dream. Or more, maybe more. So many layers of dreams that he was back in the world, back in time, his own time, reality. Here he would live, and rot. Love, and die. Here he would play with his children, calculate the chances of eternity, walk in the rain. Here in time, his own time.

But. . .

But no matter where he was. . .'

His mind had been magicked away.

By the goddess of death, and her dressed as a witch, dressed as a Wife, dressed as a boy, dressed as a bone, a bone in his hand, a walking stick!

He picked his way along.

I lean on death my walking stick, I lean on death to walk through life!

He picked his way along and came to steps, leading, down. And then more steps, down further to a dark room, and the crackling of a fire and the light of a fire. And a muddy pig hanging from the ceiling, squealing. And seven grey old men sitting by the fire, muttering. And a slaughterman in a leather apron sharpening blades on a stone. And a girl dressed as a boy was looking at him from across the room, and her eyes were glinting in the firelight, flickering, cold, and cruel.

She was talking.

But she spoke the sound of knives, sharpening.

The Storyteller's eyes married the gloom. And the squealing pig was not a pig, it was that fat woman from the cart of the hag, hanging, like a pig would hang upside down, her ankles tied to hooks at a beam. Her hair touched the floor. Huge fat tits flopped over her face, covering it, so it looked like her head was in bags, muddy bags. And squeals came out from between the bags where they pressed together, like it was a mouth between them. . .

The slaughterman's knives grated across stones.

The fat woman squealed. The druid Maol muttered, something in the corner. His bear strained at his chain, growling. The druid Caplait muttered something else, in another corner. His black girl strained at her chain, crying.

The fat woman squealed.

The Storyteller looked a question across at the Wife. But she looked back, and her eyes were cold and cruel. She whispered. But the whisper was the scrape of a knife, sharpening. The fat woman squealed, suddenly, and the Storyteller looked back at her, but it was not a woman now, it was a pig, swaying, squealing. It swung and twisted from the hooks.

The slaughterman decided on a knife.

He walked from his sharpening stone.

And now the Storyteller saw that his head was split, and all that was there was two thirds of a head, like a third had been axed away.

'What place is this,' he said, 'and who are you?'

The slaughterman said nothing. It was the girl dressed as a boy who answered. 'I am death,' she said, 'as you well know, and this is Irial the pig slaughterer.'

'Irial? From Tara?' said the Storyteller.

The slaughterman nodded his head, his two thirds of a head. 'The very same,' he said, 'and how have you been yourself, I haven't seen you round, of late.'

'Oh here and there,' said the Storyteller, 'you know the way it is. But now I've met you. . . was thinking of asking. . . that slave-girl of yours. . . Ranait. . . the pretty one. . . well I was thinking of asking. . .'

'But how much were you thinking of giving?' interrupted Irial.

'Well I'm not a rich man,' said the Storyteller, carefully.

Irial laughed. And then his hand reached out suddenly and sliced the belly of the pig. But not deeply. Into the flesh enough for it to split, but not enough to pierce the innards. He sliced, slowly.

A stream of blood ran ahead of the knife, splashing over the udders, dripping to the floor.

'Let it squeal there awhile,' said the slaughterman, pausing at his work, walking around to the Storyteller. 'The more it squeals, the better the meat'. He looked at the Storyteller, sarcastically. 'So you're not a rich man?'

'Not particularly.'

'Well you're a lot richer than I am,' came the reply. And then Irial turned back to the pig, slapped one of the hams, and then the other. The pig swayed on the hooks. Away, and back, and when it swayed back it was no longer a pig, it was the fat woman, dripping blood, screaming.

'I am an *educated* man,' said the Storyteller, 'and there's a world of difference between rich and being educated.'

'Well I'm an ignorant man,' said Irial, 'and a poor one too!'

He pushed at the body on the hook. 'Swing high,' he said, 'swing low.'

It swung.

'Yes,' said Irial, 'I am an ignorant man. And all I know is that you and me will one day swing, Storyteller, swing high, and low, waiting for death.' He looked around. 'Where is death?'

The body swayed and swung, screaming and squealing, one minute a person, and the next a pig. High and low, the Storyteller watched it go, and then come back into sight as a pig, squealing, and swayed away again, squealing, and came back again as a woman, screaming. The pig it was remained the same, at least as far as he could see, one pig looks much like the other. But as the carcass swayed from pig to woman, and back again, the woman changed. Sometimes it was the woman from the ferryman's house at the river, and other times the daughter of the blind man of Tulach Uisce. He was sorry to see her there. But not that much. Because he told himself it was a dream, and had some hidden meaning in his mind.

The carcass swayed.

'Is this woman or pig?' shouted the Storyteller again, exasperated at the vision.

'Where is death?' said Irial.

'Where is death?' said the black bear from the north, growling.

'Where is death?' said the black girl from the south, crying.

'Death,' muttered Maol the druid.

'Death,' mumbled Caplait the druid.

'Death,' said the head of the Christian girl, 'death and resurrection.'

'I am here, I am here,' said the Wife.

'But is this the body of woman or pig,' shouted the Storyteller again, exasperated at the vision.

'Neither now,' said the Wife, her knife in her hand. 'Now it is *meat*,' and as she said the word she drove her knife deep into the white belly, the knife vanishing, her hand vanishing, and her wrist suddenly cascaded with a tumble of gut and blood. The Storyteller watched, and she immediately started to skin and butcher the carcass, expertly, with little flicks and twists.

He watched. The carcass was still alive. It twisted. He watched. The twisting of the knife. The slicing of the flesh.

'Where did you learn to do that?' he asked.

'The trick is,' she said, concentrating, 'to keep it alive. . .' Her knife sliced. 'As long as possible. . .' Her knife sliced. 'Keep her squealing. . .' Her knife sliced. 'As long as possible. . .'

'To clean the meat of blood?' said the Storyteller.

'Oh no,' said the Wife, 'for the cruelty. . . and the pain. . . for the goddess. . . the goddess. . .'

She stabbed the body, deep in a fleshy part.

It squealed.

'The goddess likes the pain. . .' She stabbed the body again, in another fleshy part. 'The pain.'

It squealed.

'How did you learn,' said the Storyteller quickly, more to distract himself from the horrible scene than to know, 'how did you learn all this?'

'I danced with the wizards as a girl.'

'Is that that why Daithi laughed at me. . . when he saw I married you?'

'Perhaps. . . few men want to marry us. . . we have blood on our hands. . .'

'You certainly do. . . and not only on your hands. . .'

'You're right,' she said, 'come. . . I'll wash. . . I'm weary,' She turned to the slaughterman. 'You finish here,' she said. He nodded his two thirds of a head. It looked like someone had axed the other third away, in a neat slice.

The Storyteller looked at it, wondering. Was that another dream, or another reality? No way of knowing. No way of knowing anything really. All my thinking leads to nothing, he realised.

It was a weary thing to know.

The Slaughterman leaned up high, and cut the carcass from the hooks. It fell with a heavy flump. Parts of it slid, wetly, most of it lay there, twitching, half skinned, half alive, half dead, all horrible.

'This is the magic of the Mucklaghs,' said the wife, looking at it, smiling.

'A savage sacrifice,' said the Storyteller. 'Why are you smiling?'

'Because it's weak,' she said, 'and I am cruel. . . you knew that.'

The Storyteller shivered, and he looked for the door of the dream.

But there was no door.

It was no dream.

He had slipped through time, and everything about him was real.

Real in its own time.

'Come,' said the Wife, 'let's go before I horrify you more.'

She led him through tunnels and caves, through the alleys of the earth.

The path was not good, and he watched her feet, such pretty feet. He thought of the slavegirl Ranait, and was she safe in Ulster now?

He watched the feet of the Wife, picking along. How delicate the way they picked among the stones. As if she had eyes in her toes!

The path was definitely not good, not good at all.

Muddy, almost a stream in places.

The walls were wet to the touch. Though they were not walls really, more like a split in the rock of the earth, but here and there the split in the earth had obviously been touched by men, building, small sections, supporting, and these man-made sections knitted in to the natural earth. But did not quite knit in. It was always possible to tell where man had built, and which was the original split in the earth. It was if two different races had built this place.

And one was the gods and one was man?

But which was which?

And were they any different really?

Were the hands of man just the hands of the gods, the tools of the gods, like a saw or a hammer, cutting, building, killing, creating, destroying?

Questions, sighed the Storyteller, more questions! And now, he realised, now it was too late for questions, let alone for answers. . . too late to be worrying about the food and the meal half eaten!

'It's a long way you're leading me,' he said.

'This goes to the sea in the west.'

'The sea in the west? That's fifty miles!'

'Oh yes, to the grave of Eochaidh mac Eirce. But we're not going all the way.'

'I'm very glad to hear that.'

'In fact. . .' she stopped, and moved aside, a separate passage to the light. 'We're here. . . up there. . .'

A sheep baa'ed.

'Is that a real sheep, or a dream sheep?' he asked, coming up into the air.

'Real as this blood on my arms,' said the Wife.

She held out bloodied arms.

How real is the blood on her arms, he wondered. But asked her an entirely different question. 'Where is this place?' he looked around, in the dark, and some of the shadows here were shadows, and some familiarities.

'The Well of Clebach. . . here I'll wash.'

She stripped her tunic off and plunged in.

'Is it cold?' he called.

'Fierce cold.' She climbed out quickly. And stood beside him, very small.

'Dry me.'

'With what?'

'I don't know. . . your shirt, cloak, something. . . anything. . . I've nothing. . .'

'By the gods,' said the Storyteller. He took off his outer shirt and dried her best he could. She was very small. There wasn't much of her to dry really. She bowed her head, watching the cloth of the shirt move over her body. 'I killed the Christian girl,' she said. . . 'She didn't run away in the night.'

'I know you killed the Christian girl. Why did you kill the Christian girl?'

'The goddess told me to. . .'

'The witch. . . the crone. . . the bird. . .'

'Yes. . .'

'Why?'

'Because there was no room for her in the story. . . you either travel with me, Storyteller, or you travel with the Christian girl. . .'

'Would you not let me choose myself, choose who I travel with?'

'There is no choosing, Storyteller. . . it's chosen for us. . . please dress me.'

He picked up her tunic, and helped it over her head, her shoulders. And when it was over her head he heard her voice coming out, muffled. 'What will we tell them, of Eithne, and Fidelma?'

He pulled the tunic down over her skinny body, said nothing.

'Maybe we'll just tell them they're dead.' she said.

'They know that already. . . Laoghaire wants to know *how* they died. . .'

'Well we'll tell them the Romans killed them. . .' She shrugged. 'Details aren't important. . .'

'The details are always important. . . light is in the details. . . and the darkness in them too. . . look at you, girl. . .' He picked her belt from the ground, clasped it round her waist. 'This is no sow's dug around your waist here. . . the purse you wear. . . this is the dug of some sacrifice. . . that's a detail!'

'Oh her'. . . The Wife flapped at the purse, thoughtfully. 'She's long gone to the goddess. . .'

'You sliced it off her at the Mucklaghs.'

'Well I was very young. . . I danced with the wizards.'

'She screamed.'

'Oh yes, like a pig, it was horrible. But beautiful too.' She squeezed the purse, thoughtfully. And then shrugged coldly. 'Oh don't mind her, what matters her to us? And doesn't she live on? Around my waist and here in the Otherworld. And in your horror at the horror. Yes she lives on. In the goddess. We all live on. Don't be minding the meat we walk round in when we're breathing!'

'You're as bad as Patrick. . . you with your certainties. . .'

'Patrick's Christian girl is eaten now,' said the Wife, coldly. 'Eaten by foxes and cats and rats. . . her bones are in burrows. . . and her skull rolls. . . where is her faith in god? Where is her god?'

She walked away a way, and looked down into the water.

'Oh let's not argue gods,' said the Storyteller.

'Oh yes let's, Storyteller, let's just!' And it was the witch talking to him again, that dark figure there in the darkness, at the edge of the Well of Clebach, that was the witch. He saw her looking down into the water, and pointing. 'Let's look into that water there, the water of the Well of Clebach. . . where is the blood I washed away?'

'The water is clear. . . dark with the night, but clear and clean.' The Storyteller looked around, realising suddenly how very dark it was. 'It's very dark,' he murmured, 'where is the moon tonight?'

'Where is the daughter of the moon,' laughed the witch, 'tonight?'

Her laughter tumbled in the trickle of the stream. 'The women of Rathcroghan come here,' she said, 'come here by the day. . . every day. . . to wash away their women's blood. . . where is that blood now?'

'The water is clear. Dark, but clear and clean.'

'Where are the screams of the sacrifice?'

'They are silent. There's no sound now but the trickle of the stream.'

'The silence after suffering, after sacrifice. . . a warm silence. . . better that than the cold silence of Patrick's god. . . tell me. . . where is Patrick's god when a sacrifice squeals?'

'He is silent.'

'Yes, with a cold silence. And when a warrior dies in battle?'

'He is silent.'

'When a child weeps, with the hunger? When a mother cries? When a young man dies in war? When sickness comes to a house? Where is Patrick's god, then?'

'Silent.'

'If King Laoghaire sends great armies here. . . King Laoghaire the Son of Niall. . . Laoghaire the greatest of kings. . . if he sends his armies here there will be slaughter. . . and destruction. . . and suffering. . . where will Patrick's god be, then?'

'Silent.'

'Yes, Storyteller, silent silent silent silent silent! So *let* us argue gods. . . *my* goddess is never silent. . . she screams, she laughs, she dances with the corpses. . .'

'She is death.'

'Of course she's bloody death. . . and she always loves you. . . always waits for you. . . her arms are always ready. . . come to my arms, Storyteller.'

She held out her arms, a dark figure beside the stream.

He walked to her, and she leaned into his arms. And it wasn't the witch anymore, it was the Wife, leaning into his arms, thin and small and cold. 'Oh husband. . . I get weary.'

'It's just the cold, of the waters of the well.'

'No, it's the weariness. . . will you mind me?'

'Do you think I wouldn't?' He stroked her ugly hair. He saw her with a crown of reeds, with dabs of mud for jewels.

'Will you love me?'

'Do you think I couldn't?'

'That's settled so,' she said, freeing herself from his arms with a sudden giggle. 'Now, what will we tell them, of Eithne, and Fidelma?'

'That they are dead. . . but how did they die?'

'Oh we'll tell them the Romans killed them. It is ordinary. They were pretty girls. They went to the well to bathe. The Romans were there, and saw them naked. And wanted them. You're a man yourself, you know.'

'I know. . . but. . .'

'But nothing! Sure you'll make a handsome story of the tale. The girls were daughters of a king. . . brave and strong. . . and fought them off. . . and the Romans killed them, drowned them, in the well.'

'I know that story, I could tell it.'

'Of course you could. And the girls died virgins in the well.'

'I know, I see it, the words are waiting.'

'And they'll call this well for the girls. . . in time. . . the virgins' well. . .'

'Ogulla Well. . . I know.'

'Yes, yes. the Romans got frightened then. Because these were girls at the school of Cathbad. . . no ordinary slave girls. . . they saw that Daithi would have their heads. . . so they concocted a story. . . that Patrick met them. . . that he told them of his god. . . and they died to go to him. . .'

'What fool would believe that story?'

'A fool that wants to believe,' said the Wife, softly. 'And the world is full of fools that want to believe. And not just fools. . . a wise man who has nothing to believe, he too will believe anything. . .'

'But the story isn't true,' said the Storyteller, 'I know completely different!'

The Wife laughed. She squeezed her purse, and pointed it to him. 'Is this the dug of a pig?'

'No.'

'But you'd be happier believing it was. . .'

'Of course I would. . . I'm not some Connacht savage!'

'Well we can't all be civilised,' she mocked, 'can't all be mighty men from Tara. . . the world needs us savages too!'

'What're you saying to me anyway?'

'I'm saying, about the stories of Eithne and Fidelma. . . we lie, Storyteller, we *lie!* And soon enough it'll be the truth.'

'Is it the witch talking to me now? She doesn't know lie from truth, dream from reality. . . and she doesn't care.'

'Maybe because it doesn't matter. And anyway. . . me. . . the witch?. . . Have you eyes in your head. . . have I dark hair?'

'No.'

'And a full body.'

'No. . . but it's still the witch talking. . . she's hidden in you. . . like the the blood of sacrifice is hidden on your hand. . . or the blood of the Christian girl. . . hidden. . .'

'Oh alright. . . betimes I speak for the goddess, act for her.. . . betimes I don't. . . do you love me?'

'Betimes I do, betimes I don't. . . what will we tell King Laoghaire?'

'What does he want to believe?'

'What would be easier to believe?'

'That the girls have seen the Roman god. . . and gone to him?'

'That would be easier to believe.'

'Well will we tell him that so?' she asked.

And the Storyteller was silent for a moment, delayed his answer, because that was the querstion he didn't want to answer.

'Well?' she prompted.

He sighed, and nodded. 'There is nothing else now in Tara to believe. The bones of sacrifices are scattered by children. The sacred places are neglected. The druids are old and useless. It is all dead. All the old ways, crumbling. we are hollow trees, waiting for a storm. Only the Roman god is alive. . .'

'I wouldn't be too sure of that,' said the Wife, 'but I know what you mean. . . we live in the innards of time.'

'Some years ago I talked to Lochru and Lucatmael,' said the Storyteller.

'Those wizards at Tara. . .'

'Yes. . . they told me and anyone else who would listen. . . told me that Patrick would come. . . old axe head they called him, they saw him like that in their dreams. . .'

'From the shape of his hair. . .'

'They didn't know his name. . . they called him axe head. . . from the shape of the cut of his hair. . . they saw him in dreams. . . and they said that when he came it would be the end of the old ways. . . and they were right. . . now it *is* the end of the old ways.'

'We live in the innards of time. . . we search for the bag of the womb.'

'Aye, and we search for the seed.'

'Where will we go, husband, you and I? I am weary.'

'To Tara. Where are my horses, and where are my dogs, my black dog, my white dog? Where is Night, and where is Day?'

'They wait by the lubgort of Caplait and Mael'.

'Well you go, Wife, go and fetch them. . . you know these paths. . . and meet me here at the well. . . I would say goodbye to Eithne and Fidelma.'

⸺·

WHISPERING, WHISPERING, he heard them whispering.

And at first there were no words in that whispering.

It was the little sounds of the land.

A leaf, touching, a leaf. Water, trickling, a pebble in a tumble. Some animal shuffling. A slither, what was that, like the sound of a knife sharpening?

Whispering.

'He's here now.'

'She was here with him.'

'She's gone now.'
'I saw her going towards Rathcroghan.'
'To the guest house at Tulach Oichre.'
'But he stays here.'
'What does he do?'
Listens.

To a leaf, touching, a leaf. Water, trickling, a pebble in a tumble. Some animal slithering, its claws on a stone like the sound of a knife sharpening. And a screech in the darkness, what could that be?

A cat?

Call it a cat!

'Why is he waiting?'
'What is he watching?'

The rags on the tree, girls hang them there in a wish. Rags of their first bleeds. There was blood on them once but now they're washed in the rain. Girls hang them there in a wish. For a good husband. And an easy childbirth. And all the things girls wish for. They hang like bats in the tree.

If a man had a flying dog he could catch the flying bats!

If there was such a thing, such a thing as a flying dog.

'What does he think of, sitting there?'

He thinks of wishes.

He sees them, flying like bats over the slopes of Cruachan Ai.

They swoop in the dark.

At first it seems like madness, they way the bats swoop, and swerve, in any and every direction. But as soon as a man knows they're swooping up insects to eat, as soon as that it does not seem like madness anymore.

So many things seem mad.

Because the purpose is unseen.

The wizard girl wife, she drenches the earth in blood!

Patrick the Roman, he splashes water on poor people's heads!

Blood, and water.

Water, and blood.

So much seems madness, and meaningless.

Until we know the purpose.

Eithne the Fair, her hair is the colour of water, in the light.

Fidelma the Ruddy, her hair is the colour of blood, in the dark.

And Eithne is the seed, the source, and Fidelma is the faith, the story.

And they are sisters.

'What does he know, the Storyteller?' said the whispering.

'Our names,' said the whispering, 'and who we are.'

'Where does he go now?' asked the whispering.

'To Rathcroghan. . . he follows the wizard girl wife.'

'Oh yes,' said the whispering, 'he *will* follow her.'

'Forever,' said the little movements of the night.

'Forever,' said the sound of a knife, sharpening.

'Forever,' said a scream.

What was that?

It came from the Mucklaghs, over there.

A cat? Call it a cat!

20

THE SERVANT STOOD in the doorway. Morning crept in around him like it knew it was unwelcome. And the Storyteller looked at the Servant and at the morning and he sighed.

There were *always* mornings, and *always* young men standing in his doorway!

They brought messages, for this and for that. Different messages, about different things, oh sure enough, but they were always messages and messages are always. . . an imposition!

But oh well, but oh well, it was the part of the price for being important.

A poor man gets no messengers.

In many cases a poor man has no doorway for them to stand in!

'What is it now,' he asked, 'can't you see I'm readying for my journey home?'

'There are some travellers from the road,' said the servant.

'What road?'

'Slighe Asail. . . the road you travelled from the east. . .'

'What do they want, I am done with that road from east to west. . . I'll travel it now from west to east. . . and as for travellers on that road, I'm done with them in either direction!'

'They have a small boy. . . they met him a day from here. . . they say he is lost. . . but that he tells them he is your slaveboy. . .'

'I have no slaveboy, this is madness. . . go. . . tell them to go. . . and not be disturbing an important man in his business.'

The servant turned to go. 'Wait,' said the Wife, pausing him. Then she turned to the Storyteller. 'We *do* have a slaveboy,' her voice was thoughtful, 'we bought him on the road. . . '

'We bought no slaveboy. . . you're touched with dreams and tiredness girl!'

'But we did,' she insisted, 'that raggedy family. . . we bought them. . .'

'Oh yes. . . I suppose so. . . but how do you expect me to remember these things? I've been to hell and back!'

'And back?' murmured the Wife.

He ignored that. Better to talk about the slaveboy problem. 'Oh alright,' he sighed, 'yes I remember that family. . . that little boy. . . sure that was charity, not buying! He's gone off with his parents.'

'The boy the travellers have,' said the Servant, 'he tells them bandits killed his parents. . . and he is alone in the world. . .'

The Storyteller sighed again. Or, more like, continued the same sigh, keeping it alive, feeling he was going to have a need of it as the day progressed. 'Bandits. . . bandits. . . oh by the gods. . . what savage country is this!' He waved an arm. 'You. . . boy. . . bring. . . bring those travellers in. . .'

The servant went out.

'It must be the same child,' said the Wife. . .

It was.

Of six, or seven years, the travellers had dressed him in a man's shirt. It trailed the ground. The little boy looked up at them. Last time he had been happy, ragged, almost naked. Now he was dressed, but morose, anxious. The Storyteller thought of this. And how people wear clothes like they wear moods. And how sometimes there's no connection between the clothes and the moods.

'We found him in the whin,' said one of the travellers.

'What do you do in the whin?' asked the Storyteller, suspicious. Even though he vaguely recognised the little boy, he felt that these two chancers might be trying to get one over on him. Salesmen, they were, for sure. Spot them a mile away. Their insincerity travelling before them like the smell of cattle coming on a warm day.

'Gather roots,' was the reply, 'we gather roots. Every time we pass that spot we gather roots. . . particular type of roots. . . there's a woman buys them here. . .'

'A witch?'

'Well. . . a woman who makes medicines. . . she needs these roots. . . we gather them. . .'

'And in return we get our lodgings,' added the previously silent traveller.

'Good lodgings? asked the Storyteller, looking around at his own guest house, meaningfuly.

'Oh very good,' came the reply.

'Good food?' asked the Storyteller, looking towards the cooking pot, meaningfully.

'Oh very good,' came the reply.

'And probably free medicine thrown in. . . well. . . next time we'll know. . .'

'Know what?' murmured the Wife.

'Know to be gathering roots along our way. . . so. . . what. . . now. . . well.' The Storyteller looked in his mind for words. And there were none to say. Not on the particular problem in front of him anyway. So he said something else. 'What business do you good men do?'

'We trade cloth.'

'Where does the cloth come from?'

'Armorica. . . and beyond. . . would you like to see some. . . we have a cart outside. . . '

'Oh I think I've seen quite enough carts of cloth this journey,' said the Storyteller, 'well and enough.'

'We have linen, threaded with gold. . . from Rome itself. . . and cotton, good cotton, from Egypt.'

'Where's Egypt?' asked the wife.

'It's an area of Rome,' said the traveller.

'Jesus Christ was born in Egypt,' said the Servant.

'Jesus Christ?' said the Storyteller.

'The Son of God,' said the Servant.

'Oh by the gods,' said the Storyteller, suddenly realising. 'You, you're a Christian. . . you follow the Romans. . . Jesus Christ!'

'Yes,' he agreed, 'I am saved. I was baptised, I have learned the way of light.'

'Well,' said the Storyteller, 'learn how to cook now and we're half way there!'

'Are you sure you wouldn't like to see our linen?' said the traveller.

'Or our cotton?' said the other.

'If I buy anything now,' said the Storyteller, 'I'll have to carry it all the way back to Tara.'

'We deliver,' said the traveller, quickly.

'Buy from us here,' said the other traveller, 'and we'll leave it at your house in Tara. . . on our way back to the coast. . .'

'That's very efficient,' agreed the Storyteller, thinking. It would indeed be very churlish not to buy at least something. After all, they had brought the boy to him. Though of course the bringing of the boy had surely been inspired by hope of some reward! Not that they had really done him any favours by bringing the boy. Just another complication. But no matter. If he was churlish and mean here his name would be muddied along many of the muddy roads of Ireland! And yes, it may be true that a man can't buy his honour, but he can surely lose it by *not* buying something!

A man's good name is worth a lot more than the price of a piece of cloth.

'Alright,' he said, 'bring me in a roll of cotton, let us see the quality.'

'And a roll of that linen you mentioned,' added the Wife, 'the linen threaded with gold.'

'Linen?' The Storyteller turned to her. 'Linen, what need have I of linen. . . threaded with gold or not threaded with gold. . .'

'Your Chief Wife and the Quiet One might like dresses made,' she said.

'And of course you would have no interest in the matter at all?'

'Perhaps. . . perhaps not. . . I'm thinking by the time we get back to Tara I may be tired of being a boy. . .'

'Indeed,' said the Storyteller, 'and I'm thinking I may be tired of extravagent women.'

The travellers looked from Storyteller to Wife, working out which way the wind was blowing in the argument. Then, deciding, one of them went out and almost immediately returned with two bales of cloth, one of cotton, and one of linen, a fine looking linen threaded with gold. An *expensive* looking linen threaded with gold!

He shook out the bale of cotton. Then he shook out the bale of linen.

'This is very good cotton,' the Storyteller agreed, fingering it.

'This is lovely linen,' said the wife, holding it up in front of her, like the makings of a dress.

'Will look lovely on you,' said the first traveller.

'I think it's the gold,' said the second, 'picks up the colour of your hair.'

Picks up the colour of her hair, thought the Storyteller. Hah! If it picked up the colour of the blood on her hands it might be more to the point! But then, the blood on her hands might only be a dream, a trance, a thing of Otherworld and strangeness. While the colour of her hair was definitely real. Unfortunately.

The Wife twirled the cloth about her, the way a woman will.

The Storyteller saw in her twirling the memory of a mysterious dream.

The linen cloth was blue, pale, much paler than a dark blue sea.

The ship moved up and down.

He was someone else in the dream, in the memory of the dream, and he was leaving a woman in Armorica.

She stood on the wall, and he on the ship.

Sailors busied around.

She was a graceful woman, gentle, of the Roman people.

Her eyes were brown, soft as a deer.

Was she crying?

So hard to see.

The ship moved up and down.

Armorica sank on the horizon. First a mountain, then a hill, then it was a thread of land and then a thread and then it was gone. Forever.

And that was the dream. Lost, and gone, forever. And the Storyteller looked about the emptiness of the room. There is a time in a room full of people when there's also an emptiness there. And this was one of those times.

'It certainly suits the lady,' he heard the traveller say, like a person in a play that he was watching. But then he felt himself being drawn back into the goings-on in the room. And whether he was becoming part of the play, or they becoming part of the audience was not clear. But whatever, they were all the one again.

Lady, thought the Storyteller, *lady*? It suits the *lady*? From blood soaked wizard girl to lady, all in the shake of a bolt of cloth! By the gods!

By the gods. . . by the gods he should put his foot down on all this and run the salesmen from the place! But. . . but. . . he knew the waste of energy in playing out a game that was lost before it began and he said 'alright, alright, enough already, I'll buy, how much?'

But then, immediately, before they answered, a sudden idea. 'I'll tell you what, I'll trade you the slaveboy for the cloth.'

'For *both* bales?' asked the traveller, his eyes narrowed, as if the better to see some calculations.

'Well he has got *two* legs and *two* arms, hasn't he!'

'Oh no we can't do that,' said the Wife, dropping the makings of the dress from in front of her and clutching the little boy. 'He needs a home, a proper home.'

'*I* need a home,' said the Storyteller, 'a proper home. . . the way you spend my money I'll be on the road myself!'

'Oh don't be ridiculous,' she said, 'buy the cloth with coin and let's have no more of it.'

'Coin?' said the traveller, passing a glance to his companion.

'Yes,' said the Storyteller, 'I have some Saxon coin.'

'*Saxon* coin,' said the traveller. He looked at his companion again, meaningfully. And the companion said 'have you no gold, or silver?'

'I have yes,' said the Storyteller, 'but I want to hang onto it. What is this about Saxon coin. . . why will no-one take it. . . even that ruffian Coroticus the slave trader wouldn't take it, now you won't!'

'It's not very popular,' said the traveller.

'I know that. . . I'm asking you why?'

'The head of the king on the Saxon coin. . .'

'What about him. . .'

'They roasted him in an iron cage on a fire. . .'

'Who did?'

'Another Saxon. . . and now he's the king. . .'

'And he says that anyone who carries the coins of the other king. . .' said the second traveller.

'The roasted one?'

'Yes, anyone who carries his coins will go the same way. . .'

'Oh. I have quite a lot of Saxon coin,' said the Storyteller, gloomily. 'It seems I won't be travelling in the Saxon country!'

'But,' said the traveller, 'the son of the first king. . . the roasted king. . . he is safe among the Picts. . .'

'And they say he's gathering an army. . .'

'To get back his kingdom. . .'

'And then he will roast the second Saxon king. . . and then your coin will be valuable again. . .'

'I see,' said the Storyteller, 'well I'm thinking I'll stand back from all that until they have it sorted out. . . come. . . we'll deal in gold.'

They dealt in gold.
The travelling merchants left, happy.
The Storyteller watched them leave, gloomy.
Had he paid them too much?

⌒•

THE MIND HAS MANY ROOMS, thought the Storyteller. And a man's imagination moves from room to room, like feet might move through a well known house, down corridors, and halls, past little rooms that are best kept closed, best left to dust and spiders.

And life *itself* has many rooms, he thought next!

But the rooms where the life lives are not quite the same as the ones where the mind wanders. It's as if a man lives twice. Once with his mind, once with his body. And the two lives intertwine. But, the question is, are the two lives branches of two different trees with different roots, or are they the branches of the same tree, intertwined?

He shrugged.

There's one for the druids to be thinking over!

He added a sigh to his shrug!

How near was he now to be knowing about Eithne and Fidelma?

That was one for *him* to be thinking over. On the journey back, while his body would be moving across the desolate land, trying to stay alive, his mind would be moving from room of truth to room of truth. There would be this thought here, and that there, and in the end a story would emerge for King Laoghaire. A story for the greatest of kings. From the greatest of storytellers. A story that Laoghaire would believe. And a story that would keep the story alive. Not to mention the Storyteller.

Oh rooms, he thought, oh rooms and truth and life and death and night and day. If I get two more dogs, he mused, I'll call one Life and the other Death. And they'll run around my horse's heels, guarding me from the dangers of the desolate land. Guarding me from the darkness of the forest. But who, he wondered, who will guard me from the darkness in the mind?

He smiled.

Not the bravest of dogs nor the strongest of soldiers would take up that duty!

'What're you smiling at?' asked the Wife.

'Can a man not smile in peace?' He looked at her. And now there was this, this for the mind of many rooms to be dealing with! The Wife, and her mothering a small boy. Yes, he nodded to himself, yes it was true what they say. A man he had drunk with in Tara once had discussed this very thing. How all women become the same one, eventually. And this is why men keep on taking on new wives. Because the woman that is the same one is not really the woman they are looking for!

'But it's a hopeless quest,' said that man in Tara.

'And why is that?' the Storyteller had asked, looking nervously at the level in the jug of beer. He well knew the close relationship between that and the quality of conversation.

'Because,' said that man in Tara, what was his name, no matter, 'because a man who takes on too many women is running backwards through his life, trying to find himself when he was young. It's a hunt without a kill.'

'Sure a day's hunting,' the Storyteller had said, 'sure that can be pretty satisfying itself, even if you do go hungry in the evening.'

He sighed, remembering, old conversations.

Would that life were as easy and neat as words!

The telling of the story is a damn sight easier than living it!

He packed his saddle bags, prepared to go.

The Wife mothered the boy.

The Storyteller watched, and listened. How she coaxed the boy out of his caution, and how the child coaxed the mothering out of her. The child gave way a piece, and she a little, in a game of tiny moves, a game of fidchell really. . . but not, no not a game of fidchell really. . . because in games of chance and skill like that there is one will be the winner. . . with the Wife and the boy child there would be no winner. . . at least neither of *them* would win. Something else would win. The game would win. Life would win.

Is life a game?

And men and women and children merely players, playing it, endlessly?

And playing it without quite knowing the rules?

Perhaps.

The Storyteller smiled. And reached out his hand for a jug of beer that wasn't there. And looked across the table for a drinking companion, and he wasn't there either! No-one to bandy the words with.

The Wife stayed busy with the child, and the servant busy with the food, and him a Christian anyway... no joy in talking to them. Too damn certain about everything! Good conversation is an exploration, not an argument.

'You could talk with me,' said the witch, she moved in the morning fire. No heat in that fire yet, but a lot of dancing flames for a witch to move in.

'Oh away with you, woman, or I'll stir you into the ashes with my bone.'

'You still carry that,' she mocked, 'all the way from Tara?'

'I did, I do, it's a habit of mine... everytime I go on a journey I carry something from home... usually an ashplant... but this time a bone...'

'Well will you bring it back to Tara... or leave it here?'

'I haven't decided... I may come across a place where the bone belongs... and leave it there... or I may not... that's what I do with ashplants.'

'Do?' asked the witch in the fire.

'Yes I'd be walking along, and I suddenly see a place where the stick belongs, and I'll put it in there!'

'And the ash stick will grow into a tree... if you put it in the soil in the hedge...'

'Oh it will, surely...'

'So there are trees along the roads you've travelled... and they've grown from your ashplants...?'

'Yes, and other people's ashplants too... because its a habit of a man to carry a stick along his way... and because of this habit the roads around the country are the story of many men, and many men's journeying.'

'Perhaps that habit comes from driving cattle, perhaps he got that habit there.'

'Indeed, but even if he's not driving cattle, even if he's never driven cattle in his life, he'll still carry an ashplant.'

'It's born in him,' said the witch. 'But when you leave that bone, in some particular place on the road, will flesh cling to it? And will that flesh become a person, following you, on the way of your journey?'

'Perhaps,' said the Storyteller.

The witch came out of the fire and sat across him at the table. She wore ordinary clothes.

'Where are the jewels in your hair?' he asked.

'Did you like the jewels in my hair?' she asked, the tip of her tongue to her lip. And her eyes the eyes of a whore. And then the sudden smell of charcoal burners' smoke, in the memory.

'Yes,' said the Storyteller, but carefully, 'I did like the jewels in your hair.'

'And the flesh that clings to my bones?'

'Yes,' said the Storyteller, even more carefully.

'What colour do you see when you look in my eyes?' she asked, suddenly changing her mood, no longer playing seduction.

'Your eyes are black, witch.'

'Yes I know, thats why I asked. . . because I have a riddle for you. . . do you know what it is about colour?'

'Tell me what, *what* is it about colour?'

'Well as you know there are many colours, all the many colours, yellow and blue and red. . . and green. . .'

'I've noticed!'

'And if you add all those colours together. . . do you know what will happen then?'

'What?'

'You'll be looking at black. . .'

'I suppose I will. So your eyes are all the colours?'

'Yes. . . but another interesting thing,' said the witch. . .

'Tell me. . .'

'If you get white light, and shine it through glass. . . or water. . . you'll see all the colours again. . . yellow and blue and red. . .'

'And green,' said the Storyteller.

'Yes. So isn't it the fact that all the colours must add up to black *and* to white. . . isn't that an interesting thing?'

'It does bear thinking about.'

'But it is a side road on the path. . . the colour of my eyes. . . better for you to be worrying about the colour of your own women's eyes, and not of a witch you see in a fire. . . I ask you a question now. . .'

'What question is that?'

'Is the carrying of a bone born in a man, the way the carrying of an ashplant is?'

'I suppose some are born from cattle herders, some from storytellers,' he replied. 'And now I ask you a question.'

'Ask me a question, Storyteller.'

'Why did you come to Tara, with your wizards?'

'Was I not always *in* Tara?'

'Alright. . . I'll ask the question differently. . . why did you *appear* in Tara. . . and put a spell on the place. . .'

'For Eithne and Fidelma.'

'They are dead.'

'They wanted you to know.'

'Me? To know? Am I that important?'

'Only because you tell the story. . . they wanted themselves in the story. . .'

'How they died?'

'Not particularly. Just their names. Anyway, who can you tell. . . how they died?'

'Laoghaire. . . I can tell Laoghaire. . . I *must* tell my king, King Laoghaire. . . or he'll have my head!'

'Tell him that Maol and Caplait had them drowned? To show their power to the world? You'll tell him that? What will he do when you tell him that?'

'I suppose he'll kill an awful lot of druids.'

'And a few storytellers! And what about the other truth, the Christian truth. . . what will he do if you tell him that. . .'

'I suppose he will be sad. . . then happy. . . and follow the Christian way. . . eventually. . .'

'Which do you want?'

'But the Christian truth is a lie.'

'Which do you want? Remember. . . you would not rest on the Christian breasts of the Christian girl!' said the witch.

'What do you mean?'

'Which do you want. . . death. . . or to live with the lie?'

'I don't know what you mean. . .'

'Oh yes, oh yes you do. . . the choice is death. . . or living alone with a lie. And you are on the side of death, Storyteller, that's where your story comes from! Sure who are you, you storytellers, who are you but druids too. . . !' The witch laughed. 'If Maol and Caplait go, then so go you. . . Laoghaire will have all of your heads. . . if the blind man's tale gets back to him. . .'

'The blind man will be dead soon.'

'He's dead already. In Tulach Uisce. He drowned in his own breath. It was his own curse. His daughter sits at her window, waiting for a cart to come, to bury him.'

'Is she sad?'

'No, she thinks of you, shagging her. It's a memory for a lonely woman.'

'Does she know his story?'

'Perhaps. . . perhaps she was listening at the door. . . perhaps not. . .'

'His voice was low, he had no breath. But still she could have heard.'

'Yes she could have heard. . . and she could gossip. . . better to have her squeal on a hook than gossip is my thinking. . .'

'It's a cruel death.'

'Do you want to live, or die?'

'Live.'

'Well the druids of the Mucklaghs will come for her so. . . . .'

'How will they come for her?'

'They have a little cart. It travels the country. Drawn by an old horse. And an old woman sitting on the horse. She wears the clothes the colour of the horse.'

'I know that cart, that horse, that crone.'

'Of course you do. It follows on your journey. The daughter will hear the cart at the door. And she'll think it's come for the body of the blind man.'

'She'll go to the door.'

'But the cart has come for her,' the witch laughed, a mocking sound.

'But,' said the Storyteller, 'the daughter of the blind man. . . I'm sure she didn't hear his story. . .'

'I'm sure she didn't either,' laughed the witch. And ran her birds claw fingers through her glossy hair.

'Then why the cruel death?'

'Flesh for the bones,' said the witch, in a voice he knew. The Storyteller looked into her eyes, and one was cold, the other cruel.

'Flesh for the bones,' she repeated, 'and anyway, why not? Why not the cruel death?'

And then she said no more. Because at that moment the servant walked across the room and threw a log on the fire, and the vision of her scattered into sparks, and smoke, and different flames.

Her going was like being woken at the wrong time in a dream.

Or being woken at the right time in a dream.

The Storyteller sighed.

Why not. What was the daughter of the blind man to him? Meat on the end of his prick, meat on the druids' hook, and what was the difference? Let her scream. And if he heard it from the Mucklaghs he could call it a cat, howling in the rain.

Yes, he could call it a cat.

That'd be for the best.

He listened.

The rain fell.

It was a hard journey waiting for him.

⌒•

'DO YOU SEE HIM NOW?' asked Eithne.

'Yes sister, I see him now.'

'He sits alone. . .'

'But not alone.'

'No, and that sort of aloneness is the real loneliness.'

'He thinks of why he's here, what brought him here.'

'And of all the other places he could have been.'

'What brought him here then?'

'The story, I suppose.'

'He is a storyteller, yes, and must follow that, and preach it. . . it's a thing apart from him, a separate thing, he's a bubble in its stream.' said Fidelma.

'A bubble in a stream,' said Eithne, picking up her words like an echo. 'Just like us. . . bubbles, trickles in this water here.'

'We must go where the stream goes. . . but. . . did you ever think, did you ever think of this?'

'What, sister, what brilliant idea have you come up with now?'

'It's just this, that the bubbles and trickles in the stream, they must go where the stream goes. . . but without them, there'd be no stream at all. . . they *are* the stream. . . !'

'*We* are the stream.'

'Alive or dead.'

'Is it better to be alive, or dead?'

'Is there a difference?'

'I don't know,' said Eithne, 'he wonders that too, about life, and death. Look at him there, wondering.'

'He sits alone.'

'Is there such a thing as good, or bad, or death or life?'

'He sits alone.'

'But his bishops are around him.'

'In his small church near Magh Seilig.'

'His bishops are talking of the new church they are building. And how many more they have baptised.'

'But Patrick of Armorica thinks of home. . .'

'And a girl, a Roman girl. . .'

'She wore a blue dress. . . she stood on snakes in a mysterious dream.'

'He hears the bishops chatter on, about the new church. And he has an idea. He'll talk to his wrights, his woodcarvers, carpenters. . . and he'll have them make a statue. And the statue will be the mother of his god. . .'

'Is she a goddess too?'

'I think so. . . it's all very confusing, christianity.'

'But anyway, look what he thinks. . .'

'Yes, I see what he thinks. . . the mother of his god will look just like that Roman girl. . . in a blue dress, and her feet will be standing on snakes. . .'

'He doesn't know why she'll be like that. . . but she will!'

'Yes, Patrick writes his story too.'

'Why am I here, he wonders, among these savage people.'

'He thinks of the Storyteller of Tara. . . he met him. . . an educated man from Tara. . .'

'But still a savage. . . he travels the country with a wizard, a devil girl.'

'But still, he would have liked to talk to him. . . there were interesting things to talk to him about.'

'But their stories were so different.'
'Were they that different?'
'Not to you or me, Fidelma, not to you or me.'
'Yes it's much the same. Patrick and his god. . . and the mother of his god. . . and the son and the father and the spirit and all that complication. . .'
'Oh I couldn't be doing with it! But hasn't the Storyteller of Tara got all the same stuff too?'
'Yes. . . all that complication. His witch. His crone. His bird.'
'His sacrifice too. . . yes. . . the same. . .'
'The son of Patrick's god, he hangs there, nailed on a cross.'
'And the daughters of the Storyteller's goddess. . . they swing on the hook at Cruachan Ai?' Where is the difference, sister?'
'I see no difference.'
'What do you see?'
'I see the lonely storytellers, men, and women too, they walk the world. They listen to the gods, and hear them well, but they can only speak in the language of men. . .'
'And women too.'
'Yes, of all of us. They're the ones I see. Patrick in Magh Seilig. And the Storyteller in Tulach Oichre.'
'Yes. . . one sits with his bishops. . . they speak of life. . . eternal. . . and the other sits with his wife, and she is death. . . and will never die!'
'She plays with a child. . . see her, see her play with that child. . .'
'Death plays with children too. . . she is death. . .'
'I know.'
'And she speaks of death. . . eternal.'
'Do you see a difference, sister?'
'Between the goddess of death and the god of life? I see none.'
'And I see none.'
'Oh now I'm sad. . . and this is a lonesome place, here by the well.'
'A lonesome place to be forever.'
'Waiting. For the lonely, to sit here by the well.'
'Watching. And the lonely coming, and going.'
'On journeys that have no meaning.'
'They pause here. Some the followers of Patrick. Some the followers of the other ways. They look into the water.'

'They are coming from problems in their lives.'
'And going back to them.'
'And here is a pause in the way.'
'Ogulla Well.'
'Our well.'
'Yes. Our well, our place.'
'But. . .'
'But what, sister?'
'If we hadn't died. . .
'What then?'
'We wouldn't have lived, lived on, in death, here in this lonesome place.'
'But we did die. . .'
'Do you forgive them?'
'No. . . Never. I would have seen my father, and him an old man. And I would have been a laughter to him, and a joy. And he would have danced my children on his knee. And instead, instead my father has to see me, forever a young girl. Who am I to forgive, that?'
'You're right, sister. . . do not forgive, do not forget.'
'Patrick wouldn't like that, you not forgiving. He preaches forgiveness.'
'Ah sure who is he? A foreigner. . . from Armorica. . . how much of *his* blood is in our earth? What does he know, of forgiving, and forgetting?'
'Who do you not forgive, and what can you not forget?'
'The gods, sister, the gods.'

THE RAIN FELL, on the roof.

The child laughed, at something.

The Wife smiled, at the child.

The Servant hacked, at roots for the cooking pot.

The *Christian* Servant!

The Storyteller looked at him, wondering. If he'd known he was a Christian he'd hardly have let him share the Wife's passages! Either in a dream or reality! And which it was, well, that was still a matter of some mystery. But dream or reality, no matter, the Wife *had* screeched between them, they had played her tune!

The Storyteller thought, and suddenly realised.

The wisdom of dreams, or, in this case, more than perhaps, the wisdom of reality. Dreams, reality, tangled! Sure isn't reality only the dreams of someone else in other times? And aren't dreams just a thread, knitted through life, like the gold in that bolt of cloth over there. Who knits that dream, who tangles that thread?

What gods knit that garment?

No matter.

The thread was tangled anyway. And it was entirely appropriate that the old ways and the new ways *should* share the Wife's passages. Because what was a wife but a woman, and what was a woman but the way men lived. . . and isn't it a fact that the way of living is mostly a twisting, in pain and in pleasure, between the old, and the new.

Wasn't there be a good symbolism in that?

'What're *you* looking so wise about?' she asked, suddenly, looking over.

'Oh. . . symbolism,' he said, topping up his voice with vagueness, the way a man might water whiskey for a drunk. Sometimes a man's thinking doesn't do a women any good, just as strong drink is no favour to a drunk.

'So now we better go,' he said, 'you and I.'

'And the child. To Tara,' said the Wife, 'we will take the child to Tara.'

'You're very determined about that.'

'I saw his mother in my sight. . . she's a carcass on a tree.'

'Sure what do you care about that? Aren't you the one that dances with death?'

'I didn't say I cared. But the child needs a mother. And who better than death to look after him?'

'Whatever you say, Wife, whatever you say! Now. . . more important. . . what news will we bring. . . to Laoghaire. . . of Eithne and Fidelma?'

'Oh we'll dream it on the way,' she said, casually. She tousled the head of the boy. 'Or we'll bring him the child instead of the news.'

'And if we do not dream? Do you think we might not dream?' said the Storyteller.

'I think we will,' said the Wife, 'Oh yes, I think we will.'

'And why are you so sure?'

'Because we live in the innards of time,' said the Wife, 'and we search for the bag of the womb.'

'Aye,' said the Storyteller, 'and we search for the seed.'

'Yes,' she said, and smiled.

The witch was in the smile.

I have married death, he thought, and he shrugged the thought away. I brought her through the Lag an Aenaigh. Too late to change things now.

'Now,' he said, suddenly busy, an organised man. 'Now where are my horses?'

'They wait by the lubgort of Caplait and Maol, Husband, I have them ready.'

'And where are my dogs, my black dog and my white?'

'Night and Day are waiting too,' she said, 'I have them ready.'

'Well you go, Wife, and fetch them, and meet me at the well. . . I would walk aways, and say goodbye to Eithne and Fidelma.'

⌒·

THE STORYTELLER SAT by the Well of Clebach, the place they call Ogulla now. The water trickled into the pool. There were sheep on a distant hill. And the sound of small birds. And ribbons and rags in a tree. He could not see the birds that were twittering, but he watched the ribbons and rags in the tree and thought of them as birds, and thought of the sound of each ribbon and each rag, and he thought of each ribbon and each rag singing out a story. And each story different, but each the same. An old man prays for his son, and him in a distant land. And a girl wonders, will love ever touch her? And a mother with a sick child, she prays let my sick child live.

The Storyteller looked into the water of the pool, and it was dark and it was light. And the dark streaks wrapped around the light, and the light about the dark, like wool at a weaving. And the light in the water streaming was the hair of Eithne the Fair. . . and the dark was Fidelma, the Auburn Haired. He looked into the stream that flowed from the pool, and the water there was dark and light, and changing one from the other. So that if a man came with a cup to fill, and reached into the water to catch a cup of light, or of dark, there would be no way of knowing what would fill the cup. And even if he came looking for the light, he might not know it was the dark he drank. But both would quench his thirst. The light and dark were one, and there was no separating them.

The Storyteller heard a moaning in the sky, and looked up. And it was an aeroplane. Up there, high, the shape of a cross. And the Storyteller smiled, remembering Tara, and the burning of the witch, the witch who did not scream. She did not scream because she was no witch, she was a dream, a dream and a magic on them all.

He stood to go.

His car shone in the sun.

A good car that, a new car. And in the back window a sticker still, Caseys of Castlebar, Main Ford Dealers.

How long should a man leave a new car sticker on his back window, he wondered. Too long would be a little bit sad, but too short, well, that'd be robbing himself of a simple pleasure.

He walked to the car, thinking about this.

And a large black bird on a tumbled wall looked at him, passing.

And a witch with heavy breasts, mocked him.

And a girl dressed as a boy, smiled at him.

And a crone with twisted bones, whispered.